P9-CKJ-417
PS3525
A1772
M6
1971
84234
TERTELING LIBRARY
THE COLLEGE OF IDAHO
CALDWELL, IDAHO

THE MORTGAGED HEART

Books by Carson McCullers

The Heart Is a Lonely Hunter

Reflections in a Golden Eye

The Member of the Wedding

The Ballad of the Sad Café
and Collected Short Stories

The Square Root of Wonderful (*a play*)

Clock Without Hands

Sweet as a Pickle and Clean as a Pig
(*poetry for children*)

The Member of the Wedding (*a play*)

THE MORTGAGED HEART

❖ ❖ ❖

CARSON McCULLERS

Edited by Margarita G. Smith

HOUGHTON MIFFLIN COMPANY
19 BOSTON 71

First Printing w

ISBN: 0-395-10953-1
Library of Congress Catalog Card Number: 70-120829
Printed in the United States of America

Portions of this book were originally published as follows:
"The Russian Realists and Southern Literature" in *Decision,* copyright 1941 by Decision, Inc.; "The Flowering Dream" in *Esquire;* "The Haunted Boy," "How I Began To Write," "Our Heads Are Bowed," "Home for Christmas," "The Discovery of Christmas," "Who Has Seen the Wind?," "Art and Mr. Mahoney," "The Dual Angel," and "Stone Is Not Stone" in *Mademoiselle;* "A Hospital Christmas Eve" in *McCall's;* "Isak Dinesen: *Winter's Tales*" in *The New Republic;* "Correspondence" in *The New Yorker;* "Sucker" in *Saturday Evening Post;* "Isak Dinesen: In Praise of Radiance" in *Saturday Review;* "The Vision Shared" in *Theatre Arts,* copyright, 1950 by John D. MacArthur; "Loneliness — An American Malady" in *This Week,* copyright — 1949 — New York Herald-Tribune, Inc.; "Look Homeward Americans," "Night Watch Over Freedom," "Brooklyn Is My Neighborhood," and "We Carried Our Banners — We Were Pacifists Too" in *Vogue;* "The Mortgaged Heart" and "When We Are Lost" in *Voices,* copyright 1952 by Harold Vinal. "Like That," "Instant of the Hour After," and "Breath from the Sky" appeared in *Redbook* in October 1971 as excerpts from this volume.

The outline for "The Mute" appeared in *The Ballad of Carson McCullers* by Oliver Evans, published in 1966 by Coward-McCann, copyright © 1965 by Peter Owen. The excerpt from an early, unpublished version of Tennessee Williams' Introduction to Carson McCullers' *Reflections in a Golden Eye* is published by permission of New Directions Publishing Corporation and Miss Audrey Wood, International Famous Agency, copyright © 1971 by Tennessee Williams. The editor is grateful to the estate of Sylvia Chatfield Bates for permission to reprint Miss Bates' comments. And to Random House, Inc. for permission to reprint the passage from *Out of Africa* by Isak Dinesen, copyright 1938 by Random House, Inc.

The dead demand a double vision. A furthered zone,
Ghostly decision of apportionment. For the dead can claim
The lover's senses, the mortgaged heart.

— Carson McCullers, from "The Mortgaged Heart"

EDITOR'S ACKNOWLEDGMENTS

LIKE MANY OTHER BOOKS, this one evolved. Through several changes, the original intention to collect most of Carson McCullers' published but uncollected work in one volume remained the primary purpose, and I am grateful to the invaluable bibliographies of Robert Phillips, William T. Stanley and Stanley Stewart. This book makes no pretense at scholarship, and is not intended as a study of the author or her work — early or late. I leave that to those more objectively qualified.

I thank Floria V. Lasky, the executrix of the estate of Carson McCullers, who for twenty years was the author's friend, adviser and attorney. I also thank Robert Lantz, who opened his literary agency in the late 1950s with Carson as one of his first five clients. His admiration for her work and affection for the author have been matched by his skills in her behalf. In her will, the author appointed him literary co-executor along with me. I thank him for his cooperation with this book and express appreciation to his entire staff for their graciousness.

Jane Hawke Warwick has worked with me on Carson's papers and on this book. When Jane was Assistant Fiction Editor at *Mademoiselle,* she met Carson and accompanied her on lecture tours. Her memory is better than mine, and I respect her taste and judgment.

Appreciation is due to Joyce Hartman, New York Editor of Houghton Mifflin Company, which has published Carson since 1940 and has kept all of her books in print. Mrs. Hartman, a long-time friend of Carson's, had the original concept for this book which we all agreed was a necessary step toward completion of a Carson McCullers library.

I appreciate, too, the cooperation we have received from editors, legal representatives and publishers in clearing rights and permissions.

I would like to squeeze in very personal thanks to those few intimate friends whose love and support made it possible for me to complete my part of this joint venture. They know who they are.

CONTENTS

Essays and Articles

Poetry

INTRODUCTION

OF ALL THE CHARACTERS in the work of Carson McCullers, the one who seemed to her family and friends most like the author herself was Frankie Addams: the vulnerable, exasperating and endearing adolescent of *The Member of the Wedding* who was looking for the "we of me." However, Carson once said that she was or became in the process of writing all the characters in her work. This is probably true of most real writers who often with pain draw from their unconscious what the rest of us would just as soon keep hidden from ourselves and others. So accept the fact that Carson was not only Frankie Addams but J. T. Malone, Miss Amelia and Captain Penderton; but familiarity with the work that she was able to finish would be only a partial clue to who and what she was. This was not simply because she had not finished what she had to say, but that she was the artist, and as she often quoted, "Nothing human is alien to me."

Before her death, I would have said that I knew Carson better than anyone did — that I knew her very well indeed. This would have been the truth as I saw it at the time, and at times I am still tempted to think that I knew her the best. After all, I knew her for forty-five years and lived with her off and on for much of that time. We shared the same heritage, the same parents, the same brother, the same room that looked out on the same holly tree and Japanese magnolia, and for the first twelve years of my life, the same mahogany bed. But we were sisters — sometimes intimate friends, sometimes enemies and at times strangers.

I remember very well the day that she told me — she did not ask me — that she had appointed me co-executor of her literary estate. I was annoyed. Unable to acknowledge her constant closeness to death,

I resented her trying to force me to face it. Carson was there when I was born and would be there when I died. She had lived through enough close calls to prove to me that she was indestructible.

Her papers were no concern of mine when she was living and I had no idea what she had saved. I have been just as surprised by what is there as by what is not there. I can't find any letters from our mother who wrote her every day they were separated, but all the valentines from a year were committed for keeping. So it would seem that these archives are partially due to accidental circumstance — dependent on Carson's health and the whim of any part-time secretarial help she had from time to time. Those of us concerned with her estate hope that these files will go to a library before much longer and be made available for further study. Even then, scholars will find it difficult to distinguish the truth.

Carson saw her life one way and those intimate with her often perceived it differently. Intentionally or unintentionally, she added to the confusion about herself. An interviewer was more likely to be cannily interviewed than to extract an interview from her. Besides, she simply liked a good story and frequently embellished the more amusing ones of her life. The one person who singled out this quality in a particularly loving way was Tennessee Williams in his unpublished essay "Praise to Assenting Angels":

> The great generation of writers that emerged in the twenties, poets such as Eliot, Crane, Cummings and Wallace Stevens, prose-writers such as Faulkner, Hemingway, Fitzgerald and Katharine Anne Porter, has not been succeeded or supplemented by any new figures of corresponding stature with the sole exception of this prodigious young talent that first appeared in 1940 with the publication of her first novel, *The Heart Is a Lonely Hunter.* She was at that time a girl of twenty-two who had come to New York from Columbus, Georgia, to study music. According to the legends that surround her early period in the city, she first established her residence, quite unwittingly, in a house of prostitution, and she found the other tenants of the house friendly and sympathetic and had not the ghost of an idea of what illicit enterprise was going on there. One of the girls in this establishment became her particular

friend and undertook to guide her about the town, which Carson McCullers found confusing quite imaginably, since even to this day she hesitates to cross an urban street unattended, preferably on both sides. However a misadventure befell her. Too much trust was confided in this mischievous guide, and while she was being shown the subway route to the Juilliard School of Music, the companion and all of her tuition money, which the companion had offered to keep for her, abruptly disappeared. Carson was abandoned penniless in the subway, and some people say it took her several weeks to find her way out, and when she did finally return to the light of day, it was in Brooklyn where she became enmeshed in a vaguely similar menage whose personnel ranged from W. H. Auden to Gypsy Rose Lee. At any rate, regardless of how much fantasy this legend may contain, the career of music was abandoned in favor of writing, and somewhere, sometime, in the dank and labyrinthine mysteries of the New York subway system, possibly between some chewing-gum vendor and some weight and character analysis given by a doll Gypsy, a bronze tablet should be erected in the memory of the mischievous comrade who made away with Carson's money for the study of piano. To paraphrase a familiar cliché of screen publicity-writers, perhaps a great musician was lost but a greater writer was found . . .

The original intention of this volume was to include most of Carson's previously published but uncollected work that otherwise would require assiduous research for an interested reader. But as I read through her papers, another concept for a collection evolved. Her papers included a good number of very early unpublished stories, most of them written before she was nineteen, in the late Sylvia Chatfield Bates' evening class in writing at New York University. Several of them still had the teacher's comment attached. My first reaction to this student material was that none of it should be published. After further reading I felt that all of it should eventually be published in a small edition by a university press. Now, four years after Carson's death, I believe a few selected examples belong in this volume to round out the glimpse of Carson's growth as a writer. I say "glimpse" because although the total material in this volume spans over thirty years, for the most part it was culled from her least-known work. This book does not include all of her previously uncollected or unpublished work, but rather a selection chosen to illuminate in part the creative process and development of Carson McCullers. "Wunderkind" is reprinted here, although it appeared earlier in *The Ballad of the Sad Café* collection, because it is her first published story — a milestone in any author's life. The other early stories have either not been previously published or have never been collected in a Carson McCullers edition. The outline of "The Mute" is included as another milestone in Carson's period of development, particularly when we know it evolved as her first novel, *The Heart Is a Lonely Hunter.* As examples of her mature work, again I have chosen lesser-known stories in order to familiarize the reader with fresh material.

Many of the pieces in the Essays and Articles section were written on assignment or written after such promptings as unspecific as "Do you have any thoughts on Thanksgiving?" given out by an editor who knew her work. These "assignments" were welcome because Carson was in need of money and could take some quick time off from her fiction writing to take advantage of these suggestions. Although this kind of magazine journalism is not always her best work, a number of these pieces are included because they are little known and have never been collected.

Five of Carson's poems, published in magazines or recorded, are here. Most of her unpublished poetry is in longhand, difficult to decipher accurately, and in some cases, unfinished or uncollated; therefore, none of these poems are included.

So this book is to give some idea of the early work of a writer and to illustrate, within the range of material chosen from her least-known work, the development of that talent. My hope is that Carson would have approved. I am plagued with doubt because I wonder why Carson did not collect some of this material while she was living since money was always a problem. Her expenses were excessive — doctors, nursing care, hospitals and an invalid's more than ordinary necessities. However, writers usually think more about their current work and their future plans than about what has already been written and she may not have had the strength or the interest to put together such a book. In fact, she may have forgotten these early stories existed.

I have referred obliquely to Carson's precarious health and her suffering and I do not plan to go into detail here. As a child she was always delicate and intermittently sick in bed, even though she played tennis, rode horseback and swam in between bouts of illness. As a young adult she began experiencing strokes and by the age of thirty-one her entire left side was paralyzed. Subsequent strokes and operations limited her physical abilities even more. The myth of her typing novels with one finger probably started with her (in fact, it probably was true for a while), but for years before her death, she could not have sat at a desk or even typed in bed. Even so, writing was possible — sometimes in longhand, sometimes dictated in a voice that she hardly had the strength to project. It is a blessing in every way that, while very young, Carson gave up her design to be a concert pianist, a career which would have been impossible for her to pursue. (Of course, as any reader of Carson McCullers knows, she used her knowledge and love of music throughout her writing.) When we were children, she used to practice five hours a day. At the time, I did not think I was especially privileged to be awakened by a Bach fugue. The most graphic memory I have of those beautiful Bach-playing hands with long strong fingers was shortly before she died, when the sheets of her bed had to be changed and she was able with her good hand to pull herself over to one side of the bed. It was as if her last physical strength was still in that hand.

At the age of sixteen, Carson wrote her first novel (I think she called it *A Reed of Pan* — the manuscript no longer exists). I remember that she earned money to come to New York — her dream — by giving a series of lectures on music appreciation to a group of Mother's friends. Once in the city she gave up music as a career and turned to her other talent — writing. She studied with Sylvia Chatfield Bates and later with Whit Burnett, who with Martha Foley edited the famous *Story* magazine. She continued writing up until the last and massive brain hemorrhage seven weeks before she died at fifty on September 29, 1967.

Carson's life was tragic in so many ways that people who did not know her personally have heard of her courage but not of her ingenuousness, her folksy humor, her wit and kindness. No two of her friends can be in the same room for long before one of them begins "Remember the time that Carson . . ." and off they go with countless stories.

I think now of a time when she wanted me to straighten out her library. This was many years ago but even at that period it was difficult for her to walk with a cane for more than a few steps and she wanted to be able to tell whoever happened to be taking care of her at the time exactly where to put his hands on the Rilke poems, *Out of Africa, A Portrait of the Artist as a Young Man,* and on and on; it soon became clear that all the books she had were essential to her. Two young girls had come to help with the physical labor of making our homemade version of a library. It was obvious that the girls had not read much and had never read Carson McCullers or heard of her. They just knew that she was a writer and one asked if she had really read all those books. I was busy trying to narrow down the absolutely essential books so that they would fit in one bookcase when I heard the same girl making more polite conversation by saying, "I never did understand why that lady let Beth die in *Little Women."* I didn't want to look at Sister, but the reflex was too sudden and now, thank God, I often see her expression of that moment when I think of her, rather than the way she was those last weeks. Her smile was so sweet and bemused, and she answered gently, seriously, "Yes, I cried too."

There were sorrows and tragedies in Carson's life other than her physical illness: two stormy marriages to the same James Reeves McCullers, his death followed by that of our mother and that of a favorite aunt, and many other difficult times. But it is important to note that there were moments of joy and anticipation of joy. She had recognition from sources that pleased her and she enjoyed fame from the time she was twenty-three when *The Heart Is a Lonely Hunter* was published. There were standing ovations for the magical Broadway production of *The Member of the Wedding.* There were invitations to presidential inaugurations and teas with Edith Sitwell and Marilyn Monroe, and her long and constant friendship with Tennessee Williams. Stage-struck like Frankie, she enjoyed having her picture taken with John Huston when she visited him at his castle in Ireland. She had two works in progress before her death and movies of *Reflections in a Golden Eye* and *The Heart Is a Lonely Hunter* were in production. She had many friends who loved her, but more important a few whom she really loved.

She loved any kind of occasion, any to-do such as a party or Christmas, and she loved to plan for them. She was planning a party when she died. Other women might dread birthdays, but they were big events in her life. With her hair freshly washed, she would put on one of her best robes and wait for the telegrams, flowers, and — most important — the presents. In the South, if one had no intention of giving a birthday present or a Christmas present, a card was sent. Carson hated cards because it meant that the sender was not going to give her a present.

Well, there is much courage in this world and most of it we never see. Probably what is important here is not that Carson wrote with such incredible handicaps, but that what she wrote was beautiful and real to those of us who are willing to go with her to explore the human heart. What matters about this collection is not that it has been difficult for me but whether readers who admire her work will find it rewarding to discover these little-known writings.

I might like to think I knew Carson better than anyone did. But Tennessee Williams on his first meeting with her caught the real spirit of Carson and the Carson I like to remember. In the essay cited earlier, he wrote:

> I should like to mention my first meeting with Carson McCullers. It occurred during the summer that I thought I was dying. I was performing a great many acts of piety that summer. I had rented a rather lopsided frame house on the island of Nantucket and had filled it with a remarkably random assortment of creatures animal and human. There was a young gentleman of Mexican-Indian extraction who was an angel of goodness except when he had a drink. The trouble was that he usually had a drink. Then there was a young lady studying for the opera and another young lady who painted various bits of refuse washed up by the sea. I remember they gave a rather cold and wet odor to the upper

floor of the house where she arranged her still-lifes which she called arrangements. If the weather had been consistently bright and warm these arrangements would not have been so hard to take. But the weather was unrelentingly bleak so that the exceedingly dank climate of the arrangements did little to dispell my reflections upon things morbid. One night there was a great wind-storm. Promptly as if they had been waiting all year to make this gesture, every window on the North side of the house crashed in, and we were at the mercy of the elements. The young lady who painted the wet arrangements, the opera singer and the naturally-good-humored Mexican all were driven South to that side of the house where I was attempting to write a play that involved the Angel of Eternity. At that time a pregnant cat came into the building and gave birth to five or six kittens on the bed in our downstairs guest-room. It was about this time, immediately after the wind-storm and the invasion of cats, that Carson McCullers arrived to pay me a visit on the island, in response to the first fan-letter that I had ever written to a writer, written after I had read her latest book, *The Member of the Wedding.*

The same morning that Carson arrived the two other female visitors, if my memory serves me accurately, took their departure, the one with her portfolio of arias and the other with several cases of moist canvases and wet arrangements, neither of them thanking me too convincingly for the hospitality of the house and as they departed, casting glances of veiled compassion upon the brand new arrival.

Carson was not dismayed by the state of the house. She had been in odd places before. She took an immediate fancy to the elated young Mexican and displayed considerable fondness for the cats and insisted that she would be comfortable in the downstairs bedroom where they were boarding. Almost immediately the summer weather improved. The sun came out with an air of permanence, the wind shifted to the South and it was suddenly warm enough for bathing. At the same time, almost immediately after Carson and the sun appeared on the island, I relinquished the romantic notion that I was a dying artist. My various psychosomatic symptoms were forgotten. There was warmth and light in the house, the odor of good cooking and the nearly-forgotten sight of clean dishes and silver. Also there was some coherent talk for a change. Long evening conversations over hot rum and tea, the reading of poetry aloud, bicycle rides and wanderings along moonlit dunes, and one night there was a marvelous display of the Aurora Borealis, great quivering sheets of white radiance sweeping over the island and the ghostly white fishermen's houses and fences. That night and that mysterious phenomenon of the sky will be always associated in my mind with the discovery of our friendship, or rather, more precisely, with the spirit of this new found friend, who seemed as curiously and beautifully unworldly as that night itself . . .

MARGARITA G. SMITH

SHORT STORIES

Editor's Note

DURING THE COMPILATION of this book, I have always called this first group of stories the "Carson Smith" stories, since that is the by-line that appears on the majority of them. Much of this early material was written in 1935 and 1936 for Sylvia Chatfield Bates' evening class at New York University when Carson was eighteen and nineteen. When the teacher's comment was saved, I include it. Only two manuscripts had no by-line: "The Aliens" and the one long untitled piece. Although I can be certain that both manuscripts predate *The Heart Is a Lonely Hunter,* I can't be sure whether they were written before or after her marriage to Reeves McCullers at nineteen. None of these early stories that remained unpublished at Carson's death have been changed except for corrections of misspellings, typographical errors and some repetitions. Her own handwritten corrections on the original manuscripts have been followed as carefully as possible.

Although "Sucker" was not published until 1963 in the *Saturday Evening Post* (since then it has been widely reprinted), the magazine carried a note from the author saying: ". . . I think it was my first short story; at least it was the first story I was proud to read to my family . . . I wrote it when I was seventeen, and my daddy had just given me my first typewriter. I remember writing the story in longhand, and then painfully typing it out . . ."

As the agent's letter which we include here indicates, Carson believed enough in "Court in the West Eighties" at the time she wrote it to have had it sent out when "Sucker" was making the rounds. And although "Poldi" is obviously part of the "court," too, there is nothing in the files that would indicate that Carson made any effort to get this published. Instead, the young author lifted out a phrase that Miss Bates underlined and put it in "Wunderkind," referring to notes of music falling over each other "like a handful of marbles dropped downstairs." Attentive readers will see other such examples taken from her previously unpublished work.

Since Carson regarded "Sucker" as her first real story and, indeed, does not seem to have submitted the majority of these early manuscripts, perhaps the remaining material ("Poldi," "Breath from the Sky," "The Orphanage," "Instant of the Hour After," "The Aliens" and the last untitled piece) should be referred to as "exercises," in deference to the author. Whatever they are called, these examples of her early work are most interesting in their own right and are amazing for one so young.

"Wunderkind" was written in Miss Bates' class. In her comment she suggested that Carson make specific revisions and then submit the story to the *Story* magazine contest of 1936. Carson heeded Miss Bates' advice: it was published in *Story*'s December 1936 issue when Carson was nineteen. I include it here, even though it appeared in her collection *The Ballad of the Sad Café,* because it marks the beginning of her professional career. Although *Story* also bought "Like That" the same year, it never appeared in the magazine and was recently discovered among the *Story* magazine archives at the Princeton University Library.

"The Aliens" and the untitled piece will be more interesting to the readers who know the author's novels. Both reflect the South of the Thirties and Carson's growing social consciousness. They take on even more importance when we see them suggesting later characters and themes. Although neither may have been intended as short stories (I have a feeling they were both early attempts at novels) I include them here because they seem to stand alone as stories. I suspect that "The Aliens" came first. There were three different versions of this manuscript, but the version included here seems to me to be the most self-contained. Any attempts to continue with Felix Kerr were abandoned until Mr. Minowitz appears in the untitled material.

Although a hint of the mute in *The Heart Is a Lonely Hunter* is seen in the silent redhead in "Court in the West Eighties," we know definitely that Mr. Minowitz eventually becomes Mr. Singer. Carson herself says, in "The Flowering Dream" (p. 274 in this volume), "For a whole year I worked on *The Heart Is a Lonely Hunter* without understanding it at all. Each character was talking to a central character, but why, I didn't know . . . I had been working for five hours and I went outside. Suddenly, as I walked across a road, it occurred to me that Harry Minowitz, the character all the other characters were talking to, was a different man, a deaf mute, and immediately the name was changed to John Singer . . ." I have come to refer to this untitled piece as "a little bit of everything" since it also seems to contain the beginnings of Mick in *The Heart Is a Lonely Hunter* and of Frankie in *The Member of the Wedding.*

I have tried to give some of the more obvious examples of the foreshadowing process that goes on in these early "exercises" included in this section. Many more "exercises" were found in Carson's papers, but an effort has been made to pick those which prefigure later works and which are self-contained and unfragmented. Ultimately, the choice from all this unpublished material was arbitrary because I chose what I really liked the best.

Since this volume is to show in part the growth of a writer, included here is the working outline of "The Mute," previously published in Oliver Evans' biography *The Ballad of Carson McCullers.* When Carson was living in the South, married to James Reeves McCullers, Sylvia Chatfield Bates wrote to her suggesting that if she were working on a long piece of fiction she should submit an outline to the Houghton Mifflin Fellowship Awards contest. She sent this outline along with a few chapters, and Houghton Mifflin published the novel as *The Heart Is a Lonely Hunter* in 1940. There is no accounting for the jump from the early searching and somewhat rambling material of "The Aliens" and the untitled piece to the maturity of vision and execution seen in this outline where she focuses clearly on a major first novel. Since she did not entirely stick to the outline, it gives evidence of a further stage in her development.

With the publication of *The Heart Is a Lonely Hunter,* she became not simply a published writer, but a celebrated one at the age of twenty-three. Readers who may know very little else of Carson's work have probably read one or two of her most famous and frequently anthologized short stories. From the stories published in Carson's lifetime, those four included here under Later Stories are some that have not been as widely read. Although all of these had national magazine publication after Carson had become an established writer, three of them, "Correspondence," "Who Has Seen the Wind?" and "Art and Mr. Mahoney," were not included in *The Ballad of the Sad Café and Collected Short Stories,* which contains most of her best short stories.

At one time, Carson began adapting "Who Has Seen the Wind?" for the theater. This changed in the writing and became *The Square Root of Wonderful.* Although the original story has appeared in many anthologies, until now it has not appeared in a collection of Carson's work. "The Haunted Boy" was in later editions of her *The Ballad of the Sad Café* collection, but not the first edition, so possibly it has been missed by many of her readers.

EARLY STORIES

SUCKER

IT WAS ALWAYS like I had a room to myself. Sucker slept in my bed with me but that didn't interfere with anything. The room was mine and I used it as I wanted to. Once I remember sawing a trap door in the floor. Last year when I was a sophomore in high school I tacked on my wall some pictures of girls from magazines and one of them was just in her underwear. My mother never bothered me because she had the younger kids to look after. And Sucker thought anything I did was always swell.

Whenever I would bring any of my friends back to my room all I had to do was just glance once at Sucker and he would get up from whatever he was busy with and maybe half smile at me, and leave without saying a word. He never brought kids back there. He's twelve, four years younger than I am, and he always knew without me even telling him that I didn't want kids that age meddling with my things.

Half the time I used to forget that Sucker isn't my brother. He's my first cousin but practically ever since I remember he's been in our family. You see his folks were killed in a wreck when he was a baby. To me and my kid sisters he was like our brother.

Sucker used to always remember and believe every word I said. That's how he got his nick-name. Once a couple of years ago I told him that if he'd jump off our garage with an umbrella it would act as a parachute and he wouldn't fall hard. He did it and busted his knee. That's just one instance. And the funny thing was that no matter how many times he got fooled he would still believe me. Not that he was dumb in other ways — it was just the way he acted with me. He would look at everything I did and quietly take it in.

There is one thing I have learned, but it makes me feel guilty and is hard to figure out. If a person admires you a lot you despise him and don't care — and it is the person who doesn't notice you that you are apt to admire. This is not easy to realize. Maybelle Watts, this senior at school, acted like she was the Queen of Sheba and even humiliated me. Yet at this same time I would have done anything in the world to get her attentions. All I could think about day and night was Maybelle until I was nearly crazy. When Sucker was a little kid and on up until the time he was twelve I guess I treated him as bad as Maybelle did me.

Now that Sucker has changed so much it is a little hard to remember him as he used to be. I never imagined anything would suddenly happen that would make us both very different. I never knew that in order to get what has happened straight in my mind I would want to think back on him as he used to be and compare and try to get things settled. If I could have seen ahead maybe I would have acted different.

I never noticed him much or thought about him and when you consider how long we have had the same room together it is funny the few things I remember. He used to talk to himself a lot when he'd think he was alone — all about him fighting gangsters and being on ranches and that sort of kids' stuff. He'd get in the bathroom and stay as long as an hour and sometimes his voice would go up high and excited and you could hear him all over the house. Usually, though, he was very quiet. He didn't have many boys in the neighborhood to buddy with and his face had the look of a kid who is watching a game and waiting to be asked to play. He didn't mind wearing the sweaters and coats that I outgrew, even if the sleeves did flop down too big and make his wrists look as thin and white as a little girl's. That is how I remember him — getting a little bigger every year but still being the same. That was Sucker up until a few months ago when all this trouble began.

Maybelle was somehow mixed up in what happened so I guess I ought to start with her. Until I knew her I hadn't given much time to girls. Last fall she sat next to me in General Science class and that was when I first began to notice her. Her hair is the brightest yellow I ever saw and occasionally she will wear it set into curls with some sort of gluey stuff. Her fingernails are pointed and manicured and painted a shiny red. All during class I used to watch Maybelle, nearly all the time except when I thought she was going to look my way or when the teacher called on me. I couldn't keep my eyes off her hands, for one thing. They are very little and white except for that red stuff, and when she would turn the pages of her book she always licked her thumb and held out her little finger and turned very slowly. It is impossible to describe Maybelle. All the boys are crazy about her but she didn't even notice me. For one thing she's almost two years older than I am. Between periods I used to try and pass very close to her in the halls but she would hardly ever smile at me. All I could do was sit and look at her in class — and sometimes it was like the whole room could hear my heart beating and I wanted to holler or light out and run for Hell.

At night, in bed, I would imagine about Maybelle. Often this would keep me from sleeping until as late as one or two o'clock. Sometimes Sucker would wake up and ask me why I couldn't get settled and I'd tell him to hush his mouth. I suppose I was mean to him lots of times. I guess I wanted to ignore somebody like Maybelle did me. You could always tell by Sucker's face when his feelings were hurt. I don't remember all the ugly remarks I must have made because even when I was saying them my mind was on Maybelle.

That went on for nearly three months and then somehow she began to change. In the halls she would speak to me and every morning she copied my homework. At lunch time once I danced with her in the gym. One afternoon I got up nerve and went around to her house with a carton of cigarettes. I knew she smoked in the girls' basement and sometimes outside of school — and I didn't want to take her candy because I think that's been run into the ground. She was very nice and it seemed to me everything was going to change.

It was that night when this trouble really started. I had come into my room late and Sucker was already asleep. I felt too happy and keyed up to get in a comfortable position and I was awake thinking about Maybelle a long time. Then I dreamed about her and it seemed I kissed her. It was a surprise to wake up and see the dark. I lay still and a little while passed before I could come to and understand where I was. The house was quiet and it was a very dark night.

Sucker's voice was a shock to me. "Pete? . . ."

I didn't answer anything or even move.

"You do like me as much as if I was your own brother, don't you, Pete?"

I couldn't get over the surprise of everything and it was like this was the real dream instead of the other.

"You have liked me all the time like I was your own brother, haven't you?"

"Sure," I said.

Then I got up for a few minutes. It was cold and I was glad to come back to bed. Sucker hung on to my back. He felt little and warm and I could feel his warm breathing on my shoulder.

"No matter what you did I always knew you liked me."

I was wide awake and my mind seemed mixed up in a strange way. There was this happiness about Maybelle and all that — but at the same time something about Sucker and his voice when he said these things made me take notice. Anyway I guess you understand people better when you are happy than when something is worrying you. It was like I had never really thought about Sucker until then. I felt I had always been mean to him. One night a few weeks before I had heard him crying in the dark. He said he had lost a boy's beebee gun and was scared to let anybody know. He wanted me to tell him what to do. I was sleepy and tried to make him hush and when he wouldn't I kicked at him. That was just one of the things I remembered. It seemed to me he had always been a lonesome kid. I felt bad.

There is something about a dark cold night that makes you feel close to someone you're sleeping with. When you talk together it is like you are the only people awake in the town.

"You're a swell kid, Sucker," I said.

It seemed to me suddenly that I did like him more than anybody else I knew — more than any other boy, more than my sisters, more in a certain way even than Maybelle. I felt good all over and it was like when they play sad music in the movies. I wanted to show Sucker how much I really thought of him and make up for the way I had always treated him.

We talked for a good while that night. His voice was fast and it was like he had been saving up these things to tell me for a long time. He mentioned that he was going to try to build a canoe and that the kids down the block wouldn't let him in on their football team and I don't know what all. I talked some too and it was a good feeling to think of him taking in everything I said so seriously. I even spoke of Maybelle a little, only I made out like it was her who had been running after me all this time. He asked questions about high school and so forth. His voice was excited and he kept on talking fast like he could never get the words out in time. When I went to sleep he was still talking and I could still feel his breathing on my shoulder, warm and close.

During the next couple of weeks I saw a lot of Maybelle. She acted as though she really cared for me a little. Half the time I felt so good I hardly knew what to do with myself.

But I didn't forget about Sucker. There were a lot of old things in my bureau drawer I'd been saving — boxing gloves and Tom Swift books and second rate fishing tackle. All this I turned over to him. We had some more talks together and it was really like I was knowing him for the first time. When there was a long cut on his cheek I knew he had been monkeying around with this new first razor set of mine, but I didn't say anything. His face seemed different now. He used to look timid and sort of like he was afraid of a whack over the head. That expression was gone. His face, with those wide-open eyes and his ears sticking out and his mouth never quite shut, had the look of a person who is surprised and expecting something swell.

Once I started to point him out to Maybelle and tell her he was my kid brother. It was an afternoon when a murder mystery was on at the movie. I had earned a dollar working for my Dad and I gave Sucker a quarter to go and get candy and so forth. With the rest I took Maybelle. We were sitting near the back and I saw Sucker come in. He began to stare at the screen the minute he stepped past the ticket man and he stumbled down the aisle without noticing where he was going. I started to punch Maybelle but couldn't quite make up my mind. Sucker looked a little silly — walking like a drunk with his eyes glued to the movie. He was wiping his reading glasses on his shirt tail and his knickers flopped down. He went on until he got to the first few rows where the kids usually sit. I never did punch Maybelle. But I got to thinking it was good to have both of them at the movie with the money I earned.

I guess things went on like this for about a month or six weeks. I felt so good I couldn't settle down to study or put my mind on anything. I wanted to be friendly with everybody. There were times when I just had to talk to some person. And usually that would be Sucker. He felt as good as I did. Once he said: "Pete, I am gladder that you are like my brother than anything else in the world."

Then something happened between Maybelle and me. I never have figured out just what it was. Girls like her are hard to understand. She began to act different toward me. At first I wouldn't let myself believe this and tried to think it was just my imagination. She didn't act glad to see me anymore. Often she went out riding with this fellow on the football team who owns this yellow roadster. The car was the color of her hair and after school she would ride off with him, laughing and looking into his face. I couldn't think of anything to do about it and she was on my mind all day and night. When I did get a chance to go out with her she was snippy and didn't seem to notice me. This made me feel like something was the matter — I would worry about my shoes clopping too loud on the floor or the fly of my pants, or the bumps on my chin. Sometimes when Maybelle was around, a devil would get into me and I'd hold my face stiff and call grown men by their last names without the Mister and say rough things. In the night I would wonder what made me do all this until I was too tired for sleep.

At first I was so worried I just forgot about Sucker. Then later he began to get on my nerves. He was always hanging around until I would get back from high school, always looking like he had something to say to me or wanted me to tell him. He made me a magazine rack in his Manual Training class and one week he saved his lunch money and bought me three packs of cigarettes. He couldn't seem to take it in that I had things on my mind and didn't want to fool with him. Every afternoon it would be the same — him in my room with this waiting expression on his face. Then I wouldn't say anything or I'd maybe answer him rough-like and he would finally go on out.

I can't divide that time up and say this happened one day and that the next. For one thing I was so mixed up the weeks just slid along into each other and I felt like Hell and didn't care. Nothing definite was said or done. Maybelle still rode around with this fellow in his yellow roadster and sometimes she would smile at me and sometimes not. Every afternoon I went from one place to another where I thought she would be. Either she would act almost nice and I would begin thinking how nice things would finally clear up and she would care for me — or else she'd behave so that if she hadn't been a girl I'd have wanted to grab her by that white little neck and choke her. The more ashamed I felt for making a fool of myself the more I ran after her.

Sucker kept getting on my nerves more and more. He would look at me as though he sort of blamed me for something, but at the same time knew that it wouldn't last long. He was growing fast and for some reason began to stutter when he talked. Sometimes he had nightmares or would throw up his breakfast. Mom got him a bottle of cod liver oil.

Then the finish came between Maybelle and me. I met her going to the drug store and asked for a date. When she said no I remarked something sarcastic. She told me she was sick and tired of my being around and that she had never cared a rap about me. She said all that. I just stood there and didn't answer anything. I walked home very slowly.

For several afternoons I stayed in my room by myself. I didn't want to go anywhere or talk to anyone. When Sucker would come in and look at me sort of funny I'd yell at him to get out. I didn't want to think of Maybelle and I sat at my desk reading *Popular Mechanics* or whittling at a toothbrush rack I was making. It seemed to me I was putting that girl out of my mind pretty well.

But you can't help what happens to you at night. That is what made things how they are now.

You see a few nights after Maybelle said those words to me I dreamed about her again. It was like that first time and I was squeezing Sucker's arm so tight I woke him up. He reached for my hand.

"Pete, what's the matter with you?"

All of a sudden I felt so mad my throat choked — at myself and the dream and Maybelle and Sucker and every single person I knew. I remembered all the times Maybelle had humiliated me and everything bad that had ever happened. It seemed to me for a second that nobody would ever like me but a sap like Sucker.

"Why is it we aren't buddies like we were before? Why — ?"

"Shut your damn trap!" I threw off the cover and got up and turned on the light. He sat in the middle of the bed, his eyes blinking and scared.

There was something in me and I couldn't help myself. I don't think anybody ever gets that mad but once. Words came without me knowing what they would be. It was only afterward that I could remember each thing I said and see it all in a clear way.

"Why aren't we buddies? Because you're the dumbest slob I ever saw! Nobody cares anything about you! And just because I felt sorry for you sometimes and tried to act decent don't think I give a damn about a dumb-bunny like you!"

If I'd talked loud or hit him it wouldn't have been so bad. But my voice was slow and like I was very calm. Sucker's mouth was part way open and he looked as though he'd knocked his funny bone. His face was white and sweat came out on his forehead. He wiped it away with the back of his hand and for a minute his arm stayed raised that way as though he was holding something away from him.

"Don't you know a single thing? Haven't you ever been around at all? Why don't you get a girl friend instead of me? What kind of a sissy do you want to grow up to be anyway?"

I didn't know what was coming next. I couldn't help myself or think.

Sucker didn't move. He had on one of my pajama jackets and his neck stuck out skinny and small. His hair was damp on his forehead.

"Why do you always hang around me? Don't you know when you're not wanted?"

Afterward I could remember the change in Sucker's face. Slowly that blank look went away and he closed his mouth. His eyes got narrow and his fists shut. There had never been such a look on him before. It was like every second he was getting older. There was a hard look to his eyes you don't see usually in a kid. A drop of sweat rolled down his chin and he didn't notice. He just sat there with those eyes on me and he didn't speak and his face was hard and didn't move.

"No you don't know when you're not wanted. You're too dumb. Just like your name — a dumb Sucker."

It was like something had busted inside me. I turned off the light and sat down in the chair by the window. My legs were shaking and I was so tired I could have bawled. The room was cold and dark. I sat there for a long time and smoked a squashed cigarette I had saved. Outside the yard was black and quiet. After a while I heard Sucker lie down.

I wasn't mad any more, only tired. It seemed awful to me that I had talked like that to a kid only twelve. I couldn't take it all in. I told myself I would go over to him and try to make it up. But I just sat there in the cold until a long time had passed. I planned how I could straighten it out in the morning. Then, trying not to squeak the springs, I got back in bed.

Sucker was gone when I woke up the next day. And later when I wanted to apologize as I had planned he looked at me in this new hard way so that I couldn't say a word.

All of that was two or three months ago. Since then Sucker has grown faster than any boy I ever saw. He's almost as tall as I am and his bones have gotten heavier and bigger. He won't wear any of my old clothes any more and has bought his first pair of long pants — with some leather suspenders to hold them up. Those are just the changes that are easy to see and put into words.

Our room isn't mine at all any more. He's gotten up this gang of kids and they have a club. When they aren't digging trenches in some vacant lot and fighting they are always in my room. On the door there is some foolishness written in Mercurochrome saying "Woe to the Outsider who Enters" and signed with crossed bones and their secret initials. They have rigged up a radio and every afternoon it blares out music. Once as I was coming in I heard a boy telling something in a loud voice about what he saw in the back of his big brother's automobile. I could guess what I didn't hear. *That's what her and my brother do. It's the truth — parked in the car.* For a minute Sucker looked surprised and his face was almost like it used to be. Then he got hard and tough again. "Sure, dumbbell. We know all that." They didn't notice me. Sucker began telling them how in two years he was planning to be a trapper in Alaska.

But most of the time Sucker stays by himself. It is worse when we are alone together in the room. He sprawls across the bed in those long corduroy pants with the suspenders and just stares at me with that hard, half-sneering look. I fiddle around my desk and can't get settled because of those eyes of his. And the thing is I just have to study because I've gotten three bad cards this term already. If I flunk English I can't graduate next year. I don't want to be a bum and I just have to get my mind on it. I don't care a flip for Maybelle or any particular girl any more and it's only this thing between Sucker and me that is the trouble now. We never speak except when we have to before the family. I don't even want to call him Sucker any more and unless I forget I call him by his real name, Richard. At night I can't study with him in the room and I have to hang around the drug store, smoking and doing nothing, with the fellows who loaf there.

More than anything I want to be easy in my mind again. And I miss the way Sucker and I were for a while in a funny, sad way that before this I never would have believed. But everything is so different that there seems to be nothing I can do to get it right. I've sometimes thought if we could have it out in a big fight that would help. But I can't fight him because he's four years younger. And another thing — sometimes this look in his eyes makes me almost believe that if Sucker could he would kill me.

[*The Saturday Evening Post,* 1963]

COURT IN THE WEST EIGHTIES

IT WAS NOT UNTIL SPRING that I began to think about the man who lived in the room directly opposite to mine. All during the winter months the court between us was dark and there was a feeling of privacy about the four walls of little rooms that looked out on each other. Sounds were muffled and far away as they always seem when it is cold and windows everywhere are shut. Often it would snow and, looking out, I could see only the quiet white flakes sifting down against the gray walls, the snow-edged bottles of milk and covered crocks of food put out on the window sills, and perhaps a light coming out on the dimness in a thin line from behind closed curtains. During all this time I can remember seeing only a few incomplete glimpses of this man living across from me — his red hair through the frosty window glass, his hand reaching out on the sill to bring in his food, a flash of his calm drowsy face as he looked out on the court. I paid no more attention to him than I did to any of the other dozen or so people in that building. I did not see anything unusual about him and had no idea that I would come to think of him as I did.

There was enough to keep me busy last winter without looking at things outside my window. This was my first year at university, the first time I had been in New York. Also there was the necessity of trying to get and keep a part time job in the mornings. I have often thought that when you are an eighteen year old girl, and can't fix it so you look any older than your age, it is harder to get work than at any other time. Maybe I would say the same thing, though, if I were forty. Anyway those months seem to me now about the toughest time I've had so far. There was work (or job-hunting) in the morning, school all afternoon, study and reading at night — together with the newness and strangeness of this place. There was a queer sort of hungriness, for food and for other things too, that I could not get rid of. I was too busy to make any friends down at school and I had never been so much alone.

Late at night I would sit by the window and read. A friend of mine back home would sometimes send me three or four dollars to get certain books in secondhand book stores here that he can't get in the library. He would write for all sorts of things — books like "A Critique of Pure Reason," or "Tertium Organum," and authors like Marx and Strachey and George Soule. He has to stay back home now and help out his family because his Dad is unemployed. He had a job as a garage mechanic. He could get some sort of office work, but a mechanic's wages are better and, lying under an automobile with his back to the ground, he has a chance to think things out and make plans. Before mailing him the books I would study them myself, and although we had talked about many of the things in them in simpler words there would sometimes be a line or two that would make a dozen things I'd half known definite and sure.

Often such sentences as these would make me restless and I'd stare out the window a long time. It seems strange now to think of me standing there alone and this man asleep in his room on the other side and me not knowing anything about him and caring less. The court would be dark for the night, with the snow on the roof of the first floor down below, like a soundless pit that would never awaken.

Then gradually the spring began to come. I cannot understand why I was so unconscious of the way in which things began to change, of the milder air and the sun that began to grow stronger and light up the court and all the rooms around it. The thin, sooty-gray patches of snow disappeared and the sky was bright azure at noon. I noticed that I could wear my sweater instead of my coat, that sounds from outside were beginning to get so clear that they bothered me when reading, that every morning the sun was bright on the wall of the opposite building. But I was busy with the job I had and school and the restlessness that these books I read in my spare time made me feel. It was not until one morning when I found the heat in our building turned off and stood looking out through the open window that I realized the great change that had come about. Oddly enough, too, it was then when I saw the man with the red hair plainly for the first time.

He was standing just as I was, his hands on the window sill, looking out. The early sun shone straight in his face and I was surprised at his nearness to me and at the clarity with which I could see him. His hair, bright in the sunlight, came up from his forehead red and coarse as a sponge. I saw that his mouth was blunt at the corners, his shoulders straight and muscular under his blue pajama jacket. His eyelids drooped slightly and for some reason this gave him a look of wisdom and deliberateness. As I watched him he went inside a moment and returned with a couple of potted plants and set them on the window sill in the sun. The distance between us was so little that I could plainly see his neat blunt hands as they fondled the plants, carefully touching the roots and the soil. He was humming three notes over and over — a little pattern that was more an expression of well being than a tune. Something about the man made me feel that I could stand there watching him all morning. After a while he looked up once more at the sky, took a deep breath and went inside again.

The warmer it got the more things changed. All of us around the court began to pin back our curtains to let the air into our small rooms and move our beds close to the windows. When you can see people sleep and dress and eat you get to feel that you understand them — even if you don't know their names. Besides the man with the red hair there were others whom I began to notice now and then.

There was the cellist whose room was at a right angle with mine and the young couple living above her. Because I was at my window so much I could not help but see nearly everything that happened to them. I knew the young couple were going to have a baby soon and that, although she didn't look so well, they were very happy. I knew about the cellist's ups and downs too.

At night when I wasn't reading I would write to this friend of mine back home or type out things that happened to come into my head on the typewriter he got me when I left for New York. (He knew I would have to type out assignments at school.) The things I'd put down weren't of any importance — just thoughts that it did me good to try to get out of my mind. There would be a lot of x marks on the paper and maybe a few sentences such as: *fascism and war cannot exist for long because they are death and death is the only evil in the world,* or *it is not right that the boy next to me in Economics should have had to wear newspapers under his sweater all winter because he didn't have any overcoat,* or *what are the things that I know and can always believe?* While I would sit writing like this I would often see the man across from me and it would be as if he were somehow bound up in what I was thinking — as if he knew, maybe, the answers to the things that bothered me. He seemed so calm and sure. When the trouble we began to have in the court started I could not help but feel he was the one person able to straighten it out.

The cellist's practicing annoyed everybody, especially the girl living directly above her who was pregnant. The girl was very nervous and seemed to be having a hard time. Her face was meager above her swollen body, her little hands delicate as a sparrow's claws. The way she had her hair skinned back tightly to her head made her look like a child. Sometimes when the practicing was particularly loud she would lean down toward the cellist's room with an exasperated expression and look as though she might call out to her to stop awhile. Her husband seemed as young as she did and you could tell they were happy. Their bed was close to the window and they would often sit on it Turkish fashion, facing each other, talking and laughing. Once they were sitting that way eating some oranges and throwing the peels out the window. The wind blew a bit of a peel into the cellist's room and she screamed up to them to quit littering everyone else with their trash. The young man laughed, loud so the cellist could hear him, and the girl laid down her half finished orange and wouldn't eat anymore.

The man with the red hair was there the evening that happened. He heard the cellist and looked a long time at her and at the young couple. He had been sitting as he often did, at the chair by the window — in his pajamas, relaxed and doing nothing at all. (After he came in from work he rarely went out again.) There was something contented and kind about his face and it seemed to me he wanted to stop the tension between the rooms. He just looked, and did not even get up from his chair, but that is the feeling I had. It makes me restless to hear people scream at each other and that night I felt tired and jittery for some reason. I put the Marx book I was reading down on the table and just looked at this man and imagined about him.

I think the cellist moved in about the first of May, because during the winter I don't remember hearing her practice. The sun streamed in on her room in the late afternoon, showing up a collection of what looked to be photographs tacked on the wall. She went out often and sometimes she had a certain man in to see her. Late in the day she would sit facing the court with her cello, her knees spread wide apart to straddle the instrument, her skirts pulled up to the thighs so as not to strain the seams. Her music was raw toned and lazily played. She seemed to go into a sort of coma when she worked and her face took on a cowish look. Nearly always she had stockings drying in the window (I could see them so plainly that I could tell she sometimes only washed the feet to save wear and trouble) and some mornings there was a gimcrack tied on to the cord of the window shade.

I felt that this man across from me understood the cellist and everyone else on the court as well. I had a feeling that nothing would surprise him and that he understood more than most people. Maybe it was the secretive droop of his eyelids. I'm not sure what it was. I just knew that it was good to watch him and think about him. At night he would come in with a paper sack and carefully take his food out and eat it. Later he would put on his pajamas and do exercises in his room and after that he'd usually just sit, doing nothing, until almost midnight. He was an exquisite housekeeper, his window sill was never cluttered up. He would tend his plants every morning, the sun shining on his healthily pale face. Often he carefully watered them with a rubber bulb that looked like an ear syringe. I could never guess for sure just what his job in the day time was.

About the end of May there was another change in the court. The young man whose wife was pregnant began to quit going regularly to work. You could tell by their faces he had lost his job. In the morning he would stay at home later than usual, would pour out her milk from the quart bottle they still kept on the window sill and see that she drank the whole amount before it had time to sour. Sometimes at night after everyone else was asleep you could hear the murmuring sound of his talking. Out of a late silence he would say *listen here* so loud that it was enough to wake all of us, and then his voice would drop and he would start a low, urgent monologue to his wife. She almost never said anything. Her face seemed to get smaller and sometimes she would sit on the bed for hours with her little mouth half open like a dreaming child's.

The university term ended but I stayed on in the city because I had this five hour job and wanted to attend summer school. Not going to classes I saw even fewer people than before and stayed closer to home. I had plenty of time to realize what it meant when the young man started coming in with a pint of milk instead of a quart, when finally one day the bottle he brought home was only one of the half pint size.

It is hard to tell how you feel when you watch someone go hungry. You see their room was not more than a few yards from mine and I couldn't quit thinking about them. At first I wouldn't believe what I saw. This is not a tenement house far down on the East side, I would tell myself. We are living in a fairly good, fairly average part of town — in the West eighties. True our court is small, our rooms just big enough for a bed, a dresser and a table, and we are almost as close as tenement people. But from the street these buildings look fine; in both entrances there is a little lobby with something like marble on the floor, an elevator to save us walking up our six or eight or ten flights of stairs. From the street these buildings look almost rich and it is not possible that inside someone could starve. I would say: because their milk is cut down to a fourth of what they used to get and because I don't see him eating (giving her the sandwich he goes out to get each evening at dinner time) that is not a sign they are hungry. Because she just sits like that all day, not taking any interest in anything except the window sills where some of us keep our fruit that is because she is going to have the baby very soon now and is a little unnatural. Because he walks up and down the room and yells at her sometimes, his throat sounding choked up, that is just the ugliness in him.

After reasoning with myself like this I would always look across at the man with the red hair. It is not easy to explain about this faith I had in him. I don't know what I could have expected him to do, but the feeling was there just the same. I quit reading when I came home and would often just sit watching him for hours. Our eyes would meet and then one of us would look away. You see all of us in the court saw each other sleep and dress and live out our hours away from work, but none of us ever spoke. We were near enough to throw our food into each others' windows, near enough so that a single machine gun could have killed us all together in a flash. And still we acted as strangers.

After a while the young couple didn't have any sort of milk bottle on their window sill and the man would stay home all day, his eyes looped with brown circles and his mouth a sharp straight line. You could hear him talking in bed every night — beginning with his loud *listen here.* Out of all the court the cellist was the only one who didn't show in some little gesture that she felt the strain.

Her room was directly below theirs so she probably had never seen their faces. She practiced less than usual now and went out more. This friend of hers that I mentioned was in her place almost every night. He was dapper like a little cat — small, with a round oily face and large almond shaped eyes. Sometimes the whole court would hear them quarreling and after a while he would usually go out. One night she brought home one of those balloon-men they sell along Broadway — a long balloon for the body and a round small one for the head, painted with a grinning mouth. It was a brilliant green, the crepe paper legs were pink and the big cardboard feet black. She fastened the thing to the cord of the shade where it dangled, turning slowly and shambling its paper legs whenever a breeze came.

By the end of June I felt I could not have stayed in the court much longer. If it had not been for the man with red hair I would have moved. I would have moved before the night when everything came finally to a show down. I couldn't study, couldn't keep my mind on anything.

There was one hot night I well remember. The cellist and her friend had their light turned on and so did the young couple. The man across from me sat looking out on the court in his pajamas. He had a bottle by his chair and would draw it up to his mouth occasionally. His feet were propped on the window sill and I could see his bare crooked toes. When he had drunk a good deal he began talking to himself. I couldn't hear the words, they were merged together into one low rising and falling sound. I had a feeling, though, that he might be talking about the people in the court because he would gaze around at all the windows between swallows. It was a queer feeling — like what he was saying might straighten things out for all of us if we could only catch the words. But no matter how hard I listened I couldn't understand any of it. I just looked at his strong throat and at his calm face that even when he was tight did not lose its expression of hidden wisdom. Nothing happened. I never knew what he was saying. There was just that feeling that if his voice had been only a little less low I would have learned so very much.

It was a week later when this thing happened that brought it all to a finish. It must have been about two o'clock one night when I was waked up by a strange sound. It was dark and all the lights were out. The noise seemed to come from the court and as I listened to it I could hardly keep myself from trembling. It was not loud (I don't sleep very well or otherwise it wouldn't have waked me) but there was something animal-like about it — high and breathless, between a moan and an exclamation. It occurred to me that I had heard such a sound sometime in my life before, but it went too far back for me to remember.

I went to the window and from there it seemed to be coming from the cellist's room. All the lights were off and it was warm and black and moonless. I was standing there looking out and trying to imagine what was wrong when a shout came from the young couple's apartment that as long as I live I will never be able to forget. It was the young man and between the words there was a choking sound.

"Shut up! You bitch down there shut up! I can't stand —"

Of course I knew then what the sound had been. He left off in the middle of the sentence and the court was quiet as death. There were no *shhh*s such as usually follow a noise in the night here. A few lights were turned on, but that was all. I stood at the window feeling sick and not able to stop trembling. I looked across at the red headed man's room and in a few minutes he turned on his light. Sleepy eyed, he gazed all around the court. *Do something do something,* I wanted to call over to him. In a moment he sat down with a pipe in his chair by the window and switched off his light. Even after everybody else seemed to be sleeping again there was still the smell of his tobacco in the hot dark air.

After that night things began to get like they are now. The young couple moved and their room remained vacant. Neither the man with the red hair nor I stayed inside as much as before. I never saw the cellist's dapper looking friend again and she would practice fiercely, jabbing her bow across the strings. Early in the mornings when she would get the brassiere and stockings she had hung out to dry she would snatch them inside and turn her back to the window. The balloon-man still dangled from her shade cord, turning slowly in the air, grinning and brilliant green.

And now yesterday the man with the red hair left for good, too. It is late summer, the time people usually move. I watched him pack up all the things he had and tried not to think of never seeing him again. I thought about school starting soon and about a list of books I would make out to read. I watched him like a complete stranger. He seemed happier than he had been in a long time, humming a little tune as he packed, fondling his plants for a while before taking them in from the sill. Just before leaving he stood at the window looking out on the court for the last time. His calm face did not squint in the glare, but his eyelids drooped until they were almost shut and the sun made a haze of light around his bright hair that was almost like a sort of halo.

Tonight I have thought a long time about this man. Once I started to write my friend back home who has the mechanic's job about him, but I changed my mind. The thing is this — it would be too hard explaining to anybody else, even this friend, just how it was. You see when it comes right down to it there are so many things about him I don't know — his name, his job, even what nationality he is. He never did do anything, and I don't even know just exactly what I expected him to do. About the young couple I don't guess he could have helped it any more than I could. When I think back over the times I have watched him I can't remember a thing unusual that he ever did. When describing him nothing stands out except his hair. Altogether he might seem just like a million other men. But no matter how peculiar it sounds I still have this feeling that there is something in him that could change a lot of situations and straighten them out. And there is one point in a thing like this — as long as I feel this way, in a sense it is true.

The following letter, concerning this story and "Sucker," was found among Carson McCullers' correspondence. Maxim Lieber was her literary agent at that time.

MAXIM LIEBER
Authors' Representative

545 Fifth Avenue
New York City

MUrray Hill 2–3135 — 3136
CABLE: FERENC • NEW YORK

November 10, 1939

Mrs. Carson Smith McCullers
1519 Starke Avenue
Columbus, Georgia

DEAR MRS. MCCULLERS:

I am sorry to say that your manuscripts SUCKER and COURT IN THE WEST EIGHTIES have been rejected by the following magazines respectively; The Virginia Quarterly, The Ladies' Home Journal, Harper's, Atlantic Monthly, The New Yorker, Redbook, Harper's

Bazaar, Esquire, American Mercury, North American Review, Yale Review, Southern Review, Story, and; The Virginia Quarterly, The Atlantic Monthly, Harper's, The New Yorker, Harper's Bazaar, Coronet, North American Review, The American Mercury, The Yale Review, Story, The Southern Review, Zone, Nutmeg.

We are returning the two stories herewith.

Sincerely yours,

GERALDINE MAVOR

GM:MW

POLDI

When Hans was only a block from the hotel a chill rain began to fall, draining the color from the lights that were just being turned on along Broadway. He fastened his pale eyes on the sign reading COLTON ARMS, tucked a sheet of music under his overcoat, and hurried on. By the time he stepped inside the dingily marbled lobby his breath was coming in sharp pants and the sheet of music was crumpled.

Vaguely he smiled at a face before him. "Third floor — this time."

You could always tell how the elevator boy felt about the permanent people of the hotel. When those for whom he had the most respect stepped out on their floors he always held the door open for an extra moment in an attitude of unctuousness. Hans had to jump furtively so that the sliding door would not nip his heels.

Poldi —

He stood hesitantly in the dim corridor. From the end came the sound of a cello — playing a series of descending phrases that tumbled over each other helter skelter like a handful of marbles dropped downstairs. Stepping down to the room with the music he stood for a moment just outside the door. A wobbly lettered notice was pinned there by a thumbtack.

Poldi Klein
Please Do Not Disturb While Practicing

The first time he had seen that, he recalled, there had been an E before the ING of practicing.

The heat seemed to be very low; the folds of his coat smelled wet and let out little whiffs of coldness. Crouching over the half warm radiator that stood by the end window did not relieve him.

Poldi — I've waited for a long time. And many times I've walked outside until you're through and thought about the words I wish to say to you. Gott! How pretty — like a poem or a little song by Schumann. Start like that. Poldi —

His hand crept along the rusty metal. Warm, she always was. And if he held her it would be so that he would want to bite his tongue in two.

Hans, you know the others have meant nothing to me. Joseph, Nikolay, Harry — all the fellows I've known. And this Kurt *only three times she couldn't* that I've talked about this last week — Poof! They all are nothing.

It came to him that his hands were crushing the music. Glancing down he saw that the brutally colored back sheet was wet and faded, but that the notation inside was undamaged. Cheap stuff. Oh well —

He walked up and down the hall, rubbing his pimply forehead. The cello whirred upward in an unclear arpeggio. That concert — the Castelnuovo-Tedesco — How long was she going to keep on practicing? Once he paused and stretched out his hand toward the door knob. No, that time he had gone in and she had looked — and looked and told him —

The music rocked lushly back and forth in his mind. His fingers jerked as he tried to transcribe the orchestral score to the piano. She would be leaning forward now, her hands gliding over the fingerboard.

The sallow light from the window left most of the corridor dim. With a sudden impulse he knelt down and focussed his eye to the keyhole.

Only the wall and the corner; she must be by the window. Just the wall with its string of staring photographs — Casals, Piatigorsky, the fellow she liked best back home, Heifetz — and a couple of valentines and Christmas cards tucked in between. Nearby was the picture called Dawn of the barefooted woman holding up a rose with the dingy pink paper party hat she had gotten last New Year cocked over it.

The music swelled to a crescendo and ended with a few quick strokes. Ach! The last one a quarter tone off. Poldi —

He stood up quickly and, before the practicing should continue, knocked on the door.

"Who is it?"

"Me — H — Hans."

"All right. You can come in."

She sat in the fading light of the court window, her legs sprawled broadly to clench her cello. Expectantly she raised her eyebrows and let her bow droop to the floor.

His eyes fastened on the trickles of rain on the window glass. "I — I just came in to show you the new popular song we're playing tonight. The one you suggested."

She tugged at her skirt that had slid up above her stocking rolls and the gesture drew his gaze. The calves of her legs bulged out and there was a short run in one stocking. The pimples on his forehead deepened in color and he stared furtively at the rain again.

"Did you hear me practicing outside?"

"Yes."

"Listen, Hans, did it sound spiritual — did it sing and lift you to a higher plane?"

Her face was flushed and a drop of perspiration dribbled down the little gully between her breasts before disappearing under the neck of her frock. "Ye-es."

"I think so. I believe my playing has deepened much in the last month." Her shoulders shrugged expansively. "Life does that to me — it happens every time something like this comes up. Not that it's ever been like this before. It's only after you've suffered that you can play."

"That's what they claim."

She stared at him for a moment as though seeking a stronger confirmation, then curved her lips down petulantly. "That wolf, Hans, is driving me crazy. You know that Fauré thing — in E — well it takes in that note over and over and nearly drives me to drink. I get to dreading that E — it stands out something awful."

"You could have it shifted?"

"Well — but the next thing I take up would probably be in that key. No, that won't do any good. Besides, it costs something and I'd have to let them have my cello for a few days and what should I use? Just what, I ask you?"

When he made money she could get — "I don't notice it so much."

"It's a darn shame, I think. People who play like Hell can have good cellos and I can't even have a decent one. It's not right for me to put up with a wolf like that. It damages my playing — anybody can tell you that. How should I get any tone from that cheese box?"

A phrase from a sonata he was learning weaved itself in and out of his mind. "Poldi —" What was it now? *I love you love you.*

"And for what do I bother anyway — this lousy job we have?" With a dramatic gesture she got up and balanced her instrument in the corner of the room. When she switched on the lamp the bright circle of light made shadows follow the curves of her body.

"Listen, Hans, I'm so restless till I could scream."

The rain splashed on the window. He rubbed his forehead and watched her walk up and down the room. All at once she caught sight of the run in her stockings and, with a hiss of displeasure, spat on the end of her finger and bent over to transfer the wetness to the bottom of the run.

"Nobody has such a time with stockings as cellists. And for what? A room in a hotel and five dollars for playing trash three hours every night in the week. A pair of stockings twice every month I have to buy. And if at night I just rinse out the feet the tops run just the same."

She snatched down a pair of stockings that hung side by side with a brassiere in the window and, after peeling off the old ones, began to pull them on. Her legs were white and traced with dark hairs. There were blue veins near the knees. "Excuse me — you don't mind, do you? You seem to me like my little brother back home. And we'll get fired if I start wearing things like that down to play."

He stood at the window and looked at the rain blurred wall of the next building. Just opposite him was a milk bottle and a jar of mayonnaise on a window ledge. Below, someone had hung some clothes out to dry and forgotten to take them in; they flapped dismally in the wind and rain. A little brother — Jesus!

"And dresses," she went on impatiently. "All the time getting split at the seams because of having to stretch your knees out. But at that it's better than it used to be. Did you know me when everybody was wearing those short skirts — and I had such a time being modest when I played and still keeping with the style? Did you know me then?"

"No," Hans answered. "Two years ago the dresses were about like they are now."

"Yes, it was two years ago we first met, wasn't it?"

"You were with Harry after the con —"

"Listen, Hans." She leaned forward and looked at him urgently. She was so close that her perfume came sharp to his nostrils. "I've just been about crazy all day. It's about him, you know."

"Wh — Who?"

"You understand well enough — him — Kurt! How, Hans, he loves me, don't you think so?"

"Well — but Poldi — how many times have you seen him. You hardly know each other." He turned away from her at the Levin's when she was praising his work and —

"Oh, what does it matter if I've only been with him three times. I should worry. But the look in his eyes and the way he spoke about my playing. Such a soul he has. It comes out in his music. Have you ever heard the Beethoven funeral march sonata played so well as he did it that night?"

"It was good —"

"He told Mrs. Levin my playing had so much temperament."

He could not look at her; his grey eyes kept their focus on the rain.

"So gemütlich he is. Ein Edel Mensch! But what can I do? Huh, Hans?"

"I don't know."

"Quit looking so pouty. What would you do?"

He tried to smile. "Have — have you heard from him — he telephoned you or written?"

"No — but I'm sure it's just his delicateness. He wouldn't want me to feel offended or turn him down."

"Isn't he engaged to marry Mrs. Levin's daughter next spring?"

"Yes. But it's a mistake. What would he want with a cow like her?"

"But Poldi —"

She smoothed down the back of her hair, holding her arms above her head so that her broad breasts stood out tautly and the muscles of her underarms flexed beneath the thin silk of her dress. "At his concert, you know, I had a feeling he was playing just to me. He looked straight at me every time he bowed. That's the reason he didn't answer my letter — he's so afraid he'll hurt someone and then he can always tell me what he means in his music."

The adams-apple jutting from Hans' thin neck moved up and down as he swallowed. "You wrote to him?"

"I had to. An artist cannot subdue the greatest of the things that come to her."

"What did you say?"

"I told him how much I love him — that was ten days ago — a week after I saw him first at the Levins'."

"And you heard nothing?"

"No. But can't you see how he feels? I knew it would be that way so day before yesterday I wrote another note telling him not to worry — that I would always be the same."

Hans vaguely traced his hairline with his slender fingers. "But Poldi — there have been so many others — just since I've known you." He got up and put his finger on the photograph next to Casals'.

The face smiled at him. The lips were thick and topped by a dark moustache. On the neck there was a little round spot. Two years ago she had pointed it out to him so many times, telling him that the hicky where his violin rested used always to be so angry-red. And how she used to stroke it with her finger. How she had called it Fiddler's Ill Luck — and how between them it had gotten down to simply his Zilluck. For several moments he stared at that vague splotch on the picture, wondering if it had been photographed or was simply the smudge from the number of times she had pointed it out to him.

The eyes stared at him sharp seeing and dark. Hans' knees felt weak; he sat down again.

"Tell me, Hans, he loves — don't you think so? You think really that he loves me but is only waiting until he feels it's best to reply — you think so?"

A thin haze seemed to cover everything in the room. "Yes," he said slowly.

Her expression changed. "Hans!"

He leaned forward, trembling.

"You — you look so queer. Your nose is wiggling and your lips shake like you are ready to cry. What —"

Poldi —

A sudden laugh broke into her question. "You look like a peculiar little cat my Papa used to have."

Quickly he moved toward the window so that his face was turned away from her. The rain still slithered down the glass, silvery, half opaque. The lights of the next building were on; they shone softly through the grey twilight. Ach! Hans bit his lips. In one of the windows it looked like — like a woman — Poldi in the arms of a big man with dark hair. And on the window sill looking in, beside the bottle of milk and the mayonnaise jar, was a little yellow cat out in the rain. Slowly Hans' bony knuckles rubbed his eyelids.

Sylvia Chatfield Bates' comment, attached to "Poldi" and marked *Return for reading next time*:

This is an excellent example of the "picture" story — which means full dramatization of a short time scheme, the picturing of an almost static condition the actual narrative elements of which are in the past or in the future. The situation is rather trite, but not very. You can rescue it from triteness — as Willa Cather did in *Lucy Gayheart* — by the truth, accuracy and freshness of detail. Many a story sells on its detail; yours, so far as I have seen them, may be that sort. These details are good. Very vivid. Also a special knowledge story has a bid for success, and your special knowledge of music exhibited here sounds authentic. A musician can judge that better than I.

The average reader will want more than your static picture vividly presented — movement forward, at the very least suggested for the future. But I like this as it is. For what it is it need not be much better done.

S.C.B.

BREATH FROM THE SKY

HER PEAKED, YOUNG FACE stared for a time, unsatisfied, at the softer blue of the sky that fringed the horizon. Then with a quiver of her open mouth she rested her head again on the pillow, tilted the panama hat over her eyes, and lay motionless in the canvas striped chair. Chequered shade patterns jerked over the blanket covering her thin body. Bee drones sounded from the spirea bushes that sprayed out their white blossoms nearby.

Constance dozed for a moment. She awoke to the smothering smell of hot straw — and Miss Whelan's voice.

"Come on now. Here's your milk."

Out of her sleepy haze a question came that she had not intended to ask, that she had not even been consciously thinking about: "Where's Mother?"

Miss Whelan held the glistening bottle in her plump hands. As she poured the milk it frothed white in the sunlight and crystal frost wreathed the glass.

"Where —?" Constance repeated, letting the word slide out with her shallow release of breath.

"Out somewhere with the other kids. Mick was raising a fuss about bathing suits this morning. I guess they went to town to buy those."

Such a loud voice. Loud enough to shatter the fragile sprays of the spirea so that the thousands of tiny blossoms would float down, down, down in a magic kaleidoscope of whiteness. Silent whiteness. Leaving only the stark, prickly twigs for her to see.

"I bet your mother will be surprised when she finds where you are this morning."

"No," whispered Constance, without knowing the reason for the denial.

"I should think she would be. Your first day out and all. I know *I* didn't think the doctor would let you talk him into coming out. Especially after the time you had last night."

She stared at the nurse's face, at her white clad bulging body, at her hands serenely folded over her stomach. And then at her face again — so pink and fat that why — why wasn't the weight and the bright color uncomfortable — why didn't it sometimes droop down tiredly toward her chest — ?

Hatred made her lips tremble and her breath come more shallowly, quickly.

In a moment she said: "If I can go three hundred miles away next week — all the way to Mountain Heights — I guess it won't hurt to sit in my own side yard for a little while."

Miss Whelan moved a pudgy hand to brush back the girl's hair from her face. "Now, now," she said placidly. "The air up there'll do the trick. Don't be impatient. After pleurisy — you just have to take it easy and be careful."

Constance's teeth clamped rigidly. Don't let me cry, she thought. Don't, please, let her look at me ever again when I cry. Don't ever let her look at me or touch me again. Don't, please — Ever again.

When the nurse had moved off fatly across the lawn and gone back into the house, she forgot about crying. She watched a high breeze make the leaves of the oaks across the street flutter with a silver sheen in the sun. She let the glass of milk rest on her chest, bending her head slightly to sip now and then.

Out again. Under the blue sky. After breathing the yellow walls of her room for so many weeks in stingy hot breaths. After watching the heavy footboard of her bed, feeling it crush down on her chest. Blue sky. Cool blueness that could be sucked in until she was drenched in its color. She stared upward until a hot wetness welled in her eyes.

As soon as the car sounded from far off down the street she recognized the chugging of the engine and turned her head toward the strip of road visible from where she lay. The automobile seemed to tilt precariously as it swung into the driveway and jerked to a noisy stop. The glass of one of the rear windows had been cracked and plastered with dingy adhesive tape. Above this hung the head of a police dog, tongue palpitating, head cocked.

Mick jumped out first with the dog. "Looka there, Mother," she called in a lusty child's voice that rose up almost to a shriek. "She's *out.*"

Mrs. Lane stepped to the grass and looked at her daughter with a hollow, strained face. She drew deeply at her cigarette that she held in her nervous fingers, blew out airy grey ribbons of smoke that twisted in the sunshine.

"Well —" Constance prompted flatly.

"Hello, stranger," Mrs. Lane said with a brittle gaiety. "Who let you out?"

Mick clung to the straining dog. "See, Mother! King's trying to get to her. He hasn't forgotten Constance. See. He knows her good as anybody — don't you, boyoboyoboy —"

"Not so loud, Mick. Go lock that dog in the garage."

Lagging behind her mother and Mick was Howard — a sheepish expression on his pimply, fourteen year old face. "Hello, Sister," he mumbled after a gangling moment. "How do you feel?"

To look at the three of them, standing there in the shade from the oaks, somehow made her more tired than she had felt since she came out. Especially Mick — trying to straddle King with her muscular little legs, clinging to his flexed body that looked ready any moment to spring out at her.

"See, Mother! King —"

Mrs. Lane jerked one shoulder nervously. "Mick — Howard take that animal away this instant — now mind me — and lock him up somewhere." Her slender hands gesture without purpose. "This instant."

The children looked at Constance with sidelong gazes and moved off across the lawn toward the front porch.

"Well —" said Mrs. Lane when they were gone. "Did you just pick up and walk out?"

"The doctor said I could — finally — and he and Miss Whelan got that old rolling chair out from under the house and — helped me."

The words, so many of them at once, tired her. And when she gave a gentle gasp to catch her breath, the coughing started again. She leaned over the side of the chair, Kleenex in hand, and coughed until the stunted blade of grass on which she had fastened her stare had, like the cracks in the floor beside her bed, sunk ineffaceably into her memory. When she had finished she stuffed the Kleenex into a cardboard box beside the chair and looked at her mother — standing by the spirea bush, back turned, vacantly singeing the blossoms with the tip of her cigarette.

Constance stared from her mother to the blue sky. She felt that she must say something. "I wish I had a cigarette," she pronounced slowly, timing the syllables to her shallow breath.

Mrs. Lane turned. Her mouth, twitching slightly at the corners, stretched out in a too bright smile. "Now *that* would be pretty!" She dropped the cigarette to the grass and ground it out with the toe of her shoe. "I think maybe I'll cut them out for a while myself. My mouth feels all sore and furry — like a mangy little cat."

Constance laughed weakly. Each laugh was a huge burden that helped to sober her.

"Mother —"

"Yes."

"The doctor wanted to see you this morning. He wants you to call him."

Mrs. Lane broke off a sprig of the spirea blossoms and crushed it in her fingers. "I'll go in now and talk to him. Where's that Miss Whelan? Does she just set you out on the lawn by yourself when I'm gone — at the mercy of dogs and —"

"Hush, Mother. She's in the house. It's her afternoon off, you know, today."

"Is it? Well, it isn't afternoon."

The whisper slid out easily with her breath. "Mother —"

"Yes, Constance."

"Are — are you coming back out?" She looked away as she said it — looked at the sky that was a burning, fevered blue.

"If you want me to — I'll be out."

She watched her mother cross the lawn and turn into the gravel path that led to the front door. Her steps were as jerky as those of a little glass puppet. Each bony ankle stiffly pushing past the other, the thin bony arms rigidly swinging, the delicate neck held to one side.

She looked from the milk to the sky and back again. "Mother," her lips said, but the sound came out only in a tired exhalation.

The milk was hardly started. Two creamy stains drooped from the rim side by side. Four times, then, she had drunk. Twice on the bright cleanliness, twice with a shiver and eyes shut. Constance turned the glass half an inch and let her lips sink down on an unstained part. The milk crept cool and drowsy down her throat.

When Mrs. Lane returned she wore her white string garden gloves and carried rusty, clinking shears.

"Did you phone Doctor Reece?"

The woman's mouth moved infinitesimally at the corners as though she had just swallowed. "Yes."

"Well —"

"He thinks it best — not to put off going too long. This waiting around — The sooner you get settled the better it'll be."

"When, then?" She felt her pulse quiver at her finger tips like a bee on a flower — vibrate against the cool glass.

"How does the day after tomorrow strike you?"

She felt her breath shorten to hot, smothered gasps. She nodded.

From the house came the sound of Mick's and Howard's voices. They seemed to be arguing about the belts of their bathing suits. Mick's words merged into a scream. And then the sounds hushed.

That was why she was almost crying. She thought about water, looking down into great jade swirls of it, feeling the coolness of it on her hot limbs, splashing through it with long, effortless strokes. Cool water — the color of the sky.

"Oh, I do feel so dirty —"

Mrs. Lane held the shears poised. Her eyebrows quivered upward over the white sprays of blossoms she held. "Dirty?"

"Yes — yes. I haven't been in a bathtub for — for three months. I'm sick of being just sponged — stingily —"

Her mother crouched over to pick up a scrap of a candy wrapper from the grass, looked at it stupidly for a moment, and let it drop to the grass again.

"I want to go swimming — feel all the cool water. It isn't fair — isn't fair that I can't."

"Hush," said Mrs. Lane with testy sibilance. "Hush, Constance. You don't have to worry over nonsense."

"And my hair —" She lifted her hand to the oily knot that bumped out from the nape of her neck. "Not washed with water in — months — nasty awful hair that's going to run me wild. I can stand all the pleurisy and drains and t.b. but —"

Mrs. Lane was holding the flowers so tightly that they curled limply into each other as though ashamed. "Hush," she repeated hollowly. "This isn't necessary."

The sky burned brightly — blue jet flames. Choking and murderous to air.

"Maybe if it were just cut off short —"

The garden shears snipped shut slowly. "Here — if you want me to — I guess I could clip it. Do you really want it short?"

She turned her head to one side and feebly lifted one hand to tug at the bronze hairpins. "Yes — real short. Cut it all off."

Dank brown, the heavy hair hung several inches below the pillow. Hesitantly Mrs. Lane bent over and grasped a handful of it. The blades, blinding bright in the sun, began to shear through it slowly.

Mick appeared suddenly from behind the spirea bushes. Naked, except for her swimming trunks, her plump little chest gleamed silky white in the sun. Just above her round child's stomach were scolloped two soft lines of plumpness. "Mother! Are you giving *her* a haircut?"

Mrs. Lane held the dissevered hair gingerly, staring at it for a moment with her strained face. "Nice job," she said brightly. "No little fuzzes around your neck, I hope."

"No," said Constance, looking at her little sister.

The child held out an open hand. "Give it to me, Mother. I can stuff it into the cutest little pillow for King. I can—"

"Don't dare let her touch the filthy stuff," said Constance between her teeth. Her hand fingered the stiff, loose fringes around her neck, then sank tiredly to pluck at the grass.

Mrs. Lane crouched over and, moving the white flowers from the newspaper where she had laid them, wrapped up the hair and left the bundle lying on the ground behind the invalid's chair.

"I'll take it when I go in—"

The bees droned on in the hot stillness. The shade had grown blacker, and the little shadows that had fluttered by the side of the oak trees were still. Constance pushed the blanket down to her knees. "Have you told Papa about my going so soon?"

"Yes, I telephoned him."

"To Mountain Heights?" asked Mick, balancing herself on one bare leg and then the other.

"Yes, Mick."

"Mother, isn't that where you went to see Unca Charlie?"

"Yes."

"Is that where he sent us the cactus candy from—a long time ago?"

Lines, fine and grey as the web of a spider, cut through the pale skin around Mrs. Lane's mouth and between her eyes. "No, Mick. Mountain Heights is just the other side of Atlanta. That was Arizona."

"It was funny tasting," said Mick.

Mrs. Lane began cutting the flowers again with hurried snips. "I—I think I hear that dog of yours howling somewhere. Go tend to him—go—run along, Mick."

"You don't hear King, Mother. Howard's teaching him to shake hands out on the back porch. Please don't make me go." She laid her hands on her soft mound of stomach. "Look! You haven't said anything about my bathing suit. Aren't I nice in it, Constance?"

The sick girl looked at the flexed, eager muscles of the child before her, and then gazed back at the sky. Two words shaped themselves soundlessly on her lips.

"Gee! I wanna hurry up and get in. Did you know they're making people walk through a kind of ditch thing so you won't get sore toes this year — And they've got a new chute-ty-chute."

"Mind me this instant, Mick, and go on in the house."

The child looked at her mother and started off across the lawn. As she reached the path that led to the door she paused and, shading her eyes, looked back at them. "Can we go soon?" she asked, subdued.

"Yes, get your towels and be ready."

For several minutes the mother and daughter said nothing. Mrs. Lane moved jerkily from the spirea bushes to the fever-bright flowers that bordered the driveway, snipping hastily at the blooms, the dark shadow at her feet dogging her with noonday squatness. Constance watched her with eyes half closed against the glare, with her bony hands against the bubbling, thumping dynamo that was her chest. Finally she shaped the words on her lips and let them emerge. "Am I going up there by myself?"

"Of course, my dear. We'll just put you on a bicycle and give you a shove —"

She mashed a string of phlegm with her tongue so that she would not have to spit, and thought about repeating the question.

There were no more blooms ready for cutting. The woman looked sidewise at her daughter from over the flowers in her arm, her blue veined hand shifting its grasp on the stems. "Listen, Constance — The garden club's having some sort of a to-do today. They're all having lunch at the club — and then going to somebody's rock garden. As long as I'm taking the children over I thought I — you don't mind if I go, do you?"

"No," said Constance after a moment.

"Miss Whelan promised to stay on. Tomorrow maybe —"

She was still thinking about the question that she must repeat, but the words clung to her throat like gummy pellets of mucus and she felt that if she tried to expel them she would cry. She said instead, with no special reason: "Lovely —"

"Aren't they? Especially the spirea — so graceful and white."

"I didn't even know they'd started blooming until I got out."

"Didn't you? I brought you some in a vase last week."

"In a vase —" Constance murmured.

"At night, though. That's the time to look at them. Last night I stood by the window — and the moonlight was on them. You know how white flowers are in the moonlight —"

Suddenly she raised her bright eyes to those of her mother. "I heard you," she said half accusingly. "In the hall — tipping up and down. Late. In the living room. And I thought I heard the front door open and close. And when I was coughing once I looked at the window and I thought I saw a white dress up and down the grass like a ghost — like a —"

"Hush!" said her mother in a voice as jagged as splintered glass. "Hush. Talking is so — exhausting."

It was time for the question — as though her throat were swollen with its matured syllables. "Am I going by myself to Mountain Heights, or with Miss Whelan, or —"

"I'm going with you. I'll take you up on the train. And stay a few days until you're settled."

Her mother stood against the sun, stopping some of the glare so that she could look into her eyes. They were the color of the sky in the cool morning. They were looking at her now with a strange stillness — a hollow restfulness. Blue as the sky before the sun had burned it to its gaseous brilliance. She stared with trembling, open lips, listening to the sound her breath made. "Mother —"

The end of the word was smothered by the first cough. She leaned over the side of the chair, feeling them beat at her chest like great blows risen from some unknown part inside her. They came, one after another with equal force. And when the last toneless one had wrenched itself clear she was so tired that she hung with unresisting limpness on the chair arm, wondering if the strength to raise her dizzy head would ever again be hers.

In the gasping minute that followed, the eyes that were still before her stretched to the vastness of the sky. She looked, and breathed, and struggled up to look again.

Mrs. Lane had turned away. But in a moment her voice rang out bitterly bright. "Goodbye, pet — I'll run along now. Miss Whelan'll be out in a minute and you'd better go right in. So long —"

As she crossed the lawn Constance thought she saw a delicate shudder shake her shoulders — a movement as perceptible as that of a crystal glass that had been thumped too soundly.

Miss Whelan stood placidly in her line of vision as they left. She only had a glimpse of Howard's and Mick's half naked bodies and the towels they flapped lustily at each other's rears. Of King thrusting his panting head above the broken window glass with its dingy tape. But she heard the overfed roar of the engine, the frantic stripping of the gears as the car backed from the driveway. And even after the last sound of the motor had trailed into silence, it was as though she could still see her mother's strained white face bent over the wheel —

"What's the matter?" asked Miss Whelan calmly. "Your side's not hurting you again, I hope."

She turned her head twice on the pillow.

"There now. Once you're in again you'll be all right."

Her hands, limp and colorless as tallow, sank over the hot wetness that streamed down her cheeks. And she swam without breath in a wide, ungiving blueness like the sky's.

[*Redbook,* October 1971]

THE ORPHANAGE

HOW THE HOME came to be associated with the sinister bottle belongs to the fluid logic of childhood, for at the beginning of this episode I must have been not more than seven. But the Home, as a dwelling for the orphans in our town, might have in its mysterious ugliness been partly to blame. It was a large, gabled house, painted in a blackish green, and set back in a rake-printed front yard that was absolutely bare except for two magnolia trees. The yard was surrounded by a wrought iron fence, and the orphans were seldom to be seen there when you stopped on the sidewalk to gaze inside. The back yard, on the other hand, was for a long time a secret place to me; the Home was on a corner, and a high board fence concealed what went on inside, but when you passed there would be the sound of unseen voices and sometimes a noise like that of clanging metal. This secrecy and the mysterious noises made me very much afraid. I would often pass the Home with my Grandmother, on the way home from the main street of town, and now, in memory, it seems that we always walked by in twilight wintertime. The sounds behind the board fence seemed tinged with menace in the fading light, and the iron picket gate in front was to the touch of a finger bitter cold. The gloom of the grassless yard and even the gleams of yellow light from the narrow windows seemed somehow in keeping with the dreadful knowledge that came to me about this time.

My initiator was a little girl named Hattie, who must have been about nine or ten. I don't remember her last name, but there are some other facts about this Hattie that are unforgettable. For one thing, she told me that George Washington was her uncle. Another time she explained to me what made colored people colored. If a girl, said Hattie, kissed a boy she turned into a colored person, and when she was married her children were colored, too. Only brothers were excepted from this law. Hattie was a small child for her age, with snaggled front teeth, and greasy blond hair held back by a jeweled barrette. I was forbidden to play with her, perhaps because my Grandmother or parents sensed an unwholesome element in the relation; if this supposition is true they were quite right. I had once kissed Tit, who was my best friend but only a second cousin, so that day by day I was slowly turning into a colored person. It was summer, and day by day I was turning darker. Perhaps I had some notion that Hattie, having once revealed this fearful transformation, might somehow have the power to stop it. In the dual bondage of guilt and fear, I followed her around the neighborhood, and often she demanded nickels and dimes.

The memories of childhood have a strange shuttling quality, and areas of darkness ring the spaces of light. The memories of childhood are like clear candles in an acre of night, illuminating fixed scenes from the surrounding darkness. I don't remember where Hattie lived, but one passageway, one room, have an uncanny clarity. Nor do I know how I happened to go to this room, but anyway I was there with Hattie and my cousin, Tit. It was late afternoon, the room was not quite dark. Hattie was wearing an Indian dress, with a headband of bright red feathers, and she had asked if we knew where babies come from. The Indian feathers in her band looked, for some reason, scary to me.

"They grow in the insides of ladies," Tit said.

"If you swear you will never tell a living soul then I will show you something."

We must have sworn, though I remember a reluctance, and a dread of further revelations. Hattie climbed up on a chair and brought down something from a closet shelf. It was a bottle, with something queer and red inside.

"Do you know what this is?" she asked.

The thing inside the bottle resembled nothing I had ever seen before. It was Tit who asked: "What is it?"

Hattie waited and her face beneath the band of feathers wore a crafty expression. After some moments of suspense, she said:

"It's a dead pickled baby."

The room was very quiet. Tit and I exchanged a sidelong look of horror. I could not look again at the bottle, but Tit was gazing at it with fascinated dread.

"Whose?" he asked finally in a low voice.

"See the little old red head with the mouth. And the little teensy red legs squelched up under it. My brother brought it home when he was learning to be a drug store man."

Tit reached out a finger and touched the bottle, then put his hands behind his back. He asked again, this time in a whisper: "Whose? Whose baby?"

"It is an orphan," Hattie said.

I remember the light whispering sound of our footsteps as we tiptoed from the room, and that the passageway was dark and at the end there was a curtain. That, thank goodness, is my final recollection of this Hattie. But the pickled orphan haunted me for some time; I dreamed once that the Thing had got out of the jar and was skuttling around the Orphans' Home and I was locked in there and It was skuttling after me — Did I believe that in that gloomy, gabled house there were shelves with rows of these eerie bottles? Probably yes — and no. For the child knows two layers of reality — that of the world, which is accepted like an immense collusion of all adults — and the unacknowledged, hidden secret, the profound. In any case, I kept close to my Grandmother when in the late afternoon we passed by the Home on our way from town. At that time I knew none of the orphans, as they went to the Third Street School.

It was a few years later that two occurrences came about that brought me in a direct relation with the Home. Meanwhile, I looked on myself as a big girl, and had passed the place a thousand times, walking alone, or on skates, or bicycle. The terror had diminished to a sort of special fascination. I always stared at the Home in passing, and sometimes I would see the orphans, walking with Sunday slowness on their way to Sunday school and church, grouped in marching formation with the two biggest orphans leading and the two smallest orphans at the end. I was about eleven when changes occurred that drew me in closer as a spectator, and opened an unexpected area of romance. First, my Grandmother was made a member of the Board of the Orphans' Home. That was in the autumn. Then at the beginning of the spring term the orphans were transferred to the Seventeenth Street School, where I was going, and three of the orphans were in the room with me in the sixth grade. The transfer was made because of a change in the boundary line of the school districts. My Grandmother was elected to the Board because she enjoyed Boards, Committees, and the meetings of associations, and a former member of the Board had died at about that time.

My Grandmother visited the Home about once a month, and on her second visit I went with her. It was the best time of the week, a Friday afternoon, spacious with the sense of coming holiday. The afternoon was cold, and the late sunlight made fiery reflections on the windowpanes. Inside, the Home was quite different from the way I had imagined it. The wide hall was bare, and the rooms were uncurtained, rugless, and scantily furnished. Heat came from stoves in the dining room and in the general room that was next to the front parlor, Mrs. Wesley, the matron of the Home, was a large woman, rather hard of hearing, and she kept her mouth slightly ajar when anyone of importance spoke. She always seemed to be short of breath, and she spoke through her nose in a placid voice. My Grandmother had brought some clothes (Mrs. Wesley called them garments) donated by the various churches and they shut themselves in the cold parlor to talk. I was entrusted to a girl of my own age, named Susie, and we went out immediately to the board fenced back yard.

That first visit was awkward. Girls of all ages were playing different games. There was in the yard a joggling board, and an acting bar, and a hopscotch game was marked on the ground. Confusion made me see the yard full of children as an unassorted whole. One little girl came up to me and asked me what was my father. And, as I was slow in answering she said: "My father was a walker on the railroad." Then she ran to the acting bar and swung by her knees — her hair hung straight down from her red face and she wore brown cotton bloomers.

INSTANT OF THE HOUR AFTER

LIGHT AS SHADOWS her hands fondled his head and then came placidly to rest; the tips of her fingers hovered on his temples, throbbed to the warm slow beat inside his body, and her palms cupped his hard skull.

"Re*ver*berating va-cuity," he mumbled so that the syllables lolloped ponderously into each other.

She looked down at his lax, sound body that stretched the length of the couch. One foot — the sock wrinkled around the ankle — hung limp over the edge. And as she watched his sensitive hand left his side and crept up drunkenly to his mouth — to touch his lips that had remained pursed out and loose after his words. "Immense hollowness —" he mouthed behind his feeling fingers.

"Enough out of you tonight — my darling," she said. "The show's over and the monkey's dead."

They had turned off the heat an hour before and the apartment was beginning to chill. She looked at the clock, the hands of which pointed to one. Not much heat anyway at that hour, she thought. No draughts, though; opalescent ribbons of smoke lay motionless close to the ceiling. Speculatively her glance shifted to the whiskey bottle and the confused chessmen on the card table. To a book that lay face downward on the floor — and a lettuce leaf lying forlornly in the corner since Marshall had lost it while waving his sandwich. To the dead little butts of cigarettes and the charred matches scattered.

"Here cover up," she said absently, unfolding a blanket at the foot of the couch. "You're so susceptible to draughts."

His eyes opened and stared stolidly up at her — blue-green, the color of the sweater he wore. One of them was shot through at the corner with fragile fibers of pink, giving him somehow the guileless expression of an Easter bunny. So much younger than twenty, he always looked — With his head thrown back on her knees so that his neck was arched above his rolled collar and tender seeming with the soft outline of the cords and cartilages. With his dark hair springing from the pallor of his face.

"Vacant majesty —"

As he spoke his eyelids drooped until the eyes beneath had been narrowed to a slit that seemed to sneer at her. And she knew with a sudden start that he was not as drunk as he pretended to be.

"You needn't hold forth any longer," she said. "Phillip's gone home and there's just me."

"It's in the na-a-ature of things — that such a viewpoint — view —"

"He's gone home," she repeated. "You talked him out." She had a fleet picture of Phillip bending to pick up the cigarette butts — his agile, blond little body and his calm eyes — "He washed up the dishes we messed and even wanted to sweep the floor, but I made him leave it."

"He's a —" started Marshall.

"Seeing *you* — and how tired I was — he even offered to pull out the couch and get you to bed."

"A cute procedure —" he mouthed.

"I made him run along." She remembered for a moment his face as she shut the door between them, the sound of his footsteps going down stairs, and the feeling — half of pity for loneliness, half of warmth — that she always felt when she listened to the sounds of others going out into the night away from them.

"To listen to him — one would think his reading were rigidly narrowed to — to G. K. Chesterton and George Moore," he said, giving a drunken lilt to the words. "Who won at chess — me or him?"

"You," she said. "But you did your best work before you got so drunk."

"Drunk —" he murmured, moving his long body laxly, changing the position of his head. "God! your knees are bony. Bo-ony."

"But I thought sure you'd give him the game when you made that idiotic move with your queen's pawn." She thought of their fingers hovering over the carved precision of their pieces, brows frowned, the glow of the light on the bottle beside them.

His eyes were closed again and his hand had crumpled down on his chest. "Lousy simile —" he mumbled. "Granted about the mountain. Joyce climbed laboriously — O-O-OK — but when he reached the top — top reached —"

"You can't stand this drinking, darling —" Her hands moved over the soft angle of his chin and rested there.

"He wouldn't say the world was *fla-at.* All along that's what they said. Besides the villagers could walk around — around with their jackasses and see that for themselves. With their asses."

"Hush," she said. "You've talked about that long enough. You get on one subject and go on and on ad infinitum. And don't land anywhere."

"A crater —" he breathed huskily. "And at least after the immensity of his climb he could have expected — some lovely leaps of Hell fire — some —"

Her hand clenched on his chin and shook it. "Shut up," she said. "I heard you when you improvised on that so brilliantly before Phillip left. You were obscene. And I'd almost forgotten."

A smile crept out across his face and his blue fringed eyes looked up at her. "Obscene —? Why should you put yourself in place of those symbols — sym —"

"If it were with anyone but Phillip that you talk like that I'd — I'd leave you."

"Immense va-cuity," he said, closing his eyes again. "Dead Hollowness. Hollowness, I say. With maybe in the ashes at the bottom a —"

"Shut up."

"A squirming, fatbellied cretin."

It came to her that she must have drunk more than she realized, for the objects in the room seemed to take on a strange look of suffering. The butts of the cigarettes looked overmouthed and limp. The rug, almost brand new, seemed trampled and choked in design by the ashes.

Even the last of the whiskey lay pale and quiet in the bottle. "Does it relieve you any?" she asked with slow calm. "I hope that times like this —"

She felt his body stiffen and, like an aggravating child, he interrupted her words with a sudden burst of unmelodic humming.

She eased her thighs from beneath his head and stood up. The room seemed to have grown smaller, messier, ranker with smoke and spilled whiskey. Bright lines of white weaved before her eyes. "Get up," she said dully. "I've got to pull out this darn couch and make it up."

He folded his hands on his stomach and lay solid, unstirring.

"You are detestable," she said, opening the door of the closet and taking down the sheets and blankets that lay folded on the shelves.

When she stood above him once more, waiting for him to rise, she felt a moment of pain for the drained pallor of his face. For the shades of darkness that had crept down halfway to his cheekbones, for the pulse that always fluttered in his neck when he was drunk or fatigued.

"Oh Marshall, it's bestial for us to get all shot like this. Even if you don't have to work tomorrow — there are years — fifty of them maybe — ahead." But the words had a false ring and she could only think of tomorrow.

He struggled to sit up on the edge of the couch and when he had reached that position his head dropped down to rest in his hands. "Yes, Pollyanna," he mumbled. "Yes, my dear croaking Pol — Pol. Twenty is a lovely lovely age Blessed God."

His fingers that weaved through his hair and closed into weak fists filled her with a sudden, sharp love. Roughly she snatched at the corners of the blanket and drew them around his shoulders. "Up now. We can't fool around like this all night."

"Hollowness —" he said wearily, without closing his sagging jaw.

"Has it made you sick?"

Holding the blanket close he pulled himself to his feet and lumbered toward the card table. "Can't a person even *think* without being called obscene or sick or drunk. No. No understanding of thought. Of deep deep thought in blackness. Of rich morasses. Morrasses. With their asses."

The sheet billowed down through the air and the round swirls collapsed into wrinkles. Quickly she tucked in the corners and smoothed the blankets on top. When she turned around she saw that he sat hunched over the chessmen — ponderously trying to balance a pawn on a turreted castle. The red checked blanket hung from his shoulders and trailed behind the chair.

She thought of something clever. "You look," she said, "like a brooding king in a bad-house." She sat on the couch that had become a bed and laughed.

With an angry gesture he embrangled his hands in the chessmen so that several pieces clattered to the floor. "That's right," he said. "Laugh your silly head off. That's the way it's always been done."

The laughs shook her body as though every fiber of her muscles had lost its resistance. When she had finished the room was very still.

After a moment he pushed the blanket away from him so that it crumpled in a heap behind the chair. "He's blind," he said softly. "Almost blind."

"Watch out, there's probably a draught — Who's blind?"

"Joyce," he said.

She felt weak after her laughter and the room stood out before her with painful smallness and clarity. "That's the trouble with you, Marshall," she said. "When you get like this you go on and on so that you wear a person out."

He looked at her sullenly. "I must say you're pretty when you're drunk," he said.

"I don't get drunk — couldn't if I wanted to," she said, feeling a pain beginning to bear down behind her eyes.

"How 'bout that night when we —"

"I've told you," she said stiffly between her teeth, "I wasn't drunk. I was ill. And you would make me go out and —"

"It's all the same," he interrupted. "You were a thing of beauty hanging on to that table. It's all the same. A sick woman — a drunk woman — ugh."

Nervelessly she watched his eyelids droop down until they had hidden all the goodness in his eyes.

"And a pregnant woman," he said. "Yeah. It'll be some sweet hour like this when you come to simper your sweet sneakret into my ear. Another cute little Marshall. Ain't we fine — look what we can do. Oh, God, what dreariness."

"I loathe you," she said, watching her hands (that were surely not a part of her?) begin to tremble. "This drunk brawling in the middle of the night —"

As he smiled his mouth seemed to her to take on the same pink, slitted look that his eyes had. "You love it," he whispered soberly. "What would you do if once a week I didn't get soused. So that — glutinously — you can paw over me. And Marshall darling this and Marshall that. So you can run your greedy little fingers all over my face — Oh yes. You love me best when I suffer. You — you —"

As he lurched across the room she thought she saw that his shoulders were shaking.

"Here Mama," he taunted. "Why don't you offer to come help me point." As he slammed the door to the bathroom some vacant coathangers that had been hung on the doorknob clashed at each other with tinny sibilance.

"I'm leaving you —" she called hollowly when the noise from the coathangers had died down. But the words had no meaning to her. Limp, she sat on the bed and looked at the wilted lettuce leaf across the room. The lampshade had been knocked atilt so that it clung dangerously to the bulb — so that it made a hurtful passage of brightness across the grey disordered room.

"Leaving you," she repeated to herself — still thinking about the late-at-night squalor around them.

She remembered the sound of Phillip's footsteps as he had descended. Nightlike and hollow. She thought of the dark outside and the cold naked trees of early spring. She wanted to picture herself leaving the apartment at that hour. With Phillip maybe. But as she tried to see his face, his small calm little body, the outlines were vague and there was no expression there. She could only recall the way his hands had poked at the sugar-grained bottom of a glass with the dishcloth — as they had done when he helped her with the dishes that night. And as she thought of following the empty sounds of the footsteps they grew softer, softer — until there was only black silence left.

With a shiver she got up from the couch and moved toward the whiskey bottle on the table. The parts of her body felt like tiresome appendages; only the pain behind her eyes seemed her own. She hesitated, holding the neck of the bottle. That — or one of the Alka-Seltzers in the top bureau drawer. But the thought of the pale tablet writhing to the top of the glass, consumed by its own effervescence — seemed sharply depressing. Besides, there was just enough for one more drink. Hastily she poured, noting again how the glittering convexity of the bottle always cheated her.

It made a sharp little path of warmness down into her stomach but the rest of her body remained chill. "Oh damn," she whispered — thinking of picking up that lettuce leaf in the morning, of the cold outside, listening for any sound from Marshall in the bathroom. "Oh damn. I can never get drunk like that."

And as she stared at the empty bottle she had one of those grotesque little imaginings that were apt to come to her at that hour. She saw herself and Marshall — in the whiskey bottle. Revolting in their smallness and perfection. Skeetering angrily up and down the cold blank glass like minute monkeys. For a moment with noses flattened and stares of longing. And then after their frenzies she saw them lying in the bottom — white and exhausted — looking like fleshy specimens in a laboratory. With nothing said between them.

She was sick with the sound of the bottle as it crashed through the orange peels and paper wads in the waste basket and clanked against the tin at the bottom.

"Ah —" said Marshall, opening the door and carefully placing his foot across the threshold. "Ah — the purest enjoyment left to man. At the last sweet point — pissing."

She leaned against the frame of the closet door — pressing her cheek against the cold angle of the wood. "See if you can get undressed."

"Ah —" he repeated, sitting down on the couch that she had made. His hands left his trouser flaps and began to fumble with his belt. "All but the belt — Can't sleep with a belt buckle. Like your knees. Bo-ony."

She thought that he would lose his balance trying to jerk out the belt all at once — (once before, she remembered, that had happened). Instead he slid the leather out slowly, strap by strap, and when he was through he placed it neatly under the bed. Then he looked up at her. The lines around his mouth were drawn down — making grey threads in the pallor of his face. His eyes looked widely up at her and for a moment she thought that he would cry. "Listen —" he said slowly, clearly.

She heard only the labored sound of his swallowing.

"Listen —" he repeated. And his white face sank into his hands.

Slowly, with a rhythm not of drunkenness, his body swayed from side to side. His blue sweatered shoulders were shaking. "Lord God," he said quietly. "How I — suffer."

She found the strength to drag herself from the doorway, to straighten the lampshade, and switch off the light. In the darkness an arc of blue rocked before her eyes — to the movement of his swaying body. And from the bed came the sound of his shoes being dropped to the floor, the creaking of the springs as he rolled over toward the wall.

She lay down in the darkness and pulled up the blankets — suddenly heavy and chill feeling to her fingers. As she covered his shoulders she noticed that the springs still sputtered beneath them, and that his body was quivering. "Marshall —" she whispered. "Are you cold?"

"Those chills. One of those damn chills."

Vaguely she thought of the missing top to the hot water bottle and the empty coffee sack in the kitchen. "Damn —" she repeated vacantly.

His knees urged close to hers in the darkness and she felt his body contract to a shivering little ball. Tiredly she reached out for his head and drew it to her. Her fingers soothed the little hollow at the top of his neck, crept up the stiff shaved part to the soft hair at the top, moved on to his temples where again she could feel the beating there.

"Listen —" he repeated, turning his head upward so that she could sense his breath on her throat.

"Yes Marshall."

His hands flexed into fists that beat tensely behind her shoulders. Then he lay so still that for a moment she felt a strange fear.

"It's this —" he said in a voice drained of all tone. "My love for you, darling. At times it seems that — in some instant like this — it will destroy me."

Then she felt his hands relax to cling weakly to her back, felt the chill that had been brooding in him all the evening make his body jerk with great shudders. "Yes," she breathed, pressing his hard skull to the hollow between her breasts. "Yes —" she said as soon as words and the creaking of the springs and the rank smell of smoke in the darkness had drawn back from the place where, for the moment, all things had receded.

Sylvia Chatfield Bates' comment, attached to "Instant of the Hour After":

I like this the least of anything you have done, so you see I do not always praise you! The good points first: If I had never seen anything you had done I should have to comment on the great vividness, the acute visibility of your writing. The dramatization of every little detail is excellent, and fresh. And the characters come through the objective scenes beautifully. The "feature" of the story, is the delightful little "element of artistic piquancy," the two persons in the bottle. That is memorable and good.

Now for the other side. Again I must insist that a story should have a reason for being. Must rise, make a point, that is inside the tale itself, and at the same time outside in the world. Why should we be given all these rather disagreeable details, only at the end to hear his love is so great it will destroy him? Before that line I was waiting for something interesting, mature, vital to come out of it all, and I merely had this highly personal statement which I might think was caused by his drunkenness anyway. Can't you keep what you have, but suggest or show how they are caught, and by what; how they are being destroyed, and by what? It's a serious question. Are they really being destroyed by passion? You have used words without realizing their full meaning, and that makes for sentimentality, though this you would call anything but sentimental. It is possible to be sentimental about sophistication!

I think the thing to do is heighten the significance of the figures in the bottle. Write *to that,* and let the overtones and theme grow stronger until you have the effect of a climax, although this is really a conte of mood. Perhaps the reason you have not been successful is that the conflict is not definite enough in your mind and not brought out.

This is well worth doing over. And by the way, certain parts are not printable in a magazine, Joyce or no Joyce.

S.C.B.

[*Redbook,* October 1971]

LIKE THAT

EVEN IF SIS is five years older than me and eighteen we used always to be closer and have more fun together than most sisters. It was about the same with us and our brother Dan, too. In the summer we'd all go swimming together. At nights in the wintertime maybe we'd sit around the fire in the living room and play three-handed bridge or Michigan, with everybody putting up a nickel or a dime to the winner. The three of us could have more fun by ourselves than any family I know. That's the way it always was before this.

Not that Sis was playing down to me, either. She's smart as she can be and has read more books than anybody I ever knew — even school teachers. But in High School she never did like to priss up flirty and ride around in cars with girls and pick up the boys and park at the drug store and all that sort of thing. When she wasn't reading she'd just like to play around with me and Dan. She wasn't too grown up to fuss over a chocolate bar in the refrigerator or to stay awake most of Christmas Eve night either, say, with excitement. In some ways it was like I was heaps older than her. Even when Tuck started coming around last summer I'd sometimes have to tell her she shouldn't wear ankle socks because they might go down town or she ought to pluck out her eyebrows above her nose like the other girls do.

In one more year, next June, Tuck'll be graduated from college. He's a lanky boy with an eager look to his face. At college he's so smart he has a free scholarship. He started coming to see Sis the last summer before this one, riding in his family's car when he could get it, wearing crispy white linen suits. He came a lot last year but this summer he came even more often — before he left he was coming around for Sis every night. Tuck's O.K.

It began getting different between Sis and me a while back, I guess, although I didn't notice it at the time. It was only after a certain night this summer that I had the idea that things maybe were bound to end like they are now.

It was late when I woke up that night. When I opened my eyes I thought for a minute it must be about dawn and I was scared when I saw Sis wasn't on her side of the bed. But it was only the moonlight that shone cool looking and white outside the window and made the oak leaves hanging down over the front yard pitch black and separate seeming. It was around the first of September, but I didn't feel hot looking at the moonlight. I pulled the sheet over me and let my eyes roam around the black shapes of the furniture in our room.

I'd waked up lots of times in the night this summer. You see Sis and I have always had this room together and when she would come in and turn on the light to find her nightgown or something it woke me. I liked it. In the summer when school was out I didn't have to get up early in the morning. We would lie and talk sometimes for a good while. I'd like to hear about the places she and Tuck had been or to laugh over different things. Lots of times before that night she had talked to me privately about Tuck just like I was her age — asking me if I thought she should have said this or that when he called and giving me a hug, maybe, after. Sis was really crazy about Tuck. Once she said to me: "He's so lovely — I never in the world thought I'd know anyone like him —"

We would talk about our brother too. Dan's seventeen years old and was planning to take the co-op course at Tech in the fall. Dan had gotten older by this summer. One night he came in at four o'clock and he'd been drinking. Dad sure had it in for him the next week. So he hiked out to the country and camped with some boys for a few days. He used to talk to me and Sis about Diesel motors and going away to South America and all that, but by this summer he was quiet and not saying much to anybody in the family. Dan's real tall and thin as a rail.

He has bumps on his face now and is clumsy and not very good looking. At nights sometimes I know he wanders all around by himself, maybe going out beyond the city limits sign into the pine woods.

Thinking about such things I lay in bed wondering what time it was and when Sis would be in. That night after Sis and Dan had left I had gone down to the corner with some of the kids in the neighborhood to chunk rocks at the street light and try to kill a bat up there. At first I had the shivers and imagined it was a smallish bat like the kind in Dracula. When I saw it looked just like a moth I didn't care if they killed it or not. I was just sitting there on the curb drawing with a stick on the dusty street when Sis and Tuck rode by slowly in his car. She was sitting over very close to him. They weren't talking or smiling — just riding slowly down the street, sitting close, looking ahead. When they passed and I saw who it was I hollered to them. "Hey, Sis!" I yelled.

The car just went on slowly and nobody hollered back. I just stood there in the middle of the street feeling sort of silly with all the other kids standing around.

That hateful little old Bubber from down on the other block came up to me. "That your sister?" he asked.

I said yes.

"She sure was sitting up close to her beau," he said.

I was mad all over like I get sometimes. I hauled off and chunked all the rocks in my hand right at him. He's three years younger than me and it wasn't nice, but I couldn't stand him in the first place and he thought he was being so cute about Sis. He started holding his neck and bellering and I walked off and left them and went home and got ready to go to bed.

When I woke up I finally began to think of that too and old Bubber Davis was still in my mind when I heard the sound of a car coming up the block. Our room faces the street with only a short front yard between. You can see and hear everything from the sidewalk and the street. The car was creeping down in front of our walk and the light went slow and white along the walls of the room. It stopped on Sis's writing desk, showed up the books there plainly and half a pack of chewing gum. Then the room was dark and there was only the moonlight outside.

The door of the car didn't open but I could hear them talking. Him, that is. His voice was low and I couldn't catch any words but it was like he was explaining something over and over again. I never heard Sis say a word.

I was still awake when I heard the car door open. I heard her say, "Don't come out." And then the door slammed and there was the sound of her heels clopping up the walk, fast and light like she was running.

Mama met Sis in the hall outside our room. She had heard the front door close. She always listens out for Sis and Dan and never goes to sleep when they're still out. I sometimes wonder how she can just lie there in the dark for hours without going to sleep.

"It's one-thirty, Marian," she said. "You ought to get in before this."

Sis didn't say anything.

"Did you have a nice time?"

That's the way Mama is. I could imagine her standing there with her nightgown blowing out fat around her and her dead white legs and the blue veins showing, looking all messed up. Mama's nicer when she's dressed to go out.

"Yes, we had a grand time," Sis said. Her voice was funny— sort of like the piano in the gym at school, high and sharp on your ear. Funny.

Mama was asking more questions. Where did they go? Did they see anybody they knew? All that sort of stuff. That's the way she is.

"Goodnight," said Sis in that out of tune voice.

She opened the door of our room real quick and closed it. I started to let her know I was awake but changed my mind. Her breathing was quick and loud in the dark and she did not move at all. After a few minutes she felt in the closet for her nightgown and got in the bed. I could hear her crying.

"Did you and Tuck have a fuss?" I asked.

"No," she answered. Then she seemed to change her mind. "Yeah, it was a fuss."

There's one thing that gives me the creeps sure enough — and that's to hear somebody cry. "I wouldn't let it bother me. You'll be making up tomorrow."

The moon was coming in the window and I could see her moving her jaw from one side to the other and staring up at the ceiling. I watched her for a long time. The moonlight was cool looking and there was a wettish wind coming cool from the window. I moved over like I sometimes do to snug up with her, thinking maybe that would stop her from moving her jaw like that and crying.

She was trembling all over. When I got close to her she jumped like I'd pinched her and pushed me over quick and kicked my legs over. "Don't," she said. "Don't."

Maybe Sis had suddenly gone batty, I was thinking. She was crying in a slower and sharper way. I was a little scared and I got up to go to the bathroom a minute. While I was in there I looked out the window, down toward the corner where the street light is. I saw something then that I knew Sis would want to know about.

"You know what?" I asked when I was back in the bed.

She was lying over close to the edge as she could get, stiff. She didn't answer.

"Tuck's car is parked down by the street light. Just drawn up to the curb. I could tell because of the box and the two tires on the back. I could see it from the bathroom window."

She didn't even move.

"He must be just sitting out there. What ails you and him?"

She didn't say anything at all.

"I couldn't see him but he's probably just sitting there in the car under the street light. Just sitting there."

It was like she didn't care or had known it all along. She was as far over the edge of the bed as she could get, her legs stretched out stiff and her hands holding tight to the edge and her face on one arm.

She used always to sleep all sprawled over on my side so I'd have to push at her when it was hot and sometimes turn on the light and draw the line down the middle and show her how she really was on my side. I wouldn't have to draw any line that night, I was thinking. I felt bad. I looked out at the moonlight a long time before I could get to sleep again.

The next day was Sunday and Mama and Dad went in the morning to church because it was the anniversary of the day my aunt died. Sis said she didn't feel well and stayed in bed. Dan was out and I was there by myself so naturally I went into our room where Sis was. Her face was white as the pillow and there were circles under her eyes. There was a muscle jumping on one side of her jaw like she was chewing. She hadn't combed her hair and it flopped over the pillow, glinty red and messy and pretty. She was reading with a book held up close to her face. Her eyes didn't move when I came in. I don't think they even moved across the page.

It was roasting hot that morning. The sun made everything blazing outside so that it hurt your eyes to look. Our room was so hot that you could almost touch the air with your finger. But Sis had the sheet pulled up clear to her shoulders.

"Is Tuck coming today?" I asked. I was trying to say something that would make her look more cheerful.

"Gosh! Can't a person have *any* peace in this house?"

She never did used to say mean things like that out of a clear sky. Mean things, maybe, but not grouchy ones.

"Sure," I said. "Nobody's going to notice you."

I sat down and pretended to read. When footsteps passed on the street Sis would hold onto the book tighter and I knew she was listening hard as she could. I can tell between footsteps easy. I can even tell without looking if the person who passes is colored or not. Colored people mostly make a slurry sound between the steps. When the steps would pass Sis would loosen the hold on the book and bite at her mouth. It was the same way with passing cars.

I felt sorry for Sis. I decided then and there that I never would let any fuss with any boy make me feel or look like that. But I wanted Sis and me to get back like we'd always been. Sunday mornings are bad enough without having any other trouble.

"We fuss a lots less than most sisters do," I said. "And when we do it's all over quick, isn't it?"

She mumbled and kept staring at the same spot on the book.

"That's one good thing," I said.

She was moving her head slightly from side to side — over and over again, with her face not changing. "We never do have any real long fusses like Bubber Davis's two sisters have —"

"No." She answered like she wasn't thinking about what I'd said.

"Not one real one like that since I can remember."

In a minute she looked up the first time. "I remember one," she said suddenly.

"When?"

Her eyes looked green in the blackness under them and like they were nailing themselves into what they saw. "You had to stay in every afternoon for a week. It was a long time ago."

All of a sudden I remembered. I'd forgotten it for a long time. I hadn't wanted to remember. When she said that it came back to me all complete.

It was really a long time ago — when Sis was about thirteen. If I remember right I was mean and even more hardboiled than I am now. My aunt who I'd liked better than all my other aunts put together had had a dead baby and she had died. After the funeral Mama had told Sis and me about it. Always the things I've learned new and didn't like have made me mad — mad clean through and scared.

That wasn't what Sis was talking about, though. It was a few mornings after that when Sis started with what every big girl has each month, and of course I found out and was scared to death. Mama then explained to me about it and what she had to wear. I felt then like I'd felt about my aunt, only ten times worse. I felt different toward Sis, too, and was so mad I wanted to pitch into people and hit.

I never will forget it. Sis was standing in our room before the dresser mirror. When I remembered her face it was white like Sis's there on the pillow and with the circles under her eyes and the glinty hair to her shoulders — it was only younger.

I was sitting on the bed, biting hard at my knee. "It shows," I said. "It does too!"

She had on a sweater and a blue pleated skirt and she was so skinny all over that it did show a little.

"Anybody can tell. Right off the bat. Just to look at you anybody can tell."

Her face was white in the mirror and did not move.

"It looks terrible. I wouldn't ever ever be like that. It shows and everything."

She started crying then and told Mother and said she wasn't going back to school and such. She cried a long time. That's how ugly and hardboiled I used to be and am still sometimes. That's why I had to stay in the house every afternoon for a week a long time ago . . .

Tuck came by in his car that Sunday morning before dinner time. Sis got up and dressed in a hurry and didn't even put on any lipstick. She said they were going out to dinner. Nearly every Sunday all of us in the family stay together all day, so that was a little funny. They didn't get home until almost dark. The rest of us were sitting on the front porch drinking ice tea because of the heat when the car drove up again. After they got out of the car Dad, who had been in a very good mood all day, insisted Tuck stay for a glass of tea.

Tuck sat on the swing with Sis and he didn't lean back and his heels didn't rest on the floor — as though he was all ready to get up again. He kept changing the glass from one hand to the other and starting new conversations. He and Sis didn't look at each other except on the sly, and then it wasn't at all like they were crazy about each other. It was a funny look. Almost like they were afraid of something. Tuck left soon.

"Come sit by your Dad a minute, Puss," Dad said. Puss is a nickname he calls Sis when he feels in a specially good mood. He still likes to pet us.

She went and sat on the arm of his chair. She sat stiff like Tuck had, holding herself off a little so Dad's arm hardly went around her waist. Dad smoked his cigar and looked out on the front yard and the trees that were beginning to melt into the early dark.

"How's my big girl getting along these days?" Dad still likes to hug us up when he feels good and treat us, even Sis, like kids.

"O.K.," she said. She twisted a little bit like she wanted to get up and didn't know how to without hurting his feelings.

"You and Tuck have had a nice time together this summer, haven't you, Puss?"

"Yeah," she said. She had begun to see-saw her lower jaw again. I wanted to say something but couldn't think of anything.

Dad said: "He ought to be getting back to Tech about now, oughtn't he? When's he leaving?"

"Less than a week," she said. She got up so quick that she knocked Dad's cigar out of his fingers. She didn't even pick it up but flounced on through the front door. I could hear her half running to our room and the sound the door made when she shut it. I knew she was going to cry.

It was hotter than ever. The lawn was beginning to grow dark and the locusts were droning out so shrill and steady that you wouldn't notice them unless you thought to. The sky was bluish grey and the trees in the vacant lot across the street were dark. I kept on sitting on the front porch with Mama and Papa and hearing their low talk without listening to the words. I wanted to go in our room with Sis but I was afraid to. I wanted to ask her what was really the matter. Was hers and Tuck's fuss so bad as that or was it that she was so crazy about him that she was sad because he was leaving? For a minute I didn't think it was either one of those things. I wanted to know but I was scared to ask. I just sat there with the grown people. I never have been so lonesome as I was that night. If ever I think about being sad I just remember how it was then — sitting there looking at the long bluish shadows across the lawn and feeling like I was the only child left in the family and that Sis and Dan were dead or gone for good.

It's October now and the sun shines bright and a little cool and the sky is the color of my turquoise ring. Dan's gone to Tech. So has Tuck gone. It's not at all like it was last fall, though. I come in from High School (I go there now) and Sis maybe is just sitting by the window reading or writing to Tuck or just looking out. Sis is thinner and sometimes to me she looks in the face like a grown person. Or like, in a way, something has suddenly hurt her hard. We don't do any of the things we used to. It's good weather for fudge or for doing so many things. But no she just sits around or goes for long walks in the chilly late afternoon by herself. Sometimes she'll smile in a way that really gripes — like I was such a kid and all. Sometimes I want to cry or to hit her.

But I'm hardboiled as the next person. I can get along by myself if Sis or anybody else wants to. I'm glad I'm thirteen and still wear socks and can do what I please. I don't want to be any older if I'd get like Sis has. But I wouldn't. I wouldn't like any boy in the world as much as she does Tuck. I'd never let any boy or any thing make me act like she does. I'm not going to waste my time and try to make Sis be like she used to be. I get lonesome — sure — but I don't care. I know there's no way I can make myself stay thirteen all my life, but I know I'd never let anything really change me at all — no matter what it is.

I skate and ride my bike and go to the school football games every Friday. But when one afternoon the kids all got quiet in the gym basement and then started telling certain things — about being married and all — I got up quick so I wouldn't hear and went up and played basketball. And when some of the kids said they were going to start wearing lipstick and stockings I said I wouldn't for a hundred dollars.

You see I'd never be like Sis is now. I wouldn't. Anybody could know that if they knew me. I just wouldn't, that's all. I don't want to grow up — if it's like that.

[*Story* Magazine Archives, Princeton University Library; published by *Redbook,* October 1971]

WUNDERKIND

SHE CAME into the living room, her music satchel plopping against her winter-stockinged legs and her other arm weighted down with school books, and stood for a moment listening to the sounds from the studio. A soft procession of piano chords and the tuning of a violin. Then Mister Bilderbach called out to her in his chunky, guttural tones:

"That you, Bienchen?"

As she jerked off her mittens she saw that her fingers were twitching to the motions of the fugue she had practiced that morning. "Yes," she answered. "It's me."

"I," the voice corrected. "Just a moment."

She could hear Mister Lafkowitz talking — his words spun out in a silky, unintelligible hum. A voice almost like a woman's, she thought, compared to Mister Bilderbach's. Restlessness scattered her attention. She fumbled with her geometry book and *Le Voyage de Monsieur Perrichon* before putting them on the table. She sat down on the sofa and began to take her music from the satchel. Again she saw her hands — the quivering tendons that stretched down from her knuckles, the sore finger tip capped with curled, dingy tape. The sight sharpened the fear that had begun to torment her for the past few months.

Noiselessly, she mumbled a few phrases of encouragement to herself. A good lesson — a good lesson — like it used to be — Her lips closed as she heard the stolid sound of Mister Bilderbach's footsteps across the floor of the studio and the creaking of the door as it slid open.

For a moment she had the peculiar feeling that during most of the fifteen years of her life she had been looking at the face and shoulders that jutted from behind the door, in a silence disturbed only by the muted, blank plucking of a violin string. Mister Bilderbach. Her teacher, Mister Bilderbach. The quick eyes behind the horn-rimmed glasses; the light, thin hair and the narrow face beneath; the lips full and loose shut and the lower one pink and shining from the bites of his teeth; the forked veins in his temples throbbing plainly enough to be observed across the room.

"Aren't you a little early?" he asked, glancing at the clock on the mantelpiece that had pointed to five minutes of twelve for a month. "Josef's in here. We're running over a little sonatina by someone he knows."

"Good," she said, trying to smile. "I'll listen." She could see her fingers sinking powerless into a blur of piano keys. She felt tired — felt that if he looked at her much longer her hands might tremble.

He stood uncertain, halfway in the room. Sharply his teeth pushed down on his bright, swollen lip. "Hungry, Bienchen?" he asked. "There's some apple cake Anna made, and milk."

"I'll wait till afterward," she said. "Thanks."

"After you finish with a very fine lesson — eh?" His smile seemed to crumble at the corners.

There was a sound from behind him in the studio and Mister Lafkowitz pushed at the other panel of the door and stood beside him.

"Frances?" he said, smiling. "And how is the work coming now?"

Without meaning to, Mister Lafkowitz always made her feel clumsy and overgrown. He was such a small man himself, with a weary look when he was not holding his violin. His eyebrows curved high above his sallow, Jewish face as though asking a question, but the lids of his eyes drowsed languorous and indifferent. Today he seemed distracted. She watched him come into the room for no apparent purpose, holding his pearl-tipped bow in his still fingers, slowly gliding the white horsehair through a chalky piece of rosin. His eyes were sharp bright slits today and the linen handkerchief that flowed down from his collar darkened the shadows beneath them.

"I gather you're doing a lot now," smiled Mister Lafkowitz, although she had not yet answered the question.

She looked at Mister Bilderbach. He turned away. His heavy shoulders pushed the door open wide so that the late afternoon sun came through the window of the studio and shafted yellow over the dusty living room. Behind her teacher she could see the squat long piano, the window, and the bust of Brahms.

"No," she said to Mister Lafkowitz, "I'm doing terribly." Her thin fingers flipped at the pages of her music. "I don't know what's the matter," she said, looking at Mister Bilderbach's stooped muscular back that stood tense and listening.

Mister Lafkowitz smiled. "There are times, I suppose, when one —"

A harsh chord sounded from the piano. "Don't you think we'd better get on with this?" asked Mister Bilderbach.

"Immediately," said Mister Lafkowitz, giving the bow one more scrape before starting toward the door. She could see him pick up his violin from the top of the piano. He caught her eye and lowered the instrument. "You've seen the picture of Heime?"

Her fingers curled tight over the sharp corner of the satchel. "What picture?"

"One of Heime in the *Musical Courier* there on the table. Inside the top cover."

The sonatina began. Discordant yet somehow simple. Empty but with a sharp-cut style of its own. She reached for the magazine and opened it.

There Heime was — in the left-hand corner. Holding his violin with his fingers hooked down over the strings for a pizzicato. With his dark serge knickers strapped neatly beneath his knees, a sweater and rolled collar. It was a bad picture. Although it was snapped in profile his eyes were cut around toward the photographer and his finger looked as though it would pluck the wrong string. He seemed suffering to turn around toward the picture-taking apparatus. He was thinner — his stomach did not poke out now — but he hadn't changed much in six months.

Heime Israelsky, talented young violinist, snapped while at work in his teacher's studio on Riverside Drive. Young Master Israelsky, who will soon celebrate his fifteenth birthday, has been invited to play the Beethoven Concerta with —

That morning, after she had practiced from six until eight, her dad had made her sit down at the table with the family for breakfast. She hated breakfast; it gave her a sick feeling afterward. She would rather wait and get four chocolate bars with her twenty cents lunch money and munch them during school — bringing up little morsels from her pocket under cover of her handkerchief, stopping dead when the silver paper rattled. But this morning her dad had put a fried egg on her plate and she had known that if it burst — so that the slimy yellow oozed over the white — she would cry. And that had happened. The same feeling was upon her now. Gingerly she laid the magazine back on the table and closed her eyes.

The music in the studio seemed to be urging violently and clumsily for something that was not to be had. After a moment her thoughts drew back from Heime and the concerta and the picture — and hovered around the lesson once more. She slid over on the sofa until she could see plainly into the studio — the two of them playing, peering at the notations on the piano, lustfully drawing out all that was there.

She could not forget the memory of Mister Bilderbach's face as he had stared at her a moment ago. Her hands, still twitching unconsciously to the motions of the fugue, closed over her bony knees. Tired, she was. And with a circling, sinking away feeling like the one that often came to her just before she dropped off to sleep on the nights when she had over-practiced. Like those weary half-dreams that buzzed and carried her out into their own whirling space.

A Wunderkind — a *Wunderkind* — a *Wunderkind.* The syllables would come out rolling in the deep German way, roar against her ears and then fall to a murmur. Along with the faces circling, swelling out in distortion, diminishing to pale blobs — Mister Bilderbach, Mrs. Bilderbach, Heime, Mister Lafkowitz. Around and around in a circle revolving to the guttural *Wunderkind.* Mister Bilderbach looming large in the middle of the circle, his face urging — with the others around him.

Phrases of music seesawing crazily. Notes she had been practicing falling over each other like a handful of marbles dropped downstairs.

Bach, Debussy, Prokofieff, Brahms — timed grotesquely to the far off throb of her tired body and the buzzing circle.

Sometimes — when she had not worked more than three hours or had stayed out from high school — the dreams were not so confused. The music soared clearly in her mind and quick, precise little memories would come back — clear as the sissy "Age of Innocence" picture Heime had given her after their joint concert was over.

A *Wunderkind* — a *Wunderkind.* That was what Mister Bilderbach had called her when, at twelve, she first came to him. Older pupils had repeated the word.

Not that he had ever said the word to her. "Bienchen —" (She had a plain American name but he never used it except when her mistakes were enormous.) "Bienchen," he would say, "I know it must be terrible. Carrying around all the time a head that thick. Poor Bienchen —"

Mister Bilderbach's father had been a Dutch violinist. His mother was from Prague. He had been born in this country and had spent his youth in Germany. So many times she wished she had not been born and brought up in just Cincinnati. How do you say *cheese* in German? Mister Bilderbach, what is Dutch for *I don't understand you?*

The first day she came to the studio. After she played the whole Second Hungarian Rhapsody from memory. The room graying with twilight. His face as he leaned over the piano.

"Now we begin all over," he said that first day. "It — playing music — is more than cleverness. If a twelve-year-old girl's fingers cover so many keys to a second — that means nothing."

He tapped his broad chest and his forehead with his stubby hand. "Here and here. You are old enough to understand that." He lighted a cigarette and gently blew the first exhalation above her head. "And work — work — work — We will start now with these Bach Inventions and these little Schumann pieces." His hands moved again — this time to jerk the cord of the lamp behind her and point to the music. "I will show you how I wish this practiced. Listen carefully now."

She had been at the piano for almost three hours and was very tired. His deep voice sounded as though it had been straying inside her for a long time. She wanted to reach out and touch his muscle-flexed finger that pointed out the phrases, wanted to feel the gleaming gold band ring and the strong hairy back of his hand.

She had lessons Tuesday after school and on Saturday afternoons. Often she stayed, when the Saturday lesson was finished, for dinner, and then spent the night and took the streetcar home the next morning. Mrs. Bilderbach liked her in her calm, almost dumb way. She was much different from her husband. She was quiet and fat and slow. When she wasn't in the kitchen, cooking the rich dishes that both of them loved, she seemed to spend all her time in their bed upstairs, reading magazines or just looking with a half-smile at nothing. When they had married in Germany she had been a *lieder* singer. She didn't sing anymore (she said it was her throat). When he would call her in from the kitchen to listen to a pupil she would always smile and say that it was *gut,* very *gut.*

When Frances was thirteen it came to her one day that the Bilderbachs had no children. It seemed strange. Once she had been back in the kitchen with Mrs. Bilderbach when he had come striding in from the studio, tense with anger at some pupil who had annoyed him. His wife stood stirring the thick soup until his hand groped out and rested on her shoulder. Then she turned — stood placid — while he folded his arms about her and buried his sharp face in the white, nerveless flesh of her neck. They stood that way without moving. And then his face jerked back suddenly, the anger diminished to a quiet inexpressiveness, and he had returned to the studio.

After she had started with Mister Bilderbach and didn't have time to see anything of the people at high school, Heime had been the only friend of her own age. He was Mister Lafkowitz's pupil and would come with him to Mister Bilderbach's on evenings when she would be there. They would listen to their teachers' playing. And often they themselves went over chamber music together — Mozart sonatas or Bloch.

A *Wunderkind* — a *Wunderkind.*

Heime was a *Wunderkind.* He and she, then.

Heime had been playing the violin since he was four. He didn't have to go to school; Mister Lafkowitz's brother, who was crippled, used to teach him geometry and European history and French verbs in the afternoon. When he was thirteen he had as fine a technique as any violinist in Cincinnati — everyone said so. But playing the violin must be easier than the piano. She knew it must be.

Heime always seemed to smell of corduroy pants and the food he had eaten and rosin. Half the time, too, his hands were dirty around the knuckles and the cuffs of his shirts peeped out dingily from the sleeves of his sweater. She always watched his hands when he played — thin only at the joints with the hard little blobs of flesh bulging over the short-cut nails and the babyish-looking crease that showed so plainly in his bowing wrist.

In the dreams, as when she was awake, she could remember the concert only in a blur. She had not known it was unsuccessful for her until months after. True, the papers had praised Heime more than her. But he was much shorter than she. When they stood together on the stage he came only to her shoulders. And that made a difference with people, she knew. Also, there was the matter of the sonata they played together. The Bloch.

"No, no — I don't think that would be appropriate," Mister Bilderbach had said when the Bloch was suggested to end the programme. "Now that John Powell thing — the *Sonate Virginianesque.*"

She hadn't understood then; she wanted it to be the Bloch as much as Mister Lafkowitz and Heime.

Mister Bilderbach had given in. Later, after the reviews had said she lacked the temperament for that type of music, after they called her playing thin and lacking in feeling, she felt cheated.

"That oie oie stuff," said Mister Bilderbach, crackling the newspapers at her. "Not for you, Bienchen. Leave all that to the Heimes and vitses and skys."

A *Wunderkind.* No matter what the papers said, that was what he had called her.

Why was it Heime had done so much better at the concert than she? At school sometimes, when she was supposed to be watching someone do a geometry problem on the blackboard, the question would twist knife-like inside her. She would worry about it in bed, and even sometimes when she was supposed to be concentrating at the piano. It wasn't just the Bloch and her not being Jewish — not entirely. It wasn't that Heime didn't have to go to school and had begun his training so early, either. It was — ?

Once she thought she knew.

"Play the Fantasia and Fugue," Mister Bilderbach had demanded one evening a year ago — after he and Mister Lafkowitz had finished reading some music together.

The Bach, as she played, seemed to her well done. From the tail of her eye she could see the calm, pleased expression on Mister Bilderbach's face, see his hands rise climactically from the chair arms and then sink down loose and satisfied when the high points of the phrases had been passed successfully. She stood up from the piano when it was over, swallowing to loosen the bands that the music seemed to have drawn around her throat and chest. But —

"Frances —" Mister Lafkowitz had said then, suddenly, looking at her with his thin mouth curved and his eyes almost covered by their delicate lids. "Do you know how many children Bach had?"

She turned to him, puzzled. "A good many. Twenty some odd."

"Well then —" The corners of his smile etched themselves gently in his pale face. "He could not have been so cold — then."

Mister Bilderbach was not pleased; his guttural effulgence of German words had *Kind* in it somewhere. Mister Lafkowitz raised his eyebrows. She had caught the point easily enough, but she felt no deception in keeping her face blank and immature because that was the way Mister Bilderbach wanted her to look.

Yet such things had nothing to do with it. Nothing very much, at least, for she would grow older. Mister Bilderbach understood that, and even Mister Lafkowitz had not meant just what he said.

In the dreams Mister Bilderbach's face loomed out and contracted in the center of the whirling circle. The lip surging softly, the veins in his temples insisting.

But sometimes, before she slept, there were such clear memories; as when she pulled a hole in the heel of her stocking down, so that her shoe would hide it. "Bienchen, Bienchen!" And bringing Mrs. Bilderbach's work basket in and showing her how it should be darned and not gathered together in a lumpy heap.

And the time she graduated from Junior High.

"What you wear?" asked Mrs. Bilderbach the Sunday morning at breakfast when she told them about how they had practiced to march into the auditorium.

"An evening dress my cousin had last year."

"Ah — Bienchen!" he said, circling his warm coffee cup with his heavy hands, looking up at her with wrinkles around his laughing eyes. "I bet I know what Bienchen wants —"

He insisted. He would not believe her when she explained that she honestly didn't care at all.

"Like this, Anna," he said, pushing his napkin across the table and mincing to the other side of the room, swishing his hips, rolling up his eyes behind his horn-rimmed glasses.

The next Saturday afternoon, after her lessons, he took her to the department stores downtown. His thick fingers smoothed over the filmy nets and crackling taffetas that the saleswomen unwound from their bolts. He held colors to her face, cocking his head to one side, and selected pink. Shoes, he remembered too. He liked best some white kid pumps. They seemed a little like old ladies' shoes to her and the Red Cross label in the instep had a charity look. But it really didn't matter at all. When Mrs. Bilderbach began to cut out the dress and fit it to her with pins, he interrupted his lessons to stand by and suggest ruffles around the hips and neck and a fancy rosette on the shoulder. The music was coming along nicely then. Dresses and commencement and such made no difference.

Nothing mattered much except playing the music as it must be played, bringing out the thing that must be in her, practicing, practicing, playing so that Mister Bilderbach's face lost some of its urging look. Putting the thing into her music that Myra Hess had, and Yehudi Menuhin — even Heime!

What had begun to happen to her four months ago? The notes

began springing out with a glib, dead intonation. Adolescence, she thought. Some kids played with promise — and worked and worked until, like her, the least little thing would start them crying, and worn out with trying to get the thing across — the longing thing they felt — something queer began to happen — But not she! She was like Heime. She had to be. She —

Once it was there for sure. And you didn't lose things like that. A *Wunderkind*. . . . A *Wunderkind*. . . . Of her he said it, rolling the words in the sure, deep German way. And in the dreams even deeper, more certain than ever. With his face looming out at her, and the longing phrases of music mixed in with the zooming, circling round, round, round — A *Wunderkind*. A *Wunderkind*. . . .

This afternoon Mister Bilderbach did not show Mister Lafkowitz to the front door, as he usually did. He stayed at the piano, softly pressing a solitary note. Listening, Frances watched the violinist wind his scarf about his pale throat.

"A good picture of Heime," she said, picking up her music. "I got a letter from him a couple of months ago — telling about hearing Schnabel and Hubermann and about Carnegie Hall and things to eat at the Russian Tea Room."

To put off going into the studio a moment longer she waited until Mister Lafkowitz was ready to leave and then stood behind him as he opened the door. The frosty cold outside cut into the room. It was growing late and the air was seeped with the pale yellow of winter twilight. When the door swung to on its hinges, the house seemed darker and more silent than ever before she had known it to be.

As she went into the studio Mister Bilderbach got up from the piano and silently watched her settle herself at the keyboard.

"Well, Bienchen," he said, "this afternoon we are going to begin all over. Start from scratch. Forget the last few months."

He looked as though he were trying to act a part in a movie. His solid body swayed from toe to heel, he rubbed his hands together, and even smiled in a satisfied movie way. Then suddenly he thrust his manner brusquely aside. His heavy shoulders slouched and he began to run through the stack of music she had brought in. "The Bach — no, not yet," he murmured. "The Beethoven? Yes. The Variation Sonata. Opus 26."

The keys of the piano hemmed her in — stiff and white and dead-seeming.

"Wait a minute," he said. He stood in the curve of the piano, elbows propped, and looked at her. "Today I expect something from you. Now this sonata — it's the first Beethoven sonata you ever worked on. Every note is under control — technically — you have nothing to cope with but the music. Only music now. That's all you think about."

He rustled through the pages of her volume until he found the place. Then he pulled his teaching chair halfway across the room, turned it around and seated himself, straddling the back with his legs.

For some reason, she knew, this position of his usually had a good effect on her performance. But today she felt that she would notice him from the corner of her eye and be disturbed. His back was stiffly tilted, his legs looked tense. The heavy volume before him seemed to balance dangerously on the chair back. "Now we begin," he said with a peremptory dart of his eyes in her direction.

Her hands rounded over the keys and then sank down. The first notes were too loud, the other phrases followed dryly.

Arrestingly his hand rose up from the score. "Wait! Think a minute what you're playing. How is this beginning marked?"

"An-andante."

"All right. Don't drag it into an *adagio* then. And play deeply into the keys. Don't snatch it off shallowly that way. A graceful, deep-toned *andante* —"

She tried again. Her hands seemed separate from the music that was in her.

"Listen," he interrupted. "Which of these variations dominates the whole?"

"The dirge," she answered.

"Then prepare for that. This is an *andante* — but it's not salon stuff as you just played it. Start out softly, *piano,* and make it swell out just before the arpeggio. Make it warm and dramatic. And down here —

where it's marked *dolce* make the counter melody sing out. You know all that. We've gone over all that side of it before. Now play it. Feel it as Beethoven wrote it down. Feel that tragedy and restraint."

She could not stop looking at his hands. They seemed to rest tentatively on the music, ready to fly up as a stop signal as soon as she would begin, the gleaming flash of his ring calling her to halt. "Mister Bilderbach — maybe if I — if you let me play on through the first variation without stopping I could do better."

"I won't interrupt," he said.

Her pale face leaned over too close to the keys. She played through the first part, and, obeying a nod from him, began the second. There were no flaws that jarred on her, but the phrases shaped from her fingers before she had put into them the meaning that she felt.

When she had finished he looked up from the music and began to speak with dull bluntness: "I hardly heard those harmonic fillings in the right hand. And incidentally, this part was supposed to take on intensity, develop the foreshadowings that were supposed to be inherent in the first part. Go on with the next one, though."

She wanted to start it with subdued viciousness and progress to a feeling of deep, swollen sorrow. Her mind told her that. But her hands seemed to gum in the keys like limp macaroni and she could not imagine the music as it should be.

When the last note had stopped vibrating, he closed the book and deliberately got up from the chair. He was moving his lower jaw from side to side — and between his open lips she could glimpse the pink healthy lane to his throat and his strong, smoke-yellowed teeth. He laid the Beethoven gingerly on top of the rest of her music and propped his elbows on the smooth, black piano top once more. "No," he said simply, looking at her.

Her mouth began to quiver. "I can't help it. I —"

Suddenly he strained his lips into a smile. "Listen, Bienchen," he began in a new, forced voice. "You still play the Harmonious Blacksmith, don't you? I told you not to drop it from your repertoire."

"Yes," she said. "I practice it now and then."

His voice was the one he used for children. "It was among the first things we worked on together — remember. So strongly you used to play it — like a real blacksmith's daughter. You see, Bienchen, I know you so well — as if you were my own girl. I know what you have — I've heard you play so many things beautifully. You used to —"

He stopped in confusion and inhaled from his pulpy stub of cigarette. The smoke drowsed out from his pink lips and clung in a gray mist around her lank hair and childish forehead.

"Make it happy and simple," he said, switching on the lamp behind her and stepping back from the piano.

For a moment he stood just inside the bright circle the light made. Then impulsively he squatted down to the floor. "Vigorous," he said.

She could not stop looking at him, sitting on one heel with the other foot resting squarely before him for balance, the muscles of his strong thighs straining under the cloth of his trousers, his back straight, his elbows staunchly propped on his knees. "Simply now," he repeated with a gesture of his fleshy hands. "Think of the blacksmith — working out in the sunshine all day. Working easily and undisturbed."

She could not look down at the piano. The light brightened the hairs on the backs of his outspread hands, made the lenses of his glasses glitter.

"All of it," he urged. "Now!"

She felt that the marrows of her bones were hollow and there was no blood left in her. Her heart that had been springing against her chest all afternoon felt suddenly dead. She saw it gray and limp and shriveled at the edges like an oyster.

His face seemed to throb out in space before her, come closer with the lurching motion in the veins of his temples. In retreat, she looked down at the piano. Her lips shook like jelly and a surge of noiseless tears made the white keys blur in a watery line. "I can't," she whispered. "I don't know why, but I just can't — can't anymore."

His tense body slackened and, holding his hand to his side, he pulled himself up. She clutched her music and hurried past him.

Her coat. The mittens and galoshes. The school books and the satchel he had given her on her birthday. All from the silent room that was hers. Quickly — before he would have to speak.

As she passed through the vestibule she could not help but see his hands — held out from his body that leaned against the studio door, relaxed and purposeless. The door shut to firmly. Dragging her books and satchel she stumbled down the stone steps, turned in the wrong direction, and hurried down the street that had become confused with noise and bicycles and the games of other children.

Sylvia Chatfield Bates' comment on an earlier draft of "Wunderkind":

We disagree on your stories for I like this one. It seems to me a more than averagely successful evocation of a mood and a crisis, chiefly presented by objective details presented subjectively — that is through the veil of the mood. This is an excellent method, and not easy. That is why I like the degree of success you have attained.

Some will think this story is too long. I don't. It is no longer than many published in the same genre. However, to be on the safe side with regard to publication since you are unknown as yet, it would be quite possible to point the mood, and give the crisis in the girl's life more emphasis and importance by cutting before the climax so that we arrive at it more quickly. You can cut Hortense. It would be possible to transfer some of the material thus cut to the scene of the climax, thus expanding it. Once arrived the reader is usually willing to go slowly, but he does not want to wait too long before he knows where he is going. I use the term climax, but of course this is a mood story, so that the climax takes the form of a high moment.

The so-called stage business plus the mood make this story. Small details of gesture and property are excellent. Also it is a special knowledge story, and you know they appeal to curiosity. Please return for my files, i.e. submit for Mss 1936 & *Story* prize.

S.C.B.

[*Story*, December 1936]

THE ALIENS

IN AUGUST OF THE YEAR 1935 a Jew sat alone on one of the rear seats of a bus headed south. It was late afternoon and the Jew had been travelling since five o'clock in the morning. That is to say he had left New York at daybreak and except for a number of necessary brief stops he had been waiting patiently on his rear seat for the time when he would reach his destination. Behind him was the great city — that marvel of immensity and intricate design. And the Jew, who had set out at such an early hour on this journey, carried in him a last memory of a city strangely hollow and unreal. As the sun was rising he had walked alone in the unpeopled streets. As far ahead as he could see there were the skyscrapers, pastel mauve and yellow in color, clear and sharp as stalactites against the sky. He had listened to the sound of his own quiet footsteps and for the first time in that city he had heard on the streets the clear articulation of a single human voice. But even then there was the feeling of the multitude, some subtle warning of the raucous fury of the hours soon to come, the turmoil, the constant struggles around closing subway doors, the vast roaring of the city day. Such then was his last impression of the place he had left behind him. And now before him was the South.

The Jew, a man of about fifty years of age, was a patient traveller. He was of middle height and only slightly under average weight. As the afternoon was hot he had removed his black coat and hung it carefully on the back of his seat. He wore a blue striped shirt and gray checked trousers. And of these rather threadbare trousers he was careful to the point of anxiousness, lifting the cloth at the knee each time he crossed his legs, flicking with his handkerchief the dust that seeped in the open window. Although there was no passenger beside him he kept himself well within the limits of his portion of the seat. On the rack above him there was a cardboard lunch box and a dictionary.

The Jew was an observant person — and already with some care he had scanned each fellow passenger. Especially he had noticed the two Negroes who, although they had boarded the bus at widely separate points, had been talking and laughing together on the back seat all the afternoon. Also he watched with interest the passing landscape. He had a quiet face—this Jew — with a high, white forehead, dark eyes behind horn rimmed spectacles, and a rather strained, pale mouth. And for a patient traveller, a man of such composure, he had one annoying habit. He smoked constantly and as he smoked he quietly worried the end of his cigarette with his thumb and forefinger, rubbing and pulling out shreds of tobacco so that often the cigarette was so ragged that he was obliged to nip off the end before putting it to his lips again. His hands were slightly calloused at the fingertips and developed to a state of delicate muscular perfection; they were a pianist's hands.

At seven o'clock the long summer twilight had just begun. After a day of glare and heat the sky was now tempered to a restful greenish blue. The bus wound along a dusty unpaved road, flanked by deep fields of cotton. It was here that a halt was made to pick up a new passenger — a young man carrying a brand new cheap tin suitcase. After a moment of awkward hesitation the young man sat down beside the Jew.

"Good evenin', sir."

The Jew smiled — for the young man had a sunburned pleasant face — and replied to this greeting in a voice that was soft and slightly accented. For a while these were the only words that were said between them. The Jew looked out of the window and the young man watched him shyly from the corner of his eye. Then the Jew took down his lunch box from the rack above his head and prepared to eat his evening meal. In the box there was a sandwich made with rye bread and two lemon tarts. "Will you have some?" he asked politely.

The young man blushed. "Why, much obliged. You see, when I

come in I had to wash and I didn't get a chance to eat my supper." His sunburned hand hovered hesitantly over the two tarts until he chose the one that was stickier and a little crushed around the edges. He had a warm musical voice — with the vowels long drawn and the final consonants unsounded.

They ate in silence with the slow enjoyment of those who know the worth of food. Then when his tart was finished the Jew moistened his fingertips with his mouth and wiped them with his handkerchief. The young man watched and gravely copied him. Dark was coming. Already the pine trees in the distance were blurred and there were flickering lights in the lonely little houses set back in the fields along the way. The Jew had been looking intently out the window and at last he turned to the young man and asked with a nod of his head toward the fields outside: "What is that?"

The young man strained his eyes and saw above the trees in the distance the outline of a smokestack. "Can't tell from here," he said. "It might be a gin or even a sawmill."

"I mean out there all around — growing."

The young man was puzzled. "I can't see what it is you're talkin' about."

"The plants with the white flowers."

"Why man!" said the southerner slowly. "That's *cotton.*"

"Cotton," repeated the Jew. "Of course. I should have known."

There was a long pause in which the young man looked at the Jew with anxiety and fascination. Several times he wet his lips as though about to speak. After some deliberation he smiled genially to the Jew and nodded his head with elaborate reassurance. And then (God knows from what experience in what small-town Greek café) he leaned over so that his face was only a few inches from the Jew's and said with a labored accent: *"You Greek fallow?"*

The Jew, bewildered, shook his head.

But the young man nodded and smiled even more insistently. He repeated his question in a very loud voice. "I say *you Greek fallow?"*

The Jew drew back into his corner. "I can hear O.K. I just do not understand that idiom."

The summer twilight faded. The bus had left the dusty road and was travelling now on a paved but winding highway. The sky was a deep somber blue and the moon was white. The fields of cotton (belonging perhaps to some huge plantation) were behind them and now on either side of the road the land was fallow and uncultivated. Trees on the horizon made a dark black fringe against the blue of the sky. The atmosphere had a dusky lavender tone and perspective was curiously difficult, so that objects which were far appeared near and things close at hand seemed distant. Silence had settled in the bus. There was only the vibrant throb of the motor, so constant that by now it was scarcely realized.

The sunburned young man sighed. And the Jew glanced quickly into his face. The southerner smiled and asked the Jew in a soft voice: "Where is your home, sir?"

To this question the Jew had no immediate answer. He pulled out shreds of tobacco from the end of his cigarette until it was too mangled for further use and then stamped out the stub on the floor. "I mean to make my home in the town where I am going — Lafayetteville."

This answer, careful and oblique, was the best that the Jew could give. For it must be understood at once that this was no ordinary traveller. He was no denizen of the great city he had left behind him. The time of his journey would not be measured by hours, but by years — not by hundreds of miles, but by thousands. And even such measurements as these would be in only one sense accurate. The journey of this fugitive — for the Jew had fled from his home in Munich two years before — more nearly resembled a state of mind than a period of travelling computable by maps and timetables. Behind him was an abyss of anxious wandering, suspense, of terror and of hope. But of this he could not speak with a stranger.

"I'm only going a hundred and eight miles away," said the young man. "But this is the futherest I've ever been away from home."

The Jew raised his eyebrows with polite surprise.

"I'm going to visit with my sister who's only been wedded about a year. I think a mighty lot of this sister and now she's —" He hesitated and seemed to be rummaging in his mind for some choice and delicate expression. "She's with young." His blue eyes fastened doubtfully on the Jew as though uncertain that a man who had never before seen cotton would understand this other fundament of nature.

The Jew nodded and bit his lower lip with restrained amusement.

"Her time is just about here and her husband is cooking his tobacco. So I thought maybe I would come in handy."

"I hope she will have an easy time," the Jew said.

Here there was an interruption. By now it was quite dark and the driver of the bus pulled to the side of the road and turned on the lights inside. The sudden brightness awoke a child who had been sleeping and she began to fret. The Negroes on the back seat, for a long time silent, resumed their languorous dialogue. An old man on the front seat who spoke with the hollow insistence of the deaf began to joke with his companion.

"Are your folks already at this town where you going?" the young man asked the Jew.

"My family?" The Jew took off his spectacles, breathed on the lenses, and polished them on the sleeve of his shirt. "No, they will join me there when I have settled myself — my wife and my two daughters."

The young man leaned forward so that his elbows rested on his knees and his chin was cupped in his palms. Beneath the electric light his face was round and rosy and warm. Beads of perspiration glistened on his short upper lip. His blue eyes had a sleepy look and there was something childish about the way the soft brown bangs of his hair lay damp on his forehead. "I mean to get married sometime soon," he said. "I been picking around for a long time amongst the girls. And now I got them finally narrowed down to three."

"Three?"

"Yeah — all fine good looking girls. And that's another reason why I thought it fit to go off on this trip just now. You see when I come back I can look at them fresh and maybe make up my mind which one I want to ask."

The Jew laughed — a smooth hearty laugh that changed him completely. All trace of strain left his face, his head was thrown back, and his hands clasped tight. And although the joke was at his own expense, the southerner laughed with him. Then the Jew's laughter ended as abruptly as it had begun, finished with a great intake and release of breath that trailed off in a groan. The Jew closed his eyes for a moment and seemed to be according this morsel of fun a place in some inward repertoire of the ridiculous.

The two travellers had eaten together and had laughed together. By now they were no longer strangers. The Jew settled himself more comfortably in his seat, took a tooth-pick from his vest pocket and made use of it unobtrusively, half hiding his mouth with his hand. The young man removed his tie and unbuttoned his collar to the point where brown curling hairs showed on his chest. But it was evident that the southerner was not so much at ease as was the Jew. Something perplexed him. He seemed to be trying to frame some question that was painful and difficult to ask. He rubbed the damp bangs on his forehead and rounded his mouth as though about to whistle. At last he said: "You *are* a foreign man?"

"Yes."

"You come from abroad?"

The Jew inclined his head and waited. But the young man seemed unable to go further. And while the Jew waited for him either to speak or to be silent the bus stopped to take on a Negro woman who had signaled from the roadside. The sight of this new passenger disturbed the Jew. The Negro was of indeterminate age and, had she not been clothed in a filthy garment that served as a dress, even her sex would have been difficult at first glance to define. She was deformed — although not in any one specific limb; the body as a whole was stunted, warped and undeveloped. She wore a dilapidated felt hat, a torn black skirt and a blouse that had been roughly fashioned from a meal sack. At one corner of her mouth there was an ugly open sore and beneath her lower lip she carried a wad of snuff. The whites of her eyes were not white at all, but of a muddy yellow color veined with red. Her face as a whole had a roving, hungry, vacant look. As she walked down the aisle of the bus to take her place on the back seat the Jew turned questioningly to the young man and asked in a quiet, taut voice: "What is the matter with her?"

The young man was puzzled. "Who? You mean the nigger?"

"Sh —" the Jew cautioned, for they were on the next to the last seat and the Negro was just behind them.

But already the southerner had turned in his seat and was staring behind him with such frankness that the Jew winced. "Why there's nothing the matter with her," he said when he had completed this scrutiny. "Not that I can see."

The Jew bit his lip with embarrassment. His brows were drawn and his eyes were troubled. He sighed and looked out of the window although, because of the light in the bus and the darkness outside, there was little to be seen. He did not notice that the young man was trying to catch his eye and that several times he moved his lips as though about to speak. Then finally the young man's question was spoken. "Was you ever in Paris, France?"

The Jew said yes.

"That's one place I always wanted to go. I know this man was over there in the war and somehow all my life I wanted to go to Paris, France. But understand —" The young man stopped and looked earnestly into the Jew's face. "Understand it's not the wimming." (For, due either to the influence of the Jew's careful syllables or to some spurious attempt at elegance the young man actually pronounced the word "wimming.") "It's not because of the French girls you hear about."

"The buildings — the boulevards?"

"No," said the young man with a puzzled shake of his head. "It's not any of those things. That's how come I can't understand it. Because when I think about Paris just one thing is in my mind." He closed his eyes thoughtfully. "I always see this little narrow street with tall houses on both sides. It's dark and it's cold and raining. And nobody is in sight except this French fellow standing on the corner with his cap pulled down over his eyes." The young man looked anxiously into the Jew's face. "Now how come I would have this homesick feeling for something like that? Why — do you reckon?"

The Jew shook his head. "Maybe too much sun," he said finally.

Soon after this the young man reached his destination — a little cross roads village that appeared to be deserted. The southerner took his time about leaving the bus. He pulled down his tin suitcase from the rack and shook hands with the Jew. "Goodbye, Mister —" The fact that he did not know the name seemed to come as a sudden surprise to him. "Kerr," said the Jew. "Felix Kerr." Then the young man was gone. At the same stop the Negro woman — that derelict of humanity the sight of whom had so disturbed the Jew — left the bus also. And the Jew was alone again.

He opened his lunch box and ate the sandwich made with rye bread. Afterward he smoked a few cigarettes. For a time he sat with his face close to the window screen and tried to gather some impression of the landscape outside. Since nightfall clouds had gathered in the sky and there were no stars. Now and then he saw the dark outline of a building, vague stretches of land, or a clump of trees close to the roadside. At last he turned away.

Inside the bus the passengers had settled down for the night. A few were sleeping. He looked about him with a certain rather jaded curiosity. Once he smiled to himself, a thin smile that sharpened the corners of his mouth. But then, even before the last trace of this smile had faded, a sudden change came over him. He had been watching the deaf old man in overalls on the front seat and some small observation seemed suddenly to cause in him intense emotion. Over his face came a swift grimace of pain. Then he sat with his head bowed, his thumb pressed to his right temple and his fingers massaging his forehead.

For this Jew was grieving. Although he was careful of his checked threadbare trousers, although he had eaten with enjoyment and had laughed, although he hopefully awaited this new strange home that lay ahead of him — in spite of these things there was a long dark sorrow in his heart. He did not grieve for Ada, his good wife to whom he had been faithful for twenty-seven years, or for his little daughter, Grissel, who was a charming child. Those two — God be willing — would join him here as soon as he could prepare for them. Neither was this grief concerned with his anxiety for his friends, nor with the loss of his home, his security, and his content. The Jew sorrowed for his elder daughter, Karen, whose whereabouts and state of welfare were unknown to him.

And grief such as this is not a constant thing, demanding in measure, taking its toll in fixed proportion. Rather (for the Jew was a musician) such grief is like a subordinate but urgent theme in an orchestral work — an endless motive asserting itself with all possible variations of rhythm and tonal coloring and melodic structure, now suggested nervously in flying-spiccato passage from the strings, again emerging in the pastoral melancholy of the English horn, or sounding at times in a strident but truncated version down deep among the brasses. And this theme, although for the most part subtly concealed, affects by its sheer insistence the music as a whole far more than the apparent major melodies. And also there are times in this orchestral work when this motive which has been restrained so long will at a signal volcanically usurp all other musical ideas, commanding the full orchestra to recapitulate with fury all that hitherto had been insinuated. But with grief there is a difference here. For it is no fixed summons, such as the signal from the conductor's hand, that activates a dormant sorrow. It is the uncalculated and the indirect. So that the Jew could speak of his daughter with composure and without a quiver could pronounce her name. But when on the bus he saw a deaf man bend his head to one side to hear some bit of conversation the Jew was at the mercy of his grief. For his daughter had the habit of listening with her face turned slightly away and of looking up with one quick glance only when the speaker was done. And this old man's casual gesture was the summons that released in him the grief so long restrained — so that the Jew winced and bowed his head.

For a long time the Jew sat tense in his seat and rubbed his forehead. Then at eleven o'clock the bus made a scheduled stop. By turns the passengers hastily visited a cramped, stale urinal. Later in a café they gulped down drinks and ordered food that could be carried away and eaten with the hands. He had a beer and on his return to the bus preparted for sleep. He took from his pocket a fresh, unfolded handkerchief and, settling himself in his corner with his head resting in the crotch made by the side of the bus and the rounded back of his seat, he placed the handkerchief over his eyes to guard them from the light. He rested quietly with his legs crossed and his hands clasped loosely in his lap. By midnight he was sleeping.

Steadily, in darkness, the bus travelled southward. Sometime in the middle of the night the dense summer clouds dispersed and the sky was clear and starry. They were travelling down the long coastal plain that lies to the east of the Appalachian hills. The road wound through melancholy fields of cotton, and tobacco, through long and lonesome stretches of pine woods. The white moonlight made dreary silhouettes of the tenant shacks close by the roadside. Now and then they went through dark, sleeping towns and sometimes the bus stopped to take on or leave off some traveller. The Jew slept the heavy sleep of those who are mortally tired. Once the jolting of the bus caused his head to fall forward on his chest but this did not disturb his slumber. Then just before daylight, the bus reached a town somewhat larger than most of those through which they had been passing. The bus stopped and the driver laid his hand on the Jew's shoulder to awaken him. For at last his journey was ended.

UNTITLED PIECE

THE YOUNG MAN AT THE TABLE of the station lunch room knew neither the name nor the location of the town where he was, and he had no knowledge of the hour more exact than that it was some time between midnight and morning. He realized that he must already be in the south, but that there were many more hours journeying before he would reach home. For a long time he had sat at the table over a half finished bottle of beer, relaxed to a gangling position — with his thighs fallen loose apart and with one foot stepping on the other ankle. His hair needed cutting and hung down softly ragged over his forehead and his expression as he stared down at the table was absorbed, but mobile and quick to change with his shifting thoughts. The face was lean and suggestive of restlessness and a certain innocent, naked questioning. On the floor beside the boy were two suitcases and a packing box, each tagged neatly with a card on which was typewritten his name — Andrew Leander, and an address in one of the larger towns in Georgia.

He had come into the place in a drunken turmoil, caused partly by the swallows of corn a man on the bus had offered him, mostly by a surge of expectancy that had come to him during the last few hours of travelling. And that feeling was not unaccountable. Three years before, when he was seventeen years old, the boy had left home in an inner quandary of violence, a gawky wanderer going with fear into the unknown, expecting never to come back. And now after these three years he was returning.

Sitting at the table in the lunch room of that little nameless town, Andrew had become more calm. All during the time of his absence he had put away thoughts of his home town and his family — of his Dad and his sisters, Sara and Mick, and of the colored girl Vitalis, who worked for them. But as he sat with his beer (so completely a stranger, that it was as though he were magically suspended from the very earth) the memories of all of them at home revolved inside him with the clarity of a reel of films — sometimes precise and patterned, again in a chaos of disorder.

And there was one little episode that kept recurring again and again in his mind, although until that night he had not thought of it in years. It was about the time he and his sister made a glider in the back yard, and perhaps he kept remembering it because the things he had felt at that time were so much like the expectancy this journey now brought.

At that time they had all been kids and at the age when all the new things they learned about on the radio and in books and at the movies could set them wild with eagerness. He had been thirteen, Sara a year younger, and little Mick (she didn't count in things like this) was still in kindergarten. He and Sara had read about gliders in a science magazine in the school library and immediately they began to build one in their back yard. (They began to build it one afternoon in the middle of the week and by Saturday they had worked so hard that it was almost finished.) The article had not given any exact directions for making the glider; they had had to go by the way they imagined it should be and to use whatever materials they could find. Vitalis would not give them a sheet to cover the wings and so they had to cut up his canvas camping tent to use instead. For the frame they used some bamboo sticks and some light wood they snitched from the carpenters who were building a garage up on the next block. When it was finished the glider was not very big, and seemed very different from the ones they had seen in the movies — but he and Sara kept telling each other that it was just as good and that there was nothing to keep their ship from flight.

That Saturday was a time that none of them would ever forget. The sky was a deep, blazing blue, the color of gas flames, and at times there was a thick and sultry breeze. All morning he and Sara stayed out in the hot sun of the back yard working. Her face was strained and pale with excitement and her full, almost sullen lips were red and dry as though from a fever. She kept running back and forth to get things she thought they might need, her thin legs overgrown and clumsy, her damp hair streaming out behind her shoulders. Little Mick hung around the back steps, watching. It seemed to him then that they were as different as any sisters could be. Mick sat quietly, her hands on her fat little knees, not saying much but gazing at everything they did with a wondering look to her face and with her little mouth softly open. Even Vitalis was out there with them most of the time. She didn't know whether to believe in it or not. She was a nervous, light colored girl and there was something about the glider that excited her as much as it did the rest of them — and that scared her too. As she watched them her fingers kept fooling with her red earrings or picking at her swollen quivering lips.

They all felt that there was something wild about that day. It was like they were shut off from all other people in the world and nothing mattered except the four of them planning and working out in the quiet, sun-baked yard. It was as though they had never wanted anything except this glider and its flight from the earth up toward the hot blue sky.

It was the launching that gave them the most worry. He kept saying to Sara: "We ought to have a car to hitch it to because that's the way the real flyers get them up. Or else one of those elastic ropes like they described in the magazine."

But beside their garage was a tall pine tree, with the limbs growing high and stretching out almost as far as the house. From one of these branches hung a swing and it was from this that they intended to make their start. He and Sara took out the board seat and put in its place a larger plank. And it was from the start that the swing would give them that they would be launched.

Vitalis felt like she ought to be responsible and she was afraid. "I been having this here queer feeling all day."

There was a hot slow breeze and from the top of the pine came a gentle soughing. She held up her hands to feel the wind and stood for a moment looking at the sky — intent as some savage rapt in prayer.

"You all think just because your mother ain't living that you don't have to mind nobody. Why don't you wait till your Daddy come home and ask him? I been having this here feeling all day that something bad ghy happen from that thing."

"Hush," said Sara.

"I know it ain't no real airplane even if it do have them big wings made out of a old torn up tent. And I know you just as human as I is. And your head just as easy to bust."

But no matter what she said Vitalis believed in the glider as much as any of them. When she was in the kitchen they could see her come to the window every few minutes and stare out at them, her broad nose pressed to the glass, her dark face quivering.

By the time they were finished the sun was almost down. The sky had blanched to a pale jade color and the breeze that had been blowing most of the day seemed cooler and stronger to them. The yard was very quiet and neither he nor Sara said anything or looked at each other as they tensely balanced the glider on the swing. They had already argued about who would be the one to go up first and he had won. They called Vitalis out from the house and told her to help Sara give the final push and when she did not want to they said they would call Chandler West or some other kid in the neighborhood so she might as well be the one. Little Mick got up from the steps where she had been looking at them all day long and watched him step carefully up into the swing and squat down on the frame of the glider, gripping the wood with the rubber soles of his sneakers.

"Do you think you'll go as far as Atlanta or Cleveland?" she asked. Cleveland was the place where their cousin lived and that was how she knew the name.

It seemed to him as he crouched in there trying to keep his balance that already he was leaving the ground. He could feel his heart beating almost in his throat and his hands were shaking.

Vitalis said: "And even if this slow little wind do carry you up in the air, what you ghy do then? Is you just ghy fly around up there all night like you is an angel?"

"Will you be back in time for supper, Drew?" Mick asked.

Sara looked like she didn't hear anything that was said. There were drops of sweat on her forehead and he could hear her breath coming quick and shallow. She and Vitalis each took a rope of the swing and pulled with all their strength. Even little Mick helped them balance the glider. It seemed like it took them hours to hoist him up as far as their head while he waited, crouched tensely, with his jaw stiff and his eyes half closed. During that moment he thought of himself soaring up and up into the cool blue sky and the joy of it was such as he never felt before.

Then came the part that afterward was the hardest to understand. As soon as the glider left the swing it crashed and he fell so hard that for a long time his stomach moved round and round in dizzy turns and he felt like someone was standing on his chest so that he could not breathe. But for some reason that did not matter at all. He got up from the ground and it was as though he would not let himself believe what had happened. He had not fallen on the glider and it was not hurt except for a little tear in the wing. He undid his belt buckle and tried to take a deep breath. He and Sara did not talk but kept themselves busy getting ready for the next take-off. And the queer thing was that they both knew that this second trial would be just like the first and that their glider would not fly. In a part of them they knew this but there was something that would not let them think about it — the wanting and the excitement that would not let them be quiet or stop to reason.

Vitalis was different and her voice went up high and sing-song. "Here Andrew done almost bust hisself wide open and still you all ghy keep on with this thing. Time you all is near bout twenty-five and old as I is you'll learn some sense."

Even Mick began to talk. She was always a quiet kid and hadn't said more than ten words all the time she had been hanging around. That was the way she always was. She just looked with her little mouth half open and seemed to wonder about and take in everything you did or said without trying to answer. "When I'm twelve years old and a big girl I'm going to fly and I'm not going to fall. You just wait and see."

"Quit your talking like that," Vitalis said. She did not want to watch them so she went into the house. Now and then they could see her dark face peering out at them from the kitchen window. He had to launch Sara by himself.

When she got into the glider it was almost dark. She crashed even worse than he did but she did not act like she was hurt and at first he did not notice the bump over her eye and the long bloody smear on her knee where the skin had scraped off. The glider was not even damaged much this time and it was like they were really wild as Vitalis made them out to be. "Just one more time I'm going to try," Sara said. "It keeps sticking to the seat and when I fix that it's just got to go up." She ran into the house, stepping light on the leg she had hurt, and came back with a hunk of butter on a piece of waxed bread wrapper to grease the swing. Vitalis's high singing voice called out to them from the kitchen but no one answered.

After the third time it was all over. He let Sara go because he was too heavy for her to launch. Their glider was smashed so you wouldn't know what it was and he had to help Sara get up from the ground this time. Her eye was swollen and she looked sick. She stood with her weight on one foot and when she pulled up her skirt to show him a big bruise on her thigh, her leg was trembling so that she almost lost her balance. Everything was over and he felt dead and empty inside.

It was almost dark and they stood there for a while just looking at each other. Mick still sat on the steps, watching them with a scared look and not saying anything. Their faces were white in the half-darkness and the smells of supper from the kitchen were strong in the hot still air. It was very quiet and again it seemed that lonely feeling came to him like they were the only people in the world.

Finally, Sara said: "I don't care. I'm glad anyway even if it didn't work. I'd rather for it to be like it is now than not to have tried to build it. I don't care."

He broke off a piece of the pine bark and looked at Vitalis moving around in the soft yellow light of the kitchen.

"It ought to have worked though. It ought to have flown. I just can't see why it didn't."

In the dark sky there was a white star shining. Very slowly they walked across the yard toward their back steps and they were glad that their faces were half secret in the darkness. Quietly they went into the house and after that Vitalis was the only one who ever spoke of what had happened on that day.

The young man finished his beer on the table and motioned to the sleepy waiter to bring him another. All at once he decided not to take the next bus, but to stay in this strange town until morning. He half closed his eyes to shut out the crude light, the few weary travellers waiting at the tables, the dirty checked cloth before him.

It seemed to him that no one had ever felt just as he did. The past, the seventeen years of his life when he was at home, was before him like a dark and complex arabesque. But it was not a pattern to be comprehended at a glance, being more like a musical work that unfolds contrapuntally voice by voice and cannot be understood until after the time that it takes to reproduce it. It took shape in a vague design, less composed of events than of emotions. The last three years in New York did not enter into this pattern at all and were no more than a dark background to reflect for the moment the clarity of what had passed before. And through all this, in counterpart to the interwoven feelings, there was music in his mind.

Music had always meant a lot to him and Sara. Long ago, before Mick was even born and when their mother was still living, they would blow together on combs wrapped in toilet paper. Later there were harps from the ten cent store and the sad wordless songs that colored people sang. Then Sara began to take music lessons and although she didn't like either her teacher or the pieces she was given, she stuck to her practicing pretty well. She liked to pick out the jazz songs she heard or just to sit at the piano, playing aimless notes that weren't music at all.

He was about twelve when the family got a radio and after that things began to change. They began to dial to symphony orchestras and programmes that were very different from the ones they had listened to before. In a way this music was strange to them and again it was like something they had been waiting for all of their lives. Then their Dad gave them a portable Victrola one Christmas and some Italian opera records. Over and over they would wind up their Victrola and finally they wore the records out — there began to be scratching noises in the music and the singers sounded like they were holding their noses. The next year they got some Wagner and Beethoven.

All of that was before the time when Sara tried to run away from home. Because they lived in the same house and were together so much he was slow to notice the way she was changing. Of course she was growing very fast and couldn't wear a dress two months before her wrists would be showing and the skirt would be shorter than her bony knees — but that wasn't what it was. She reminded him of someone who had been sleepily stumbling through a dark room when a light was turned on. Often there was a lost, dazed look about her face that was hard to understand.

She would throw herself into first one thing and then another. For a while there were movies. She went to the show every Saturday with him and Chandler West and the rest of the kids, but when it was over and they had seen everything through she wouldn't come out with them but would stay on in the movie until almost dark. She always started looking at the picture as soon as she passed the ticket man and would stumble down the aisle without ever looking at the seats until she has almost reached the screen — then she would sit on about the third row with her neck bent back and her mouth not quite closed. Even after she had seen everything through twice she would keep turning back to look as she walked out of the show so that she would bump into people and was almost like somebody drunk. On week days she would save all but a dime of her lunch money and buy movie magazines. She had the pictures of Clive Brook and four or five other stars tacked up on the wall of her room and when she would go to the drug store to buy the magazines she would get a chocolate milk and look through all they had, then buy the ones with the most in them about the stars she liked. Movies were all she cared about for about three months. Then all of a sudden that was over and she didn't even go to the show anymore on Saturdays.

Then there was the Girl Scout Camp she and the girls she knew were going on, out at a lake about twenty miles from town. That was all she talked about the month beforehand. She would priss around in front of the mirror in the khaki shorts and boy's shirts they were supposed to have, her hair slicked back close to her head, thinking it was grand to try to act like a boy. But after she had been on the camp just four days he came in one afternoon and found her playing the Victrola. She had made one of the counsellors bring her home and she looked all done in. She said all they did was swim and run races and shoot bows and arrows. And there weren't any mattresses on the cots and at night there were mosquitoes and she had growing pains in her legs and couldn't sleep. "I just ran and ran and then lay awake in the dark all night," she kept saying. "That's all there was to it." He laughed at her, but when she started crying — not in the way kids like Mick bawled but slowly and unsobbing — it was almost like he was part of her and crying, too. For a long time they sat on the floor together, playing their records. They were always a lot closer than most brothers and sisters.

Music to them was something like the glider should have been. But it wasn't sudden like that and it didn't let them down. Maybe it was like whiskey was to their Dad. They knew it was something that would stay with them always.

Sara played the piano more and more after she got to high school. She didn't like it there any more than he did and sometimes she would even worry him into writing excuses for her and signing their Dad's name. The first term she got seven bad cards. Their Dad never knew what to do about Sara and whenever she did something wrong he would just clear his throat and look at her in an embarrassed way like he didn't know how to say what was in his mind. Sara looked like pictures of their mother and he loved her a lot — but it was in a funny sort of timid way. He didn't fuss at all about the bad cards. She was just twelve and that was young to be in high school anyway.

There is a time when everybody wants to run away — no matter how well they get along with their family. They feel they have to leave because of something they have done, or something they want to do, or maybe they don't know why it is they run away. Maybe it is a kind of slow hunger that makes them feel like they have to get out and go in search of something. He ran away from home once when he was eleven. A girl on the next block took her money out of the school savings bank and got a bus to Hollywood because the actress she had a crush on answered one of her letters and said that if she was ever in California to drop in and see her and swim in her swimming pool. Her folks couldn't get in touch with her for ten days and then her mother went out to Hollywood to bring her back. She had swum in the actress's pool and was trying to get a job in the movies. She was not sorry to come back home. Even Chandler West who was always slow and dumb tried to run away. Although Chandler had lived across the street from them all their lives there was something about him no one could ever understand. Even as little kids he and Sara felt that. It happened after Chandler had failed all his subjects at school, most of them for the second time. He said afterward that he wanted to build a hut up in the Canadian woods and live there by himself as a trapper. He was too dumb to hitch hike and he just kept walking toward the north until finally he was arrested for sleeping in a ditch and sent home. His mother had almost gone crazy and while he was gone her eyes were wild and like an animal's. You would think that Chandler was the only person that she had ever loved. And maybe it was from her that he was running away, too.

So there was nothing very peculiar about what Sara did — that is unless you were a grown person like their Dad who just didn't understand things like that. There wasn't any real reason for her wanting to leave. It was just the way she had begun to feel in the last year. Maybe music had something to do with it. Or it might have been because she had grown so much and just didn't know what to do with herself.

It happened on her thirteenth birthday and it was Monday morning. Vitalis had the breakfast table fixed nice with flowers and a new table cloth. Sara didn't seem any different that morning from any other time. But suddenly as she was eating her grits she saw a kinky hair on her plate and she burst out crying. Vitalis's feelings were hurt because she had tried to have breakfast so nice that morning. Sara grabbed her school books and went out the door. She said she wasn't mad with anybody about anything but that she was leaving home for good. He knew she was just talking and would just stay away until school was out. If it hadn't been for Vitalis their Dad would never have known about it. Sara went up the street running and when she came to the vacant lot at the corner she threw all her school books in the high grass there. When he went to pick them up there were papers scattered everywhere in the wind — homework and funny things she had drawn in her tablet.

Vitalis phoned their Dad who had already gone to work and he came home in the automobile. He was very worried and serious. He kept pulling his lower lip tight against his teeth and clearing his throat. All three of them got in the automobile to go find her. The rest would have been funny if you hadn't been mixed up in it. They found her after about half an hour — walking down the road between high school and downtown. But when their Dad blew the horn she wouldn't get in the car, or even look around at them. She just kept going with her head in the air and her pleated skirt switching above her skinny knees. Their Dad had never been so nervous and mad. He couldn't get out and chase a girl down the street and so he had to just creep the car along behind her and blow the horn. They passed kids going to school who stared and giggled and it was awful. He was madder with Sara than their Dad. If they had had a closed car he would have leaned back and hid his face. But it was a Model T Ford and there wasn't anything to do but shuffle his feet and try to look like he didn't care.

After a while she gave up and got in the car. Their Dad didn't know what to say and all of them were stiff and quiet. Sara was shamed and sad. She tried to cover it up by humming to herself in a don't-care way. They got out quietly at the high school. But that wasn't the end.

The next month Uncle Jim, who was kin to them on their mother's side, came down from Detroit on the way to spend his vacation in Florida. Aunt Esther, his wife, was with him. She was a Jew and played the violin. Both of them had always liked Sara a lot — and in their Christmas boxes her present was always better than his or Mick's. They didn't have any children and there was something about them that was different from most married people. The first night they sat up very late with their Dad and maybe he told them all about Sara. Anyway, before they left, their Dad asked Sara how she would like to go to school a year in Detroit and live with them. Right away she said that she would like it — she had never been farther away from home than Atlanta and she wanted to sleep on a train and live in a strange place and see snow in the winter time.

It happened so quickly that he could not get it into his head. He had not thought about the time when any of them would ever be away for long. He knew their Dad felt Sara was growing to the age where maybe she needed somebody who was at home more than he was. And the climate might do her good in Detroit and they didn't have many kinfolks. Before they were even born Uncle Jim had lived at their house a year — when he was still young and before he left for the north. But still he could not understand their Dad's letting her go. She left in a week — because the school term had only been going a month and they didn't want to waste more time. It was so sudden that it didn't give him time to think. She was to be gone ten months and that seemed almost as long as forever. He did not know that it would be almost twice that time before he would again see her. He felt dazed and it was like a dream when they said goodbye.

That winter the house was a lonesome place. Mick was too little to think about anything but eating and sleeping and drawing on colored paper at kindergarten. When he would come in from school all the rooms seemed quiet and more than empty. Only in the kitchen was it any different and there Vitalis was always cooking and singing to herself and it was warm and full of good smells and life. If he did not go out he would usually hang around there and watch her and they would talk while she fixed him something to eat. She knew about the lonesome feeling and was good to him.

Most afternoons he was out with Chandler West and the rest of the gang of boys who were sophomores at high school. They had a club and a scrub football team. The vacant lot on the corner of the block was sold and the buyer began to build a house. When the carpenters and bricklayers left in the late afternoon the gang would climb up on the roof or run through the naked incompleted rooms. It was strange the way he felt about this house. Every afternoon he would take off his shoes and socks so he wouldn't slip and climb to the sharp pointed top of the roof. Then he would stand there, holding his hands out for balance and look around at all that lay below him or at the pale twilight sky. From underneath the boys would be scuffling together and calling out to each other — their voices were changing and the empty rooms made long drawn echoes, so that the sounds seemed not human and unrelated to words.

Standing there alone on the roof he always felt he had to shout out — but he did not know what it was he wanted to say. It seemed like if he could put this thing into words he would no longer be a boy with big rough bare feet and hands that hung down clumsy from the outgrown sleeves of his lumberjack. He would be a great man, a kind of God, and what he called out would make things that bothered him and all other people plain and simple. His voice would be great and like music and men and women would come out of their houses and listen to him and because they knew that what he said was true they would all be like one person and would understand everything in the world. But no matter how big this feeling was he could never put any of it into words. He would balance there choked and ready to burst and if his voice had not been squeaky and changing he would have tried to yell out the music of one of their Wagner records. He could do nothing. And when the rest of the gang would come out from the house and look up at him he felt a sudden panic, as though his corduroy pants had dropped from him. To cover up his nakedness he would yell something silly like *Friends Romans Countrymen* or *Shake-Spear Kick Him In The Rear* and then he would climb down feeling empty and shamed and more lonesome than anybody else in the world.

On Saturday mornings he worked down at his Dad's store. This was a long narrow jeweller's shop in the middle of one of the main business blocks downtown. Down the length of the place was a bright glass showcase with the sections displaying stones and silver. His Dad's watchmaking bench was in the very front of the shop, looking out on the front window and the street. Day after day he would sit there over his work — a large man, more than six feet tall, and with hands that at first looked too big for their delicate work. But after you watched his Dad awhile that first feeling changed. People who noticed his hands always wanted to stare at them — they were fat and seemed without bones or muscles and the skin, darkened with acids, was smooth as old silk. His hands did not seem to belong to the rest of him, to his bent broad back and his strained muscular neck. When he worked at a hard job his whole face would show it. The eye that wore his jeweller's glass would stare down round and intent and distorted while the other was squinted almost shut. His whole big face looked crooked and his mouth gaped open with strain. Although when he was not busy he liked to stare out at the heads and shoulders of the people passing on the street, he never glanced at them while he was at work.

At the store his Dad usually gave him odd jobs such as that of polishing silverware or running errands. Sometimes he cleaned watch springs with a brush soaked in gasoline. Occasionally if there were several customers in the place and the salesgirl was busy he would awkwardly stand behind the counter and try to make a sale. But most of the time there was nothing much for him to do except hang around. He hated staying at the store on Saturdays because he could always think of so many other things he wanted to do. There were long stretches when the store would be very quiet — with only the droning ticks of the watches or the echoing sounds of a clock striking.

On the days when Harry Minowitz was there this was different. Harry took in the extra work of two or three jewellers in the town and his Dad let him use the bench at the back of the store in exchange for certain jobs. There was nothing that Harry didn't know about even the finest of watch mechanics and because of this (and for other reasons too) he had the nickname of "The Wizard." His Dad didn't like Jews because there were a couple in town who were slick as grease and bad on other jewellers' business. So it was funny the way he depended on Harry.

Harry was small and pale and he always seemed tired. His nose was large for his peaked face and next to his eyes it was the first thing you noticed. Perhaps that was because he had the habit of slowly rubbing it with his thumb and second finger when he was thinking, gently feeling the hump on it and pressing down the tip. When he was in doubt about a question put to him he would not shrug or shake his head — but slowly turn his slender hands palm upward and suck in his hollow cheeks. Usually a cigarette drooped from his mouth and his thin lips seemed too relaxed to hold it. His dark eyes had a way of staring sharply at a person, then the lids would suddenly droop down as though he understood everything and was still bored. At the same time there was a certain jauntiness about him. His clothes were dapper and he wore a stiff derby hat at an angle on the back of his head. Nothing could ever surprise Harry, but in his own quiet way he could always laugh at everything, even himself. He had come to the town ten years before and he lived alone in a small room on one of the overcrowded streets down by the river. Though he seemed to know half the people in the town by their names and faces he had few friends and was a solitary man.

During the winter after Sara left when Andrew worked at the store every Saturday he liked to watch Harry and think about him. There was a time when he would rather have been noticed and admired by him than any other person. He had never tried to ape his Dad like some boys did. But there was something sure and nonchalant about Harry that seemed wonderful to him. He had lived in cities like Los Angeles and New York and he knew languages and people that were strange to men like his Dad. He wanted to be good friends with Harry but he didn't know how to go about it. When they were together something made him talk loud and hold his face stiff and call grown men by their last names without the Mister. Then he would be embarrassed, stumble over his big feet and get in everybody's way. He felt that Harry saw through all of this and was laughing. This made him mad. There were times when if Minowitz hadn't been so old he would have picked a fight with him and tried to bash his ears in. But although Harry looked like he might be any age he knew that he must be around thirty — and a nearly six foot tall boy of fourteen couldn't fight with a smaller man who was that much older.

Then one morning Harry brought "the dolls" to the store. That was the name somebody gave to the set of chessmen he had worked on for ten years. At first it was a surprise to realize that even Harry could be a crank about something — he had known that he liked chess and owned a fine set of pieces, but that was all. He learned that Harry would go anywhere to find a partner who could give him a good game. And next to playing he liked to just fondle and work with these little doll-like men. They had been carved years ago by a friend of his father — out of ebony and some light hard wood. Some of the pieces had shrunken little Chinese faces and all of the parts were curious and beautiful. For years Harry had worked in his spare time to inlay this set with chased gold.

It was these chessmen that made them friends. When Harry saw how interested he was he began to tell him about the work and also to explain the moves in a chess game. Within a few weeks he learned how to play a fair game for a beginner. And after that he and Harry would play together often on Saturdays in the back of the store. He got so that even at night when he couldn't sleep he would think about chess. He hadn't thought that he could ever like a game so much.

Sometimes Harry would have him up to his place for an evening. The room he lived in was very neat and bare. They would sit silently over a little card table, going through the game without a word. As Harry played his face was as pale and frozen looking as one of his little carved pieces — only his sharp black eyebrows moved and his fingers as he slowly rubbed his nose. The first few times he left as soon as the games were over because he was afraid Harry might get tired of him if he stayed longer and think he was just a boring kid. But before he knew it all that was changed and they would talk sometimes until late at night. There were times when he would feel almost like a drunk man and try to put into words all the things he had kept stored up for a long time. He would talk and talk until he was breathless and his cheeks burned — about the things he wanted to do and see and make up his mind about. Harry listened with his head cocked to one side and his unsurprised silence made what he wanted to say come faster and even more clearly than he had thought it.

Harry was always quiet, but the things he did mention suggested more than he ever said. He had a younger brother named Baruch who was a pianist studying in New York. The way he would speak of his brother showed that he cared more about him than he did anyone else. Andrew tried to imagine Baruch — and in his mind he was bigger and surer and knew more than any of the kids in his gang. Often when he thought of this boy there was a sad longing feeling because they didn't know each other. Harry had other brothers — one who had a cigarette shop in Cincinnati, and another who was a piano tuner. You could tell he was close to all his family. But this Baruch was his favorite.

Sometimes when he would hurry down the dark streets on the way home he would feel a peculiar quiver of fear inside him. He didn't know why. It was like he had given all he had to a stranger who might cheat him. He wanted to run run run through the dark streets without stopping. Once when this happened he stopped on a corner and leaned against the lamp post and began to try to remember exactly what he had said. A panic came over him because it seemed that the thing he had tried to tell was too naked. He didn't know why this was so. The words jangled in his head and mocked him.

"Don't you ever hate being yourself? I mean like the times when you wake up suddenly and say I am I and you feel smothered. It's like everything you do and think about is at loose ends and nothing fits together. There ought to be a time when you see everything like you're looking through a periscope. A kind of a — colossal periscope where nothing is left out and everything in the world fits in with every other thing. And no matter what happens after that it won't — won't stick out like a sore thumb and make you lose your balance. That's one reason I like chess because it's sort of that way. And music — I mean good music. Most jazz and theme songs in the movies are like something a kid like Mick would draw on a piece of tablet paper — maybe a sort of shaky line all erased and messy. But the other music is sometimes like a great fine design and for a minute it makes you that way too. But about that sort of periscope — there's really no such thing. And maybe that's what everybody wants and they just don't know it. They try one thing after another but that want is never really gone. Never."

And when he had finished talking Harry's face was still pale and frozen, like one of his wizened chess kings. He had nodded his head and that was all. Andrew hated him. But even so he knew that the next week he would go back.

That year he often went out roaming through the town. Not only did he get to know all the streets in the suburb where he lived, and those of the main blocks downtown, and the Negro sections — but he began to be familiar, also, with that part of town called South Highlands. This was the place where the most important business of the town, the three cotton factories, was situated. For a mile up the river there was nothing but these mills and the glutted little streets of shacks where the workers lived. This huge section seemed almost entirely separate from the rest of the town and when Andrew first began to go there he felt almost as though he were a hundred miles from home. Some afternoons he would walk up and down the steep foul sidestreets for hours. He just walked without speaking to anybody with his hands in his pockets, and the more he saw the more there was this feeling that he would have to keep walking on and on through those streets until his mind was settled. He saw things there that scared him in an entirely new way — new, because it was not for himself he was afraid and he couldn't even put the reason into thought. But the fear kept on in him and sometimes it seemed it would almost choke him. Always people sitting on their front steps or standing in doorways would stare at him — and most of the faces were a pale yellow and had no expression except that of watching without any special interest. The streets were always full of kids in overalls. Once he saw a boy as old as he was piss on his own front steps when there were girls around. Another time a half grown fellow tried to trip him up and they had to fight. He had never been much of a fighter but in a scrap he always used his fists and butted with his head. But this boy was different. He fought like a cat and scratched and bit and kept snarling under his breath. The funny thing was that the fight was almost over and he felt himself on the ground and being choked when the fellow suddenly got limp like an old sack and in a minute more he gave up. Then when they were on their feet and just looking at each other he, the boy, did a crazy thing. He spat at him and slunk down to the ground and lay there on his back. The spit landed on his shoe and was thick like he had been saving it up a long time. But he looked down at him lying there on the ground and he felt sick and didn't even think about making him fight again. It was a cold day but the boy didn't have on anything but a pair of overalls and his chest was nothing but bones and his stomach stuck way out. He felt sick like he had hit a baby or a girl or somebody that should have been fighting on his side. The hoarse wailing whistles that marked the change in the mill shifts called out to him.

But even after that there was something in him that made him still walk the streets of South Highlands. He was looking for something but he didn't know what it was.

In the Negro sections he felt none of this dim fear. Those parts of the town were a sort of home to him — especially the little street called Sherman's Quarter where Vitalis lived. This street was on the edge of the City Limits and was only a few blocks from his own house. Most of the colored people there did yard work or cooked for white people or took in washing. Behind the Quarter were the long miles of fields and pine woods where he would go on camping trips. As a kid he knew the names of everybody living anywhere near. When he would go camping he used to borrow a certain skinny little hound from an old man at the end of the Quarter and if he brought back a possum or a fish sometimes they would cook it and eat together. He knew the backs of those houses like his own yard — the black washpots, the barrel hoops, the plum bushes, the privies, the old automobile body without wheels that had set for years behind one of the houses. He knew the Quarter on Sunday mornings when the women would comb and plait their children's hair in the sun on the front steps, when the grown girls would walk up and down in their trailing bright silk dresses, and the men would watch and softly whistle blues songs. And after supper time he knew it too. Then the light from the oil lamps would flicker from the houses and throw out long shadows. And there was the smell of smoke and fish and corn. And somebody was always dancing or playing the harp.

But there was one time when the Quarter was strange to him, and that was late at night. Several times on his way home late from hunting or when he was just restless, he had walked through the street at that time. The doors were all closed to the moonlight and the houses looked shrunk and had the look of shanties that have been empty a long time. At the same time there was that silence that never comes to a deserted place — and can only be sensed where there are many people sleeping. But as he would listen to this utter quietness he would always gradually become aware of a sound, and it was this that made the Quarter strange to him in the late night. The sound was never the same and it seemed always to come from a different place. Once it was like a girl laughing — softly laughing on and on. Again it was the low moan of a man in the darkness. The sound was like music except that it had no shape — it made him pause to hear and quiver as would a song. And when he would go home to bed the sound would still be inside him; he would twist in the darkness and his hard brown limbs would chafe each other because he could find no rest.

He never told Harry Minowitz about any of his walks. He could not imagine trying to tell anyone about that sound, least of all Harry, because it was a secret thing.

And he never talked to Harry about Vitalis.

When after school he would go back to the kitchen to Vitalis there were three words he always said. It was like answering *present* at the school roll-call. He would put down his books and stand in the doorway a moment and say: "I'm so hungry." The little sentence never changed and often he would not realize he had even spoken. Sometimes when he had just finished all the food he could eat and was still sitting there in the chair before the stove, restless but somehow not wanting to leave, he would mechanically mouth those three words. Just watching Vitalis brought them to his mind.

"You eats more than any lanky boy I ever seen," she would say. "What the matter with you? I believe you just eats cause you want to do something and you don't know what else to do."

But she always had food for him. Maybe pot liquor and cornbread or biscuit and syrup. Sometimes she even made candy just for him or cut off a piece of the steak they were going to have for supper.

Watching Vitalis was almost as good as eating and his eyes would follow her around. She was not coal black like some colored girls and her hair was always neatly plaited and shining with oil. Early every morning Sylvester, her boy-friend, walked to work with her and she usually wore a fancy red satin dress and earrings and high heeled green shoes. Then when she got in the house she would take off her shoes and wiggle her toes a while before putting on the bedroom slippers she wore to work in. She always hung her satin dress on the back porch and changed to a gingham one she kept at the house. She had the walk of colored people who have carried baskets of clothes on their heads. Vitalis was good and there wasn't anybody else like her.

Their talks together were warm and idle. What she didn't understand didn't gnaw on her and bother her. Sometimes he would blurt out things to her — and in a way it was like talking to himself. Her answers were always comfortable. They would make him feel like a kid again and he would laugh. One day he told her a little about Harry.

"I seen him down to your Daddy's store many a time. He a puny little white man, ain't he? You know this here is a funny thing — nearly bout all little puny peoples is biggety. The littler they is the larger they thinks they is. Just watch the way they rares up they heads when they walk. Great big mens — like Sylvester and like you ghy be — they ain't that way at all. When they be about six foots tall they liable to act soft and shamed like chilluns. Once I knowed a little biggety dwarf man name Hunch. I wish you could have seed the way on a Sunday he would commence to walk around. He carried a great big umbrella and he would priss down them streets by hisself like he was God —"

Then there was a morning when he came into the kitchen after playing a new Beethoven record he had gotten. The music had been in his head half the night and he had waked up early so as to play it awhile before school time. When he came into the kitchen Vitalis was changing her shoes. "Honey," she said. "You ought to been here a minute ago. I come in the kitchen and you was playing that there gramaphone in your room. Sound like band music folks march by. Then I done looked down at the floor and you know what I seen? A whole fambly of little mices the size of your finger, setting up on their hind legs and dancing. That the truth. Them rats really does like such music."

Maybe it was for words like this that he was always going in to Vitalis and saying, "I'm so hungry." It wasn't only for warmed up food and coffee she would give him.

Sometimes they would talk about Sara. All the eighteen months that she was away she hardly ever wrote. And then the letter would just be about Aunt Esther and her music lessons and what they were going to have for dinner that night. He knew she was changed. And he had a feeling she was in trouble or something important was happening to her. But it got so that Sara was very vague to him — and it was terrible but when he tried to remember her face he couldn't see it clearly. She got to be almost like their dead mother to him.

So it was Harry Minowitz and Vitalis who were nearest to him during that time. Vitalis and Harry. When he tried to think of them together he would have to laugh. It was like putting red with lavender — or a Bach fugue with a sad nigger whistling. Everything he knew seemed that way. Nothing fitted.

Sara came back but that didn't change things much. They weren't close like they had been before. Their Dad had thought it was time for her to come home but she didn't seem glad to be back with her own family. And all the next year she would often get very quiet and just stare ahead like she was homesick. They didn't go with the same crowd of boys and girls anymore and often they didn't even wait for each other to walk to school in the mornings. Sara had learned a lot of music in Detroit and her piano playing was different and very careful. He could tell that she had loved their Aunt Esther a lot but for some reason she didn't talk about her much.

The trouble was that he saw Sara in a hazy way at that time. That was the way everything looked to him then. Crazy and upsidedown. And he was getting to be a man and he did not know what was going to come. And always he was hungry and always he felt that something was just about to happen. And that happening he felt would be terrible and would destroy him. But he would not mold that prescience into thought. Even the time — the two long years after Sara returned — seemed to have passed through his body and not his mind. It was just long months of either floundering or quiet vacantness. And when he thought back over it there was little that he could realize.

He was getting to be a man and he was seventeen years old.

It was then that the thing happened that he had expected without knowing in his mind. This thing he had never imagined and afterward it seemed to have leapt up out of nowhere — to his mind it seemed that way but there was another part of him where this was not so.

The time was late summer and in a few weeks he was planning to leave for Atlanta to enter Tech. He did not want to go to Tech — but it was cheap because he could take the co-op course and his Dad wanted him to graduate from there and be an engineer. There didn't seem to be anything else that he could do and in a way he was eager to leave home so that he could live in a new place by himself. That late summer afternoon he was walking in the woods behind Sherman's Quarter, thinking of this and of a hundred vague things. Remembering all the other times when he had walked through those woods made him restless and he felt lost and alone.

It was almost sundown when he left the woods and started through the street where Vitalis lived. Although it was Sunday afternoon the houses were very quiet and everyone seemed to be gone. The air was sultry and there was the smell of sun-baked pine straw. On the edges of the little street were trampled weeds and a few early goldenrods. As he was walking past the houses, his ankles grey with the lazy swirls of dust that his footsteps made and his eyes tired from the sun, he suddenly heard Vitalis speak to him.

"What you doing round this way, Andrew?"

She was sitting on her front steps and seemed to be alone in the empty Quarter. "Nothing," he said. "Just wandering around."

"They having a big funeral down at our church. It the preacher dead this time. Everybody done gone but me. I just now got away from your house. Even Sylvester done gone."

He didn't know what to say but just the sight of her made him mumble, "Gosh I'm so hungry. All this walking around. And thirsty —"

"I'll get you some."

She got up slowly and he noticed for the first time that she was barefooted and her green shoes and stockings were on the porch. She stooped to put them on. "I done taken these off cause ever body done gone except a sick lady in one of them end houses. These here green shoes has always scrunched my toes — and sometimes the ground sure do feel good to my feets."

On the little stoop behind the house he drank the cool water and dashed some of it into his burning face. Again he felt as though he were hearing that strange sound he had heard late at night along this street. When he went back through the house where Vitalis had been waiting for him he felt his body tremble. He did not know why they both paused a moment in the dim little room. It was very quiet and a clock ticked slowly. There was a kewpie doll with a gauze sash on the mantlepiece and the air was close and musty.

"What ails you, Andrew? Why you shaking so? What is it ails you, Honey?"

It wasn't him and it wasn't her. It was the thing in both of them. It was the strange sound he had heard there late at night. It was the dim room and the quietness. And all the afternoons he had spent with her in the kitchen. And all his hunger and the times when he had been alone. After it happened that was what he thought.

Later she went out of the house with him and they stood by a pine tree on the edge of the woods. "Andrew, quit your looking at me like that," she kept saying. "Everthing is all right. Don't you worry none about that."

It was like he was staring at her from the bottom of a well and that was all he could think.

"That ain't nothing real wrong. It ain't the first time with me and you a grown man. Quit your looking at me like that, Andrew."

This had never been in his mind. But it had been there waiting and had crept up and smothered his other thoughts — And this was not the only thing that would do him that way. Always. Always.

"Us didn't mean nothing. Sylvester ain't ghy ever know — or your Daddy. Us haven't arranged this. Us haven't done no real sin."

He had imagined how it would be when he was twenty. And she had a pale face like a flower and that was all he knew of her.

"Peoples can't plan on everthing."

He left her. Harry's chessmen, those precise and shrunken little dolls, neat problems in geometry, music that spun itself out immense and symmetrical. He was lost lost and it seemed to him that the end had surely come. He wanted to put his hands on all that had happened to him in his life, to grasp it to him and shape it whole. He was lost lost. He was alone and naked. And along with the chessmen and the music he suddenly remembered an aerial map of New York that he had seen — with the sharp skyscrapers and the blocks neatly plotted. He wanted to go far away and Atlanta was too near his home. He remembered the map of New York, frozen and delicate it was and he knew that was where he was going. That was all that he knew.

In the restaurant of the town where he had gotten off of the bus Andrew Leander finished the last of his beers. The place was closing and there would not be a bus to Georgia until morning. He could not get Vitalis and Sara and Harry and his Dad from his mind. And there were others beside them. He realized suddenly that he had hardly remembered Chandler. Chandler West who lived across the street — whom he had been with so often and who was at the same time so obscure. And the girl who wore red fingernail polish at high school. And the little rat of a boy named Peeper whom he had once talked with at South Highlands.

He got up from the table and picked up his bags. He was the last one in the restaurant and the waiter was ready to lock up. For a moment he hung around near the door that opened into the dark quiet street.

When he had first sat down at the table everything had seemed for the first time so clear. And now he was more lost than ever. But somehow it didn't matter. He felt strong. In that dark sleepy place he was a stranger — but after three years he was going home. Not just to Georgia but to a nearer home than that. He was drunk and there was power in him to shape things. He thought of all of them at home whom he had loved. And it would not be himself but through all of them that he would find this pattern. He felt drunk and sick for home. He wanted to go out and lift up his voice and search in the night for all that he wanted. He was drunk drunk. He was Andrew Leander.

"Say," he said to the boy who was waiting to lock the door. "Can you give me the name of some place around here where I can get a room for the night?"

The boy gave him some directions and in the surface of his mind he noted them. The street was dark and silent and he stood a moment longer in the open doorway. "Say," he said again. "I got off the bus half drunk. Will you tell me the name of this place?"

AUTHOR'S OUTLINE OF "THE MUTE"
(*later published as* The Heart Is a Lonely Hunter)

General Remarks

THE BROAD PRINCIPAL THEME of this book is indicated in the first dozen pages. This is the theme of man's revolt against his own inner isolation and his urge to express himself as fully as is possible. Surrounding this general idea there are several counter themes and some of these may be stated briefly as follows: (1) There is a deep need in man to express himself by creating some unifying principle or God. A personal God created by a man is a reflection of himself and in substance this God is most often inferior to his creator. (2) In a disorganized society these individual Gods or principles are likely to be chimerical and fantastic. (3) Each man must express himself in his own way — but this is often denied to him by a wasteful, short-sighted society. (4) Human beings are innately cooperative, but an unnatural social tradition makes them behave in ways that are not in accord with their deepest nature. (5) Some men are heroes by nature in that they will give all that is in them without regard to the effort or to the personal returns.

Of course these themes are never stated nakedly in the book. Their overtones are felt through the characters and situations. Much will depend upon the insight of the reader and the care with which the book is read. In some parts the underlying ideas will be concealed far down below the surface of a scene and at other times these ideas will be shown with a certain emphasis. In the last few pages the various motifs which have been recurring from time to time throughout the book are drawn sharply together and the work ends with a sense of cohesive finality.

The general outline of this work can be expressed very simply. It is the story of five isolated, lonely people in their search for expression and spiritual integration with something greater than themselves. One of these five persons is a deaf mute, John Singer — and it is around him that the whole book pivots. Because of their loneliness these other four people see in the mute a certain mystic superiority and he becomes in a sense their ideal. Because of Singer's infirmity his outward character is vague and unlimited. His friends are able to impute to him all the qualities which they would wish for him to have. Each one of these four people creates his understanding of the mute from his own desires. Singer can read lips and understand what is said to him. In his eternal silence there is something compelling. Each one of these persons makes the mute the repository for his most personal feelings and ideas.

This situation between the four people and the mute has an almost exact parallel in the relation between Singer and his deaf-mute friend, Antonapoulos. Singer is the only person who could attribute to Antonapoulos dignity and a certain wisdom. Singer's love for Antonapoulos threads through the whole book from the first page until the very end. No part of Singer is left untouched by this love and when they are separated his life is meaningless and he is only marking time until he can be with his friend again. Yet the four people who count themselves as Singer's friends know nothing about Antonapoulos at all until the book is nearly ended. The irony of this situation grows slowly and steadily more apparent as the story progresses.

When Antonapoulos dies finally of Bright's disease Singer, overwhelmed by loneliness and despondency, turns on the gas and kills himself. Only then do these other four characters begin to understand the real Singer at all.

About this central idea there is much of the quality and tone of a legend. All the parts dealing directly with Singer are written in the simple style of a parable.

Before the reasons why this situation came about can be fully understood it is necessary to know each of the principal characters in some detail. But the characters cannot be described adequately without the events which happen to them being involved. Nearly all of the happenings in the book spring directly from the characters. During the space of this book each person is shown in his strongest and most typical actions.

Of course it must be understood that none of these personal characteristics are told in the didactic manner in which they are set down here. They are implied in one successive scene after another — and it is only at the end, when the sum of these implications is considered, that the real characters are understood in all of their deeper aspects.

Characters and Events

JOHN SINGER

Of all the main characters in the book Singer is the simplest. Because of his deaf-mutism he is isolated from the ordinary human emotions of other people to a psychopathic degree. He is very observant and intuitive. On the surface he is a model of kindness and cooperativeness — but nothing which goes on around him disturbs his inner self. All of his deeper emotions are involved in the only friend to whom he can express himself, Antonapoulos. In the second chapter Biff Brannon thinks of Singer's eyes as being "cold and gentle as a cat's." It is this same remoteness that gives him an air of wisdom and superiority.

Singer is the first character in the book only in the sense that he is the symbol of isolation and thwarted expression and because the story pivots about him. In reality each one of his satellites is of far more importance than himself. The book will take all of its body and strength in the development of the four people who revolve about the mute.

The parts concerning Singer are never treated in a subjective manner. The style is oblique. This is partly because the mute, although he is educated, does not think in words but in visual impressions. That, of course, is a natural outcome of his deafness. Except when he is understood through the eyes of other people the style is for the main part simple and declarative. No attempt will be made to enter intimately into his subconscious. He is a flat character in the sense that from the second chapter on through the rest of the book his essential self does not change.

At his death there is a strange little note from the cousin of Antonapoulos found in his pocket:

> DEAR MR. SINGER,
> No address on corner of letters. They all sent back to me. Spiros Antonapoulos died and was buried with his kidneys last month. Sorry to tell same but no use writing letters to the dead.
> Yours truly,
> CHARLES PARKER

When the man is considered in his deepest nature (because of his inner character and peculiar situation) his suicide at the death of Antonapoulos is a necessity.

MICK KELLY

Mick is perhaps the most outstanding character in the book. Because of her age and her temperament her relation with the mute is more accentuated than any other person's. At the beginning of the second part of the work she steps out boldly — and from then on, up until the last section, she commands more space and interest than anyone else. Her story is that of the violent struggle of a gifted child to get what she needs from an unyielding environment. When Mick first appears she is at the age of thirteen, and when the book ends she is fourteen months older. Many things of great importance happen to her during this time. At the beginning she is a crude child on the threshold of a period of quick awakening and development. Her energy and the possibilities before her are without limits. She begins to go forward boldly in the face of all obstacles before her and during the next few months there is great development. In the end, after the finances of her family have completely given way, she has to get a job working ten hours a day in a ten-cent store. Her tragedy does not come in any way from herself — she is robbed of her freedom and energy by an unprincipled and wasteful society.

To Mick music is the symbol of beauty and freedom. She has had no musical background at all and her chances for educating herself are very small. Her family does not have a radio and in the summer she roams around the streets of the town pulling her two baby brothers in a wagon and listening to any music she can hear from other people's houses. She begins reading at the public library and from books she learns some of the things she needs to know. In the fall when she enters the Vocational High School she arranges to have rudimentary lessons on the piano with a girl in her class. In exchange for the lessons she does all the girl's homework in algebra and arithmetic and gives her also fifteen cents a week from her lunch money. During the afternoon Mick can sometimes practice on the piano in the gymnasium — but the place is always noisy and overcrowded and she never knows when she will be interrupted suddenly by a blow on the head from a basketball.

Her love for music is instinctive, and her taste is naturally never pure at this stage. At first there is Mozart. After that she learns about Beethoven. From then on she goes hungrily from one composer to another whenever she gets a chance to hear them on other people's radios — Bach, Brahms, Wagner, Sibelius, etc. Her information is often very garbled but always the feeling is there. Mick's love for music is intensely creative. She is always making up little tunes for herself — and she plans to compose great symphonies and operas. Her plans are always definite in a certain way. She will conduct all of her music herself and her initials will always be written in big red letters on the curtains of the stage. She will conduct her music either in a red satin evening dress or else she will wear a real man's evening suit. Mick is thoroughly egoistic — and the crudely childish side of her nature comes in side by side with the mature.

Mick must always have some person to love and admire. Her childhood was a series of passionate, reasonless admirations for a motley cavalcade of persons, one after another. And now she centers this undirected love on Singer. He gives her a book about Beethoven on her birthday and his room is always quiet and comfortable. In her imagination she makes the mute just the sort of teacher and friend that she needs. He is the only person who seems to show any interest in her at all. She confides in the mute — and when an important crisis occurs at the end of the book it is to him that she wants to turn for help.

This crisis, although on the surface the most striking thing that happens to Mick, is really subordinate to her feeling for Singer and to her struggle against the social forces working against her. In the fall when she enters Vocational High she prefers to take "mechanical shop" with the boys rather than attend the stenographic classes. In this class she meets a fifteen-year-old boy, Harry West, and gradually they become good comrades. They are attracted to each other by a similar intensity of character and by their mutual interest in mechanics. Harry, like Mick, is made restless by an abundance of undirected energy. In the spring they try to construct a glider together in the Kellys' backyard and, although because of inadequate materials they can never get the contraption to fly, they work at it very hard together. All of this time their friendship is blunt and childish.

In the late spring Mick and Harry begin going out together on Saturday for little trips in the country. Harry has a bicycle and they go out about ten miles from town to a certain creek in the woods. Feelings that neither of them fully understands begin to come about between them. The outcome is very abrupt. They start to the country one Saturday afternoon in great excitement and full of childish animal energy — and before they return they have, without any premeditation at all, experienced each other sexually. It is absolutely necessary that this facet of the book be treated with extreme reticence. What has happened is made plain through a short, halting dialogue between Mick and Harry in which a great deal is implied but very little is actually said.

Although it is plain that this premature experience will affect both of them deeply, there is the feeling that the eventual results will be more serious for Harry than for Mick. Their actions are rather more mature than would be expected. However, they both decide that they will never want to marry or have the same experience again. They are both stunned by a sense of evil. They decide that they will never see each other again — and that night Harry takes a can of soup from his kitchen shelf, breaks his nickel bank, and hitchhikes from the town to Atlanta where he hopes to find some sort of job.

The restraint with which this scene between Mick and Harry must be told cannot be stressed too strongly.

For a while Mick is greatly oppressed by this that has happened to her. She turns to her music more vehemently than ever. She has always looked on sex with a cold, infantile remoteness — and now the experience she has had seems to be uniquely personal and strange. She tries ruthlessly to forget about it, but the secret weighs on her mind. She feels that if she can just tell some person about it she would be easier. But she is not close enough to her sisters and her mother to confide in them, and she has no especial friends of her own age. She wants to tell Mr. Singer and she tries to imagine how to go about this. She is still taking consolation in the possibility that she might be able to confide in Mr. Singer about this when the mute kills himself.

After the death of Singer, Mick feels very alone and defenseless. She works even harder than ever with her music. But the pressing economic condition of her family which has been growing steadily worse all through the past months is now just about as bad as it can be. The two elder children in the family are barely able to support themselves and can be of no help to their parents. It is essential that Mick get work of some kind. She fights this bitterly, for she wants to go back at least one more year to High School and to have some sort of chance with her music. But nothing can be done and at the beginning of the summer she gets a job working from eight-thirty to six-thirty as a clerk in a ten-cent store. The work is very wearing, but when the manager wants any of the girls to stay overtime he always picks Mick — for she can stand longer and endure more fatigue than any other person in the store.

The essential traits of Mick Kelly are great creative energy and courage. She is defeated by society on all the main issues before she can even begin, but still there is something in her and in those like her that cannot and will not ever be destroyed.

JAKE BLOUNT

Jake's struggle with social conditions is direct and conscious. The spirit of revolution is very strong in him. His deepest motive is to do all that he can to change the predatory, unnatural social conditions existing today. It is his tragedy that his energies can find no channel in which to flow. He is fettered by abstractions and conflicting ideas — and in practical application he can do no more than throw himself against windmills. He feels that the present social tradition is soon to collapse completely, but his dreams of the civilization of the future are alternately full of hope and of distrust.

His attitude toward his fellow man vacillates continually between hate and the most unselfish love. His attitude toward the principles of communism are much the same as his attitude toward man. Deep inside him he is an earnest communist, but he feels that in concrete application all communistic societies up until the present have degenerated into bureaucracies. He is unwilling to compromise and his is the attitude of all or nothing. His inner and outward motives are so contradictory at times that it is hardly an exaggeration to speak of the man as being deranged. The burden which he has taken on himself is too much for him.

Jake is the product of his peculiar environment. During the time of this book he is twenty-nine years old. He was born in a textile town in South Carolina, a town very similar to the one in which the action of this book takes place. His childhood was passed among conditions of absolute poverty and degradation. At the age of nine years (this was the time of the last World War) he was working fourteen hours a day in a cotton mill. He had to snatch for himself whatever education he could get. At twelve he left home on his own initiative and his self-teachings and wanderings began. At one time or another he has lived and worked in almost every section of this country.

Jake's inner instability reflects markedly on his outer personality. In physique he suggests a stunted giant. He is nervous and irritable. All of his life he has had difficulty in keeping his lips from betraying his emotions — in order to overcome this he has grown a flourishing mustache which only accentuates this weakness and gives him a comic, jerky look. Because of his nervous whims it is hard for him to get along with his neighbors and people hold aloof from him. This causes him either to drop into self-conscious buffoonery or else to take on an exaggerated misplaced dignity.

If Jake cannot act he has to talk. The mute is an excellent repository for conversation. Singer attracts Jake because of his seeming stability and calm. He is a stranger in the town and the circumstance of his loneliness makes him seek out the mute. Talking to Singer and spending the evening with him becomes a sedative habit with him. At the end, when the mute is dead, he feels as though he had lost a certain inner ballast. He has the vague feeling that he has been tricked, too, and that all of the conclusions and visions that he has told the mute are forever lost.

Jake depends heavily on alcohol — and he can drink in tremendous quantities with no seeming ill effect. Occasionally he will try to break himself of this habit, but he is as unable to discipline himself in this as he is in more important matters.

Jake's stay in the town ends in a fiasco. As usual, he has been trying during these months to do what he can to right social injustice. At the end of the book the growing resentment between the Negroes and the white factory workers who patronize the show is nourished by several trifling quarrels between individuals. Day by day one thing leads to another and then late on Saturday night there is a wild brawl. (This scene occurs during the week after Singer's death.) All the white workers fight bitterly against the Negroes. Jake tries to keep order for a while and then he, too, loses control of himself and goes berserk. The fight grows into an affair in which there is no organization at all and each man is simply fighting for himself. This brawl is finally broken up by the police and several persons are arrested. Jake escapes but the fight seems to him to be a symbol of his own life. Singer is dead and he leaves the town just as he came to it — a stranger.

DR. BENEDICT MADY COPELAND

Dr. Copeland presents the bitter spectacle of the educated Negro in the South. Dr. Copeland, like Jake Blount, is warped by his long years of effort to do his part to change certain existing conditions. At the opening of the book he is fifty-one years old, but already he is an old man.

He has practiced among the Negroes of the town for twenty-five years. He has always felt, though, that his work as a doctor was only secondary to his efforts at teaching his people. His ideas are laboriously thought out and inflexible. For a long while he was interested mainly in birth control, as he felt that indiscriminate sexual relations and haphazard and prolific propagation were responsible in a large part for the weakness of the Negro. He is greatly opposed to miscegenation — but this opposition comes mainly from personal pride and resentment. The great flaw in all of his theories is that he will not admit the racial culture of the Negro. Theoretically he is against the grafting of the Negroid way of living to the Caucasian. His ideal would be a race of Negro ascetics.

Parallel with Dr. Copeland's ambition for his race is his love for his family. But because of his inflexibility his relations with his four children are a complete failure. His own temperament is partly responsible for this, too. All of his life Dr. Copeland has gone against the grain of his own racial nature. His passionate asceticism and the strain of his work have their effect on him. At home, when he felt the children escaping from his influence, he was subject to wild and sudden outbreaks of rage. This lack of control was finally the cause of his separation from his wife and children.

While still a young man Dr. Copeland suffered at one time from pulmonary tuberculosis, a disease to which the Negro is particularly susceptible. His illness was arrested — but now when he is fifty-one years old his left lung is involved again. If there were an adequate sanatorium he would enter it for treatment — but of course there is no decent hospital for Negroes in the state. He ignores the disease and keeps up his practice — although now his work is not as extensive as it was in the past.

To Dr. Copeland the mute seems to be the embodiment of the control and asceticism of a certain type of white man. All of his life Dr. Copeland has suffered because of slights and humiliations from the white race. Singer's politeness and consideration make Dr. Copeland pitiably grateful. He is always careful to keep up his "dignity" with the mute — but Singer's friendship is of great importance to him.

The mute's face has a slightly Semitic cast and Dr. Copeland thinks that he is a Jew. The Jewish people, because they are a racially persecuted minority, have always interested Dr. Copeland. Two of his heroes are Jews — Benedict Spinoza and Karl Marx.

Dr. Copeland realizes very fully and bitterly that his life work has been a failure. Although he is respected to the point of awe by most of the Negroes of the town his teachings have been too foreign to the nature of the race to have any palpable effect.

In the beginning of the book Dr. Copeland's economic situation is very uncertain. His house and most of his medical equipment are mortgaged. For fifteen years he had received a small but steady income from his work as a member of the staff of the city hospital — but his personal ideas about social situations have led to his discharge. As a pretext for dismissal he was accused, and rightly, of performing abortions in certain cases where a child was an economic impossibility. Since the loss of this post, Dr. Copeland has had no dependable income. His patients are for the most part totally unable to pay fees for treatment. His illness is a hindrance and he steadily loses ground. At the end the house is taken away from him and after a lifetime of service he is left a pauper. His wife's relations take him out to spend the short remaining part of his life on their farm in the country.

BIFF BRANNON

Of the four people who revolve around the mute Biff is the most disinterested. It is typical of him that he is always the observer. About Biff there is much that is austere and classical. In contrast with the driving enthusiasms of Mick and Jake and Dr. Copeland, Biff is nearly always coldly reflective. The second chapter of the book opens with him and in the closing pages his meditations bring the work to a thoughtful and objective finish.

Biff's humorous aspects are to be brought out in all the parts dealing with him. Technically he is a thoroughly rounded character in that he will be seen completely from all sides. At the time the book opens he is forty-four years old and has spent the best part of his life standing behind the cash register in the restaurant and making his own particular observations. He has a passion for detail. It is typical of him that he has a small room in the back of his place devoted to a complete and neatly catalogued file of the daily evening newspaper dating back without a break for eighteen years. His problem is to get the main outlines of a situation from all the cluttering details in his mind, and he goes about this with his own painstaking patience.

Biff is strongly influenced by his own specific sexual experiences. At forty-four years he is prematurely impotent — and the cause of this lies in psychic as well as physical reasons. He has been married to Alice for twenty-three years. From the beginning their marriage was a mistake, and it has endured mainly because of economic necessity and habit.

Perhaps as a compensation for his own dilemma Biff comes to his own curious conclusion that marital relations are not the primary functions of the sexual impulse. He believes that human beings are fundamentally ambi-sexual — and for confirmation he turns to the periods of childhood and senility.

Two persons have a great emotional hold on Biff. These are Mick Kelly and a certain old man named Mr. Alfred Simms. Mick has been coming in the restaurant all through her childhood to get candy with her brother and to play the slot machine. She is always friendly with Biff, but of course she has no idea of his feelings for her. As a matter of fact, Biff is not exactly clear himself on that point, either. Mr. Simms is a pitiable, fragile old fellow whose senses are muddled. During middle life he had been a wealthy man but now he is penniless and alone. The old man keeps up a great pretense of being a busy person of affairs. Every day he comes out on the street in clean ragged clothes and holding an old woman's pocket-book. He goes from one bank to another in an effort to "settle his accounts." Mr. Simms used to like to come into Biff's restaurant and sit for a little while. He always sat at a table quietly and never disturbed anyone. With his queer clothes and the big pocket-book clutched against his chest he looked like an old woman. At that time Biff did not have any particular interest in Mr. Simms. He would kindly pour him out a beer now and then, but he did not think much about him.

One night (this was a few weeks before the opening of the book) the restaurant was crowded and the table where Mr. Simms was sitting was needed. Alice insisted that Biff put the old man out. Biff was used to ejecting all sorts of people from the place and he went up to the old man without thinking much about it and asked him if he thought the table was a park bench. Mr. Simms did not understand at first and smiled up happily at Biff. Then Biff was disconcerted and he repeated the words in a much rougher way than he had intended. Tears came to the old man's eyes. He tried to keep up his dignity before the people around him, fumbled uselessly in his pocket-book and went out crushed.

This little episode is described here in some detail because of its effect on Biff. The happening is made clear in a chapter in the second part of the book. All through the story Biff's thoughts are continually going back to the old man. His treatment of Mr. Simms comes to be for him the embodiment of all the evil he has ever done. At the same time the old man is the symbol of the declining period of life which Biff is now approaching.

Mick brings up in Biff nostalgic feelings of youth and heroism. She is at the age where she possesses both the qualities of a girl and of a boy. Also, Biff has always wanted to have a little daughter and of course she reminds him of this, too. At the end of the book, when Mick begins to mature, Biff's feelings for her slowly diminish.

Toward his wife Biff is entirely cold. When Alice dies in the second part of the book Biff feels not the slightest pity or regret for her at all. His only remorse is that he did not ever fully understand Alice as a person. It piques him that he could have lived so long with a woman and still understand her so confusedly. After her death Biff takes off the crepe paper streamers from under the electric fans and sews mourning tokens on his sleeves. These gestures are not so much for Alice as they are a reflection of his own feeling for his approaching decline and death. After his wife dies certain female elements become more pronounced in Biff. He begins to rinse his hair in lemon juice and to take exaggerated care of his skin. Alice had always been a much better business manager than Biff and after her death the restaurant begins to stagnate.

In spite of certain quirks in Biff's nature he is perhaps the most balanced person in the book. He has that faculty for seeing the things which happen around him with cold objectivity — without instinctively connecting them with himself. He sees and hears and remembers everything. He is curious to a comic degree. And nearly always, despite the vast amount of details in his mind, he can work his way patiently to the very skeleton of a situation and see affairs in their entirety.

Biff is far too wary to be drawn into any mystic admiration of Singer. He likes the mute and is of course very curious about him. Singer occupies a good deal of his thoughts and he values his reserve and common sense. He is the only one of the four main characters who sees the situation as it really is. In the last few pages he threads through the details of the story and arrives at the most salient points. In his reflections at the end Biff himself thinks of the word "parable" in connection with what has happened — and of course this is the only time that this designation is used. His reflections bring the book to a close with a final, objective roundness.

SUBORDINATE CHARACTERS

There are several minor characters who play very important parts in the story. None of these persons are treated in a subjective manner — and from the point of view of the novel the things that happen to them are of more importance in the effects on the main characters than because of the change that they bring about among these characters.

Spiros Antonapoulos

Antonapoulos has been described with complete detail in the first chapter. His mental, sexual and spiritual development is that of a child of about seven years old.

Portia Copeland Jones, Highboy Jones, and Willie Copeland

A great deal of interest is centered around these three characters. Portia is the most dominant member of this trio. In actual space she occupies almost as much of the book as any one of the main characters, except Mick — but she is always placed in a subordinate position. Portia is the embodiment of the maternal instincts. Highboy, her husband, and Willie, her brother, are inseparable from herself. These three characters are just the opposite of Dr. Copeland and the other central characters in that they make no effort to go against circumstance.

The tragedy that comes to this group plays an important part on all the phases of the book. At the beginning of the second section Willie is arrested on a charge of burglary. He was walking down a side alley after midnight and two young white boys told him they were looking for someone, gave him a dollar, and instructed him to whistle when the person they were looking for came down the alley. Only when Willie saw two policemen coming toward him did he realize what had happened. In the meantime the boys had broken in a drug store. Later in the fall Willie is sentenced along with them for a year of hard labor. All of this is revealed through Portia as she tells this great trouble to the Kelly children. "Willie he so busy looking at that dollar bill he don't have no time to think. And then they asks him how come he run when he seen them police. They might just as soon ask how come a person jerk their hand off a hot stove when they lays it there by mistake."

This is the first of their trouble. Now that the household arrangements are disturbed, Highboy begins keeping company with another girl. This too is told by Portia to the Kelly children and Dr. Copeland: "I could realize this better if she were a light-colored, good-looking girl. But she at least ten shades blacker than I is. She the ugliest girl I ever seen. She walk like she haves a egg between her legs and don't want to break it. She not even clean."

The most brutal tragedy in the book comes to these three people. Willie and four other Negroes were guilty of some little misbehavior on the chain-gang where they were working. It was February and the camp was stationed a couple of hundred miles north of the town. As punishment they were put together in a solitary room. Their shoes were taken off and their feet suspended. They were left like this for three full days. It was cold and as their blood did not circulate the boys' feet froze and they developed gangrene. One boy died of pneumonia and the other four had to have one or both of their feet amputated. They were all manual laborers and of course this completely took away their means for future livelihood. This part is of course revealed by Portia, too. It is told in only a few blunt broken paragraphs and left at that.

This happening has a great effect on the main characters. Dr. Copeland is shattered by the news and is in delirium for several weeks. Mick feels all the impact of the horror. Biff had formerly employed Willie in his restaurant and he broods over all the aspects of the affair.

Jake wants to bring it all to light and make of it a national example. But this is impossible for several reasons. Willie is terribly afraid—for it has been impressed upon him at the camp to keep quiet about what has been done to him. The state has been careful to separate the boys immediately after the happening and they have lost track of each other. Also, Willie and the other boys are really children in a certain way—they do not understand what their cooperation would mean. Suffering had strained their nerves so much that during the three days and nights in the room they had quarreled angrily among themselves and when it was over they had no wish to see each other again. From the long view their childish bitterness toward each other and lack of cooperation is the worst part of the whole tragedy.

Highboy comes back to Portia after Willie returns and, handicapped by Willie's infirmity, the three of them start their way of living all over again.

The thread of this story runs through the whole book. Most of it is told through Portia's own vivid, rhythmic language at intervals as it happens.

Harry West

Harry has already been briefly described in the section given to Mick. During the first part of the year, when he and Mick started their friendship, he was infatuated with a certain little flirting girl at High School. His eyes had always given him much trouble and he wore thick-lensed glasses. The girl thought the glasses made him look sissy and he tried to stumble around without them for several months. This aggravated his eye trouble. His friendship with Mick is very different from his infatuation with the other little girl at High School.

Harry has the exaggeratedly developed sense of right and wrong that sometimes is a characteristic of adolescence. He is also of a brooding nature. There is the implication that his abrupt experience with Mick will leave its mark on him for a long time.

Lily Mae Jenkins

Lily Mae is an abandoned, waifish Negro homosexual who haunts the Sunny Dixie Show where Jake works. He is always dancing. His mind and feelings are childish and he is totally unfit to earn his living. Because of his skill in music and dancing he is a friend of Willie's. He is always half starved and he hangs around Portia's kitchen constantly in the hopes of getting a meal. When Highboy and Willie are gone Portia takes some comfort in Lily Mae.

Lily Mae is presented in the book in exactly the same naive way that his friends understand him. Portia describes Lily Mae to Dr. Copeland in this manner: "Lily Mae is right pitiful now. I don't know if you ever noticed any boys like this but he cares for mens instead of girls. When he were younger he used to be real cute. He were all the time dressing up in girls' clothes and laughing. Everybody thought he were real cute then. But now he getting old and he seem different. He all the time hungry and he real pitiful. He loves to come set and talk with me in the kitchen. He dances for me and I gives him a little dinner."

The Kelly Children — Bill, Hazel, Etta, Bubber and Ralph

No great interest is focussed on any of these children individually. They are all seen through the eyes of Mick. All three of the older children are confused, in varying degrees, by the problem of trying to find their places in a society that is not prepared to absorb them. Each one of these youngsters is seen sharply — but not with complex fullness.

It is Mick's permanent duty to nurse Bubber and the baby during all the time when she is not actually at school. This chore is something of a burden for an adventurous roamer like Mick — but she has a warm and deep affection for these youngest children. At one time she makes these rambling remarks concerning her sisters and brothers as a whole: "A person's got to fight for every single little thing they ever get. And I've noticed a lot of times that the farther down a kid comes in a family the better the kid really is. Youngest kids are always the toughest. I'm pretty hard because I have a lot of them on top of me. Bubber — he looks sick but he's got guts underneath that. If all this is true Ralph sure ought to be a real strong one when he's big enough to get around. Even though he's just thirteen months old I can read something hard and tough in that Ralph's face already."

INTERRELATIONS OF CHARACTERS

It can easily be seen that in spirit Dr. Copeland, Mick Kelly and Jake Blount are very similar. Each one of these three people has struggled to progress to his own mental proportions in spite of fettering circumstances. They are like plants that have had to grow under a rock from the beginning. The great effort of each of them has been to give and there has been no thought of personal returns.

The likeness between Dr. Copeland and Jake Blount is so marked that they might be called spiritual brothers. The greatest real difference between them is one of race and of years. Dr. Copeland's earlier life was spent in more favorable circumstances and from the start his duty was clear to him. The injustices inflicted on the Negro race are much more plainly marked than the ancient vastly scattered mismanagements of capitalism as a whole. Dr. Copeland was able to set to work immediately in a certain narrow sphere, while the conditions which Jake hates are too fluid for him to get his shoulder to them. Dr. Copeland has the simplicity and dignity of a person who has lived all of his life in one place and given the best of himself to one work. Jake has the jerky nervousness of a man whose inner and outer life has been no more stable than a whirlwind.

The conscientiousness of both of these men is heightened by artificial stimulation — Dr. Copeland is running a diurnal temperature and Jake is drinking steadily every day. In certain persons the effects of these stimulants can be very much the same.

Dr. Copeland and Jake come into direct contact with each other only once during the book. Casual encounters are not considered here. They meet and misunderstand each other in the second chapter when Jake tries to make the doctor come into Biff's restaurant and drink with him. After that they see each other once on the stairs at the Kelly boarding house and then on two occasions they meet briefly in Singer's room. But the only time they directly confront each other takes place in Dr. Copeland's own house under dramatic circumstances.

This is the night in which Willie has come home from the prison hospital. Dr. Copeland is in bed with an inflammation of the pleura, delirious and thought to be dying. The crippled Willie is on the cot in the kitchen and a swarm of friends and neighbors are trying to crowd in through the back door to see and hear of Willie's situation. Jake has heard of the whole affair from Portia and when Singer goes to sit with Dr. Copeland during the night Jake asks to accompany him.

Jake comes to the house with the intention of questioning Willie as closely as possible. But before the evening is over he is drawn to Dr. Copeland and it is he, instead of Singer, who sits through the night with the sick man. In the kitchen Willie is meeting his friends for the first time in almost a year. At first in the back of the house there is a sullen atmosphere of grief and hopelessness. Willie's story is repeated over and over in sullen monotones. Then this atmosphere begins to change. Willie sits up on the cot and begins to play his harp. Lily Mae starts dancing. As the evening progresses the atmosphere changes to a wild artificial release of merriment.

This is the background for Jake's meeting with Dr. Copeland. The two men are together in the bedroom and the sounds from the kitchen come in during the night through the closed door. Jake is drunk and Dr. Copeland is almost out of his head with fever. Yet their dialogue comes from the marrow of their inner selves. They both lapse into the rhythmic, illiterate vernacularisms of their early childhood. The inner purpose of each man is seen fully by the other. In the course of a few hours these two men, after a lifetime of isolation, come as close to each other as it is possible for two human beings to be. Very early in the morning Singer drops by the house before going to work and he finds them both asleep together, Jake sprawled loosely on the foot of the bed and Dr. Copeland sleeping with healthy naturalness.

The interrelations between the other characters will not have to be described in such detail. Mick, Jake and Biff see each other frequently. Each one of these people occupies a certain key position in the town; Mick is nearly always on the streets. At the restaurant Biff comes in frequent contact with all the main characters except Dr. Copeland. Jake is constantly watching a whole cross-section of the town at the show where he works — later when he drives a taxi he becomes acquainted with nearly all of the characters, major and minor, in the book. Mick's relations toward each of these people are childish and matter of fact. Biff, except for his affinity for Mick, is coldly appraising. Certain small scenes and developments take place between all of these people in a variety of combinations.

On the whole the interrelations between the people of this book can be described as being like the spokes of a wheel — with Singer representing the center point. This situation, with all of its attendant irony, expresses the most important theme of the book.

General Structure and Outline

TIME

The first chapter serves as a prelude to the book and the reckoning of time starts with Chapter Two. The story covers a period of fourteen months — from May until the July of the following year.

The whole work is divided into three parts. The body of the book is contained in the middle section. In the actual number of pages this is the longest of the three parts and nearly all of the months in the time scheme take place in this division.

Part I

The first writing of Part I is already completed and so there is no need to take up this section in detail. The time extends from the middle of May to the middle of July. Each of the main characters is introduced in detail. The salient points of each person are clearly implied and the general direction each character will take is indicated. The tale of Singer and Antonapoulos is told. The meetings of each one of the main characters with Singer are presented — and the general web of the book is begun.

Part II

There is a quickening of movement at the beginning of this middle section. There will be more than a dozen chapters in this part, but the handling of these chapters is much more flexible than in Part I. Many of the chapters are very short and they are more dependent upon each other than the first six chapters. Almost half of the actual space is devoted to Mick, her growth and progress, and the increasing intensity of her admiration for Singer. Her story, and the separate parts developed from her point of view, weave in and out of the chapters about the other characters.

This part opens with Mick on one of her nocturnal wanderings. During the summer she has been hearing concerts under unusual circumstances. She has found out that in certain wealthier districts in the town a few families get fairly good programs on their radios. There is one house in particular that tunes in every Friday evening for a certain symphony concert. Of course the windows are all open at this time of the year and the music can be heard very plainly from the outside. Mick saunters into the yard at night just before the program is to begin and sits down in the dark behind the shrubbery under the living room window. Sometimes after the concert she will stand looking in at the family in the house for some time before going on. Because she gets so much from their radio she is half in love with all of the people in the house.

It would take many dozens of pages to go into a synopsis of this second part in complete detail. A complete and explanatory account would take actually longer than the whole part as it will be when it is completed — for a good book implies a great deal more than the words actually say. For convenience it is best to set down a few skeleton notations with the purpose of getting the sequence of events into a pattern. These rough notes mean very little in themselves and can only be understood after a thorough reading of the part of these remarks which goes under the heading of Characters and Events. This rough outline is still in a tentative stage and is only meant to be indicative of the general formation of this central part.

LATE SUMMER

Mick's night wandering and the concert. Resumé of the growth that is taking place in Mick this summer. On the morning after the concert Portia tells Mick and the other Kelly children of Willie's arrest. Mick's morning wanderings.

Jake Blount's experience at the Sunny Dixie Show.

AUTUMN

Mick's first day at Vocational High.

Dr. Copeland on his medical rounds. Another visit from Portia in which she tells her father that Highboy has left her.

Mick becomes acquainted with Harry West.

Biff's wife, Alice, dies — his meditations.

Mick and her music again. Mick's sister, Etta, takes French leave of her family and tries to run away to Hollywood, but returns in a few days. Mick goes with the little girl who teaches her music to a "real" piano lesson. She experiences a great embarrassment when she boldly tells the teacher she is a musician and sits down to try to play on a "real" piano. (This takes place at the house where Mick was listening to the concert at the opening of this section — and Mick already knows this teacher and her family quite well after watching them through the window during the summer.)

WINTER

Christmas. Dr. Copeland gives his two annual Christmas parties — one in the morning for children and another in the late afternoon for adults. These parties have been given by him every year for two decades and he serves refreshments to his patients and then makes a short talk. The relation between Dr. Copeland and the human material with which he works is brought out clearly.

Singer visits Antonapoulos.

Jake Blount's experience in the town as a ten-cent taxi driver.

Mick and Singer. Mick begins plans for the glider with Harry West.

The tragedy of Willie and the other four boys is told by Portia in the Kelly kitchen to Mick, Jake Blount and Singer.

SPRING

Further meditations of Biff Brannon — and scene between Mick and Biff at the restaurant.

Mick and her music again — Mick and Harry work on the glider.

Willie returns. The meeting of Dr. Copeland and Jake.

The experience between Harry and Mick comes to its abrupt fulfillment and finish. Harry's departure. Mick's oppressive secret. The Kellys' financial condition. Mick's energetic plans and her music.

Singer's death.

*

This outline does not indicate the main web of the story — that of the relations of each main character with the mute. These relations are so gradual and so much a part of the persons themselves that it is impossible to put them down in such blunt notations. However, from these notes a general idea of the time scheme and of sequence can be gathered.

Part III

Singer's death overshadows all of the final section of the book. In actual length this part requires about the same number of pages as does the first part. In technical treatment the similarity between these sections is pronounced. This part takes place during the months of June and July. There are four chapters and each of the main characters is given his last presentation. A rough outline of this conclusive part may be suggested as follows:

Dr. Copeland. The finish of his work and teachings — his departure to the country. Portia, Willie and Highboy start again.

Jake Blount. Jake writes curious social manifestoes and distributes them through the town. The brawl at the Sunny Dixie Show; Jake prepares to leave the town.

Mick Kelly. Mick begins her new work at the ten-cent store.

Biff Brannon. Final scene between Biff, Mick and Jake at the restaurant. Meditations of Biff concluded.

PLACE — THE TOWN

This story, in its essence, could have occurred at any place and in any time. But as the book is written, however, there are many aspects of the content which are peculiar to the America of this decade — and more specifically to the southern part of the United States. The town is never mentioned in the book by its name. The town is located in the very western part of Georgia, bordering the Chattahoochee River and just across the boundary line from Alabama. The population of the town is around 40,000 — and about one third of the people in the town are

Negroes. This is a typical factory community and nearly all of the business set-up centers around the textile mills and small retail stores.

Industrial organization has made no headway at all among the workers in the town. Conditions of great poverty prevail. The average cotton mill worker is very unlike the miner or a worker in the automobile industry — south of Gastonia, S.C., the average cotton mill worker has been conditioned to a very apathetic, listless state. For the most part he makes no effort to determine the causes of poverty and unemployment. His immediate resentment is directed toward the only social group beneath him — the Negro. When the mills are slack this town is veritably a place of lost and hungry people.

TECHNIQUE AND SUMMARY

This book is planned according to a definite and balanced design. The form is contrapuntal throughout. Like a voice in a fugue each one of the main characters is an entirety in himself — but his personality takes on a new richness when contrasted and woven in with the other characters in the book.

It is in the actual style in which the book will be written that the work's affinity to contrapuntal music is seen most clearly. There are five distinct styles of writing — one for each of the main characters who is treated subjectively and an objective, legendary style for the mute. The object in each of these methods of writing is to come as close as possible to the inner psychic rhythms of the character from whose point of view it is written. This likeness between style and character is fairly plain in the first part — but this closeness progresses gradually in each instance until at the end the style expresses the inner man just as deeply as is possible without lapsing into the unintelligible unconscious.

This book will be complete in all of its phases. No loose ends will be left dangling and at the close there will be a feeling of balanced completion. The fundamental idea of the book is ironic — but the reader is not left with a sense of futility. The book reflects the past and also indicates the future. A few of the people in this book come very near to being heroes and they are not the only human beings of their kind. Because of the essence of these people there is the feeling that, no matter how many times their efforts are wasted and their personal ideals are shown to be false, they will someday be united and they will come into their own.

[*The Ballad of Carson McCullers* by Oliver Evans, published by Coward-McCann in 1966]

LATER STORIES

CORRESPONDENCE

113 Whitehall Street
Darien, Conn.
United States
November 3, 1941

Manoel García,
Calle São José 120,
Rio de Janeiro,
Brazil,
South America

Dear Manoel:

I guess seeing the American address on this letter you already know what it is. Your name was on the list tacked on the blackboard at High School of South American students we could correspond with. I was the one who picked your name.

Maybe I ought to tell you something about myself. I am a girl going on fourteen years of age and this is my first year at High School. It is hard to describe myself exactly. I am tall and my figure is not very good on account of I have grown too rapidly. My eyes are blue and I don't know exactly what color you would call my hair unless it would be a light brown. I like to play baseball and make scientific experiments (like with a chemical set) and read all kinds of books.

All my life I wanted to get to travel but the furtherest I have ever been away from home is Portsmouth, New Hampshire. Lately I have thought a whole lot about South America. Since choosing your name off the list I have thought a whole lot about you also and imagined how you are. I have seen photographs of the harbor in Rio de Janeiro and I can picture you in my mind's eye walking around the beach in the sun. I imagine you with liquid black eyes, brown skin, and black curly hair. I have always been crazy about South Americans although I did not know any of them and I always wanted to travel all over South America and especially to Rio de Janeiro.

As long as we are going to be friends and correspond I think we ought to know serious things about each other right away. Recently I have thought a whole lot about life. I have pondered over a great many things such as why we were put on the earth. I have decided that I do not believe in God. On the other hand I am not an atheist and I think there is some kind of a reason for everything and life is not in vain. When you die I think I believe that something happens to the soul.

I have not decided just exactly what I am going to be and it worries me. Sometimes I think I want to be an arctic explorer and other times I plan on being a newspaper reporter and working in to being a writer. For years I wished to be an actress, especially a tragic actress taking sad roles like Greta Garbo. This summer however when I got up a performance of Camille and I played Camille it was a terrible failure. The show was given in our garage and I can't explain to you what a terrible failure it was. So now I think mostly about newspaper reporting, especially foreign corresponding.

I do not feel exactly like the other Freshmen at High School. I feel like I am different from them. When I have a girl to spend the night with me on Friday night all they want to do is meet people down at the drug store near here and so forth and at night when we lie in the bed if I bring up serious subjects they are likely to go to sleep. They don't care anything much about foreign countries. It is not that I am terribly unpopular or anything like that but I am just not so crazy about the other Freshmen and they are not so crazy about me.

I thought a long time about you, Manoel, before writing this letter. And I have this strong feeling we would get along together. Do you like dogs? I have an airdale named Thomas and he is a one man dog. I feel like I have known you for a very long time and that we could discuss all sorts of things together. My Spanish is not so good naturally as this is my first term on it. But I intend to study diligently so that between us we can make out what we are saying when we meet each other.

I have thought about a lot of things. Would you like to come and spend your summer vacation with me next summer? I think that would be marvelous. Also other plans have been in my mind. Maybe next year after we have a visit together you could stay in my home and go to High School here and I could swap with you and stay in your home and go to South American High School. How does that strike you? I have not yet spoken to my parents about it because I am waiting until I get your opinion on it. I am looking forward exceedingly to hearing from you and find out if I am right about our feeling so much alike about life and other things. You can write to me anything that you want to, as I have said before that I feel I already know you so well. *Adiós* and I send you every possible good wish.

Your affectionate friend,

HENKY EVANS

P.S. My first name is really Henrietta but the family and people in the neighborhood all call me Henky because Henrietta sounds sort of sissy. I am sending this air mail so that it will get to you quicker. *Adiós* again.

*

113 WHITEHALL STREET
DARIEN, CONN.,
U.S.A.
NOVEMBER 25, 1941

Manoel García,
Calle São José 120,
Rio de Janeiro,
Brazil,
South America

DEAR MANOEL:

Three weeks have gone by and I would have thought that by now there would be a letter from you. But it is entirely possible that communications take much longer than I had figured on, especially on account of the war. I read all the papers and the state of the world prays on my mind. I had not thought I would write to you again until I heard from you but as I said it must take a long time these days for things to reach foreign countries.

Today I am not at school. Yesterday morning when I woke up I was all broken out and swollen and red so that it looked like I had small pox at least. But when the doctor came he said it was hives. I took medicine and since then I have been sick in bed. I have been studying Latin as I am mighty close to flunking it. I will be glad when these hives go away.

There was one thing I forgot in my first letter. I think we ought to exchange pictures. Do you have a photograph of yourself, if so please send it as I want to really be sure if you look like what I think you do. I am enclosing a snapshot. The dog scratching himself in the corner is my dog Thomas and the house in the background is our house. The sun was in my eyes and that is why my face is all screwed up like that.

I was reading a very interesting book the other day about the reincarnation of souls. That means, in case you have not happened to read about it, that you live a lot of lives and are one person in one century and another one later on. It is very interesting. The more I think about it the more I believe it is true. What opinions do you have about it?

One thing I have always found it hard to realize is that about how when it is winter here it is summer below the equator. Of course I know why this is so, but at the same time it always strikes me as peculiar. Of course you are used to it. I have to keep remembering that it is now spring where you are, even if it is November. While the trees are bare here and the furnace is going it is just starting spring in Rio de Janeiro.

Every afternoon I wait for the postman. I have a strong feeling or a kind of a hunch that I will hear from you on this afternoon's mail or tomorrow. Communications must take longer than I had figured on even by air mail.

Affectionately yours,

HENKY EVANS

113 WHITEHALL STREET
DARIEN, CONN.,
U.S.A.
DECEMBER 29, 1941

Manoel García,
Calle São José 120,
Rio de Janeiro,
Brazil,
South America

DEAR MANOEL GARCÍA:

I cannot possibly understand why I have not heard from you. Didn't you receive my two letters? Many other people in the class have had letters from South Americans a long time ago. Nearly two months have gone by since I started the correspondence.

Recently it came over me that maybe you have not been able to find anybody who knows English down there and can translate what I wrote. But it seems to me that you would have been able to find somebody and anyway it was understood that the South Americans whose names were on the list were studying English.

Maybe both the letters were lost. I realize how communications can sometimes go astray, especially on account of the war. But even if one letter was lost it seems to me like the other one would have arrived there all right. I just cannot understand it.

But perchance there is some reason I do not know about. Maybe you have been very sick in the hospital or maybe your family moved from your last address. I may hear from you very soon and it will all be straightened out. If there has been some such mistake please do not think that I am mad with you for not hearing sooner. I still sincerely want us to be friends and carry on the correspondence because I have always been so crazy about foreign countries and South America and I felt like I knew you right at the first.

I am all right and I hope you are the same. I won a five pound box of cherry candy in a benefit raffle given to raise money for the needy at Christmas.

As soon as you get this please answer and explain what is wrong, otherwise I just cannot understand what has happened. I beg to remain,

Sincerely yours,

HENRIETTA EVANS

*

113 WHITEHALL STREET
DARIEN, CONN.,
U.S.A.
JANUARY 20, 1942

Mr. Manoel García,
Calle São José 120,
Rio de Janeiro,
Brazil,
South America

DEAR MR. GARCÍA:

I have sent you three letters in all good faith and expected you to fulfill your part in the idea of American and South American students corresponding like it was supposed to be. Nearly every other person in the class got letters and some even friendship gifts, even though they were not especially crazy about foreign countries like I was. I expected to hear every day and gave you the benefits of all the doubts. But now I realize what a grave mistake I made.

All I want to know is this. Why would you have your name put on the list if you did not intend to fulfill your part in the agreement? All I want to say is that if I had known then what I know now I most assuredly would have picked out some other South American.

Yrs. truly,

MISS HENRIETTA HILL EVANS

P.S. I cannot waste any more of my valuable time writing to you.

[*The New Yorker*, February 7, 1942]

ART AND MR. MAHONEY

HE WAS A LARGE MAN, a contractor, and he was the husband of the small, sharp Mrs. Mahoney who was so active in club and cultural affairs. A canny businessman (he owned a brick yard and planing mill), Mr. Mahoney lumbered with tractable amiability in the lead of the artistic Mrs. Mahoney. Mr. Mahoney was well drilled; he was accustomed to speak of "repertory," to listen to lectures and concerts with the proper expression of meek sorrow. He could talk about abstract art, he had even taken part in two of the Little Theatre productions, once as a butler, the other time as a Roman soldier. Mr. Mahoney, diligently trained, so many times admonished — how could he have brought upon them such disgrace?

The pianist that night was José Iturbi, and it was the first concert of the season, a gala night. The Mahoneys had worked very hard during the Three Arts League drive. Mr. Mahoney had sold more than thirty season tickets on his own. To business acquaintances, the men downtown, he spoke of the projected concerts as "a pride to the community" and "a cultural necessity." The Mahoneys had donated the use of their car and had entertained subscribers at a lawn fete — with three white-coated colored boys handing refreshments, and their newly built Tudor house waxed and flowered for the occasion. The Mahoneys' position as sponsors of art and culture was well earned.

The start of the fatal evening gave no hint of what was to come. Mr. Mahoney sang in the shower and dressed himself with detailed care. He had brought an orchid from Duff's Flower Shop. When Ellie came in from her room — they had adjoining separate rooms in the new house — he was brushed and gleaming in his dinner jacket, and Ellie wore the orchid on the shoulder of her blue crepe dress. She was pleased and, patting his arm, she said: "You look so handsome tonight, Terence. Downright distinguished."

Mr. Mahoney's stout body bridled with happiness, and his ruddy face with the forked-veined temples blushed. "You are always beautiful, Ellie. Always so beautiful. Sometimes I don't understand why you married a —"

She stopped him with a kiss.

There was to be a reception after the concert at the Harlows', and of course the Mahoneys were invited. Mrs. Harlow was the "bell cow" in this pasture of the finer things. Oh, how Ellie did despise such country-raised expressions! But Mr. Mahoney had forgotten all the times he had been called down as he gallantly placed Ellie's wrap about her shoulders.

The irony was that, up until the moment of his ignominy, Mr. Mahoney had enjoyed the concert more than any concert that he had ever heard. There was none of that wriggling, tedious Bach. There was some marchy-sounding music and often he was on foot-patting familiarity with the tunes. As he sat there, enjoying the music, he glanced occasionally at Ellie. Her face bore the expression of fixed, inconsolable grief that it always assumed when she listened to classical concert music. Between the numbers she put her hand to her forehead with a distracted air, as though the endurance of such emotion had been too much for her. Mr. Mahoney clapped his pink, plump hands with gusto, glad of a chance to move and respond.

In the intermission the Mahoneys filed sedately down the aisle to the lobby. Mr. Mahoney found himself stuck with old Mrs. Walker.

"I'm looking forward to the Chopin," she said. "I always love minor music, don't you?"

"I guess you enjoy your misery," Mr. Mahoney answered.

Miss Walker, the English teacher, spoke up promptly. "It's Mother's melancholy Celtic soul. She's of Irish descent, you know."

Feeling he had somehow made a mistake, Mr. Mahoney said awkwardly, "I like minor music all right."

Tip Mayberry took Mr. Mahoney's arm and spoke to him chummily. "This fellow can certainly rattle the old ivories."

Mr. Mahoney answered with reserve, "He has a very brilliant technique."

"It's still an hour to go," Tip Mayberry complained. "I wish me and you could slip out of here."

Mr. Mahoney moved discreetly away.

Mr. Mahoney loved the atmosphere of Little Theatre plays and concerts — the chiffon and corsages and decorous dinner jackets. He was warm with pride and pleasure as he went sociably about the lobby of the high school auditorium, greeting the ladies, speaking with reverent authority of movements and mazurkas.

It was during the first number after the intermission that the calamity came. It was a long Chopin sonata: the first movement thundering, the second jerking and mercurial. The third movement he followed knowingly with tapping foot — the rigid funeral march with a sad waltzy bit in the middle; the end of the funeral march came with a chorded final crash. The pianist lifted up his hand and even leaned back a little on the piano stool.

Mr. Mahoney clapped. He was so dead sure it was the end that he clapped heartily half a dozen times before he realized, to his horror, that he clapped alone. With swift fiendish energy José Iturbi attacked the piano keys again.

Mr. Mahoney sat stiff with agony. The next moments were the most dreadful in his memory. The red veins in his temples swelled and darkened. He clasped his offending hands between his thighs.

If only Ellie had made some comforting secret sign. But when he dared to glance at Ellie, her face was frozen and she gazed at the stage with desperate attentiveness. After some endless minutes of humiliation, Mr. Mahoney reached his hand timidly toward Ellie's crepe-covered thigh. Mrs. Mahoney moved away from him and crossed her legs.

For almost an hour Mr. Mahoney had to suffer this public shame. Once he caught a glimpse of Tip Mayberry, and an alien evil shafted through his gentle heart. Tip did not know a sonata from the *Slit Belly*

Blues. Yet there he sat, smug, unnoticed. Mrs. Mahoney refused to meet her husband's anguished eyes.

They had to go on to the party. He admitted it was the only proper thing to do. They drove there in silence, but when he had parked the car before the Harlow house Mrs. Mahoney said, "I should think that anybody with a grain of sense knows enough not to clap until everybody else is clapping."

It was for him a miserable party. The guests gathered around José Iturbi and were introduced. (They all knew who had clapped except Mr. Iturbi; he was as cordial to Mr. Mahoney as to the others.) Mr. Mahoney stood in the corner behind the concert-grand piano drinking Scotch. Old Mrs. Walker and Miss Walker hovered with the "bell cow" around Mr. Iturbi. Ellie was looking at the titles in the bookcase. She took out a book and even read for a little while with her back to the room. In the corner he was alone through a good many highballs. And it was Tip Mayberry who finally joined him. "I guess after all those tickets you sold you were entitled to an extra clap." He gave Mr. Mahoney a slow wink of covert brotherhood which Mr. Mahoney at that moment was almost willing to admit.

[*Mademoiselle,* February 1949]

THE HAUNTED BOY

*H*UGH LOOKED for his mother at the corner, but she was not in the yard. Sometimes she would be out fooling with the border of spring flowers — the candytuft, the sweet William, the lobelias (she had taught him the names) — but today the green front lawn with the borders of many-colored flowers was empty under the frail sunshine of the mid-April afternoon. Hugh raced up the sidewalk, and John followed him. They finished the front steps with two bounds, and the door slammed after them.

"Mamma!" Hugh called.

It was then, in the unanswering silence as they stood in the empty, wax-floored hall, that Hugh felt there was something wrong. There was no fire in the grate of the sitting room, and since he was used to the flicker of firelight during the cold months, the room on this first warm day seemed strangely naked and cheerless. Hugh shivered. He was glad John was there. The sun shone on a red piece in the flowered rug. Red-bright, red-dark, red-dead — Hugh sickened with a sudden chill remembrance of "the other time." The red darkened to a dizzy black.

"What's the matter, Brown?" John asked. "You look so white."

Hugh shook himself and put his hand to his forehead. "Nothing. Let's go back to the kitchen."

"I can't stay but just a minute," John said. "I'm obligated to sell those tickets. I have to eat and run."

The kitchen, with the fresh checked towels and clean pans, was now the best room in the house. And on the enameled table there was a lemon pie that she had made. Assured by the everyday kitchen and the pie, Hugh stepped back into the hall and raised his face again to call upstairs.

"Mother! Oh, Mamma!"

Again there was no answer.

"My mother made this pie," he said. Quickly he found a knife and cut into the pie — to dispel the gathering sense of dread.

"Think you ought to cut it, Brown?"

"Sure thing, Laney."

They called each other by their last names this spring, unless they happened to forget. To Hugh it seemed sporty and grown and somehow grand. Hugh liked John better than any other boy at school. John was two years older than Hugh, and compared to him the other boys seemed like a silly crowd of punks. John was the best student in the sophomore class, brainy but not the least bit a teacher's pet, and he was the best athlete too. Hugh was a freshman and didn't have so many friends that first year of high school — he had somehow cut himself off, because he was so afraid.

"Mamma always has me something nice for after school." Hugh put a big piece of pie on a saucer for John — for Laney.

"This pie is certainly super."

"The crust is made of crunched-up graham crackers instead of regular pie dough," Hugh said, "because pie dough is a lot of trouble. We think this graham-cracker pastry is just as good. Naturally, my mother can make regular pie dough if she wants to."

Hugh could not keep still; he walked up and down the kitchen, eating the pie wedge he carried on the palm of his hand. His brown hair was mussed with nervous rakings, and his gentle gold-brown eyes were haunted with pained perplexity. John, who remained seated at the table, sensed Hugh's uneasiness and wrapped one gangling leg around the other.

"I'm really obligated to sell those Glee Club tickets."

"Don't go. You have the whole afternoon." He was afraid of the empty house. He needed John, he needed someone; most of all he needed to hear his mother's voice and know she was in the house with him. "Maybe Mamma is taking a bath," he said. "I'll holler again."

The answer to his third call too was silence.

"I guess your mother must have gone to the movie or gone shopping or something."

"No," Hugh said. "She would have left a note. She always does when she's gone when I come home from school."

"We haven't looked for a note," John said. "Maybe she left it under the door mat or somewhere in the living room."

Hugh was inconsolable. "No. She would have left it right under this pie. She knows I always run first to the kitchen."

"Maybe she had a phone call or thought of something she suddenly wanted to do."

"She *might* have," he said. "I remember she said to Daddy that one of these days she was going to buy herself some new clothes." This flash of hope did not survive its expression. He pushed his hair back and started from the room. "I guess I'd better go upstairs. I ought to go upstairs while you are here."

He stood with his arm around the newel post; the smell of varnished stairs, the sight of the closed white bathroom door at the top revived again "the other time." He clung to the newel post, and his feet would not move to climb the stairs. The red turned again to whirling, sick dark. Hugh sat down. *Stick your head between your legs,* he ordered, remembering Scout first aid.

"Hugh," John called. "Hugh!"

The dizziness clearing, Hugh accepted a fresh chagrin — Laney was calling him by his ordinary first name; he thought he was a sissy about his mother, unworthy of being called by his last name in the grand, sporty way they used before. The dizziness cleared when he returned to the kitchen.

"Brown," said John, and the chagrin disappeared. "Does this establishment have anything pertaining to a cow? A white, fluid liquid. In French they call it *lait.* Here we call it plain old milk."

The stupidity of shock lightened. "Oh. Laney, I am a dope! Please excuse me. I clean forgot." Hugh fetched the milk from the refrigerator and found two glasses. "I didn't think. My mind was on something else."

"I know," John said. After a moment he asked in a calm voice, looking steadily at Hugh's eyes: "Why are you so worried about your mother? Is she sick, Hugh?"

Hugh knew now that the first name was not a slight; it was because John was talking too serious to be sporty. He liked John better than any friend he had ever had. He felt more natural sitting across the kitchen table from John, somehow safer. As he looked into John's gray, peaceful eyes, the balm of affection soothed the dread.

John asked again, still steadily: "Hugh, is your mother sick?"

Hugh could have answered no other boy. He had talked with no one about his mother, except his father, and even those intimacies had been rare, oblique. They could approach the subject only when they were occupied with something else, doing carpentry work or the two times they hunted in the woods together — or when they were cooking supper or washing dishes.

"She's not exactly sick," he said, "but Daddy and I have been worried about her. At least, we used to be worried for a while."

John asked: "Is it a kind of heart trouble?"

Hugh's voice was strained. "Did you hear about that fight I had with that slob Clem Roberts? I scraped his slob face on the gravel walk and nearly killed him sure enough. He's still got scars or at least he did have a bandage on for two days. I had to stay in school every afternoon for a week. But I nearly killed him. I would have if Mr. Paxton hadn't come along and dragged me off."

"I heard about it."

"You know why I wanted to kill him?"

For a moment John's eyes flickered away.

Hugh tensed himself; his raw boy hands clutched the table edge; he took a deep, hoarse breath. "That slob was telling everybody that my mother was in Milledgeville. He was spreading it around that my mother was crazy."

"The dirty bastard."

Hugh said in a clear, defeated voice, "My mother *was* in Milledgeville. But that doesn't mean that she was crazy," he added quickly. "In that big State hospital, there are buildings for people who are crazy, and there are other buildings, for people who are just sick. Mamma was sick for a while. Daddy and me discussed it and decided that the hospital in Milledgeville was the place where there were the best doctors and she would get the best care. But she was the furtherest from crazy than anybody in the world. You know Mamma, John." He said again: "I ought to go upstairs."

John said: "I have always thought that your mother is one of the nicest ladies in this town."

"You see, Mamma had a peculiar thing happen, and afterward she was blue."

Confession, the first deep-rooted words, opened the festered secrecy of the boy's heart, and he continued more rapidly, urgent and finding unforeseen relief.

"Last year my mother thought she was going to have a little baby. She talked it over with Daddy and me," he said proudly. "We wanted a girl. I was going to choose the name. We were so tickled. I hunted up all my old toys — my electric train and the tracks . . . I was going to name her Crystal — how does that name strike you for a girl? It reminds me of something bright and dainty."

"Was the little baby born dead?"

Even with John, Hugh's ears turned hot; his cold hands touched them. "No, it was what they call a tumor. That's what happened to my mother. They had to operate at the hospital here." He was embarrassed and his voice was very low. "Then she had something called change of life." The words were terrible to Hugh. "And afterward she was blue. Daddy said it was a shock to her nervous system. It's something that happens to ladies; she was just blue and run-down."

Although there was no red, no red in the kitchen anywhere, Hugh was approaching "the other time."

"One day, she just sort of gave up — one day last fall." Hugh's eyes were wide open and glaring: again he climbed the stairs and opened the bathroom door — he put his hand to his eyes to shut out the memory. "She tried to — hurt herself. I found her when I came in from school."

John reached out and carefully stroked Hugh's sweatered arm.

"Don't worry. A lot of people have to go to hospitals because they are run-down and blue. Could happen to anybody."

"We had to put her in the hospital — the best hospital." The recollection of those long, long months was stained with a dull loneliness, as cruel in its lasting unappeasement as "the other time" — how long had it lasted? In the hospital Mamma could walk around and she always had on shoes.

John said carefully: "This pie is certainly super."

"My mother is a super cook. She cooks things like meat pie and salmon loaf — as well as steaks and hot dogs."

"I hate to eat and run," John said.

Hugh was so frightened of being left alone that he felt the alarm in his own loud heart.

"Don't go," he urged. "Let's talk for a little while."

"Talk about what?"

Hugh could not tell him. Not even John Laney. He could tell no one of the empty house and the horror of the time before. "Do you ever cry?" he asked John. "I don't."

"I do sometimes," John admitted.

"I wish I had known you better when Mother was away. Daddy and me used to go hunting nearly every Saturday. We *lived* on quail and dove. I bet you would have liked that." He added in a lower tone, "On Sunday we went to the hospital."

John said: "It's kind of a delicate proposition selling those tickets. A lot of people don't enjoy the High School Glee Club operettas. Unless they know someone in it personally, they'd rather stay home with a good TV show. A lot of people buy tickets on the basis of being public-spirited."

"We're going to get a television set real soon."

"I couldn't exist without television," John said.

Hugh's voice was apologetic. "Daddy wants to clean up the hospital bills first because as everybody knows sickness is a very expensive proposition. Then we'll get TV."

John lifted his milk glass. "Skoal," he said. "That's a Swedish word you say before you drink. A good-luck word."

"You know so many foreign words and languages."

"Not so many," John said truthfully. "Just 'kaput' and 'adios' and 'skoal' and stuff we learn in French class. That's not much."

"That's *beaucoup,*" said Hugh, and he felt witty and pleased with himself.

Suddenly the stored tension burst into physical activity. Hugh grabbed the basketball out on the porch and rushed into the back yard. He dribbled the ball several times and aimed at the goal his father had put up on his last birthday. When he missed he bounced the ball to John, who had come after him. It was good to be outdoors and the relief of natural play brought Hugh the first line of a poem. "My heart is like a basketball." Usually when a poem came to him he would lie sprawled on the living room floor, studying to hunt rhymes, his tongue working on the side of his mouth. His mother would call him Shelley-Poe when she stepped over him, and sometimes she would put her foot lightly on his behind. His mother always liked his poems; today the second line came quickly, like magic. He said it out loud to John: " 'My heart is like a basketball, bounding with glee down the hall.' How do you like that for the start of a poem?"

"Sounds kind of crazy to me," John said. Then he corrected himself hastily. "I mean it sounds — odd. Odd, I meant."

Hugh realized why John changed the word, and the elation of play and poems left him instantly. He caught the ball and stood with it cradled in his arms. The afternoon was golden and the wisteria vine on the porch was in full, unshattered bloom. The wisteria was like lavender waterfalls. The fresh breeze smelled of sun-warmed flowers. The sunlit sky was blue and cloudless. It was the first warm day of spring.

"I have to shove off," John said.

"No!" Hugh's voice was desperate. "Don't you want another piece of pie? I never heard of anybody eating just one piece of pie."

He steered John into the house and this time he called only out of habit because he always called on coming in. "Mother!" He was cold after the bright, sunny outdoors. He was cold not only because of the weather but because he was so scared.

"My mother has been home a month and every afternoon she's always here when I come home from school. Always, always."

They stood in the kitchen looking at the lemon pie. And to Hugh the cut pie looked somehow — odd. As they stood motionless in the kitchen the silence was creepy and odd too.

"Doesn't this house seem quiet to you?"

"It's because you don't have television. We put on our TV at seven o'clock and it stays on all day and night until we go to bed. Whether anybody's in the living room or not. There're plays and skits and gags going on continually."

"We have a radio, of course, and a vic."

"But that's not the company of a good TV. You won't know when your mother is in the house or not when you get TV."

Hugh didn't answer. Their footsteps sounded hollow in the hall. He felt sick as he stood on the first step with his arm around the newel post. "If you could just come upstairs for a minute —"

John's voice was suddenly impatient and loud. "How many times have I told you I'm obligated to sell those tickets. You have to be public-spirited about things like Glee Clubs."

"Just for a second — I have something important to show you upstairs."

John did not ask what it was and Hugh sought desperately to name something important enough to get John upstairs. He said finally: "I'm assembling a hi-fi machine. You have to know a lot about electronics — my father is helping me."

But even when he spoke he knew John did not for a second believe the lie. Who would buy a hi-fi when they didn't have television? He hated John, as you hate people you have to need so badly. He had to say something more and he straightened his shoulders.

"I just want you to know how much I value your friendship. During these past months I had somehow cut myself off from people."

"That's O.K., Brown. You oughtn't to be so sensitive because your mother was — where she was."

John had his hand on the door and Hugh was trembling. "I thought if you could come up for just a minute —"

John looked at him with anxious, puzzled eyes. Then he asked slowly: "Is there something you are scared of upstairs?"

Hugh wanted to tell him everything. But he could not tell what his mother had done that September afternoon. It was too terrible and — odd. It was like something a *patient* would do, and not like his mother at all. Although his eyes were wild with terror and his body trembled he said: "I'm not scared."

"Well, so long. I'm sorry I have to go — but to be obligated is to be obligated."

John closed the front door and he was alone in the empty house. Nothing could save him now. Even if a whole crowd of boys were listening to TV in the living room, laughing at funny gags and jokes, it would still not help him. He had to go upstairs and find her. He sought courage from the last thing John had said, and repeated the words aloud: "To be obligated is to be obligated." But the words did not give him any of John's thoughtlessness and courage; they were creepy and strange in the silence.

He turned slowly to go upstairs. His heart was not like a basketball but like a fast, jazz drum, beating faster and faster as he climbed the stairs. His feet dragged as though he waded through knee-deep water and he held on to the bannisters. The house looked odd, crazy. As he looked down at the ground-floor table with the vase of fresh spring flowers that too looked somehow peculiar. There was a mirror on the second floor and his own face startled him, so crazy did it seem to him. The initial of his high school sweater was backward and wrong in the reflection and his mouth was open like an asylum idiot. He shut his mouth and he looked better. Still the objects he saw — the table downstairs, the sofa upstairs — looked somehow cracked or jarred because of the dread in him, although they were the familiar things of everyday. He fastened his eyes on the closed door at the right of the stairs and the fast, jazz drum beat faster.

He opened the bathroom door and for a moment the dread that had haunted him all that afternoon made him see again the room as he had seen it "the other time." His mother lay on the floor and there was blood everywhere. His mother lay there dead and there was blood everywhere, on her slashed wrist, and a pool of blood had trickled to the bathtub and lay dammed there. Hugh touched the doorframe and steadied himself. Then the room settled and he realized this was not "the other time." The April sunlight brightened the clean white tiles. There was only bathroom brightness and the sunny window. He went to the bedroom and saw the empty bed with the rose-colored spread. The lady things were on the dresser. The room was as it always looked and nothing had happened . . . nothing had happened and he flung himself on the quilted rose bed and cried from relief and a strained, bleak tiredness that had lasted so long. The sobs jerked his whole body and quieted his jazz, fast heart.

Hugh had not cried all those months. He had not cried at "the other time," when he found his mother alone in that empty house with blood everywhere. He had not cried but he made a Scout mistake. He had first lifted his mother's heavy, bloody body before he tried to bandage her. He had not cried when he called his father. He had not cried those few days when they were deciding what to do. He hadn't even cried when the doctor suggested Milledgeville, or when he and his father took her to the hospital in the car — although his father cried on the way home. He had not cried at the meals they made — steak every night for a whole month so that they felt steak was running out of their eyes, their ears; then they had switched to hot dogs, and ate them until hot dogs ran out of their ears, their eyes. They got in ruts of food and were messy about the kitchen, so that it was never nice except the Saturday the cleaning woman came. He did not cry those lonesome afternoons after he had the fight with Clem Roberts and felt the other boys were thinking queer things of his mother. He stayed at home in the messy kitchen, eating Fig Newtons or chocolate bars. Or he went to see a neighbor's television — Miss Richards, an old maid who saw old-maid shows. He had not cried when his father drank too much so that it took his appetite and Hugh had to eat alone. He had not even cried on those long, waiting Sundays when they went to Milledgeville and he twice saw a lady on a porch without any shoes on and talking to herself.

A lady who was a patient and who struck at him with a horror he could not name. He did not cry when at first his mother would say: *Don't punish me by making me stay here. Let me go home.* He had not cried at the terrible words that haunted him — "change of life" — "crazy" — "Milledgeville" — he could not cry all during those long months strained with dullness and want and dread.

He still sobbed on the rose bedspread, which was soft and cool against his wet cheeks. He was sobbing so loud that he did not hear the front door open, did not even hear his mother call or the footsteps on the stairs. He still sobbed when his mother touched him and burrowed his face hard in the spread. He even stiffened his legs and kicked his feet.

"Why, Loveyboy," his mother said, calling him a long-ago child name. "What's happened?"

He sobbed even louder, although his mother tried to turn his face to her. He wanted her to worry. He did not turn around until she had finally left the bed, and then he looked at her. She had on a different dress — blue silk it looked like in the pale spring light.

"Darling, what's happened?"

The terror of the afternoon was over, but he could not tell it to his mother. He could not tell her what he had feared, or explain the horror of things that were never there at all — but had once been there.

"Why did you do it?"

"The first warm day I just suddenly decided to buy myself some new clothes."

But he was not talking about clothes; he was thinking about "the other time" and the grudge that had started when he saw the blood and horror and felt *why did she do this to me.* He thought of the grudge against the mother he loved the most in the world. All those last, sad months the anger had bounced against the love with guilt between.

"I bought two dresses and two petticoats. How do you like them?"

"I hate them!" Hugh said angrily. "Your slip is showing."

She turned around twice and the petticoat showed terribly. "It's supposed to show, goofy. It's the style."

"I still don't like it."

"I ate a sandwich at the tearoom with two cups of cocoa and then went to Mendel's. There were so many pretty things I couldn't seem to get away. I bought these two dresses and look, Hugh! The shoes!"

His mother went to the bed and switched on the light so he could see. The shoes were flat-heeled and *blue*—with diamond sparkles on the toes. He did not know how to criticize. "They look more like evening shoes than things you wear on the street."

"I have never owned any colored shoes before. I couldn't resist them."

His mother sort of danced over toward the window, making the petticoat twirl under the new dress. Hugh had stopped crying now, but he was still angry.

"I don't like it because it makes you look like you're trying to seem young, and I bet you are forty years old."

His mother stopped dancing and stood still at the window. Her face was suddenly quiet and sad. "I'll be forty-three years old in June."

He had hurt her and suddenly the anger vanished and there was only love. "Mamma, I shouldn't have said that."

"I realized when I was shopping that I hadn't been in a store for more than a year. Imagine!"

Hugh could not stand the sad quietness and the mother he loved so much. He could not stand his love or his mother's prettiness. He wiped the tears on the sleeve of his sweater and got up from the bed. "I have never seen you so pretty, or a dress and slip so pretty." He crouched down before his mother and touched the bright shoes. "The shoes are really super."

"I thought the minute I laid eyes on them that you would like them." She pulled Hugh up and kissed him on the cheek. "Now I've got lipstick on you."

Hugh quoted a witty remark he had heard before as he scrubbed off the lipstick. "It only shows I'm popular."

"Hugh, why were you crying when I came in? Did something at school upset you?"

"It was only that when I came in and found you gone and no note or anything—"

"I forgot all about a note."

"And all afternoon I felt — John Laney came in but he had to go sell Glee Club tickets. All afternoon I felt —"

"What? What was the matter?"

But he could not tell the mother he loved about the terror and the cause. He said at last: "All afternoon I felt — odd."

Afterward when his father came home he called Hugh to come out into the back yard with him. His father had a worried look — as though he spied a valuable tool Hugh had left outside. But there was no tool and the basketball was put back in its place on the back porch.

"Son," his father said, "there's something I want to tell you."

"Yes, sir?"

"Your mother said that you had been crying this afternoon." His father did not wait for him to explain. "I just want us to have a close understanding with each other. Is there anything about school — or girls — or something that puzzles you? Why were you crying?"

Hugh looked back at the afternoon and already it was far away, distant as a peculiar view seen at the wrong end of a telescope.

"I don't know," he said. "I guess maybe I was somehow nervous."

His father put his arm around his shoulder. "Nobody can be nervous before they are sixteen years old. You have a long way to go."

"I know."

"I have never seen your mother look so well. She looks so gay and pretty, better than she's looked in years. Don't you realize that?"

"The slip — the petticoat is supposed to show. It's a new style."

"Soon it will be summer," his father said. "And we'll go on picnics — the three of us." The words brought an instant vision of glare on the yellow creek and the summer-leaved, adventurous woods. His father added: "I came out here to tell you something else."

"Yes, sir?"

"I just want you to know that I realize how fine you were all that bad time. How fine, how damn fine."

His father was using a swear word as if he were talking to a grown man. His father was not a person to hand out compliments — always he was strict with report cards and tools left around. His father never praised him or used grown words or anything. Hugh felt his face grow hot and he touched it with his cold hands.

"I just wanted to tell you that, Son." He shook Hugh by the shoulder. "You'll be taller than your old man in a year or so." Quickly his father went into the house, leaving Hugh to the sweet and unaccustomed aftermath of praise.

Hugh stood in the darkening yard after the sunset colors faded in the west and the wisteria was dark purple. The kitchen light was on and he saw his mother fixing dinner. He knew that something was finished; the terror was far from him now, also the anger that had bounced with love, the dread and guilt. Although he felt he would never cry again — or at least not until he was sixteen — in the brightness of his tears glistened the safe, lighted kitchen, now that he was no longer a haunted boy, now that he was glad somehow, and not afraid.

[*Mademoiselle,* November 1955]

WHO HAS SEEN THE WIND?

ALL AFTERNOON Ken Harris had been sitting before a blank page of the typewriter. It was winter and snowing. The snow muted traffic and the Village apartment was so quiet that the alarm clock bothered him. He worked in the bedroom as the room with his wife's things calmed him and made him feel less alone. His prelunch drink (or was it an eye opener?) had been dulled by the can of chili con carne he had eaten alone in the kitchen. At four o'clock he put the clock in the clothes hamper, then returned to the typewriter. The paper was still blank and the white page blanched his spirit. Yet there was a time (how long ago?) when a song at the corner, a voice from childhood, and the panorama of memory condensed the past so that the random and actual were transfigured into a novel, a story — there was a time when the empty page summoned and sorted memory and he felt that ghostly mastery of his art. A time, in short, when he was a writer and writing almost every day. Working hard, he carefully broke the backs of sentences, *x*'d out offending phrases and changed repeated words. Now he sat there, hunched and somehow fearful, a blond man in his late thirties, with circles under his oyster blue eyes and a full, pale mouth. It was the scalding wind of his Texas childhood he was thinking about as he gazed out of his window at the New York falling snow. Then suddenly a valve of memory opened and he said the words as he typed them:

> Who has seen the wind?
> Neither you nor I:
> But when the trees bow down their heads
> The wind is passing by.

The nursery verse seemed to him so sinister that as he sat thinking about it the sweat of tension dampened his palms. He jerked the page from the typewriter and, tearing it into many pieces, let it fall in the wastepaper basket. He was relieved that he was going to a party at six o'clock, glad to quit the silent apartment, the torn verse, and to walk in the cold but comforting street.

The subway had the dim light of underground and after the smell of snow the air was fetid. Ken noticed a man lying down on a bench, but he did not wonder about the stranger's history as he might have done another time. He watched the swaying front car of the oncoming express and shrank back from the cindery wind. He saw the doors open and close — it was his train — and stared forlornly as the subway ground noisily away. A sadness fretted him as he waited for the next one.

The Rodgers' apartment was in a penthouse far uptown and already the party had begun. There was the wash of mingled voices and the smell of gin and cocktail canapés. As he stood with Esther Rodgers in the entrance of the crowded rooms he said:

"Nowadays when I enter a crowded party I think of that last party of the Duc de Guermantes."

"What?" asked Esther.

"You remember when Proust — the I, the narrator — looked at all the familiar faces and brooded about the alterations of time? Magnificent passage — I read it every year."

Esther looked disturbed. "There's so much noise. Is your wife coming?"

Ken's face quivered a little and he took a Martini the maid was passing. "She'll be along when she leaves her office."

"Marian works so hard — all those manuscripts to read."

"When I find myself at a party like this it's always almost exactly the same. Yet there is the awful difference. As though the key lowered, shifted. The awful difference of years that are passing, the trickery and terror of time, Proust . . ."

But his hostess had gone and he was left standing alone in the crowded party room. He looked at faces he had seen at parties these last thirteen years — yes, they had aged. Esther was now quite fat and her velvet dress was too tight — dissipated, he thought, and whisky-bloated. There was a change — thirteen years ago when he published *The Night of Darkness* Esther would have fairly eaten him up and never left him alone at the fringe of the room. He had been the fair-haired boy, those days. The fair-haired boy of the Bitch Goddess — was the Bitch Goddess success, money, youth? He saw two young Southern writers at the window — and in ten years their capital of youth would be claimed by the Bitch Goddess. It pleased Ken to think of this and he ate a ham doodad that was passed.

Then he saw someone across the room whom he admired. She was Mabel Goodley, the painter and set-designer. Her blond hair was short and shining and her glasses glittered in the light. Mabel had always loved *The Night* and had given a party for him when he got his Guggenheim. More important, she had felt his second book was better than the first one, in spite of the stupidity of the critics. He started toward Mabel but was stopped by John Howards, an editor he used to see sometimes at parties.

"Hi there," Howards said, "what are you writing these days, or is it a fair question?"

This was a remark Ken loathed. There were a number of answers — sometimes he said he was finishing a long novel, other times he said he was deliberately lying fallow. There was no good answer, no matter what he said. His scrotum tightened and he tried desperately to look unconcerned.

"I well remember the stir *The Doorless Room* made in the literary world of those days — a fine book."

Howards was tall and he wore a brown tweed suit. Ken looked up at him aghast, steeling himself against the sudden attack. But the brown eyes were strangely innocent and Ken could not recognize the guile. A woman with tight pearls around her throat said after a painful moment, "But dear, Mr. Harris didn't write *The Doorless Room.*"

"Oh," Howards said helplessly.

Ken looked at the woman's pearls and wanted to choke her. "It couldn't matter less."

The editor persisted, trying to make amends. "But your name is Ken Harris. And you're married to the Marian Campbell who is fiction editor at —"

The woman said quickly: "Ken Harris wrote *The Night of Darkness* — a fine book."

Harris noticed that the woman's throat was lovely with the pearls and the black dress. His face lightened until she said: "It was about ten or fifteen years ago, wasn't it"

"I remember," the editor said. "A fine book. How could I have confused it? How long will it be before we can look forward to a second book?"

"I wrote a second book," Ken said. "It sank without a ripple. It failed." He added defensively, "The critics were more obtuse even than usual. And I'm not the best-seller type."

"Too bad," said the editor. "It's a casualty of the trade sometimes."

"The book was better than *The Night.* Some critics thought it was obscure. They said the same thing of Joyce." He added, with the writer's loyalty to his last creation, "It's a much better book than the first, and I feel I'm still just starting to do my real work."

"That's the spirit," the editor said. "The main thing is to keep plugging away. What are you writing now — if that's a fair question?"

The violence swelled suddenly. "It's none of your business." Ken had not spoken very loudly but the words carried and there was a sudden area of silence in the cocktail room. "None of your Goddam business."

In the quiet room there came the voice of old Mrs. Beckstein, who was deaf and sitting in a corner chair. "Why are you buying so many quilts?"

The spinster daughter, who was with her mother always, guarding her like royalty or some sacred animal, translating between the mother and the world, said firmly, "Mr. Brown was saying . . ."

The babble of the party resumed and Ken went to the drink table, took another Martini and dipped a piece of cauliflower in some sauce. He ate and drank with his back to the noisy room. Then he took a third Martini and threaded his way to Mabel Goodley. He sat on an ottoman beside her, careful of his drink and somewhat formal. "It's been such a tiring day," he said.

"What have you been doing?"

"Sitting on my can."

"A writer I used to know once got sacroiliac trouble from sitting so long. Could that be coming on you?"

"No," he said. "You are the only honest person in this room."

He had tried so many different ways when the blank pages started. He had tried to write in bed, and for a time he had changed to longhand. He had thought of Proust in his cork-lined room and for a month he had used ear-stoppers — but work went no better and the rubber started some fungus ailment. They had moved to Brooklyn Heights, but that did not help. When he learned that Thomas Wolfe had written standing up with his manuscript on the icebox he had even tried that too. But he only kept opening the icebox and eating. . . . He had tried writing drunk — when the ideas and images were marvelous at the time but changed so unhappily when read afterward. He had written early in the morning and dead sober and miserable. He had thought of Thoreau and Walden. He had dreamed of manual labor and an apple farm. If he could just go for long walks on the moors then the light of creation would come again — but where are the moors of New York?

He consoled himself with the writers who had felt they failed and whose fame was established after death. When he was twenty he daydreamed that he would die at thirty and his name would be blazoned after his death. When he was twenty-five and had finished *The Night of Darkness* he daydreamed that he would die famous, a writer's writer, at thirty-five with a body of work accomplished and the Nobel Prize awarded on his deathbed. But now that he was nearly forty with two books — one a success, the other a defended failure — he did not daydream about his death.

"I wonder why I keep on writing," he said. "It's a frustrating life."

He had vaguely expected that Mabel, his friend, might say something about his being a born writer, might even remind him of his duty to his talent, that she might even mention "genius," that magic word which turns hardship and outward failure to somber glory. But Mabel's answer dismayed him. "I guess writing is like the theatre. Once you write or act it gets in your blood."

He despised actors — vain, posey, always unemployed. "I don't think of acting as a creative art, it's just interpretive. Whereas the writer must hew the phantom rock —"

He saw his wife enter from the vestibule. Marian was tall and slim with straight, short black hair, and she was wearing a plain black dress, an office-looking dress without ornament. They had married thirteen years ago, the year *The Night* had come out, and for a long time he had trembled with love. There were times he awaited her with the soaring wonder of the lover and the sweet trembling when at last he saw her. Those were the times when they made love almost every night and often in the early morning. That first year she had even occasionally come home from the office at her lunch hour and they had loved each other naked in the city daylight. At last desire had steadied and love no longer made his body tremble. He was working on a second book and the going was rough. Then he got a Guggenheim and they had gone to Mexico, as the war was on in Europe. His book was abandoned and, although the flush of success was still on him, he was unsatisfied. He wanted to write, to write, to write — but month after month passed and he wrote nothing. Marian said he was drinking too much and marking time and he threw a glass of rum in her face. Then he knelt on the floor and cried. He was for the first time in a foreign country and the time was automatically valuable because it was a foreign country. He would write of the blue of the noon sky, the Mexican shadows, the water-fresh mountain air. But day followed day — always of value because it was a foreign country — and he wrote nothing. He did not even learn Spanish, and it annoyed him when Marian talked to the cook and other Mexicans. (It was easier for a woman to pick up a foreign language and besides she knew French.) And the very cheapness of Mexico made life expensive; he spent money like trick money or stage money and the Guggenheim check was always spent in advance. But he was in a foreign country and sooner or later the Mexican days would be of value to him as a writer. Then a strange thing happened after eight months: with practically no warning Marian took a plane to New York. He had to interrupt his Guggenheim year to follow her. And then she would not live with him — or let him live in her apartment. She said it was like living with twenty Roman emperors rolled into one and she was through. Marian got a job as an assistant fiction editor on a fashion magazine and he lived in a cold-water flat — their marriage had failed and they were separated, although he still tried to follow her around. The Guggenheim people would not renew his fellowship and he soon spent the advance on his new book.

About this time there was a morning he never forgot, although nothing, absolutely nothing, had happened. It was a sunny autumn day with the sky fair and green above the skyscrapers. He had gone to a cafeteria for breakfast and sat in the bright window. People passed quickly on the street, all of them going somewhere. Inside the cafeteria there was a breakfast bustle, the clatter of trays and the noise of many voices. People came in and ate and went away, and everyone seemed assured and certain of destination. They seemed to take for granted a destination that was not merely the routine of jobs and appointments. Although most of the people were alone they seemed somehow a part of each other, a part of the clear autumn city. While he alone seemed separate, an isolate cipher in the pattern of the destined city. His marmalade was glazed by sunlight and he spread it on a piece of toast but did not eat. The coffee had a purplish sheen and there was a faint mark of old lipstick on the rim of the cup. It was an hour of desolation, although nothing at all happened.

Now at the cocktail party, years later, the noise, the assurance and the sense of his own separateness recalled the cafeteria breakfast and this hour was still more desolate because of the sliding passage of time.

"There's Marian," Mabel said. "She looks tired, thinner."

"If the damned Guggenheim had renewed my fellowship I was going to take Marian to Europe for a year," he said. "The damned Guggenheim — they don't give grants to creative writers any more. Just physicists — people like that who are preparing for another war."

The war had come as a relief to Ken. He was glad to abandon the book that was going badly, relieved to turn from his "phantom rock" to the general experience of those days — for surely the war was the great experience of his generation. He was graduated from Officers' Training School and when Marian saw him in his uniform she cried and loved him and there was no further talk of divorce. On his last leave they made love often as they used to do in the first months of marriage. It rained every day in England and once he was invited by a lord to his castle. He crossed on D-Day and his battalion went all the way to Schmitz. In a cellar in a ruined town he saw a cat sniffing the face of a corpse. He was afraid, but it was not the blank terror of the cafeteria or the anxiety of a white page on the typewriter. Something was always happening — he found three Westphalian hams in the chimney of a peasant's house and he broke his arm in an automobile accident. The war was the great experience of his generation, and to a writer every day was automatically of value because it was the war. But when it was over what was there to write about — the calm cat and the corpse, the lord in England, the broken arm?

In the Village apartment he returned to the book he had left so long. For a time, that year after the war, there was the sense of a writer's gladness when he has written. A time when the voice from childhood, a song on the corner, all fitted. In the strange euphoria of his lonely work the world was synthesized. He was writing of another time, another place. He was writing of his youth in the windy, gritty Texas city that was his home town. He wrote of the rebellion of youth and the longing for the brilliant cities, the homesickness for a place he'd never seen. While he was writing *One Summer Evening* he was living in an apartment in New York but his inner life was in Texas and the distance was more than space: it was the sad distance between middle age and youth. So when he was writing his book he was split between two realities — his New York daily life and the remembered cadence of his Texas youth. When the book was published and the reviews were careless or unkind, he took it well, he thought, until the days of desolation stretched one into the other and the terror started. He did odd things at this time. Once he locked himself in the bathroom and stood holding a bottle of Lysol in his hand, just standing there holding the Lysol, trembling and terrified. He stood there for half an hour until with a great effort he slowly poured the Lysol in the lavatory. Then he lay on the bed and wept until, toward the end of the afternoon, he went to sleep. Another time he sat in the open window and let a dozen blank pages of paper float down the six stories to the street below. The wind blew the papers as he dropped them one by one, and he felt a strange elation as he watched them float away. It was less the meaninglessness of these actions than the extreme tension accompanying them that made Ken realize he was sick.

Marian suggested he go to a psychiatrist and he said psychiatry had become an avant-garde method of playing with yourself. Then he laughed, but Marian did not laugh and his solitary laughter finished in a chill of fear. In the end Marian went to the psychiatrist and Ken was jealous of them both — of the doctor because he was the arbiter of the unhappy marriage and of her because she was calmer and he was more unhinged. That year he wrote some television scripts, made a couple of thousand dollars and bought Marian a leopard coat.

"Are you doing any more television programs?" Mabel Goodley asked.

"Naw," he said, "I'm trying very hard to get into my next book. You're the only honest person I know. I can talk with you . . ."

Freed by alcohol and secure in friendship (for after all Mabel was one of his favorite people), he began to talk of the book he had tried so long to do: "The dominant theme is the theme of self-betrayal and the central character is a small-town lawyer named Winkle. The setting is laid in Texas — my home town — and most of the scenes take place in the grimy office in the town's courthouse. In the opening of the book Winkle is faced with this situation . . ." Ken unfurled his story passionately, telling of the various characters and the motivations involved. When Marian came up he was still talking and he gestured to her not to interrupt him as he talked on, looking straight into Mabel's spectacled blue eyes. Then suddenly he had the uncanny sensation of a déjà vu. He felt he had told Mabel his book before — in the same place and in the same circumstance. Even the way the curtain moved was the same. Only Mabel's blue eyes brightened with tears behind the glasses, and he was joyful that she was so much moved. "So Winkle then was impelled to divorce —" his voice faltered. "I have the strange feeling I have told you this before . . ."

Mabel waited for a moment and he was silent. "You have, Ken," she said finally. "About six or seven years ago, and at a party very much like this one."

He could not stand the pity in her eyes or the shame that pulsed in his own body. He staggered up and stumbled over his drink.

After the roar in the cocktail room the little terrace was absolutely silent. Except for the wind, which increased the sense of desertion and solitude. To dull his shame Ken said aloud something inconsequential: "Why, what on earth —" and he smiled with weak anguish. But his shame still smoldered and he put his cold hand to his hot, throbbing forehead. It was no longer snowing, but the wind lifted flurries of snow on the white terrace. The length of the terrace was about six footsteps and Ken walked very slowly, watching with growing attention his blunted footsteps in his narrow shoes. Why did he watch those footsteps with such tension? And why was he standing there, alone on the winter terrace where the light from the party room laid a sickly yellow rectangle on the snow? And the footsteps? At the end of the terrace there was a little fence about waist-high. When he leaned against the fence he knew it was very loose and he felt he *had known that it would be loose* and remained leaning against it. The penthouse was on the fifteenth floor and the lights from the city glowed before him. He was thinking that if he gave the rickety fence one push he would fall, but he remained calm against the sagging fence, his mind somehow sheltered, content.

He felt inexcusably disturbed when a voice called from the terrace. It was Marian and she cried softly: "Aah! Aah!" Then after a moment she added: "Ken, come here. What are you doing out there?" Ken stood up. Then with his balance righted he gave the fence a slight push. It did not break. "This fence is rotten — snow probably. I wonder how many people have ever committed suicide here."

"How many?"

"Sure. It's such an easy thing."

"Come back."

Very carefully he walked on the backward footprints he had made before. "It must be an inch of snow." He stooped down and felt the snow with his middle finger. "No, two inches."

"I'm cold." Marian put her hand on his coat, opened the door and steered him into the party. The room was quieter now and people were going home. In the bright light, after the dark outside, Ken saw that Marian looked tired. Her black eyes were reproachful, harried, and Ken could not bear to look into them.

"Hon, do your sinuses bother you?"

Lightly her forefinger stroked her forehead and the bridge of her nose. "It worries me so when you get in this condition."

"Condition! Me?"

"Let's put on our things and go."

But he could not stand the look in Marian's eyes and he hated her for inferring he was drunk. "I'm going to Jim Johnson's party later."

After the search for overcoats and the ragged good-bys a little group went down in the elevator and stood on the sidewalk, whistling for cabs. They discussed addresses, and Marian, the editor and Ken shared the first taxi going downtown. Ken's shame was lulled a little, and in the taxi he began to talk about Mabel.

"It's so sad about Mabel," he said.

"What do you mean?" Marian asked.

"Everything. She's obviously going apart at the seams. Disintegrating, poor thing."

Marian, who did not like the conversation, said to Howards: "Shall we go through the park? It's nice when it snows, and quicker."

"I'll go on to Fifth and Fourteenth Street," Howards said. He said to the driver: "Go through the park, please."

"The trouble with Mabel is she is a has-been. Ten years ago she used to be an honest painter and set-designer. Maybe it's a failure of imagination or drinking too much. She's lost her honesty and does the same thing over and over — repeats over and over."

"Nonsense," Marian said. "She gets better every year and she's made a lot of money."

They were driving through the park and Ken watched the winter landscape. The snow was heavy on the park trees and occasionally the wind slid the banked snow from the boughs, although the trees did not bow down. In the taxi Ken began to recite the old nursery verse about the wind, and again the words left sinister echoes and his cold palms dampened.

"I haven't thought of that jingle in years," John Howards said.

"Jingle? It's as harrowing as Dostoevski."

"I remember we used to sing it in kindergarten. And when a child had a birthday there would be a blue or pink ribbon on the tiny chair and we would then sing *Happy Birthday*."

John Howards was hunched on the edge of the seat next to Marian. It was hard to imagine this tall, lumbering editor in his huge galoshes singing in a kindergarten years ago.

Ken asked: "Where did you come from?"

"Kalamazoo," Howards said.

"I always wondered if there really was such a place or a — figure of speech."

"It was and is such a place." Howards said. "The family moved to Detroit when I was ten years old." Again Ken felt a sense of strangeness and thought that there are certain people who have preserved so little of childhood that the mention of kindergarten chairs and family moves seem somehow outlandish. He suddenly conceived a story written about such a man — he would call it *The Man in the Tweed Suit* — and he brooded silently as the story evolved in his mind with a brief flash of the old elation that came so seldom now.

"The weatherman says it's going down to zero tonight," Marian said.

"You can drop me here," Howards said to the driver as he opened his wallet and handed some money to Marian. "Thanks for letting me share the cab. And that's my part," he added with a smile. "It's so good to see you again. Let's have lunch one of these days and bring your husband if he would care to come." After he stumbled out of the taxi he called to Ken, "I'm looking forward to your next book, Harris."

"Idiot," Ken said after the cab started again. "I'll drop you home and then stop for a moment at Jim Johnson's."

"Who's he — why do you have to go?"

"He's a painter I know and I was invited."

"You take up with so many people these days. You go around with one crowd and then shift to another."

Ken knew that the observation was true, but he could not help it. In the past few years he would associate with one group — for a long time he and Marian had different circles of friends — until he would get drunk or make a scene so that the whole periphery was unpleasant to him and he felt angry and unwanted. Then he would change to another circle — and every change was to a group less stable than the one before, with shabbier apartments and cheaper drinks. Now he was glad to go wherever he was invited, to strangers where a voice might guide him and the flimsy sheaves of alcohol solace his jagged nerves.

"Ken, why don't you get help? I can't go on with this."

"Why, what's the matter?"

"You know," she said. He could feel her tense and stiff in the taxicab. "Are you really going on to another party? Can't you see you are destroying yourself? Why were you leaning against that terrace fence? Don't you realize you are — sick? Come home."

The words disturbed him, but he could not bear the thought of going home with Marian tonight. He had a presentiment that if they were alone in the apartment something dreadful might come about, and his nerves warned him of this undefined disaster.

In the old days after a cocktail party they would be glad to go home alone, talk over the party with a few quiet drinks, raid the icebox and go to bed, secure against the world outside. Then one evening after a party something had happened — he had a blackout and said or did something he could not remember and did not want to remember; afterward there was only the smashed typewriter and shafts of shameful recollection that he could not face and the memory of her fearful eyes. Marian stopped drinking and tried to talk him into joining AA. He went with her to a meeting and even stayed on the wagon with her for five days — until the horror of the unremembered night was a little distant. Afterward, when he had to drink alone, he resented her milk and her eternal coffee and she resented his drinking liquor. In this tense situation he felt the psychiatrist was somehow responsible and wondered if he had hypnotized Marian. Anyway now the evenings were spoiled and unnatural. Now he could feel her sitting upright in the taxi and he wanted to kiss her as in the old days when they were going home after a party. But her body was stiff in his embrace.

"Hon, let's be like we used to be. Let's go home and get a buzz on peacefully and hash over the evening. You used to love to do that. You used to enjoy a few drinks when we were quiet, alone. Drink with me and cozy like in the old days. I'll skip the other party if you will. Please, Hon. You're not one bit alcoholic. And it makes me feel like a lush your not drinking — I feel unnatural. And you're not a bit alcoholic, no more than I am."

"I'll fix a bowl of soup and you can turn in." But her voice was hopeless and sounded smug to Ken. Then she said: "I've tried so hard to keep our marriage and to help you. But it's like struggling in quicksand. There's so much behind the drinking and I'm so tired."

"I'll be just a minute at the party — go on with me."

"I can't go on."

The cab stopped and Marian paid the fare. She asked as she left the cab, "Do you have enough money to go on? — if you must go on."

"Naturally."

Jim Johnson's apartment was way over on the West Side, in a Puerto Rican neighborhood. Open garbage cans stood out on the curb and wind blew papers on the snowy sidewalk. When the taxi stopped Ken was so inattentive that the driver had to call him. He looked at the meter and opened his billfold — he had not one single dollar bill, only fifty cents, which was not enough. "I've run out of money, except this fifty cents," Ken said, handing the driver the money. "What shall I do?"

The driver looked at him. "Nothing, just get out. There's nothing to be done."

Ken got out. "Fifteen cents over and no tip — sorry —"

"You should have taken the money from the lady."

This party was held on the walk-up top floor of a cold-water flat and layered smells of cooking were at each landing of the stairs. The room was crowded, cold, and the gas jets were burning blue on the stove, the oven open for warmth. Since there was little furniture except a studio couch, most of the guests sat on the floor. There were rows of canvases propped against the wall and on an easel a picture of a purple junk yard and two green suns. Ken sat down on the floor next to a pink-cheeked young man wearing a brown leather jacket.

"It's always somehow soothing to sit in a painter's studio. Painters don't have the problems writers have. Who ever heard of a painter getting stuck? They have something to work with — the canvas to be prepared, the brush and so on. Where is a blank page — painters aren't neurotic as many writers are."

"I don't know," the young man said. "Didn't van Gogh cut off his ear?"

"Still the smell of paint, the colors and the activity is soothing. Not like a blank page and a silent room. Painters can whistle when they work or even talk to people."

"I know a painter once who killed his wife."

When Ken was offered rum punch or sherry, he took sherry and it tasted metallic as though coins had been soaked in it.

"You a painter?"

"No," said the young man. "A writer — that is, I write."

"What is your name?"

"It wouldn't mean anything to you. I haven't published my book yet." After a pause he added: "I had a short story in *Bolder Accent* — it's one of the little magazines — maybe you've heard of it."

"How long have you been writing?"

"Eight — ten years. Of course I have to do part-time jobs on the outside, enough to eat and pay the rent."

"What kind of jobs do you do?"

"All kinds. Once for a year I had a job in a morgue. It was wonderful pay and I could do my own work four or five hours every day. But after about a year I began to feel the job was not good for my work. All those cadavers — so I changed to a job frying hot dogs at Coney Island. Now I'm a night clerk in a real crummy hotel. But I can work at home all afternoon and at night I can think over my book — and there's lots of human interest on the job. Future stories, you know."

"What makes you think you are a writer?"

The eagerness faded from the young man's face and when he pressed his fingers to his flushed cheek they left white marks. "Just because I know. I have worked so hard and I have faith in my talent." He went on after a pause. "Of course one story in a little magazine after ten years is not such a brilliant beginning. But think of the struggles nearly every writer has — even the great geniuses. I have time and determination — and when this last novel finally breaks into print the world will recognize the talent."

The open earnestness of the young man was distasteful to Ken, for he felt in it something that he himself had long since lost. "Talent," he said bitterly. "A small, one-story talent — that is the most treacherous thing that God can give. To work on and on, hoping, believing until youth is wasted — I have seen this sort of thing so much. A small talent is God's greatest curse."

"But how do you know I have a small talent — how do you know it's not great? You don't know — you've never read a word I've written!" he said indignantly.

"I wasn't thinking about you in particular. I was just talking abstractly."

The smell of gas was strong in the room — smoke lay in drafty layers close to the low ceiling. The floor was cold and Ken reached for a pillow nearby and sat on it. "What kind of things do you write?"

"My last book is about a man called Brown — I wanted it to be a common name, as a symbol of general humanity. He loves his wife and he has to kill her because —"

"Don't say anything more. A writer should never tell his work in advance. Besides, I've heard it all before."

"How could you? I never told you, finished telling —"

"It's the same thing in the end," Ken said. "I heard the whole thing seven years — eight years ago in this room."

The flushed face paled suddenly. "Mr. Harris, although you've written two published books, I think you're a mean man." His voice rose. "Don't pick on me!"

The young man stood up, zipped his leather jacket and stood sullenly in a corner of the room.

After some moments Ken began to wonder why he was there. He knew no one at the party except his host and the picture of the garbage dump and the two suns irritated him. In the room of strangers there was no voice to guide him and the sherry was sharp in his dry mouth. Without saying good-by to anyone Ken left the room and went downstairs.

He remembered he had no money and would have to walk home. It was still snowing, and the wind shrilled at the street corners and the temperature was nearing zero. He was many blocks away from home when he saw a drug store at a familiar corner and the thought of hot coffee came to him. If he could just drink some really hot coffee, holding his hands around the cup, then his brain would clear and he would have the strength to hurry home and face his wife and the thing that was going to happen when he was home. Then something occurred that in the beginning seemed ordinary, even natural. A man in a Homburg hat was about to pass him on the deserted street and when they were quite near Ken said: "Hello there, it's about zero, isn't it?"

The man hesitated for a moment.

"Wait," he went on. "I'm in something of a predicament. I've lost my money — never mind how — and I wonder if you would give me change for a cup of coffee."

When the words were spoken Ken realized suddenly that the situation was not ordinary and he and the stranger exchanged that look of mutual shame, distrust, between the beggar and the begged. Ken stood with his hands in his pockets — he had lost his gloves somewhere — and the stranger glanced a final time at him, then hurried away.

"Wait," Ken called. "You think I'm a mugger — I'm not! I'm a writer — I'm not a criminal."

The stranger hurried to the other side of the street, his brief case bouncing against his knees as he moved. Ken reached home after midnight.

Marian was in bed with a glass of milk on the bedside table. He made himself a highball and brought it in the bedroom, although usually these days he gulped liquor in secret and quickly.

"Where is the clock?"

"In the clothes hamper."

He found the clock and put it on the table by the milk. Marian gave him a strange stare.

"How was your party?"

"Awful." After a while he added, "This city is a desolate place. The parties, the people — the suspicious strangers."

"You are the one who always likes parties."

"No, I don't. Not any more." He sat on the twin bed beside Marian and suddenly the tears came to his eyes. "Hon, what happened to the apple farm?"

"Apple farm?"

"*Our* apple farm — don't you remember?"

"It was so many years ago and so much has happened."

But although the dream had long since been forgotten, its freshness was renewed again. He could see the apple blossoms in the spring rain, the gray old farmhouse. He was milking at dawn, then tending the vegetable garden with the green curled lettuce, the dusty summer corn, the eggplant and the purple cabbages iridescent in the dew. The country breakfast would be pancakes and the sausage of home-raised pork. When morning chores and breakfast were done, he would work at his novel for four hours, then in the afternoon there were fences to be mended, wood to be split. He saw the farm in all its weathers — the snowbound spells when he would finish a whole short novel at one stretch; the mild, sweet, luminous days of May; the green summer pond where he fished for their own trout; the blue October and the apples. The dream, unblemished by reality, was vivid, exact.

"And in the evening," he said, seeing the firelight and the rise and fall of shadows on the farmhouse wall, "we would really study Shakespeare, and read the Bible all the way through."

For a moment Marian was caught in the dream. "That was the first year we were married," she said in a tone of injury or surprise. "And after the apple farm was started we were going to start a child."

"I remember," he said vaguely, although this was a part he had quite forgotten. He saw an indefinite little boy of six or so in denim jeans . . . then the child vanished and he saw himself clearly, on the horse — or rather mule — carrying the finished manuscript of a great novel on the way to the nearest village to post it to the publisher.

"We could live on almost nothing — and live well. I would do all the work — manual work is what pays nowadays — raise everything we eat. We'll have our own hogs and a cow and chickens." After a pause he added, "There won't even be a liquor bill. I will make cider and applejack. Have a press and all."

"I'm tired," Marian said, and she touched her fingers to her forehead.

"There will be no more New York parties and in the evening we'll read the Bible all the way through. I've never read the Bible all the way through, have you?"

"No," she said, "but you don't have to have an apple farm to read the Bible."

"Maybe I have to have the apple farm to read the Bible and to write well too."

"Well, tant pis." The French phrase infuriated him; for a year before they were married she had taught French in high school and occasionally when she was peeved or disappointed with him she used a French phrase that often he did not understand.

He felt a gathering tension between them that he wanted at all cost to wear through. He sat on the bed, hunched and miserable, gazing at the prints on the bedroom wall. "You see, something so screwy has happened to my sights. When I was young I was sure I was going to be a great writer. And then the years passed — I settled on being a fine minor writer. Can you feel the dying fall of this?"

"No, I'm exhausted," she said after a while. "I have been thinking of the Bible too, this last year. One of the first commandments is *Thou shalt have no other gods before me!* But you and other people like you have made a god of this — illusion. You disregard all other responsibilities — family, finances and even self-respect. You disregard anything that might interfere with your strange god. The golden calf was nothing to this."

"And after settling to be a minor writer I had to lower my sights still further. I wrote scripts for television and tried to become a competent hack. But I failed even to carry that through. Can you understand the horror? I've even become mean-hearted, jealous — I was never that way before. I was a pretty good person when I was happy. The last and final thing is to give up and get a job writing advertising. Can you understand the horror?"

"I've often thought that might be a solution. Anything, darling, to restore your self-respect."

"Yes," he said. "But I'd rather get a job in a morgue or fry hot dogs."

Her eyes were apprehensive. "It's late. Get to bed."

"At the apple farm I would work so hard — laboring work as well as writing. And it would be peaceful and — safe. Why can't we do it, Baby-love?"

She was cutting a hangnail and did not even look at him.

"Maybe I could borrow from your Aunt Rose — in a strictly legal, banking way. With business mortgages on the farm and the crops. And I would dedicate the first book to her."

"Borrow from — not my Aunt Rose!" Marian put the scissors on the table. "I'm going to sleep."

"Why don't you believe in me — and the apple farm? Why don't you want it? It would be so peaceful and — safe. We would be alone and far away — why don't you want it?"

Her black eyes were wide open and he saw in them an expression he had seen only once before. "Because," she said deliberately, "I wouldn't be alone and far away with you on that crazy apple farm for anything — without doctors, friends and help." The apprehension had quickened to fright and her eyes glowed with fear. Her hands picked at the sheet.

Ken's voice was shocked. "Baby, you're not afraid of me! Why, I wouldn't touch your smallest eyelash. I don't even want the wind to blow on you — I couldn't hurt —"

Marian settled her pillow and, turning her back, lay down. "All right. Good night."

For a while he sat dazed, then he knelt on the floor beside Marian's bed and his hand rested gently on her buttocks. The dull pulse of desire was prompted by the touch. "Come! I'll take off my clothes. Let's cozy." He waited, but she did not move or answer.

"Come, Baby-love."

"No," she said. But his love was rising and he did not notice her words — his hand trembled and the fingernails were dingy against the white blanket. "No more," she said. "Not ever."

"Please, love. Then afterward we can be at peace and can sleep. Darling, darling, you're all I have. You're the gold in my life!"

Marian pushed his hand away and sat up abruptly. The fear was replaced by a flash of anger, and the blue vein was prominent on her temple. "Gold in your life —" Her voice intended irony but somehow failed. "In any case — I'm your bread and butter."

The insult of the words reached him slowly, then anger leaped as sudden as a flame, "I — I —"

"You think you're the only one who has been disappointed. I married a writer who I thought would become a great writer. I was glad to support you — I thought it would pay off. So I worked at an office while you could sit there — lowering your sights. God, what has happened to us?"

"I — I —" But rage would not yet let him speak.

"Maybe you could have been helped. If you had gone to the doctor when that block started. We've both known for a long time you are — sick."

Again he saw the expression he had seen before — it was the look that was the only thing he remembered in that awful blackout — the black eyes brilliant with fear and the prominent temple vein. He caught, reflected the same expression, so that their eyes were fixed for a time, blazing with terror.

Unable to stand this, Ken picked up the scissors from the bedside table and held them above his head, his eyes fixed on her temple vein. "Sick!" he said at last. "You mean — crazy. I'll teach you to be afraid that I am crazy. I'll teach you to talk about bread and butter. I'll teach you to think I'm crazy!"

Marian's eyes sparkled with alarm and she tried weakly to move. The vein writhed in her temple. "Don't you move." Then with a great effort he opened his hand and the scissors fell on the carpeted floor. "Sorry," he said. "Excuse me." After a dazed look around the room he saw the typewriter and went to it quickly.

"I'll take the typewriter in the living room. I didn't finish my quota today — you have to be disciplined about things like that."

He sat at the typewriter in the living room, alternating X and R for the sound. After some lines of this he paused and said in an empty voice: "This story is sitting up on its hind legs at last." Then he began to write: *The lazy brown fox jumped over the cunning dog.* He wrote this a number of times, then leaned back in his chair.

"Dearest Pie," he said urgently. "You know how I love you. You're the only woman I ever thought about. You're my life. Don't you understand, my dearest Pie?"

She didn't answer and the apartment was silent except for the rumble of the radiator pipes.

"Forgive me," he said. "I'm so sorry I picked up the scissors. You know I wouldn't even pinch you too hard. Tell me you forgive me. Please, please tell me."

Still there was no answer.

"I'm going to be a good husband. I'll even get a job in an advertising office. I'll be a Sunday poet — writing only on weekends and holidays. I will, my darling, I will!" he said desperately. "Although I'd much rather fry hot dogs in the morgue."

Was it the snow that made the rooms so silent? He was conscious of his own heart beating and he wrote:

Why am I so afraid
Why am I so afraid
Why am I so afraid???

He got up and in the kitchen opened the icebox door. "Hon, I'm going to fix you something good to eat. What's that dark thing in the saucer in the corner? Why, it's the liver from last Sunday's dinner — you're crazy about chicken liver or would you rather have something piping hot like soup? Which, Hon?"

There was no sound.

"I bet you haven't even eaten a bite of supper. You must be exhausted — with those awful parties and drinking and walking — without a living bite. I have to take care of you. We'll eat and afterward we can cozy."

He stood still, listening. Then, with the grease-jelled chicken liver in his hands, he tiptoed to the bedroom. The room and bath were both empty. Carefully he placed the chicken liver on the white bureau scarf. Then he stood in the doorway, his foot raised to walk and left suspended for some moments. Afterward he opened closets, even the broom closet in the kitchen, looked behind furniture and peered under the bed. Marian was nowhere at all. Finally he realized that the leopard coat and her purse were gone. He was panting when he sat down to telephone.

"Hey, Doctor. Ken Harris speaking. My wife has disappeared. Just walked out while I was writing at the typewriter. Is she with you? Did she phone?" He made squares and wavy lines on the pad. "Hell yes, we quarreled! I picked up the scissors — no, I did not touch her! I wouldn't hurt her little fingernail. No, she's not hurt —how did you get that idea?" Ken listened. "I just want to tell you this. I know you have hypnotized my wife — poisoned her mind against me. If anything happens between my wife and me I'm going to kill you. I'll go up to your nosy Park Avenue office and kill you dead."

Alone in the empty, silent rooms, he felt an undefinable fear that reminded him of his ghost-haunted babyhood. He sat on the bed, his shoes still on, cradling his knees with both arms. A line of poetry came to him. "My love, my love, my love, why have you left me alone?" He sobbed and bit his trousered knee.

After a while he called the places he thought she might be, accused friends of interfering with their marriage or of hiding Marian . . .

When he called Mabel Goodley he had forgotten the episode of the early evening and he said he wanted to come around to see her. When she said it was three o'clock and she had to get up in the morning he asked what friends were for if not for times like this. And he accused her of hiding Marian, of interfering with their marriage and of being in cahoots with the evil psychiatrist. . . .

At the end of the night it stopped snowing. The early dawn was pearl gray and the day would be fair and very cold. At sunrise Ken put on his overcoat and went downstairs. At that hour there was no one on the street. The sun dappled the fresh snow with gold, and shadows were cold lavender. His senses searched the frozen radiance of the morning and he was thinking he should have written about such a day — that was what he had really meant to write.

A hunched and haggard figure with luminous, lost eyes, Ken plodded slowly toward the subway. He thought of the wheels of the train and the gritty wind, the roar. He wondered if it was true that in the final moment of death the brain blazes with all the images of the past — the apple trees, the loves, the cadence of lost voices — all fused and vivid in the dying brain. He walked very slowly, his eyes fixed on his solitary footsteps and the blank snow ahead.

A mounted policeman was passing along the curb near him. The horse's breath showed in the still, cold air and his eyes were purple, liquid.

"Hey, Officer. I have something to report. My wife picked up the scissors at me — aiming for that little blue vein. Then she left the apartment. My wife is very sick — crazy. She ought to be helped before something awful happens. She didn't eat a bite of supper — not even the little chicken liver."

Ken plodded on laboriously, and the officer watched him as he went away. Ken's destination was as uncontrollable as the unseen wind and Ken thought only of his footsteps and the unmarked way ahead.

[*Mademoiselle,* September 1956]

ESSAYS AND ARTICLES

Editor's Note

FASHION MAGAZINES in America have long been a home for some of the finest writing from this country and abroad. Certainly *Harper's Bazaar, Vogue* and *Mademoiselle* are outstanding examples of this contribution to both readers and writers, which in turn has enhanced the reputations of the magazines. *Harper's Bazaar* published some of Carson's finest fiction: *The Ballad of the Sad Café;* "A Tree, a Rock, a Cloud"; and *Reflections in a Golden Eye.* Since all of these are now among her readily available work, they are not included in this volume. *Vogue* published articles by Carson and *Mademoiselle* published stories, articles and poems. Most of Carson's nonfiction is gathered together in this section. What is omitted are those pieces that are either similar in content to the ones chosen or that simply don't hold up as well as the bulk of her writing.

The articles have been arranged loosely by subject. There was hardly a family we knew that was not involved in some way with World War II. The servicemen were our contemporaries: Reeves (Carson's husband) volunteered for the Rangers, our brother Lamar for the Navy and our cousins and in-laws and friends were in the service. Carson's commitment involved in part, as it did for most of us, a very personal concern.

There are as many articles on Christmas (three are included here) as there are on World War II and one of them written during the war years. Christmas was Carson's favorite holiday and fall and winter her favorite times of the year. Often her work evokes a longing for the cold and snow as seen in Frankie Addams' dreams of Winter Hill, or she summons the autumn with her descriptions of a "hunting dawn," the making of cane syrup, or slaughtering day after the first frost. Mother's fruitcakes were baked before Thanksgiving and were so famous that the time our house burned down when we were children, the only thing that our brother thought was valuable enough to save were a few freshly baked fruitcakes soaking in good bourbon and wrapped in linen napkins and not to be cut until Christmas. When Carson suffered her massive brain hemorrhage at the end of the summer of 1967, she had completed most of her Christmas shopping which she conducted by phone, through the mail or with the good services of her friends.

It is fitting that the very last writing of Carson's was a brief piece on Christmas for *McCall's.* It was published after she died. In this, she tells of reading "The Dead" to her young hospital roommate. Mother always read this story aloud to us at Christmastime. No doubt it was Carson who introduced Mother to James Joyce's work and "The Dead" became a family favorite.

The rest of the nonfiction published in a range of magazines, including the now defunct *Decision* edited by Klaus Mann, is for the most part concerned with writing — her own and that of other writers. "The Flowering Dream" is actually some of the notes from a longer work still in progress at the time of her death.

In addition to being able to detect suggestions of characters that appear in her fiction, such as the unlikely pair in "Brooklyn Is My Neighbourhood" who bear a similarity to Miss Amelia and Cousin Lymon in *The Ballad of the Sad Café,* the reader can see Carson's themes weaving throughout all that she wrote — predominantly the search for identity, the ecclesiastical sense of time and chance, and love.

THE WAR YEARS

LOOK HOMEWARD, AMERICANS

FROM THE WINDOWS of my rooms in Brooklyn, there is a view of the Manhattan sky-line. The sky-scrapers, pastel mauve and yellow in colour, rise up sharp as stalagmites against the sky. My windows overlook the harbour, the grey East River, and the Brooklyn Bridge. In the night, there are the lonesome calls of the boats on the river and at sea. This water-front neighbourhood is the place where Thomas Wolfe used to live, and Hart Crane. Often when I am loafing by the window, looking out at the lights and the bright traffic crossing the Bridge, I think of them. And I am homesick in a way that they were often homesick.

It is a curious emotion, this certain homesickness I have in mind. With Americans, it is a national trait, as native to us as the roller-coaster or the jukebox. It is no simple longing for the home town or the country of our birth. The emotion is Janus-faced: we are torn between a nostalgia for the familiar and an urge for the foreign and strange. As often as not, we are homesick most for the places we have never known.

All men are lonely. But sometimes it seems to me that we Americans are the loneliest of all. Our hunger for foreign places and new ways has been with us almost like a national disease. Our literature is stamped with a quality of longing and unrest, and our writers have been great wanderers. Poe turned inward to discover an eerie and glowing world of his own. Whitman, that noblest of vagabonds, saw life as a broad open road. Henry James abandoned his own adolescent country for England and the airy decadence of nineteenth-century drawing-rooms. Melville sent out his Captain Ahab to self-destruction in the mad sailing for the great white whale. And Wolfe and Crane — they wandered for a lifetime, and I am not sure they knew themselves just what it was they sought.

But these writers, our spokesmen, are dead. And although the harbour and the Bridge instinctively make me think of them, I have these days remembered also a friend of mine from whom I got a card a couple of weeks ago.

My friend is named Lester, and he lives down in North Carolina. Lester is about twenty years old with a gangling body and a pleasant, sunburned face. He has some responsibility, as he is the eldest child in the family and his father is dead. He and his mother have a little store and filling-station on Highway U.S. 1. This road runs from New York down through to Miami. It cuts through the long coastal plain that lies between the Appalachian Hills and the Atlantic. There are thousands of stands and filling-stations on this highway.

Lester takes care of the gas-pump and waits behind the counter of the store. This filling-station is out in the country a few miles from the town where I used to live, so sometimes when I was out walking in the woods I would stop in and warm myself by the stove and drink a glass of beer. Coming out of the pine woods and crossing the grey winter fields, it was good to see the lights ahead.

In the afternoon, the store would be cosy and quiet, with the air smelling of sawdust and smoke, and with the sleepy ticking of a clock the only sound in the room. Sometimes Lester would be out hunting and would come in as I was drinking my beer. He would come in from the frosty twilight with his wet-nosed hound, and maybe in his sack there would be a couple of quail for his mother to fry at suppertime. Other days, if the weather were warm, I would watch Lester just sitting on a crate by the gas-pump, a peaceful halo of flies around his head, waiting for some tourist to pass along the road and stop for service.

Lester was a great traveller. He had hitch-hiked a good deal and seen much of the country. But mostly he had travelled in his mind. On the shelf behind the counter of the store there were stacks of old *National Geographics* and a collection of atlases. When I knew Lester first it was long before the war had started, and the maps were different then. "Paris, France," Lester would say to me. "That's where I mean to go someday. And Russia and India and down in the jungles of Africa —"

It was a passion with Lester — this hunger to know the world. As he talked of the cities of Europe, his grey eyes widened, and there was about them a quality of quiet craziness. Sometimes as we were sitting there, a car would pull up to the gas-pump, and the manner in which Lester treated the customer would depend on several things. If the driver were known to him, someone from those parts, Lester did not put himself to much trouble. But if the licence plate were from some distant place, such as New York or California, he polished the windshield lovingly, and his voice became gentle and slurred.

He had a deft way of extracting information as to the places the tourist had seen in his lifetime. Once a man stopped who had lived in Paris, and Lester made friends with him and got him drunk on white-lightning so that the customer had to stay overnight in the town.

Lester did not often talk about the places he had actually seen, but he knew much of America. A couple of years before he had gone into the C.C.C. and had been sent out to the forests of Oregon. He had passed over the prairies of the Middle West and seen the tawny wheat-fields under the summer sun. He had crossed the Rockies and looked out on the magnificence of the Pacific Ocean.

Then later, after a year in the Oregon camp, he had stayed for a while with an uncle in San Diego. On his way home again, he had hitch-hiked and taken a zigzagged course — through Arizona, Texas, the delta of the Mississippi. He had seen south Georgia in peach time and discovered the lazy grandeur of Charleston. He had come back to North Carolina in time for the tobacco harvest, after having been away from home two years.

But about this odyssey Lester did not talk much. His longing was never for home, or for the places he had seen and known and made a part of himself. He hungered always for the alien, the country far away and unattainable. And in the meantime he was wretched in his own countryside, and waited by the gas-pump thinking always of distant things.

When the war started, Lester did not concern himself as much with the happenings in Europe as I had expected. He was convinced that the war could not last longer than a few months because Hitler would run out of gasoline. Then in the late spring I went away and did not hear from him until his card reached me this autumn. He mentioned the tobacco crop and told me his hound had got mange. At the end he wrote: "Look at what happened to the places I meant to go. There is certainly one thing about this war. It leaves you no place to be homesick for."

A lonely little store and gas-pump down on Highway U.S. 1 seems far away from the harbour of Manhattan. And Lester, a foot-loose adolescent, does not appear to have very much in common with our poets of the time before the war — with Wolfe and Hart Crane. But their longing, their restlessness, their turning to the unknown is the same.

There are thousands of Lesters, but poets come rarely and are the spiritual syntheses of their time and place. And the world of these poets, and of all of us who lived before this debacle, has been ruthlessly amputated from the world of today. Frontiers, both of the earth and of the spirit, were open to them and have since been closed to us. America is now isolated in a way that we never before could have foreseen.

The Manhattan harbour is quiet this year. Wolfe and Hart Crane no longer wander in these water-front streets — Wolfe maddened by unfocused longing. Hart Crane sick for a nameless place and broken and inflamed by drink. The harbour, yes, is quieter now, and the great ships from abroad do not come to port so often any more. Most of the boats I see from my windows are the small sort that did not go out far from shore. In the late autumn afternoons, a soft fog veils the sky-line of Manhattan. There is a sadness about this scene. And no wonder — a sky-line facing outward toward the Atlantic and the grim convulsions of the world beyond. Not only sad, but somehow hopeless.

So we must turn inward. This singular emotion, the nostalgia that has been so much a part of our national character, must be converted to good use. What our seekers have sought for we must find. And this is a great, a creative task. America is youthful, but it can not always be young. Like an adolescent who must part with his broken family, America feels now the shock of transition. But a new and serene maturity will come if it is worked for. We must make a new declaration of independence, a spiritual rather than a political one this time. No place to be homesick for. We must now be homesick for our own familiar land, this land that is worthy of our nostalgia.

[*Vogue,* December 1, 1940]

NIGHT WATCH OVER FREEDOM

ON THIS NIGHT — the last dark evening of the old year and the first morning of the new — there will be listeners over all the earth. Big Ben will sound at midnight. It may be that in the last hour the Clock Tower itself will be damaged or destroyed. But even so the bells of Big Ben will be heard. For there is a tense listening independent of the ear, a listening that causes the blood to wait and the heart itself for a moment to be hushed.

England will hear Big Ben in darkness. Perhaps as the hour is tolled, there will be the roar of explosives and the deathly murmur of bombing planes — or the night may be a quiet one over there. In any case the bell will sound in our mind's ear. And these will be among the listeners: the sentries keeping watch over the dark channel; the city people in the air-raid shelters; and the homeless who huddle together on the platforms of the tubes; old farmers in wayside pubs. In the wards of hospitals the hurt and restless they also will hear. And somewhere a frightened child with an upturned face. A rough, rosy soldier on duty at an airport will blow warm breath into his cupped hands, stamp on the frosty ground, and stand silent for a moment at midnight. These, then, will hear — for the sound will echo through the cities and all the countryside of the dark island.

Nor will the echoes stop there. The time will not actually be midnight everywhere. But the twelve slow strokes will for a moment seem to effect a synthesis of time throughout the world. In the defeated lands Big Ben will bring hope and, to the souls of many, a fevered quiver of rebellion. And if the people of the Axis countries were allowed to hear this bell who knows what their feelings and their doubts might be?

We in America will be listeners on this New Year. In all the states the tones of Big Ben will be broadcast. From Oregon to Georgia, in the homes of the comfortable who taste egg-nog from silver cups and in the grim tenements of the poor, the English New Year will be heard. Down in the South it will be early evening. Quiet, orange firelight will flicker on kitchen walls, and in the cupboards there will be the hog-jowl and the black-eyed peas to bring good fortune in the coming year. On the Pacific coast the sun will still be shining. In the Northern homes, with the cold blue glow of snow outside, the gathered families will wait for the hour.

On this night, London may be grey with fog, or the clean moonlight may make of the Clock Tower a silhouette against the winter sky. But when the bells sound it will be the heartbeat of warring Britain—somber, resonant, and deeply sure. Yes, Big Ben will ring again this New Year, and over all the earth there will be listeners.

[*Vogue,* January 1, 1941]

BROOKLYN IS MY NEIGHBOURHOOD

BROOKLYN, in a dignified way, is a fantastic place. The street where I now live has a quietness and sense of permanence that seem to belong to the nineteenth century. The street is very short. At one end, there are comfortable old houses, with gracious façades and pleasant backyards in the rear. Down on the next block, the street becomes more heterogeneous, for there is a fire station; a convent; and a small candy factory. The street is bordered with maple-trees, and in the autumn the children rake up the leaves and make bonfires in the gutter.

It is strange in New York to find yourself living in a real neighbourhood. I buy my coal from the man who lives next-door. And I am very curious about the old lady living on my right. She has a mania for picking up stray, starving dogs. Besides a dozen of these dogs, she keeps a little green, shrewd monkey as her pet and chief companion. She is said to be very rich and very stingy. The druggist on the corner has told me she was once in jail for smashing the windows of a saloon in a temperance riot.

"The square of the hypotenuse of a right triangle is equal to —"

On coming into the corner drug store in the evening, you are apt to hear a desperate voice repeating some such maxim. Mr. Parker, the druggist, sits behind the counter after supper, struggling with his daughter's homework — she can't seem to get on well in school. Mr. Parker has owned his store for thirty years. He has a pale face, with watery grey eyes and a silky little yellow mustache that he wets and combs out frequently. He is rather like a cat. And when I weigh myself, he sidles up quietly beside me and peers over my shoulder as I adjust the scale. When the weights are balanced, he always gives me a quick little glance, but he has never made any comment, nor indicated in any way whether he thought I weighed too little or too much.

On every other subject, Mr. Parker is very talkative. He has always lived in Brooklyn, and his mind is a rag-bag for odd scraps of information. For instance, in our neighbourhood there is a narrow alley called Love Lane. "The alley comes by its name," he told me, "because more than a century ago two bachelors by the name of DeBevoise lived in the corner house with their niece, a girl of such beauty that her suitors mooned in the alley half the night, writing poetry on the fence." These same old uncles, Mr. Parker added, cultivated the first strawberries sold in New York in their back garden. It is pleasant to think of this old household — the parlour with the coloured glass windows glowing in the candlelight, the two old gentlemen brooding quietly over a game of chess, and the young niece, demure on a footstool, eating strawberries and cream.

"The square of the hypotenuse —" As you go out of the drug store, Mr. Parker's voice will carry on where he had left off, and his daughter will sit there, sadly popping her chewing-gum.

Comparing the Brooklyn that I know with Manhattan is like comparing a comfortable and complacent duenna to her more brilliant and neurotic sister. Things move more slowly out here (the street-cars still rattle leisurely down most of the main streets), and there is a feeling for tradition.

The history of Brooklyn is not so exciting as it is respectable. In the middle of the past century, many of the liberal intellectuals lived here, and Brooklyn was a hot-bed of abolitionist activity. Walt Whitman worked on the *Brooklyn Daily Eagle* until his anti-slavery editorials cost him his job. Henry Ward Beecher used to preach at the old Plymouth Church. Talleyrand lived here on Fulton Street during his exile in America, and he used to walk primly every day beneath the elm-trees. Whittier stayed frequently at the old Hooper home.

*

The first native of Brooklyn I got to know when I first came out here was the electrician who did some work at my house. He is a lively young Italian with a warm, quick face and a pleasant way of whistling operatic arias while on the job. On the third day he was working for me, he brought in a bottle of bright homemade wine, as his first child, a boy, had been born the night before. The wine was sour and clean to the tongue, and when we had drunk some of it the electrician invited me to a little supper to be held a week later at his house on the other side of Brooklyn, near Sheepshead Bay. The party was a fine occasion. The old grandfather who had come over from Italy sixty years ago was there. At night, the old man fishes for eels out in the Bay, and when the weather is fine he spends most of the day lying in a cart in the backyard, out in the sun. He had the face of a charming old satyr, and he held the new baby with the casualness of one who has walked the floor with many babies in his day.

"He is very ugly, this little one," he kept saying. "But it is clear that he will be smart. Smart and very ugly."

The food at the party was rich, wholesome Italian fare—*provolone* cheese, salami, pastries, and more of the red wine. A stream of kinsmen and neighbours kept coming in and out of the house all evening. This family had lived in the same house near the Bay for three generations, and the grandfather had not been out of Brooklyn for years.

Here in Brooklyn there is always the feeling of the sea. On the streets near the water-front, the air has a fresh, coarse smell, and there are many seagulls. One of the most gaudy streets I know stretches between Brooklyn Bridge and the Navy Yard. At three o'clock in the morning, when the rest of the city is silent and dark, you can come suddenly on a little area as vivacious as a country fair. It is Sand Street, the place where sailors spend their evenings when they come here to port. At any hour of the night some excitement is going on in Sand Street. The sunburned sailors swagger up and down the sidewalks with their girls. The bars are crowded, and there are dancing, music, and straight liquor at cheap prices.

*

These Sand Street bars have their own curious traditions also. Some of the women you find there are vivid old dowagers of the street who have such names as The Duchess or Submarine Mary. Every tooth in Submarine Mary's head is made of solid gold — and her smile is rich-looking and satisfied. She and the rest of these old habitués are greatly respected. They have a stable list of sailor pals and are known from Buenos Aires to Zanzibar. They are conscious of their fame and don't bother to dance or flirt like the younger girls, but sit comfortably in the centre of the room with their knitting, keeping a sharp eye on all that goes on. In one bar, there is a little hunchback who struts in proudly every evening, and is petted by everyone, given free drinks, and treated as a sort of mascot by the proprietor. There is a saying among sailors that when they die they want to go to Sand Street.

Cutting through the business and financial centre of Brooklyn is Fulton Street. Here are to be found dozens of junk and antique shops that are exciting to people who like old and fabulous things. I came to be quite at home in these places, as I bought most of my furniture there. If you know what you are about, there are good bargains to be found — old carved sideboards, elegant pier-glasses, beautiful Lazy Susans, and other odd pieces can be bought at half the price you would pay anywhere else. These shops have a musty, poky atmosphere, and the people who own them are an incredible crew.

The woman from whom I got most of my things is called Miss Kate. She is lean, dark, and haggard, and she suffers much from cold. When you go into the junk-shop, you will most likely find her hovering over a little coal stove in the back room. She sleeps every night wrapped in a Persian rug and lying on a green velvet Victorian couch. She has one of the handsomest and dirtiest faces I can remember.

Across the street from Miss Kate, there is a competitor with whom she often quarrels violently over prices — but still she always refers to him as "Ein Edler Mensch," and once when he was to be evicted for failure to pay the rent she put up the cash for him.

"Miss Kate is a good woman," this competitor said to me. "But she dislikes washing herself. So she only bathes once a year, when it is summer. I expect she's just about the dirtiest woman in Brooklyn." His voice as he said this was not at all malicious; rather, there was in it a quality of wondering pride. That is one of the things I love best about Brooklyn. Everyone is not expected to be exactly like everyone else.

[*Vogue,* March 1, 1941]

WE CARRIED OUR BANNERS—WE WERE PACIFISTS, TOO

*I*T IS THE SUMMER of 1941, and I am helping a friend to pack. My friend is called Mac, and he lives in a room across the hall from me. In the late afternoon, when the weather was fine and the sky over the city a pale grey-blue, we have often met up on the roof.

Mac would sit leaning against a chimney, usually with a book, as after office hours he goes to night classes at N.Y.U. Nearly always Sugar would be on the roof with him, her head resting on one of his knees. Sugar is a very small, very smart terrier who has the most finicky of manners. Now as we are packing, Sugar sits in the corner of the room, and occasionally she whines and gives a little shiver, as she knows that something is happening that she does not understand. We are packing because Mac has volunteered for the Army and has been accepted; he is going off to fight.

The room is in mad disorder — with books, clothes, and phonograph records on the floor. Scattered about are old newspapers with their blunt, black head-lines of destruction, their captions of ruin. Mac sorts out his possessions quickly, not hesitating about the things he can take with him and the things he will leave behind. Much must be left.

Mac is twenty-three — with a short, wiry body and red hair. He has a freckled face, and his expression is now rather sombre and scowling, as he is cutting a wisdom tooth and keeps feeling out the sore spot with his tongue. As we crate the records with excelsior and nail the boxes of books, we are both of us intent on that inward reckoning that departure and great change bring about.

What few words we say aloud are only the flotsam of thoughts within us. Our meditations probably follow the same track. Our backgrounds are similar. We have known secure childhoods, in homes neither rich nor very poor. We have had our share of formal education and have been allowed to seek for and to affirm our own spiritual values. In short, we have grown up as Americans. And we have much to think over, much to remember, and not a little to regret.

"But why did it take me so long? Huh?" Mac is saying. "Glued to the radio, talking, talking. Doing nothing. Why? Answer me that one!"

Sugar looks up at the sound of his voice. Mac has had her for six years. She sits across the table from him when he has his meals at home, and eats exactly what he eats — eggs for breakfast, carrots, anything. Whenever he offers her some special dainty he holds it close to her nose, and before taking it she has a pretty way of raising her right paw in a gesture halfway between begging and benediction.

But Mac pays no attention to Sugar now.

"There is this," he says. "A virtue is a virtue only insofar as it leads to good. But when it can be used as a weakness, as an instrument to make way for evil. . . ."

Mac balls up a sweater and throws it on a pile of clothes in the corner. "You know what I mean."

I do know what he means. We were all of us pacifists. In our adolescence and our youth, we had no notion that we would ever have to fight. War was evil. The last World War had no place in our memories, but we had heard and read all about it. Our heroes in childhood were not soldiers, but great adventurers.

There was Byrd. There was Lindbergh — I thought he was wonderful and wrote him a long letter to tell him so. But that was in 1927, ages ago.

Then later in High School. My High School was like any one of thousands of High Schools in America. On Thursdays, we studied a subject called current events. My teacher had a great spirit and a passion to instil in us the horrors of war. She need not have been so anxious; we were born to the pacifist point of view.

I remember the physical gestures and peculiarities of this teacher better than anything ever said in class — the way she rapped the top of her head with a pencil to emphasize a point, the way that, when she was exasperated, she took off her glasses, pressed her fingers to her eyeballs, and said, "Oh pshaw! Pshaw! Pshaw!" There was always a giggle when this happened, and she would put her glasses back on and peer all around resentfully.

A disarmament conference — the League of Nations — a new party in the German Reich led by a man called Hitler. None of these things meant very much. Everybody knew there could never be another war. What country could start such a thing again? And if in the future it happened — why that would be in Europe. And American faces would never rot in European mud again.

"They told the truth. They were right," Mac says, and I look up at him. He is still packing books. Among them are *Company K, A Farewell to Arms, The Road to War,* and *The Enormous Room.* It was in our adolescence that the culmination of all the agony and destruction of the past war was finally expressed. The influence of these books on us can not be exaggerated. Mac arranges the volumes in stacks according to their size.

"They were right, but only for their time. They could not have realized then that there are worse things even than war. You know?"

"Yes," I answer.

The books are now packed in their boxes, and Mac stops off for a rest. He goes over to the medicine cabinet, opens his mouth very wide, and paints his sore gum with iodine. Then he sits down on a packing-case, his forehead propped on his fists, his face pink and sweating.

"Listen!" Mac says suddenly. "Do you remember May the first, 1935? Can you think back that far?"

Sugar looks up at him, and, as he gives her no notice, she sighs so deeply that her ribs stand out, and she drops her head down on her paws.

"That May day was my first year at University, and I was a member of a students' club. We marched in the parade. I was carrying a big banner AGAINST WAR AND FASCISM. Everything was either black or white. War was evil, Fascism was evil — they were the same. We never knew then that we would ever have to choose between them."

"They were marching that year in Germany, too," I said quickly. "But they weren't choosing the banners they marched to."

"Yeah," Mac says. "They were marching all right."

Mac starts folding his good suit to put into the bag. "It was Spain," he says. "It was Spain that waked most of us up. . . .

"That was the first round, and we lost it. Then afterward we were forced to pull our punches for so long that most of us just gave up. We didn't make this war, so why should we have to fight in it. Why I ask you? Let's just sit around punch drunk and see what happens. Maybe that gorilla on the other side won't even notice that we're in the ring."

There is truth in what he has just said. The last year has a weird, drunken quality. The *Blitzkreig* — the collapse of Europe — funereal radio voices affirming each new loss — the debris that was once Democracy. We in America have not been able to grasp it all at once. We were prepared to fight for the betterment of Democracy, and to fight with Democratic means — that in itself is no paltry battle.

We never knew that the full force of our barrage would have to be turned outward in order to escape complete annihilation. We have been demoralized. It has taken us long, too long, to come to terms with our inward selves, to adjust our traditions to necessity, to reach the state of conviction that impels action. We have had to re-examine our ideals, and to leave much behind. We have had to face a moral crisis for which we were scantily equipped. But at last we have reached our conclusions and are ready to act. We have come through.

Democracy — intellectual and moral freedom, the liberty to work and live in the way most productive for us, the right to establish our individual spiritual values — that is the breath of the American ideal. And we Americans will fight to preserve it. We have clenched our giant fist; it will not open until we are victorious.

"Thank the Lord it's over," Mac says.

He may be speaking of the past indecisions, or of the packing. We have finished. The room has a sad, naked look with the boxes and suitcases piled up on the dusty floor. Mac goes down-stairs for beer, and when he comes back we close the door and go up to the roof. It is a quiet, warm late afternoon. Wet clothes are hanging on a line, and pigeons strut along the parapet. We sit resting with our backs against a chimney.

Mac opens the beer. Because of the warmth, the foam geysers up over the neck of the bottle and spills on his hand and arm. He holds out his arm to Sugar, and she licks it daintily. Evidently the taste pleases her, for very slowly she raises her right paw and begs for more; he draws her in between his knees and scratches her behind the ears. To-morrow Sugar will be sent on the train to Mac's brother in Delaware.

For a long time we are silent. When Mac speaks his voice is controlled and quiet:

"They say we know what we are fighting against, but that we don't make ourselves plain about what we are fighting for. They want us to stop off to form slogans. It is like asking a man who is being choked and in danger of suffocation why he puts up a struggle. He does not say to himself that he fights because with his wind-pipe clutched he can not get air. He does not remind himself that air contains oxygen, and it is by the process of oxidation that the body derives the energy by which it functions. He does not lie still and tell himself that he has three minutes of grace in which to find out his reasons for wanting to fight off his oppressor and to breathe. A man in such peril simply fights. He fights for release, for air, for life, and he struggles with every ounce of power in his body. He does not stop fighting until all trace of consciousness has left him, or until breath has been granted him once more."

Dark comes on. An airplane cruises in the deepening sky. Mac does not say anything further, there is no more need to talk. To-morrow he will be in the Army.

And Mac, the thousands of others like him, does not face the struggle ahead of us with hopped-up, specious feelings of glory. He knows what it will cost his generation in personal self-denial and in suffering. But he is done with questioning, finished with doubt.

[*Vogue,* July 15, 1941]

OUR HEADS ARE BOWED

ON THANKSGIVING, this November 1945, the day that is set aside for ritual gratitude to God, our heads are bowed. This day of thanks is a national day, and never has our country had more to be grateful for, and at the same time never have we so needed godly counsel. After the long years of universal agony and waste, the war is ended; today we rejoice in peace. But there is a gravity in our rejoicing, the sense of loss, the quiet sternness of power when combined with conscience. In a world of shattered cities and ruin, our land is one of the very few that has escaped the physical destruction of this war, a country of unblemished wholeness on this globe of misery and stunned want. It is with the deference proper to the suffering of unreckoned others that on this day our heads are bowed.

Thanksgiving is essentially a family day. It is the Thursday of November when the separate members of the family assemble to join in a day of shared feasting, mutual prayer. It comes at the end of the harvest season, when the bright grain is barned and the fruits of the earth have matured in all their lavish varieties — a season of golden richness before the fallow of the wintertime. But although our earth has been undisturbed by the wreck of war, we have known a more insidious disruption. These last Thanksgivings have been marked by absences. Our husbands, brothers and loved ones have been missing from the family gatherings; the strength of the nation has been away. So that at best our feasts were bleak. A great part of those who have been absent will not be in our homes today. They will observe another Thanksgiving in unfamiliar weathers and distant lands. And there are others coming homeward on the seas. But peace for most of us has restored a measure of serenity. The torn nerves can become more tranquil, the individual anguish of suspense has been eased or put at rest. It is in the time of greatest calamity, war, that human beings realize how fugitive is personal happiness and what a fragile grasp we bring to the guidance of our personal lives. For war and chance are indivisible. The sense of hazard is now quieted, and on this day of gratitude the homes of most of us can be free of anxiety and alarm. Many of us are fortunate in having our soldiers close to us at home and able to lead our prayer. For our soldiers, whether at home or far away, who have endured the ghastliness of war and suffered the terrors and miseries of battle that made possible the peace, our heads are bowed.

There is no family on this day who will not reflect the sorrow of those of us who have been dealt a deeper loss. There are our men in hospitals; most of these can with the aid of science — that science that can work equally for darkness as well as light — be cured and returned to us soon. But there are others who will never be whole again; the mutilated, blind and permanently maimed. For those who have suffered such affliction, we can only promise that the acknowledgment of our debt will endure through all our generation. The prisoners of war are home or soon will be here; we pray that those who have suffered the willful torments of our enemies will, with our love and patient care, soon overcome the shock, the debilitation, and regain the peace of health again. There are those loved ones who will never join with us in prayer again, those who have made the mute and final sacrifice of life. For the families of the dead only exquisite understanding of a poet can be trusted now.

> All the whole world is living without war,
> And yet I cannot find out any peace.

We pause in the voiceless prayer that those who have known this extremity of loss will find the strength to resist lasting despair, and will, through patience and sorrow, succeed to peace. For the grieving today our heads are bowed.

This is a national day, and we are a proud nation. Our land is broad, a country of many toils and many weathers. In another way our land is varied. We have not grown strong from bigotry and reasonless exclusions. We have grown mighty, not through prejudice and insularity, but by the peoples of many nations and the genius of varied racial strains. Our pride is not the narrow, distrustful pride of the weak. It is the pride of a generous nation, able to absorb the human gifts with which it has been endowed; and we pray that our pride will be free of all bigotry — the pride of the great as well as the strong. For this our heads are bowed.

On Thanksgiving, 1945, we pray for a rare wisdom. The last of the weapons of this past war have made it certain that, if peace cannot be maintained, the future of mankind is precarious as it has never been in all of history. This past war has left whole continents of hunger, of the dazed lost. We pray that as a nation we will have the wisdom to justly and generously use our power, to work with others so that a lasting order can be secured. With the grave knowledge of our responsibility we pray for clarity of spirit, moral might. The soul of humanity must not be exceeded by the amoral mind. And so it is for the greatest of all blessings, wisdom of heart, that today, in humility, our heads are bowed. Amen.

[*Mademoiselle,* November 1945]

CHRISTMAS

HOME FOR CHRISTMAS

SOMETIMES IN AUGUST, weary of the vacant, broiling afternoon, my younger brother and sister and I would gather in the dense shade under the oak tree in the back yard and talk of Christmas and sing carols. Once after such a conclave, when the tunes of the carols still lingered in the heat-shimmered air, I remember climbing up into the tree-house and sitting there alone for a long time.

Brother called up: "What are you doing?"

"Thinking," I answered.

"What are you thinking about?"

"I don't know."

"Well, how can you be thinking when you don't know what you are thinking about?"

I did not want to talk with my brother. I was experiencing the first wonder about the mystery of Time. Here I was, on this August afternoon, in the tree-house, in the burnt, jaded yard, sick and tired of all our summer ways. (I had read *Little Women* for the second time, *Hans Brinker and the Silver Skates, Little Men,* and *Twenty Thousand Leagues under the Sea.* I had read movie magazines and even tried to read love stories in the *Woman's Home Companion* — I was so sick of everything.) How could it be that I was I and now was now when in four months it would be Christmas, wintertime, cold weather, twilight and the glory of the Christmas tree? I puzzled about the *now* and *later* and rubbed the inside of my elbow until there was a little roll of dirt between my forefinger and thumb. Would the *now* I of the tree-house and the August afternoon be the same *I* of winter, firelight and the Christmas tree? I wondered.

My brother repeated: "You say you are thinking but you don't know what you are thinking about. What are you really doing up there? Have you got some secret candy?"

September came, and my mother opened the cedar chest and we tried on winter coats and last year's sweaters to see if they would do again. She took the three of us downtown and bought us new shoes and school clothes.

Christmas was nearer on the September Sunday that Daddy rounded us up in the car and drove us out on dusty country roads to pick elderberry blooms. Daddy made wine from elderberry blossoms — it was a yellow-white wine, the color of weak winter sun. The wine was dry to the wry side — indeed, some years it turned to vinegar. The wine was served at Christmastime with slices of fruitcake when company came. On November Sundays we went to the woods with a big basket of fried chicken dinner, thermos jug and coffee-pot. We hunted partridge berries in the pine woods near our town. These scarlet berries grew hidden underneath the glossy brown pine needles that lay in a slick carpet beneath the tall wind-singing trees. The bright berries were a Christmas decoration, lasting in water through the whole season.

In December the windows downtown were filled with toys, and my brother and sister and I were given two dollars apiece to buy our Christmas presents. We patronized the ten-cent stores, choosing between jackstones, pencil boxes, water colors and satin handkerchief holders. We would each buy a nickel's worth of lump milk chocolate at the candy counter to mouth as we trudged from counter to counter, choice to choice. It was exacting and final — taking several afternoons — for the dime stores would not take back or exchange.

Mother made fruitcakes, and for weeks ahead the family picked out the nut meats of pecans and walnuts, careful of the bitter layer of the pecans that lined your mouth with nasty fur. At the last I was allowed to blanch the almonds, pinching the scalded nuts so that they sometimes hit the ceiling or bounced across the room. Mother cut slices of citron and crystallized pineapple, figs and dates, and candied cherries were added whole. We cut rounds of brown paper to line the pans.

Usually the cakes were mixed and put into the oven when we were in school. Late in the afternoon the cakes would be finished, wrapped in white napkins on the breakfast-room table. Later they would be soaked in brandy. These fruitcakes were famous in our town, and Mother gave them often as Christmas gifts. When company came thin slices of fruitcake, wine and coffee were always served. When you held a slice of fruitcake to the window or the firelight the slice was translucent, pale citron green and yellow and red, with the glow and richness of our church windows.

Daddy was a jeweler, and his store was kept open until midnight all Christmas week. I, as the eldest child, was allowed to stay up late with Mother until Daddy came home. Mother was always nervous without a "man in the house." (On those rare occasions when Daddy had to stay overnight on business in Atlanta, the children were armed with a hammer, saw and a monkey wrench. When pressed about her anxieties Mother claimed she was afraid of "escaped convicts or crazy people." I never saw an escaped convict, but once a "crazy" person did come to see us. She was an old, old lady dressed in elegant black taffeta, my mother's second cousin once removed, and came on a tranquil Sunday morning and announced that she had always liked our house and she intended to stay with us until she died. Her sons and daughters and grandchildren gathered around to plead with her as she sat rocking in our front porch rocking chair and she left not unwillingly when they promised a car ride and ice cream.) Nothing ever happened on those evenings in Christmas week, but I felt grown, aged suddenly by trust and dignity. Mother confided in secrecy what the younger children were getting from Santa Claus. I knew where the Santa Claus things were hidden, and was appointed to see that my brother and sister did not go into the back-room closet or the wardrobe in our parents' room.

Christmas Eve was the longest day, but it was lined with the glory of tomorrow. The sitting-room smelled of floor wax and the clean, cold odor of the spruce tree. The Christmas tree stood in a corner of the front room, tall as the ceiling, majestic, undecorated. It was our family custom that the tree was not decorated until after we children were in bed on Christmas Eve night. We went to bed very early, as soon as it was winter dark. I lay in the bed beside my sister and tried to keep her awake.

"You want to guess again about your Santa Claus?"

"We've already done that so much," she said.

My sister slept. And there again was another puzzle. How could it be that when she opened her eyes it would be Christmas while I lay awake in the dark for hours and hours? The time was the same for both of us, and yet not at all the same. What was it? How? I thought of Bethlehem and cherry candy, Jesus and skyrockets. It was dark when I awoke. We were allowed to get up on Christmas at five o'clock. Later I found out that Daddy juggled the clock Christmas Eve so that five o'clock was actually six. Anyway it was always still dark when we rushed in to dress by the kitchen stove. The rule was that we dress and eat breakfast before we could go in to the Christmas tree. On Christmas morning we always had fish roe, bacon and grits for breakfast. I grudged every mouthful — for who wanted to fill up on breakfast when there in the sitting-room was candy, at least three whole boxes? After breakfast we lined up, and carols were started. Our voices rose naked and mysterious as we filed through the door to the sitting-room. The carol, unfinished, ended in raw yells of joy.

The Christmas tree glittered in the glorious, candlelit room. There were bicycles and bundles wrapped in tissue paper. Our stockings hanging from the mantlepiece bulged with oranges, nuts and smaller presents. The next hours were paradise. The blue dawn at the window brightened, and the candles were blown out. By nine o'clock we had ridden the wheel presents and dressed in the clothes gifts. We visited the neighborhood children and were visited in turn. Our cousins came and grown relatives from distant neighborhoods. All through the morning we ate chocolates. At two or three o'clock the Christmas dinner was served. The dining-room table had been let out with extra leaves and the very best linen was laid — satin damask with a rose design. Daddy asked the blessing, then stood up to carve the turkey. Dressing, rice and giblet gravy were served. There were cut-glass dishes of sparkling jellies and stateliness of festal wine. For dessert there was always sillabub or charlotte and fruitcake. The afternoon was almost over when dinner was done.

At twilight I sat on the front steps, jaded by too much pleasure, sick at the stomach and worn out. The boy next door skated down the street in his new Indian suit. A girl spun around on a crackling son-of-a-gun. My brother waved sparklers. Christmas was over. I thought of the monotony of Time ahead, unsolaced by the distant glow of paler festivals, the year that stretched before another Christmas — eternity.

[*Mademoiselle,* December 1949]

THE DISCOVERY OF CHRISTMAS

THE CHRISTMAS of my fifth year, when we still lived in the old downtown Georgia home, I had just recovered from scarlet fever, and that Christmas Day I overcame a rivalry that like the fever had mottled and blanched my sickened heart. This rivalry that changed to love overshadowed my discovery that Santa Claus and Jesus were not the kin I had supposed.

The scarlet fever came first. In November my brother Budge and I were quarantined in the back room and for six weeks' time hovered over thermometers, potties, alcohol rubs and Rosa Henderson. Rosa was the practical nurse who cared for us, as Mother had deserted me for my hated rival — the new baby sister. Mother would half-open the door and pass the presents that came to the house to Rosa, calling out some words before she shut the door. She did not bring the baby and I was glad of that. There were many presents and Rosa put them in a big soapbox between the beds of my brother and me. There were games, modeling clay, paint sets, cutting-out scissors and engines.

Budge was much littler than I was. He was too little to count straight, to play Parcheesi, to wipe himself. He could only model squashed balls and cut out easy, big round things like magazine pictures of Santa Claus. Then his tongue would wiggle out of the corner of his mouth because of the difficulty. I cut out the hard things and paper dolls. When he played the harp it made a sickening shriek. I played *Dixie* and Christmas carols.

Toward dark Rosa read aloud to us. She read *Child Life,* storybooks or a *True Confessions* magazine. Her soft, stumbling voice would rise and fall in the quiet room as firelit shadows staggered gold and gray upon the walls. At that time there were only the changing tones of her colored voice and the changing walls in the firelight. Except sometimes the baby cried and I felt as if a worm crawled inside me and played the harp to drown out the sound.

It was late fall when the quarantine began and through the closed windows we could see the autumn leaves falling against the blue sky and sunlight. We sang:

> Come, little leaves, said the wind one day,
> Come o'er the meadows with me and play . . .

Then suddenly one morning Jack Frost silvered the grass and roof tops. Rosa mentioned that Christmas was not long away.

"How long?"

"About as long as that settlelord chain, I reckon." Toward the end of the quarantine we had been making a Celluloid chain of many different colors. I puzzled about the answer and Budge thought and put his tongue on the corner of his mouth. Rosa added, "Christmas is on the twenty-fifth of December — directly I will count the days. If you listen you can hear the reindeers come galloping from the North Pole. It's not long."

"Will we be loose from this old room by then?"

"I trust the Lord."

A sudden terrible thought came to me. "Are people ever sick on Christmas?"

"Yes, Baby." Rosa was making supper toast by the fire, turning it carefully with a long toast fork. Her voice was like torn paper when she said again, "My little son died on Christmas Day."

"Died! Sherman died!"

"You know it isn't Sherman," she said sternly. "Sherman comes to our winder every day and you know it." Sherman was a big boy and after school he would stand by our window and Rosa would open it from the bottom and talk with him a long time and sometimes give him a dime to go to the store. Sherman held his nose all the time he was at the window so that his voice twanged, like a ukulele string. "It was Sherman's little brother — a long time ago."

"Was he sick with scarlet fever?"

"No. He burned to death on Christmas morning. He was just a baby and Sherman put him down on the hearth to play with him. Then — childlike — Sherman forgot about him and left him alone on the hearth. The fire popped and a spark caught his little nightgown, and by the time I knew about it my baby was — that was how come I got this here wrinkled white scar on my neck."

"Was your baby like our new baby?"

"Near 'bout the same age."

I thought about it a long time before I said: "Was Sherman glad?"

"Why, what shape of thoughts is in your head, Sister?"

"I don't like babies," I said.

"You will like the baby later on. Just like you love your brother now."

"Bonny smells bad," I said.

"Most every child don't like the new baby until they get used to it."

"Are *every* and *ever* the same?" I asked.

Those were the days when we were peeling. Every day Budge and I peeled strips and patches of skin and saved them in a pillbox.

"I wonder what we're going to do with all this skin we've saved?"

"Face that when the time comes, Sister. Enjoy it while you can."

"I wonder what we're going to do with this long chain we've made." I looked at the chain that was piled in the box between the beds of my brother and me. It covered all the other toys — the dolls, engines and all.

The quarantine ended and the joy of our release battled with a sudden, inexplicable grief: all our toys were going to be burned. Every toy, the chain, even the peeled skin, which seemed the most terrible loss of all.

"It's on account of the germs," Rosa said. "Everything burned and the beds and mattresses will go to the germ disinfectory man. And the room scoured with Lysol."

I stood on the threshold of the room after the germ man had gone.

There were no echoes of toys — no beds, no furniture. The room was bitter cold, and the damp floor was sharp-smelling, the windows wet. My heart shut with the closing door.

Mother had sewed me a red dress for the Christmas season. Budge and I were free to walk in all the rooms and go out of the yard. But I was not happy. The baby was always in my mother's lap. Mary, the cook, would say, "Goosa-goosa-ga," and Daddy would throw the baby in the air.

There was a terrible song that Christmas:

> Hang up the baby's stocking;
> Be sure you don't forget —
> The dear little dimpled darling!
> She ne'er saw Christmas yet . . .

I hated the whining tune and the words so much that I put my fingers in my ears and hummed *Dixie* until the talk changed to Santa's reindeer, the North Pole and the magic of Christmas.

Three days before Christmas the real and the magic collided so suddenly that my world of understanding was instantly scattered. For some reason I don't remember now, I opened the door of the scarlet-fever room and stopped on the threshold, spellbound and trembling. The room rioted before my unbelieving eyes. Nothing familiar was there and the space was filled with everything Budge and I had written on the Santa Claus list and sent up the chimney. All that and even more — so that the room was like a Santa Claus room in a department store. There were a tricycle, a doll, a train with tracks and a child's table and four chairs. I doubted the reality of what I saw and looked at the familiar tree outside the window and at a crack on the ceiling I knew well. Then I moved around with the light, secret way of a child who meddles. I touched the table, the toys with a careful forefinger. They were touchable, real. Then I saw a wonderful, unasked-for thing — a green monkey with an organ grinder. The monkey wore a scarlet coat and looked very real with his monkey-anxious face and worried eyes. I loved the monkey but did not dare touch him. I looked around the Santa Claus room a last time. There was a hush, a stasis in my heart that follows the shock of revelation. I closed the door and walked away slowly, weighed by too much wisdom.

Mother was knitting in the front room and the baby was there in her play pen.

I took a big breath and said in a demanding voice: "Why are the Santa Claus things in the back room?"

Mother had the stumbling look of someone who is telling a story. "Why, Sister, Santa Claus asked your father if he could store some things in the back room."

I didn't believe it and said: "I think that Santa Claus is only parents."

"Why, Sister, darling!"

"I wondered about chimneys. Butch doesn't even have a chimney but Santa Claus always comes to him."

"Sometimes he walks in the door."

For the first time I knew my mother was telling me stories and I was thinking. "Is Jesus real? Santa Claus and Jesus are close kin, I know."

Mamma put down her knitting. "Santa Claus is toys and stores and Jesus is church."

This mention of church brought to me thoughts of boredom, colored windows, organ music, restlessness. I hated church and Jesus if church was Jesus. I loved only Santa Claus and he was not real.

Mother tried again: "Jesus is as the holy infant — like Bonny. The Christ child."

This was the worst of all. I squatted on the floor and bawled in the baby's face, "Santa Claus is only parents! Jesus is —"

The baby began to cry and Mother picked her up and cuddled her in her lap. "Now you behave yourself, young lady; you're making Bonny cry."

"I hate that old ugly Bonny," I wailed and went to the hall to cry.

Christmas Day was like a twice-done happening. I played with the monkey under the tree and helped Budge lay the tracks for the train. The baby had blocks and a rubber doll and she cried and didn't play.

Budge and I ate a whole layer of our box of Treasure Island chocolates and by afternoon we were jaded by play and candy.

Later I was sitting on the floor alone in the Christmasy room except for the baby in her play pen. The bright tree glowed in the winter light. Suddenly I thought of Rosa Henderson and the baby who was burned on Christmas Day. I looked at Bonny and glanced around the room. Mother and Daddy had gone to visit my Uncle Will, and Mary was in the kitchen. I was alone. Carefully I lifted the baby and put her on the hearth. In the unclear conscious of five years old I did not feel that I was doing wrong. I wondered if the fire would pop and went to the back room with my brother, sad and troubled.

It was our family custom to have fireworks on Christmas night. Daddy would light a bonfire after dark and we would shoot Roman candles and skyrockets. I remembered. The box of fireworks was on the mantlepiece of the back room and I opened it and selected two Roman candles. I asked Budge, "Do you want to do something fun?" I knew clearly this was wrong. But, angry and sad, I wanted to do wrong. I held the Roman candles to the fire and gave one to Budge. "Watch here."

I thought I remembered the fireworks, but I had never seen anything like this. After a hiss and sputter the Roman candles, violent and alive, shot in streams of yellow and red. We stood on opposite sides of the room and the blazing fireworks ricocheted from wall to wall in an arch of splendor and terror. It lasted a long time and we stood transfixed in the radiant, fearful room. When finally it was finished, my hostile feelings had disappeared. I was quiet in the very silent room.

I thought I heard the baby cry, but when I ran to the living room I knew she was not crying nor had she been burned and gone up the chimney. She had turned over and was crawling toward the Christmas tree. Her little-fingered hands were on the floor, her nightgown was hiked over her diapers. I had never seen Bonny crawl before and I watched her with the first feelings of love and pride, the old hostility gone forever.

I played with Bonny with a heart cleansed of jealousy and joyful for the first time in many months. I was reconciled that Santa Claus was only family but with this new tranquility, I felt maybe my family and Jesus were somehow kin. Soon afterward, when we moved to a new house in the suburbs, I taught Bonny how to walk and even let her hold the monkey while I played the organ grinder.

[*Mademoiselle,* December 1953]

A HOSPITAL CHRISTMAS EVE

I MET CAROL a few days before the Christmas when we were both patients in the hospital for physical therapy. Carol was a very busy girl; she painted in watercolors, drew with crayons, and most of all she planned for her future. At that time, she was planning for a Christmas Eve party, for it was to be the first time in her life that she was going to walk with her new prosthetic legs to a party.

Carol was an amputee. She had been born with legs so twisted that when she was nineteen years old, she had them amputated.

On this Christmas Eve, there were loads of visitors in the ward, families and friends of the patients' and parties organized by the hospital. But for Carol it was a catastrophe. The party she had yearned to go to was denied her because one of the legs was being repaired. It was going to ruin her Christmas Eve, and when I looked at her, I saw that silently, bitterly, she was weeping.

I asked her to come over to see me. She was very adept at her wheelchair and came over, still crying.

"Of all the times in the year this leg had to be fixed — just when I was so looking forward to walking to the party and showing my friends my new legs."

We talked for a while, and I read to her the most living piece of literature, except for the Bible, that I know. James Joyce's "The Dead."

> A few light taps upon the pane made him turn to the window. It had begun to snow again. He watched sleepily the flakes, silver and dark, falling obliquely against the lamplight. The time had come for him to set out on his journey westward. Yes, the newspapers were right: snow was general all over Ireland. It was falling on every part of the dark central plain, on the treeless hills, falling softly upon the Bog of Allen

> and, farther westward, softly falling into the dark mutinous Shannon waves. It was falling, too, upon every part of the lonely churchyard on the hill where Michael Furey lay buried. It lay thickly drifted on the crooked crosses and headstones, on the spears of the little gate, on the barren thorns. His soul swooned slowly as he heard the snow falling faintly through the universe and faintly falling, like the descent of their last end, upon all the living and the dead.

I read it as much to comfort myself as to comfort her, and the beauty of the language brought peace and loveliness to both of us on that Christmas Eve in that hospital ward.

She was a girl of magnificent courage, accepting the infirmities of her life with grace and equanimity. Still, I knew that she was troubled about the party, because she repeated, "Tonight of all nights, when I was going to walk in and show my friends."

The doctors also were troubled, and suddenly, like a rising wind, there was a small commotion in the corridor. News was being passed around that Carol's leg was going to be fixed in time and she could go to her party, after all. There was general rejoicing in the nine-bed ward, and Carol wept again, with excitement.

When it was time for the party to begin, Carol was dressed immaculately and wearing her finest clothes. Her legs were brought to her, and she used the skills for walking that she had been taught so very recently. A doctor looked in the doorway to see how she was getting on, and the therapist said, "Good girl, Carol."

She checked the straps on her prosthetic legs, and then she struggled to get into a standing position, and with her head held high, she walked proudly down the corridor of the ward to where her friends were waiting for her.

I knew that the long months of suffering, heroism, hard work and courage had paid off and that Carol would really be all right.

The last time I heard from her, she was attending college, joining in all the student activities, and was planning to teach physio-therapy after graduation.

[*McCall's,* December 1967, published posthumously]

WRITERS AND WRITING

HOW I BEGAN TO WRITE

*I*N OUR OLD GEORGIA HOME we used to have two sitting-rooms — a back one and a front one — with folding doors between. These were the family living-rooms and the theatre of my shows. The front sitting-room was the auditorium, the back sitting-room the stage. The sliding doors the curtain. In wintertime the firelight flickered dark and glowing on the walnut doors, and in the last strained moments before the curtain you noticed the ticking of the clock on the mantlepiece, the old tall clock with the glass front of painted swans. In summertime the rooms were stifling until the time for curtain, and the clock was silenced by sounds of yard-boy whistling and distant radios. In winter, frost flowers bloomed on the windowpanes (the winters in Georgia are very cold), and the rooms were drafty, quiet. The open summer lifted the curtains with each breeze, and there were the smells of sun-hot flowers and, toward twilight, watered grass. In winter we had cocoa after the show and in summer orange crush or lemonade. Winter and summer the cakes were always the same. They were made by Lucille, the cook we had in those days, and I have never tasted cakes as good as those cakes we used to have. The secret of their goodness lay, I believe, in the fact that they were always cakes that failed. They were chocolate raisin cupcakes that did not rise, so that there was no proper cupcake cap — the cakes were dank, flat and dense with raisins. The charm of those cakes was alogether accidental.

As the eldest child in our family I was the custodian, the counter of the cakes, the boss of all our shows. The repertory was eclectic, running from hashed-over movies to Shakespeare and shows I made up and sometimes wrote down in my nickel Big Chief notebooks. The cast was everlastingly the same — my younger brother, Baby Sister and myself. The cast was the most serious handicap. Baby Sister was in those days a stomachy ten-year old who was terrible in death scenes, fainting spells and such-like necessary parts. When Baby Sister swooned to a sudden death she would prudently look around beforehand and fall very carefully on sofa or chair. (Once, I remember, such a death fall broke both legs of one of Mama's favorite chairs.)

As director of the shows I could put up with terrible acting, but there was one thing I simply could not stand. Sometimes, after coaching and drilling half the afternoon, the actors would decide to abandon the whole project just before curtain time and wander out into the yard to play. "I struggle and work on a show all afternoon, and now you run out on me," I would yell, past endurance at these times. "You're nothing but children! Children! I've got a good mind to shoot you dead." But they only gulped the drinks and ran out with the cakes.

The props were impromptu, limited only by Mama's modest interdictions. The top drawer of the linen closet was out of bounds and we had to make do with second-best towels and tablecloths and sheets in the plays that called for nurses, nuns and ghosts.

The sitting-room shows ended when first I discovered Eugene O'Neill. It was the summer when I found his books down in the library and put his picture on the mantlepiece in the back sitting-room. By autumn I was writing a three-acter about revenge and incest — the curtain rose on a graveyard and, after scenes of assorted misery, fell on a catafalque. The cast consisted of a blind man, several idiots and a mean old woman of one hundred years. The play was impractical for performance under the old conditions in the sitting rooms. I gave what I called a "reading" to my patient parents and a visiting aunt.

Next, I believe, it was Nietzsche and a play called *The Fire of Life.* The play had two characters — Jesus Christ and Friedrich Nietzsche — and the point I prized about the play was that it was written in verses that rhymed. I gave a reading of this play, too, and afterward the children came in from the yard, and we drank cocoa and ate the fallen, lovely raisin cakes in the back sitting-room by the fire. "Jesus?" my aunt asked when she was told. "Well, religion is a nice subject anyway."

*

By that winter the family rooms, the whole town, seemed to pinch and cramp my adolescent heart. I longed for wanderings. I longed especially for New York. The firelight on the walnut folding doors would sadden me, and the tedious sound of the old swan clock. I dreamed of the distant city of skyscrapers and snow, and New York was the happy mise en scène of that first novel I wrote when I was fifteen years old. The details of the book were queer: ticket collectors on the subway, New York front yards — but by that time it did not matter, for already I had begun another journey. That was the year of Dostoevski, Chekhov and Tolstoy — and there were the intimations of an unsuspected region equidistant from New York. Old Russia and our Georgia rooms, the marvelous solitary region of simple stories and the inward mind.

[*Mademoiselle,* September 1948]

THE RUSSIAN REALISTS AND SOUTHERN LITERATURE

*I*N THE SOUTH during the past fifteen years a genre of writing has come about that is sufficiently homogeneous to have led critics to label it "the Gothic School." This tag, however, is unfortunate. The effect of a Gothic tale may be similar to that of a Faulkner story in its evocation of horror, beauty, and emotional ambivalence — but this effect evolves from opposite sources; in the former the means used are romantic or supernatural, in the latter a peculiar and intense realism. Modern Southern writing seems rather to be most indebted to Russian literature, to be the progeny of the Russian realists. And this influence is not accidental. The circumstances under which Southern literature has been produced are strikingly like those under which the Russians functioned. In both old Russia and the South up to the present time a dominant characteristic was the cheapness of human life.

Toward the end of the nineteenth century the Russian novelists, particularly Dostoievsky, were criticized harshly for their so called "cruelty." This same objection is now being raised against the new Southern writers. On first thought the accusation seems puzzling. Art, from the time of the Greek tragedians on, has unhesitatingly portrayed violence, madness, murder, and destruction. No single instance of "cruelty" in Russian or Southern writing could not be matched or outdone by the Greeks, the Elizabethans, or, for that matter, the creators of the Old Testament. Therefore it is not the specific "cruelty" itself that is shocking, but the manner in which it is presented. And it is in this approach to life and suffering that the Southerners are so indebted to the Russians. The technique briefly is this: a bold and outwardly callous juxtaposition of the tragic with the humorous, the immense with the trivial, the sacred with the bawdy, the whole soul of a man with a materialistic detail.

To the reader accustomed to the classical traditions this method has a repellent quality. If, for instance, a child dies and the life and death of this child is presented in a single sentence, and if the author passes over this without comment or apparent pity but goes on with no shift in tone to some trivial detail — this method of presentation seems cynical. The reader is used to having the relative values of an emotional experience categorized by the author. And when the author disclaims this responsibility the reader is confused and offended.

Marmeladov's funeral supper in *Crime and Punishment* and *As I Lay Dying,* by William Faulkner, are good examples of this type of realism. The two works have much in common. Both deal with the subject of death. In both there is a fusion of anguish and farce that acts on the reader with an almost physical force. Marveladov's violent death, Katerina Ivanovna's agitation about the supper, the details of the food served, the clerk "who had not a word to say for himself and smelt abominably" — on the surface the whole situation would seem to be a hopeless emotional rag-bag. In the face of agony and starvation the reader suddenly finds himself laughing at the absurdities between Katerina Ivanovna and the landlady, or smiling at the antics of the little Pole. And unconsciously after the laughter the reader feels guilty; he senses that the author has duped him in some way.

Farce and tragedy have always been used as foils for each other. But it is rare, except in the works of the Russians and the Southerners, that they are superimposed one upon the other so that their effects are experienced simultaneously. It is this emotional composite that has brought about the accusations of "cruelty." D. S. Mirsky, in commenting on a passage from Dostoievsky, says: "Though the element of humor is unmistakably present, it is a kind of humor that requires a rather peculiar constitution to amuse."

In Faulkner's *As I Lay Dying,* this fusion is complete. The story deals with the funeral journey made by Anse Bundren to bury his wife. He is taking the body to his wife's family graveyard some forty miles away; the journey takes him and his children several days and in the course of it the body decomposes in the heat and they meet with a mad plethora of disasters. They lose their mules while fording a stream, one son breaks his leg and it becomes gangrenous, another son goes mad, the daughter is seduced — a more unholy cortege could hardly be imagined. But the immensities of these disasters are given no more accent than the most inconsequential happenings. Anse throughout the story has his mind on the false teeth he is going to buy when he reaches the town. The girl is concerned with some cake she has brought with her to sell. The boy with the gangrenous leg keeps saying of the pain, "It don't bother me none," and his main worry is that his box of carpenter's tools will be lost on the way. The author reports this confusion of values but takes on himself no spiritual responsibility.

To understand this attitude one has to know the South. The South and old Russia have much in common sociologically. The South has always been a section apart from the rest of the United States, having interests and a personality distinctly its own. Economically and in other ways it has been used as a sort of colony to the rest of the nation. The poverty is unlike anything known in other parts of this country. In social structure there is a division of classes similar to that in old Russia. The South is the only part of the nation having a definite peasant class. But in spite of social divisions the people of the South are homogeneous. The Southerner and the Russian are both "types" in that they have certain recognizable and national psychological traits. Hedonistic, imaginative, lazy, and emotional — there is surely a cousinly resemblance.

In both the South and old Russia the cheapness of life is realized at every turn. The thing itself, the material detail, has an exaggerated value. Life is plentiful; children are born and they die, or if they do not die they live and struggle. And in the fight to maintain existence the whole life and suffering of a human being can be bound up in ten acres of washed out land, in a mule, in a bale of cotton. In Chekhov's, "The Peasants," the loss of the samovar in the hut is as sad, if not sadder, than the death of Nikolai or the cruelty of the old grandmother. And in *Tobacco Road,* Jeeter Lester's bargain, the swapping of his daughter for seven dollars and a throw-in, is symbolical. Life, death, the experiences of the spirit, these come and go and we do not know for what reason; but the *thing* is there, it remains to plague or comfort, and its value is immutable.

Gogol is credited to be the first of the realists. In "The Overcoat" the little clerk identifies his whole life with his new winter cloak, and loses heart and dies when it is stolen. From the time of Gogol, or from about 1850 until 1900, imaginative writing in Russia can be regarded as one artistic growth. Chekhov differs certainly from Aksakov and from Turgenev, but taken all in all the approach to their material and the general technique is the same. Morally the attitude is this: human beings are neither good nor evil, they are only unhappy and more or less adjusted to their unhappiness. People are born into a world of confusion, a society in which the system of values is so uncertain that who can say if a man is worth more than a load of hay, or if life itself is precious enough to justify the struggle to obtain the material objects necessary for its maintenance. This attitude was perhaps characteristic of all Russians during those times, and the writers only reported exactly what was true in their time and place. It is the unconscious moral approach, the fundamental spiritual basis of their work. But this by no means precludes a higher conscious level. And it is in the great philosophical novels that the culmination of Russian realism has been reached.

In the space of fourteen years, from 1866 to 1880, Dostoievsky wrote his four masterpieces: *Crime and Punishment, The Idiot, The Possessed,* and *The Brothers Karamazov.* These works are extremely complex. Dostoievsky, in the true Russian tradition, approaches life from a completely unbiased point of view; the evil, the confusion of life, he reports with the sharpest candor, fusing the most diverse emotions into a composite whole. But in addition to this he employs the analytical approach. It is almost as though having long looked on life and having faithfully reflected what he has seen in his art, he is appalled both by life itself and by what he has written. And unable to reject either, or to delude himself, he assumes the supreme responsibility and answers the riddle of life itself. But to do so he would have to be a Messiah. Sociologically these problems could never be altogether solved, and besides Dostoievsky was indifferent to economic theories. And it is in his role as a Messiah that Dostoievsky fails to meet the responsibility he has assumed. The questions he poses are too immense. They are like angry demands to God. Why has man let himself be demeaned and allowed his spirit to be corrupted by matter? Why is there evil? Why poverty and suffering? Dostoievsky demands magnificently, but his solution, the "new Christianity," does not answer; it is almost as though he uses Christ as a contrivance.

The "solution" to *Crime and Punishment* is a personal solution, the problems were metaphysical and universal. Raskolnikov is a symbol of the tragic inability of man to find an inward harmony with this world of disorder. The problem deals with the evils of society, and Raskolnikov is only a result of this discordance. By withdrawal, by personal expiation, by the recognition of a personal God, a Raskolnikov may or may not find a subjective state of grace. But if so only a collateral issue has been resolved; the basic problem remains untouched. It is like trying to reach the Q.E.D. of a geometrical problem by means of primer arithmetic.

As a moral analyst Tolstoi is clearer. He not only demands why, but what and how as well. From the time he was about fifty years of age his *Confessions* give us a beautiful record of a human being in conflict with a world of disharmony. "I felt," he wrote, "that something had broken within me on which my life had always rested, that I had nothing left to hold on to, and that morally my life had stopped." He goes on to admit that from an outward point of view his own personal life was ideal — he was in good health, unworried by finances, content in his family. Yet the whole of life around him seemed grotesquely out of balance. He writes: "The meaningless absurdity of life — it is the only incontestable knowledge accessible to man." Tolstoi's conversion is too well known to need more than mention here. In essence it is the same as Raskolnikov's as it is a purely solitary spiritual experience and fails to solve the problem as a whole.

But the measure of success achieved by these metaphysical and moral explorations is not of the greatest importance in itself. Their value is primarily catalytic. It is the way in which these moral probings affect the work as a whole that counts. And the effect is enormous. For Dostoievsky, Tolstoi, and the minor moralists brought to Russian realism one element that had hitherto been obscure or lacking. That is the element of passion.

Gogol has an imaginative creativeness that is overwhelming. As a satirist he has few equals, and his purely technical equipment is enormous. But of passion he has not a trace. Aksakov, Turgenev, Herzen, Chekhov, diverse as their separate geniuses are, they are alike in lacking this particular level of emotion. In the work of Dostoievsky and Tolstoi it is as though Russian literature suddenly closed its fist, and the whole literary organism was affected; there was a new tenseness, a gathering together of resources, a radically tightened nervous tone. With the moralists Russian realism reached its most fervent and glorious phase.

From the viewpoint of artistic merit it would be absurd to compare the new Southern writers with the Russians. It is only in their approach to their material that analogies can be drawn. The first real novel (this does not include old romances) to be written in the South did not appear until after 1900, when Russian realism was already on the decline. *Barren Ground,* by Ellen Glasgow, marked the beginning of an uncertain period of development, and Southern literature can only be considered to have made its start during the past fifteen years. But with the arrival of Caldwell and Faulkner a new and vital outgrowth began. And the South at the present time boils with literary energy. W. J. Cash in *The Mind of the South* says that if these days you shoot off a gun at random below the Mason-Dixon line you are bound by the law of averages to hit a writer.

An observer should not criticize a work of art on the grounds that it lacks certain qualities that the artist himself never intended to include. The writer has the prerogative of limiting his own scope, of staking the boundaries of his own kingdom. This must be remembered when attempting to appraise the work now being done in the South.

The Southern writers have reacted to their environment in just the same manner as the Russians prior to the time of Dostoievsky and

Tolstoi. They have transposed the painful substance of life around them as accurately as possible, without taking the part of emotional panderer between the truth as it is and the feelings of the reader. The "cruelty" of which the Southerners have been accused is at bottom only a sort of naïveté, an acceptance of spiritual inconsistencies without asking the reason why, without attempting to propose an answer. Undeniably there is an infantile quality about this clarity of vision and rejection of responsibility.

But literature in the South is a young growth, and it cannot be blamed because of its youth. One can only speculate about the possible course of its development or retrogression. Southern writing has reached the limits of a moral realism; something more must be added if it is to continue to flourish. As yet there has been no forerunner of an analytical moralist such as Tolstoi or a mystic like Dostoievsky. But the material with which Southern literature deals seems to demand of itself that certain basic questions be posed. If and when this group of writers is able to assume a philosophical responsibility, the whole tone and structure of their work will be enriched, and Southern writing will enter a more complete and vigorous stage in its evolution.

[*Decision,* July 1941]

LONELINESS . . . AN AMERICAN MALADY

THIS CITY, NEW YORK — consider the people in it, the eight million of us. An English friend of mine, when asked why he lived in New York City, said that he liked it here because he could be so alone. While it was my friend's desire to be alone, the aloneness of many Americans who live in cities is an involuntary and fearful thing. It has been said that loneliness is the great American malady. What is the nature of this loneliness? It would seem essentially to be a quest for identity.

To the spectator, the amateur philosopher, no motive among the complex ricochets of our desires and rejections seems stronger or more enduring than the will of the individual to claim his identity and belong. From infancy to death, the human being is obsessed by these dual motives. During our first weeks of life, the question of identity shares urgency with the need for milk. The baby reaches for his toes, then explores the bars of his crib; again and again he compares the difference between his own body and the objects around him, and in the wavering, infant eyes there comes a pristine wonder.

Consciousness of self is the first abstract problem that the human being solves. Indeed, it is this self-consciousness that removes us from lower animals. This primitive grasp of identity develops with constantly shifting emphasis through all our years. Perhaps maturity is simply the history of those mutations that reveal to the individual the relation between himself and the world in which he finds himself.

After the first establishment of identity there comes the imperative need to lose this new-found sense of separateness and to belong to something larger and more powerful than the weak, lonely self. The sense of moral isolation is intolerable to us.

In *The Member of the Wedding* the lovely 12-year-old girl, Frankie Addams, articulates this universal need: "The trouble with me is that for a long time I have just been an *I* person. All people belong to a *We* except me. Not to belong to a *We* makes you too lonesome."

Love is the bridge that leads from the *I* sense to the *We,* and there is a paradox about personal love. Love of another individual opens a new relation between the personality and the world. The lover responds in a new way to nature and may even write poetry. Love is affirmation; it motivates the *yes* responses and the sense of wider communication. Love casts out fear, and in the security of this togetherness we find contentment, courage. We no longer fear the age-old haunting questions: "Who am I?" "Why am I?" "Where am I going?" — and having cast out fear, we can be honest and charitable.

For fear is a primary source of evil. And when the question "Who am I?" recurs and is unanswered, then fear and frustration project a negative attitude. The bewildered soul can answer only: "Since I do not understand 'Who I am,' I only know what I am *not.*" The corollary of this emotional incertitude is snobbism, intolerance and racial hate. The xenophobic individual can only reject and destroy, as the xenophobic nation inevitably makes war.

The loneliness of Americans does not have its source in xenophobia; as a nation we are an outgoing people, reaching always for immediate contacts, further experience. But we tend to seek out things as individuals, alone. The European, secure in his family ties and rigid class loyalties, knows little of the moral loneliness that is native to us Americans. While the European artists tend to form groups or aesthetic schools, the American artist is the eternal maverick — not only from society in the way of all creative minds, but within the orbit of his own art.

Thoreau took to the woods to seek the ultimate meaning of his life. His creed was simplicity and his *modus vivendi* the deliberate stripping of external life to the Spartan necessities in order that his inward life could freely flourish. His objective, as he put it, was to back the world into a corner. And in that way did he discover "What a man thinks of himself, that it is which determines, or rather indicates, his fate."

On the other hand, Thomas Wolfe turned to the city, and in his wanderings around New York he continued his frenetic and lifelong search for the lost brother, the magic door. He too backed the world into a corner, and as he passed among the city's millions, returning their stares, he experienced "That silent meeting [that] is the summary of all the meetings of men's lives."

Whether in the pastoral joys of country life or in the labyrinthine city, we Americans are always seeking. We wander, question. But the answer waits in each separate heart — the answer of our own identity and the way by which we can master loneliness and feel that at last we belong.

[*This Week,* December 19, 1949]

THE VISION SHARED

I WONDER WHY I accepted this assignment. The ingenuities of aesthetics have never been my problems. Flight, in itself, interests me and I am indifferent to salting the bird's tail. Finding myself so awkwardly committed, I am reminded of a similar contretemps that happened in France three years ago. Soon after our arrival in Paris a charming gentleman came to see us and talked a good deal to me in French as rapid as a waterfall and equally intelligible to me. I understood nothing except that our caller wanted something rather urgently from me. So with amiability but little sense I spoke one of my few French words: "Oui." The caller pumped my hand and bowed out saying, "Ah, bon! Ah, bon!" He came twice again and the mysterious procedure was repeated. But things are strange in a new country and I didn't trouble myself until the day a friend came to our hotel and asked what in the world I was up to now. She took from her purse a card and I read it ten times and fell on the bed. The card was a nicely printed invitation to La Salle Richelieu at the Sorbonne to hear Carson McCullers lecture on a comparison between modern French and American literature. This was scheduled for the very next evening. My husband read the card and started packing. I telephoned an old friend from the American Embassy and he came to us. He laughed and I cried and we all drank brandy for some hours. After rationalization he said, "Since you obviously cannot lecture in French at the Sorbonne tomorrow evening, try to think of what you *can* do?" I watched my husband packing, then I thought of a recently finished poem. Our friend, a former literary critic, heard the poem and thought that it would do. He wrote a little apology in French for me that began: "*Je regrette beaucoup mais je ne parle pas français*—" The next evening I went to La Salle Richelieu, said my poem and sat there on the platform, trying to look intelligent as two critics debated the aspects of the two literatures in a language I did not understand.

I should rather say a poem now than write on the subject: "What is a Play?" For, first, I doubt the wisdom of arbitrary qualifications when an art form is concerned; and, secondly, my creative life has done nothing to equip me for formal aesthetic evaluations. For the writing of prose or poems—and I do not think there should be any immutable distinction between the two forms—this writing is a wandering creation. By that I mean that a given passage or paragraph draws astray the imagination with sensual allusions, nuances of feelings, vibrations of memory or desire. An aesthetic criticism has an opposite function. The attention of the reader should not be encouraged to wander or day dream, but should be fixed with lucid extroversion, cerebral and finite.

The function of the artist is to execute his own indigenous vision, and having done that, to keep faith with this vision. (At the risk of sounding pontifical I use the words "artist" and "vision," because of the sake of accuracy and to differentiate between the professional writers who are concerned with different aims.) Unfortunately it must be recognized that the artist is threatened by multiple pressures in the commercial world of publishers, producers, editors of magazines. The publisher says this character must not die and the book should end on an "up beat," or the producer wants phony dramatics, or friends and onlookers suggest this or that alternative. The professional writer may accede to these demands and concentrate on the ball and the bleachers. But once a creative writer is convinced of his own intentions, he must protect his work from alien persuasion. It is often a solitary position. We are afraid when we feel ourselves alone. And there is another special fear that torments the creator when he is too long assailed.

For the parallel function of a work of art is to be communicable. Of what value is a creation that cannot be shared? The vision that blazes in a madman's eye is valueless to us. So when the artist finds a creation rejected there is the fear that his own mind has retreated to a solitary uncommunicable state.

I believe that this communication is often dependent on time, for it is difficult for the many to catch the tune of something new. I think of James Joyce's long, embattled years against publishers, prudery, and finally international piracy. Or we can think of Proust's Jovian patience and faith in the magnitude of his own labors. Sometimes communication comes too late for the part of the artist that is mortal. Poe died before he saw his vision shared. Before retreating into his madness Nietzsche cried out in a letter to Cosima Wagner, "If there were only two in the world to understand me!" For all artists realize that the vision is valueless unless it can be shared.

At the same time, any form of art can only develop by means of single mutations by individual creators. If only traditional conventions are used an art will die, and the widening of an art form is bound to seem strange at first, and awkward. Any growing thing must go through awkward stages. The creator who is misunderstood because of his breach of convention may say to himself, "I seem strange to you, but anyway I am alive."

It seemed to me after my first experiences that the theatre was the most pragmatic of all art media. The first question of ordinary producers is: "Will it get across on Broadway?" The merit of a play is a secondary consideration and they shy from any play whose formula has not been proved a number of times.

The Member of the Wedding is unconventional because it is not a *literal* kind of play. It is an *inward* play and the conflicts are inward conflicts. The antagonist is not personified, but is a human condition of life; the sense of moral isolation. In this respect, *The Member of the Wedding* has an affinity with classical plays — which we are not used to in the modern theatre where the protagonist and antagonist are present in palpable conflict on the stage. The play has other abstract values; it is concerned with the weight of time, the hazard of human existence, bolts of chance. The reaction of the characters to these abstract phenomena projects the movement of the play. Some observers who failed to apprehend this *modus operandi* felt the play to be fragmentary because they did not account for this aesthetic concept.

This design was intuitive. Each creative work is determined by its own chemistry; the artist can only precipitate the inherent reactions if he approached the work subjectively. I must say I did not realize the proper dimensions of this play, the values of the unseen qualities involved, until the work had taken on its own life. An uncanny aspect of creation is that the artist approaches his destiny (or the destiny of his work) circuitously and only when the chemistry is sufficiently advanced does he realize the dimension of his work. I know that was my experience in writing *The Member of the Wedding.*

I foresaw that this play had also another problem as a lyric tragicomedy. The funniness and the grief are often co-existent in a single line and I did not know how an audience would respond to this. But Ethel Waters, Julie Harris, and Brandon de Wilde, under the superb direction of Harold Clurman, brought to their fugue-like parts a dazzling precision and harmony.

Some observers have wondered if any drama as unconventional as this should be called a play. I cannot comment on that. I only know that *The Member of the Wedding* is a vision that a number of artists have realized with fidelity and love.

[*Theatre Arts,* April 1950]

ISAK DINESEN:

Winter's Tales, by Isak Dinesen. New York:

Random House. 313 pages. $2.50.

IN THE WORLD of nature, a sudden variation of type is an event of greatest interest to scientists, who call the result of this phenomenon a "sport." In the world of literature a similar mutation has no definitive name, but it is a rare and wonderful occurrence and such a book is not soon forgotten. In the year 1934 a literary sport of this type was a book by an unknown European writing under an assumed name. The book was a collection of stories so entirely unique in their very intention that among contemporary works they had a strangely anachronistic effect; the book was reminiscent of nothing written in this century, and to make analogies and comparisons one had to think back to Boccaccio, or perhaps to the German romantics. For to begin with, the author had reverted to a medium of expression that in these days is almost obsolete, the most ancient and the purest form of fiction: the tale. *Seven Gothic Tales,* by Isak Dinesen, is a group of exquisite, weird, almost strangely brilliant stories; their appearance marked the debut of an extraordinary talent.

The second book by Isak Dinesen followed about four years later, and those who had expected a similar performance were surprised, but hardly disappointed. *Out of Africa,* a book concerning the years that the author lived on a coffee plantation in British Kenya, is a simple and tender personal document, written with a controlled and elegiac severity altogether different from the dark Gothic recklessness of the tales. Meanwhile, the identity of the author had been revealed; Isak Dinesen is the pen name of a Danish woman, who writes in English.

Winter's Tales is in suite with her first book. Traditionally, the tale has a dual purpose: to delight and to point a moral. Isak Dinesen unquestionably fulfills the first of these requirements. She is lavish with the use of the tale-teller's chief stock-in-trade, the delight of astonishment. Masquerade, trickery, swift twists of fortune are only the cruder kinds of astonishment. The real surprise is in the writing itself: the unexpected, slightly archaic word combinations, the tightrope grace of the sentences themselves. She writes of the green beech forests in Denmark in the month of May, or of a young scribe looking out into the snowy Parisian night beneath the shadow of Notre Dame—and immediately the image has come alive within the matrix of its proper atmosphere.

The second purpose of the tale, the moral point, may need some explanation. For the morality of the tale is odd and arbitrary, having little or no relation to ordinary everyday ethics, and determined solely by the tale-teller himself. In the true tale the characters are bound in the end to get what is coming to them; however, the justice is an erratic justice. Thus in the first story of this new collection, "The Sailor-Boy's Tale," the young protagonist rescues a falcon caught in the rigging of a mast, and because of this action he is later spared punishment for a murder he has committed. The tale-teller assumes the responsibility of God, and grants to his characters a moral freedom accountable only to the author himself. And furthermore, he ensures the characters the necessary worldly power to use this freedom; therefore, the characters of the tale are traditionally the aristocratic and the royal, if not in the flesh. Isak Dinesen writes of foot-loose travelers, of despots and a king, and of "that fascinating and irresistible personage, perhaps the most fascinating and irresistible in the whole world: the dreamer whose dreams come true." It is this quality of headlong freedom and recklessness that gives to the characters of *Winter's Tales* their suave and often crazy charm.

Each of these eleven tales is a graceful and finished story. "Sorrow Acre," perhaps the best, deals with the tyranny and defeat of an old lord by a victim more powerful than he. "Peter and Rosa" is an idyll of two young dreamers. "Alkmene" tells of a slightly mad young girl who went to town to watch a public execution. However, there is no story in *Winter's Tales* of quite the same freakish brilliance as the best of the *Seven Gothic Tales.* Perhaps this slight sense of disappointment is due to the fact that, having already once entered the imagination of Isak Dinesen, as a traveler enters a foreign land, the delight of surprise on a return visit is not too keen. But by any standards, except the precedent that Isak Dinesen has set for herself, these are tales of the highest excellence.

CARSON MCCULLERS

[*The New Republic,* June 7, 1943]

ISAK DINESEN:

IN PRAISE OF RADIANCE

*I*N 1938 I VISITED some friends who have a fine bookstore in Charleston. The first evening they asked if I had read *Out of Africa,* and I said I hadn't. They told me it was a beautiful book and that I must read it. I turned my head away and said I was in no state for reading, since at the time I was just finishing my novel *The Heart Is a Lonely Hunter.* I had imagined that it was a book about big-game hunting and I do not like to read about animals killed just for sport. All during the weekend there were references to *Out of Africa.* On Sunday, when I was leaving, they very quietly put *Out of Africa* in my lap, without words. My husband was driving so I was free to read. I opened to the first page:

> I had a farm in Africa, at the foot of the Ngong Hills. The Equator runs across these highlands, a hundred miles to the North, and the farm lay at an altitude of over six thousand feet. In the daytime you felt that you had got high up, near to the sun, but the early mornings and evenings were limpid and restful and the nights were cold.
>
> The geographical position, and the height of the land combined to create a landscape that had not its like in all the world. There was no fat on it and no luxuriance anywhere; it was Africa distilled up through six thousand feet, like the strong and refined essence of a continent. The colours were dry and burnt, like the colours in pottery. The trees had a light delicate foliage, the structure of which was different from that of the trees in Europe; it did not grow in bows or cupolas, but in horizontal layers, and the formation gave to the tall solitary trees a likeness to the palms, or a heroic and romantic air like full-rigged ships with their sails clewed up, and to the edge of a wood a strange appearance as if the whole wood were faintly vibrating. Upon the grass of the great plains the crooked bare old thorn-trees were scattered, and the grass was spiced

> like thyme and bog-myrtle; in some places the scent was so strong, that it smarted in the nostrils. All the flowers that you found on the plains, or upon the creepers and liana in the native forest, were diminutive like flowers of the downs — only just in the beginning of the long rains a number of big, massive heavy-scented lilies sprang out on the plains. The views were immensely wide. Everything that you saw made for greatness and freedom, and unequalled nobility.

We started driving in the early afternoon and I was so dazed by the poetry and truth of this great book, that when night came I continued reading *Out of Africa* with a flashlight. I kept thinking that this beauty and this truth could not go on, but page after page I was more enchanted. At the end of the book, I knew that Isak Dinesen had written a great dirge of the Continent of Africa. I knew that sublime security that a great, great writer can give to a reader. With her simplicity and "unequalled nobility" I realized that this was one of the most radiant books of my life.

The burning deserts, the jungles, the hills opened my heart to Africa. Open to my heart, also, were the animals and that radiant being, Isak Dinesen. Farmer, doctor, lion hunter, if need be. Because of *Out of Africa,* I loved Isak Dinesen. When she would ride through a maise grassland, I would ride with her. Her dogs, her farm, "Lulu," became my friends, and the natives for whom she had such great affection — Farsh, Kamante, and all the people on the farm — I loved also. I had read *Out of Africa* so much and with so much love that the author had become my imaginary friend. Although I never wrote to her or sought to meet her, she was there in her stillness, her serenity, and her great wisdom to comfort me. In this book, shining with her humanity, of that great and tragic continent, her people became my people and her landscape my landscape.

Naturally, I wanted to read her other works, and the next book I read was *Seven Gothic Tales.* Instead of the radiance of *Out of Africa,* the *Tales* have a quite different quality. They are brilliant, controlled, and each gives the air of a deliberate work of artistry. One realizes that the author is writing in a foreign language because of the strange, archaic quality of her beautiful prose. They had the quality of a luminous, sulphuric glow. When I was ill or out of sorts with the world, I would turn to *Out of Africa,* which never failed to comfort and support me — and when I wanted to be lifted out of my life, I would read *Seven Gothic Tales* or *Winter's Tales* or, much later, *The Last Tales.*

About two years ago, the Academy of Arts and Letters, of which I am a member, wrote to me that it had invited Isak Dinesen as an honorary member and guest. I hesitated to meet her because Isak Dinesen had been so fixed in my heart, I was afraid that the actual would disturb this image. However, I did go to the dinner and at cocktail time when I met the Academy's president, I asked of him a great favor. I asked if I could sit near her at the dinner party. To my astonishment and joy he said that she had wanted to sit with me, and so the place cards were already on the table. He also asked me how we should address her since her name was the Baroness Karen Blixen-Finecke. All I could say to him was that I was not going to call her "Butch" at the first meeting. I said, "I feel the best thing is 'Baroness,' so I will call her 'Baroness,' " which I did until we were on a first-name basis and she asked me to call her Tanya, which is her English name.

How can one think of a radiant being? I had only seen a picture of her when she was in her twenties: strong, live, wonderfully beautiful, and with one of her Scotch deerhounds in the shade of the African jungle. I had not thought visually about her person. When I met her, she was very, very frail and old but as she talked her face was lit like a candle in an old church. My heart trembled when I saw her fragility.

When she spoke at the Academy dinner that evening, something happened which I had never seen there before. When she finished her talk, every member rose to applaud her.

At the dinner she said she would like to meet Marilyn Monroe. Since I had met Marilyn several times, and since Arthur Miller was at the next table, I told her I thought that could be very easily arranged. So, I had the great honor of inviting my imaginary friend, Isak Dinesen, to meet Marilyn Monroe, with Arthur Miller, for luncheon in my home.

Tanya was a magnificent conversationalist and loved to talk. Marilyn, with her beautiful blue eyes, listened in a "once-upon-a-time-way," as did we all. Tanya talked about her friends Berkley Cole and Dennis Finch-Hatton. She talked always with such warmth that the listeners didn't have to try to interrupt or change her marvelous conversation.

Tanya ate only oysters and drank only champagne. At the luncheon we had many oysters and for the big eaters several large soufflés. Arthur asked what doctor put her on that diet of nothing but oysters and champagne. She looked at him and said rather sharply, "Doctor? The doctors are horrified by my diet but I love champagne and I love oysters and they agree with me." Then she added, "It is sad, though, when oysters are not in season, for then I have to turn back to asparagus in those dreary months." Arthur mentioned something about protein and Tanya said, "I don't know anything about that but I am old and I eat what I want and what agrees with me." Then she went back to her reminiscences of friends in Africa.

It was a great delight for her to be with colored people. Ida, my housekeeper, is colored, and so are my yardmen, Jesse and Sam. After lunch everybody danced and sang. A friend of Ida's had brought in a motion picture camera, and there were pictures of Tanya dancing with Marilyn, me dancing with Arthur, and a great round of general dancing. I love to remember this for I never met Tanya again. Since writers seldom write to each other, our communication was infrequent but not vague. She sent me flowers when I was ill and lovely pictures of her cows and her darling dog in Rungsted Kyst.

When I was asked to go to lecture at the Cheltenham Festival in England last year, I wrote Tanya and asked if she could possibly join me in London. I received a letter from Clara that she not only could not come to London but she could scarcely move from room to room. Soon afterward, I read that this most radiant being had died.

In London, Cecil Beaton called me and said he had spent an afternoon with Tanya two weeks before her death. He invited me to tea. I went to Cecil's extraordinary house. The walls of the sitting room were black velvet and there was a magnificent orange portrait of Cecil by Bebe Berard, whom I loved very much, and who died about a decade ago. In that setting I could see vivacious Tanya with her delicate gestures, drinking champagne instead of tea, enchanting her listeners, enjoying her tales of long ago. I can imagine that she would have enjoyed the chic of the decor.

Cecil said that he was in Denmark two weeks before her death and had called Tanya. He told her he had an appointment in Spain. Tanya said then, "Well, that means, Cecil, I will never see you again and it makes me very sad." Thereupon, Cecil broke his appointment in Spain. Before he had time to hire a car to go to Rungsted Kyst, she called back and said, "Cecil, we have always been such good friends and I hate to have our friendship end on such a disappointing note." Cecil said, "I am just leaving for Rungsted Kyst, and I shall see you this afternoon." Tanya met him at the door, and the driver, seeing her, took off his hat and gave her a full bow from the waist. Cecil asked if she was suffering and she said that the drugs they had given her were sufficient and that she was in no pain. Cecil gave me copies of the last photographs of her: aged and exquisite, she was among her beloved possessions, portraits of her ancestors, the chandeliers, and the beautiful old furniture. Clara wrote me later that she was buried under her favorite beech tree near the shore of Rungsted Kyst.

[*Saturday Review,* March 16, 1963]

THE FLOWERING DREAM: Notes on Writing

WHEN I WAS A CHILD of about four, I was walking with my nurse past a convent. For once, the convent doors were open. And I saw the children eating ice-cream cones, playing on iron swings, and I watched, fascinated. I wanted to go in, but my nurse said no, I was not Catholic. The next day, the gate was shut. But, year by year, I thought of what was going on, of this wonderful party, where I was shut out. I wanted to climb the wall, but I was too little. I beat on the wall once, and I knew all the time that there was a marvelous party going on, but I couldn't get in.

Spiritual isolation is the basis of most of my themes. My first book was concerned with this, almost entirely, and all of my books since, in one way or another. Love, and especially love of a person who is incapable of returning or receiving it, is at the heart of my selection of grotesque figures to write about — people whose physical incapacity is a symbol of their spiritual incapacity to love or receive love — their spiritual isolation.

To understand a work, it is important for the artist to be emotionally right on dead center; to see, to know, to experience the things he is writing about. Long before Harold Clurman, who, bless his heart, directed *The Member of the Wedding,* I think I had directed every fly and gnat in that room years ago.

The dimensions of a work of art are seldom realized by the author until the work is accomplished. It is like a flowering dream. Ideas grow, budding silently, and there are a thousand illuminations coming day by day as the work progresses. A seed grows in writing as in nature. The seed of the idea is developed by both labor and the unconscious, and the struggle that goes on between them.

I understand only particles. I understand the characters, but the novel itself is not in focus. The focus comes at random moments which no one can understand, least of all the author. For me, they usually follow great effort. To me, these illuminations are the grace of labor. All of my work has happened this way. It is at once the hazard and the beauty that a writer has to depend on such illuminations. After months of confusion and labor, when the idea has flowered, the collusion is Divine. It always comes from the subconscious and cannot be controlled. For a whole year I worked on *The Heart Is a Lonely Hunter* without understanding it at all. Each character was talking to a central character, but why, I didn't know. I'd almost decided that the book was no novel, that I should chop it up into short stories. But I could feel the mutilation in my body when I had that idea, and I was in despair. I had been working for five hours and I went outside. Suddenly, as I walked across a road, it occurred to me that Harry Minowitz, the character all the other characters were talking to, was a different man, a deaf mute, and immediately the name was changed to John Singer. The whole focus of the novel was fixed and I was for the first time committed with my whole soul to *The Heart Is a Lonely Hunter.*

What to know and what not to know? John Brown, from the American Embassy, was here to visit, and he pointed his long forefinger and said, "I admire you, Carson, for your ignorance." I said, "Why?" He asked, "When was the Battle of Hastings, and what was it about? When was the Battle of Waterloo, and what was that about?" I said, "John, I don't think I care much." He said, "That's what I mean. You don't clutter your mind with the facts of life."

When I was nearly finished with *The Heart Is a Lonely Hunter,* my husband mentioned that there was a convention of deaf mutes in a town near-by and he assumed that I would want to go and observe them. I told him that it was the last thing I wanted to do because I already had made my conception of deaf mutes and didn't want it to be disturbed. I presume James Joyce had the same attitude when he lived abroad and never visited his home again, feeling his Dublin was fixed forever — which it is.

A writer's main asset is intuition; too many facts impede intuition. A writer needs to know so many things, but there are so many things he doesn't need to know — he needs to know human things even if they aren't "wholesome," as they call it.

Every day, I read the New York *Daily News,* and very soberly. It is interesting to know the name of the lover's lane where the stabbing took place, and the circumstances which the *New York Times* never reports. In that unsolved murder in Staten Island, it is interesting to know that the doctor and his wife, when they were stabbed, were wearing Mormon nightgowns, three-quarter length. Lizzie Borden's breakfast, on the sweltering summer day she killed her father, was mutton soup. Always details provoke more ideas than any generality could furnish. When Christ was pierced in His *left* side, it is more moving and evocative than if He were just pierced.

One cannot explain accusations of morbidity. A writer can only say he writes from the seed which flowers later in the subconscious. Nature is not abnormal, only lifelessness is abnormal. Anything that pulses and moves and walks around the room, no matter what thing it is doing, is natural and human to a writer. The fact that John Singer, in *The Heart Is a Lonely Hunter,* is a deaf-and-dumb man is a symbol, and the fact that Captain Penderton, in *Reflections in a Golden Eye,* is homosexual, is also a symbol, of handicap and impotence. The deaf mute, Singer, is a symbol of infirmity, and he loves a person who is incapable of receiving his love. Symbols suggest the story and theme and incident, and they are so interwoven that one cannot understand consciously where the suggestion begins. I become the characters I write about. I am so immersed in them that their motives are my own. When I write about a thief, I become one; when I write about Captain Penderton, I become a homosexual man; when I write about a deaf mute, I become dumb during the time of the story. I become the characters I write about and I bless the Latin poet Terence who said, "Nothing human is alien to me."

When I wrote the stage version of *The Member of the Wedding,* I was at the time paralyzed, and my outward situation was miserable indeed; but when I finished that script, I wrote to a friend of mine, "Oh, how wonderful it is to be a writer, I have never been so happy. . . ."

When work does not go well, no life is more miserable than that of a writer. But when it does go well, when the illumination has focused a work so that it goes limpidly and flows, there is no gladness like it.

Why does one write? Truly it is financially the most ill-rewarded occupation in the world. My lawyer has figured out how much I made from the book *The Member of the Wedding,* and it is, over the five years I worked on it, twenty-eight cents a day. Then the irony is, the play *The Member of the Wedding* had made so much money that I've had to give eighty per cent to the government — which I'm happy, or at least *have* to be happy, to do.

It must be that one writes from some subconscious need for communication, for self-expression. Writing is a wandering, dreaming occupation. The intellect is submerged beneath the unconscious — the thinking mind is best controlled by the imagination. Yet writing is not utterly amorphous and unintellectual. Some of the best novels and prose are as exact as a telephone number, but few prose writers can achieve this because of the refinement of passion and poetry that is necessary. I don't like the word prose; it's too prosaic. Good prose should be fused with the light of poetry; prose should be like poetry, poetry should make sense like prose.

*

I like to think of Anne Frank and her immense communication, which was the communication not only of a twelve-year-old child, but a communication of conscience and courage.

Here truly there was isolation, but physical rather than spiritual isolation. Several years ago, Anne Frank's father made an appointment to see me at the Hotel Continental in Paris. We talked together and he asked me if I would dramatize the diary of his daughter. He also gave me the book, which I had not yet read. But as I was reading the book, I was so upset that I broke out in a rash on my hands and feet, and I had to tell him that under the circumstances I could not do the play.

Paradox is a clue to communication, for what is *not* often leads to the awareness of what *is*. Nietzsche once wrote to Cosima Wagner, "If only three people could understand me." Cosima understood him and years later a man called Adolf Hitler built a whole philosophical system around a misunderstanding of Nietzsche. It is paradoxical that a great philosopher like Nietzsche and a great musician like Richard Wagner could have contributed so much to the world's suffering in this century. Partial understanding for an ignorant person is a warped and subjective understanding, and it was with this type of understanding that the philosophy of Nietzsche and the creations of Richard Wagner were the mainstay of Hitler's emotional appeal to the German people. He was able to juggle great ideas into the despair of his time, which we must remember was a real despair.

When someone asks me who has influenced my work, I point to O'Neill, the Russians, Faulkner, Flaubert. *Madame Bovary* seems to be written with divine economy. It is one of the most painfully written novels, and one of the most painfully considered, of any age. *Madame Bovary* is a composite of the realistic voice of Flaubert's century, of the realism versus the romantic mind of his times. In its lucidity and faultless grace, it seems to have flown straight from Flaubert's pen without an interruption in thought. For the first time, he was dealing with his truth as a writer.

*

It is only with imagination and reality that you get to know the things a novel requires. Reality alone has never been that important to me. A teacher once said that one should write about one's own back yard; and by this, I suppose, she meant one should write about the things that one knows most intimately. But what is more intimate than one's own imagination? The imagination combines memory with insight, combines reality with the dream.

People ask me why I don't go back to the South more often. But the South is a very emotional experience for me, fraught with all the memories of my childhood. When I go back South I always get into arguments, so that a visit to Columbus in Georgia is a stirring up of love and antagonism. The locale of my books might always be Southern, and the South always my homeland. I love the voices of Negroes — like brown rivers. I feel that in the short trips when I do go to the South, in my own memory and in the newspaper articles, I still have my own reality.

Many authors find it hard to write about new environments that they did not know in childhood. The voices reheard from childhood have a truer pitch. And the foliage — the trees of childhood — are remembered more exactly. When I work from within a different locale from the South, I have to wonder what time the flowers are in bloom — and what flowers? I hardly let characters speak unless they are Southern. Wolfe wrote brilliantly of Brooklyn, but more brilliantly of the Southern cadence and ways of speech. This is particularly true of Southern writers because it is not only their speech and the foliage, but their entire culture — which makes it a homeland within a homeland. No matter what the politics, the degree or non-degree of liberalism in a Southern writer, he is still bound to this peculiar regionalism of language and voices and foliage and memory.

Few Southern writers are truly cosmopolitan. When Faulkner writes about the R.A.F. and France, he is somehow not convincing — while I'm convinced in almost every line about Yoknapatawpha County. Indeed, to me *The Sound and the Fury* is probably the greatest American novel. It has an authenticity, a grandeur and, most of all, a tenderness that stems from the combination of reality and the dream that is the divine collusion.

Hemingway, on the contrary, is the most cosmopolitan of all the American writers. He is at home in Paris, in Spain, in America, the Indian stories of his childhood. Perhaps it is his style, which is a delivery, a beautifully worked out form of expression. As expert as Hemingway is at producing and convincing the reader of his various outlooks, emotionally he is a wanderer. In Hemingway's style some things are masked in the emotional content of his work. If I prefer Faulkner to Hemingway, it's because I am more touched by the familiar — the writing that reminds me of my own childhood and sets a standard for a remembering of the language. Hemingway seems to me to use language as a style of writing.

The writer by nature of his profession is a dreamer and a conscious dreamer. How, without love and the intuition that comes from love, can a human being place himself in the situation of another human being? He must imagine, and imagination takes humility, love, and great courage. How can you create a character without love and the struggle that goes with love?

For many years I have been working on a novel called *Clock Without Hands,* and will probably finish it in about two more years. My books take a long time. This novel is in process day by day of being focused. As a writer, I've always worked very hard. But as a writer, I've also known that hard work is not enough. In the process of hard work, there must come an illumination, a divine spark that puts the work into focus and balance.

When I asked Tennessee Williams how he first thought of *The Glass Menagerie,* he said it was suggested by a glass curtain he saw at the house of one of his grandfather's parishioners. From then on it became what he called a memory play. How the recollection of that glass curtain fitted into the memories of his boyhood, neither he nor I could understand, but then the unconscious is not easily understood.

How does creation begin in any art? As Tennessee wrote *The Glass Menagerie* as a memory play, I wrote "Wunderkind" when I was seventeen years old, and it was a memory, although not the reality of the memory — it was a foreshortening of that memory. It was about a young music student. I didn't write about my real music teacher — I wrote about the music we studied together because I thought it was truer. The imagination is truer than the reality.

The passionate, individual love — the old Tristan-Isolde love, the Eros love — is inferior to the love of God, to fellowship, to the love of Agape — the Greek god of the feast, the God of brotherly love — and of man. This is what I tried to show in *The Ballad of the Sad Café* in the strange love of Miss Amelia for the little hunchback, Cousin Lymon.

The writer's work is predicated not only on his personality but by the region in which he was born. I wonder sometimes if what they call the "Gothic" school of Southern writing, in which the grotesque is paralleled with the sublime, is not due largely to the cheapness of human life in the South. The Russians are like the Southern writers in that respect. In my childhood, the South was almost a feudal society. But the South is complicated by the racial problem more severely than the Russian society. To many a poor Southerner, the only pride that he has is the fact that he is white, and when one's self-pride is so pitiably debased, how can one learn to love? Above all, love is the main generator of all good writing. Love, passion, compassion are all welded together.

In any communication, a thing says to one person quite a different thing from what it says to another, but writing, in essence, is communication; and communication is the only access to love — to love, to conscience, to nature, to God, and to the dream. For myself, the further I go into my own work and the more I read of those I love, the more aware I am of the dream and the logic of God, which indeed is a Divine collusion.

[*Esquire*, December 1959]

POETRY

Editor's Note

Carson's concentration in her early writing was not on poetry as is often the case with beginners. She began with plays and a novel and although all of her fiction is musical and poetic, she did not write poetry as such until she was a well-established author. In later years, she liked to have her manuscript in progress read aloud, partially because her vision was more affected by the strokes than she let on and reading was difficult for her, but also, I think, because she listened for the rhythm and the cadence of the language — the sound as well as the meaning of the words.

Although Carson did publish *Sweet as a Pickle, Clean as a Pig,* a collection of verse for children which she thoroughly enjoyed writing, she published little of her other poetry. What she did publish or record is collected here. Much of what remains in her files is unfinished — that is, there are often several versions of the same poem or handwritten manuscripts that are unclear.

Carson always liked to share her poems on a personal level. "The Dual Angel," which was written in France in 1951, was sent out as her Christmas card that year. She often recited poems for her friends in her soft voice. At the M-G-M recording she recited from memory, as usual, and somehow left out four lines of "Saraband," which on the record is titled "Select Your Sorrows If You Can."

About her poetry, I remember best one evening at a university lecture. After she had recited "Stone Is Not Stone" in her gentle Southern voice, there was a long silence. Then suddenly a young student stood up and said, "Mrs. McCullers, I love you."

The Mortgaged Heart

The dead demand a double vision. A furthered zone,
Ghostly decision of apportionment. For the dead can claim
The lover's senses, the mortgaged heart.

Watch twice the orchard blossoms in gray rain
And to the cold rose skies bring twin surprise.
Endure each summons once, and once again;
Experience multiplied by two — the duty recognized.
Instruct the quivering spirit, instant nerve
To schizophrenic master serve,
Or like a homeless Doppelgänger
Blind love might wander.

The mortgage of the dead is known.
Prepare the cherished wreath, the garland door.
But the secluded ash, the humble bone —
Do the dead know?

[*Voices,* September–December 1952. In somewhat different form, this poem appeared earlier in *New Directions* X, 1948.]

When We Are Lost

When we are lost what image tells?
Nothing resembles nothing. Yet nothing
Is not blank. It is configured Hell:
Of noticed clocks on winter afternoons, malignant stars,
Demanding furniture. All unrelated
And with air between.

The terror. Is it of Space, of Time?
Or the joined trickery of both conceptions?
To the lost, transfixed among the self-inflicted ruins,
All that is non-air (if this indeed is not deception)
Is agony immobilized. While Time,
The endless idiot, runs screaming round the world.

[*Voices,* September–December 1952 and, in somewhat different form, in *New Directions* X, 1948. Also recorded for MGM records under the title "When We Are Lost What Image Tells?"]

The Dual Angel

A Meditation on Origin and Choice

INCANTATION TO LUCIFER

Angel disarmed, lay down your cunning, finally tell
The currents, stops and altitudes between Heaven and Hell.
Or were the scalding stars too loud for your celestial velleities,
The everlasting zones of emptiness uncanny to your imperious
hand?
Did you admit the shocks and shuttles of the circumstance,
And were the aeons ever sinister
Or were they just vulgar as a marathon dance?
Did you keep camping all through chaos
Comparing colors of infinity to neon lights?

Forever were you inconsolable during the downward flight
Spurning the comfort of affinity and rose, the rest of sunset, clarity,
Avoiding rainbows in that desperate clash against the stars?
Your tearless wizardry soon caught the rhyme
Of universe, the planetary chimes, atomic quandary.
It took you only a zone or two to riddle
The top-secret density relating Space to Time.

Did once your hurtling senses turn
To paradise that you had robbed and spurned?
Did you once wonder, one time weep?
As earth nears, turn again defaulting eyes to paradise,
Defaulting eyes, turn once again
With the presentiment of further bliss
Before you shudder with the first and final kiss.

HYMEN, O HYMEN

It was the time when the newest star was inchoate
And there were only revolving seas and land still malleable.
There was no garden at that time — but there was God.
For when the sun burst God chose the minority side of firmament
And settled on earth to study an experiment.

We know nothing of that meeting, nothing at all
Only the protean firelight fearful on the wall.
Since we only know it happened it's anybody's guess
How abdicated angel asked for and found God's rest.

Ecce, the emperor of velocity and glare
The splendor from his awful odyssey, his starlit hair
Landed on a rim of ocean, striding to shore
The radiant grace and arrogance before
The blue-veined instep faltered and slowly dimmed the pirate eyes.
Ecce, the quailing emperor against a violet sea and the primeval skies.
Behold this homage to a majesty almost impossible to explain
For after the heavenly holdup God was left rather plain.
Deliberate and unadorned, but after all what need
Of scepter had the hand that hewed the Universe?
And ruler of infinity has little use for speed.
His visage black with wind and sun, almighty hand vibrant with strife
Feeling in blank mysterious seas the secret miracle of life.
Imagine the encounter when the polarities chance
When stars of love and sorrow met Satan's jeweled glance.

We are told nothing of conception, really nothing at all.
Only the firelit symbols of an antique nurse scary and changing on the wall.

We are told nothing
Of the vibrato of desire remorseless
Until the solar-plexal swinging
Orchestrates to all flesh singing.
Post coitum, omnia tristia sunt.
Sadness, then sleep, the blaze of noon, love's gladness.

There was no witness of this bridal night
Only azoic seascape and interlocking angels' might.
So now we speculate with filial wonder,
Fabricate that night of love and ponder
On the quietude of Satan in our Father's arms:
Velocity stilled, the restful shade.
Satan we can understand — but what was God's will
That cosmic night before we were made?

The next day He completed His experiment
Found in the seas that atom He willed alive
Nursed in His awesome hand, taught to survive
The shock of creation, watched with His love and care
Astride in ocean and unknowing that Satan's ocean-skipping eye was there
Envisaging end in the beginning, wrestling with God's life,
The eye of guile had sliced the atom with Satanic knife.

LOVE AND THE RIND OF TIME

What is Time that man should be so mindful:
The earth is aged 500 thousand millions of years,
Allowing some hundred thousand millions of margin for error
And man evolving a mere half-million years of consciousness, twilight and terror
Only a flicker of eternity divides us from unknowing beast
And how far are we from the fern, the rose, essential yeast?

Indeed in these light aeons how far
From animal to evening star?

Skip time for now and fix the eye upon eternity
Eye gazing backward or forward it is the same
Whether Mozart or short-order cook with an infirmity
Except the illuminations alter their shafts
Except we would rather be Mozart, we want to last as long as possible, to radiate, to sing
Although in eternity it may be the same thing.

In God's cosmos according to report
Nothing lapses, no gene is lost
After centuries may bustle in the sport
Which will in time command the line.

Those who find it a little harder to live
And therefore live a little harder,
As struggling gene in oceanic plant
Predestine voluntary cells that give
The evolutionary turn to fish, then beast
With multiplying brain that dominates earth's feasts.
From weed to dinosaur through the peripheries of stars
From furtherest star imperiled on the rind of time,
How long to core of love in human mind?

THE DUAL ANGEL

The world dazed by Satanic glares
Like country children spangled-eyed at county fairs
Seeing no terror in trapeze, kinetic thrill of zones above listening,
And the unheeded shrill of the world lost, rocketing in space,
Despairs of those who are struck down upon Hell's floor and die — or crawl awhile a little more.

The screams are heard by blasted ears within the radiation zone
And hanging eyes upon a cheek must see the charred and iridescent
craze —
Earth orphaned by atom, each man alone.
The furious intellect relating furtherest space to beyondest time,
Exalting abstractions, vaulting the 1 2 3,
Defaulting from the simplest kinship, disjoining man from man,
Seeing across oceans, and stumbling on a grain of sand. Almighty
God!

After the half a million years this is the century of decision
Between obscenest suicide and Man's transfigured vision.
Here are the flowering plant, beast and the dual angel,
The living who struggles with the weight of dead and,
Recognizing victory, surmises radiance in lead.

FATHER, UPON THY IMAGE WE ARE SPANNED

Why are we split upon our double nature, how are we planned?
Father, upon what image are we spanned?
Turning helpless in the garden of right and wrong
Mocked by the reversibles of good and evil
Heir of the exile. Lucifer, and brother of Thy universal Son
Who said *it is finished* when Thy synthesis was just begun.
We suffer the sorrow of separation and division
With a heart that blazes with Christ's vision:
That though we be deviously natured, dual-planned,
Father, upon Thy image we are spanned.

AVE

[*Mademoiselle,* July 1952, and *Botteghe Oscure* IX, 1952. On copies sent to friends at Christmas 1951, Carson McCullers noted that it had been written "August 1951, London–December 1951, Nyack."]

Stone Is Not Stone

There was a time when stone was stone
And a face on the street was a finished face.
Between the Thing, myself and God alone
There was an instant symmetry.
Since you have altered all my world this trinity is twisted:

Stone is not stone
And faces like the fractioned characters in dreams are incomplete
Until in the child's inchoate face
I recognize your exiled eyes.
The soldier climbs the glaring stair leaving your shadow.
Tonight, this torn room sleeps
Beneath the starlight bent by you.

[*Mademoiselle,* July 1957. Also recorded for M-G-M records under the title, "There Was a Time When Stone Was Stone." An earlier version, called "Twisted Trinity," appeared in *Decision* II, 1941.]

Saraband

Select your sorrows if you can,
Edit your ironies, even grieve with guile.
Adjust to a world divided
Which demands your candid senses stoop to labyrinthine wiles
What natural alchemy lends
To the scrubby grocery boy with dirty hair
The lustre of Apollo, or Golden Hyacinth's fabled stare.
If you must cross the April park, be brisk:
Avoid the cadence of the evening, eyes from afar
Lest you be held as a security risk
Solicit only the evening star.

Your desperate nerves fuse laughter with disaster
And higgledy piggledy giggle once begun
Crown a host of unassorted sorrows
You never could manage one by one.
The world that jibes your tenderness
Jails your lust.
Bewildered by the paradox of all your musts
Turning from horizon to horizon, noonday to dusk:
It may be only you can understand:
On a mild sea afternoon of blue and gold
When the sky is a mild blue of a Chinese bowl
The bones of Hart Crane, sailors and the drugstore man
Beat on the ocean's floor the same saraband.

[Recorded for M-G-M records under the title, "Select Your Sorrows If You Can."]